The Trouble with His Lordship's Trousers

Ladies Most Unlikely
Book One

Jayne Fresina

A TWISTED E PUBLISHING BOOK

The Trouble with His Lordship's Trousers
Ladies Most Unlikely, Book One
Copyright © 2016 by Jayne Fresina

Cover design by K Designs
All cover art and logo copyright © 2016, Twisted E-Publishing, LLC

ISBN-13: 978-1530918188
ISBN-10: 1530918189

In Regency London, Georgiana Hathaway has no intention of falling into the conventional trap of marriage and motherhood. She has so much more to do with her life, and a few tortuous years at 'The Particular Establishment for the Advantage of Respectable Ladies' has done nothing to change her mind. In fact, she's already taken the first steps to carve out a career, by anonymously crafting a scandalous, satirical column, called *His Lordship's Trousers*, for her father's newspaper.

But as the misadventures of her comical rake become the most talked-about story in London, and the naughty column earns greater popularity, it is also bound to gain critics. How much trouble can "His Lordship's Trousers" get her into? She's about to find out.

Meanwhile, "Dead Harry" Thrasher eagerly reads that wicked column every week. It is one of the few things— other than the obituaries— that make him laugh out loud these days. He lives vicariously through that fictional rake's antics, because his own life is suspended in time and he sees no reason to move forward. After all, when a man's obituary has been printed in the newspaper, not once but twice, he has a tendency to believe it. What's the point of a life over which man has no control? What, exactly, has he been saved so many times for? He's about to find out.

When Dead Harry meets Miss Hathaway, they will both find their worlds, and their long-ingrained opinions, at risk. She does not want to fall in love with a man when everybody knows the male animal only gets in the way of a girl's ambitions. And Harry may have survived a "mortal" wound, and eight hundred and fifty days stranded alone on an uncharted island, but can the very private life of this semi-recluse survive the reckless curiosity and impertinent sauce of Miss Georgiana Hathaway?

He's a naval war hero— even if he does have an aversion to decent clothing and polite behavior— so if this young woman thinks to conquer him and put his life in order, she'd better have a battle strategy. It's been a while since he enjoyed a skirmish at sea, but Harry has a feeling he'll love every moment of this one.

DEDICATION

Dedicated to all those in the middle.

Chapter One

When Dead Harry met the Wickedest Chit
November, 1814

"That's Dead Harry Thrasher," she heard someone whisper. "They say he's not fit to be out in proper society these days."

"Out in society? My dear, after what happened to him, he shouldn't even be alive. Hence the name. They simply cannot explain how he survived death. Twice."

Georgiana Hathaway, perched on the stairs, dangling the remains of a charred wig from a fishing hook through the railings, and having brought the music and conversation to a halt, might expect to be the center of attention at that moment. But no, it was the subject of these whispers—a powerfully enigmatic gentleman, unshaven and with wildly unkempt hair— who made heads turn. Standing at the foot of the stairs, he laughed raucously and unapologetically. The only man there, apparently, who dared.

Below her swaying hook, Viscount Fairbanks, whose wig she'd just fished off his head, lost much of his previous hauteur, as well as the color in his face. Plucking at the extravagant ruffles of his neck-cloth with long, spindly fingers, he backed away from "Dead Harry", as if the other man might lunge at him and take a chunk of flesh. And her sister Maria, who was, in actual fact, the cause of all this, jumped to her feet, snapped her fan shut and cried out in ungrateful despair, "Georgiana Hathaway, you are the wickedest chit that ever breathed air."

Anybody would think that this had not been done entirely for Maria! As if Georgiana had not acted purely on her sister's behalf. But someone had to take the vain and haughty Viscount Fairbanks and his wig down a peg or two, and it seemed as if only Georgiana— and Dead Harry

Thrasher— appreciated the fact.

So how had all this come about? Very simply, it began when a certain restless young lady was forbidden from attending the party. Confined instead to her room that evening, Georgiana had made the most of her solitary state, not to consider her misdemeanors and repent, but to dwell upon the many injustices she perceived as being committed against her over the span of her sixteen years.

"You, sister, are not properly 'out' yet and certainly not prepared for such an elegant party," Maria had primly assured her earlier that day.

"I shall be seventeen in another month."

"Age is not always a good measure of one's suitability for good company. Besides," Maria looked her up and down, "you always manage to ruin things. This is my greatest opportunity, and I cannot afford to have you running wild like an escaped piglet."

"But I've attended parties before. In our old home."

"Where there was nobody to impress. Certain things matter more in London than they did in the country. Tonight we shall not play foolish children's games and dash about, all hot and silly. There will be important people of fashion here, people of consequence in society. There will be... " she had lowered her voice with great reverence, "... conversation."

"I know how to talk."

"Sadly, you do. I always said it was a mistake that they encouraged you to learn," Maria replied. "But this will be civil, intelligent, genteel conversation, with very grand people, including," she caught her breath and shivered, "Viscount Fairbanks." Maria loved the effect of a dramatic pause.

"So? I'm sure he puts his breeches on one leg at a time, like anybody else."

"And there! One does not talk of a gentleman's breeches. You prove my case for me. What would we want with *you* at such a noble gathering? No, no, you can take a nursery supper with the little ones and then stay in your room."

Determined not to miss out entirely on this fine parade of human absurdity, Georgiana had crept out of her room to hide on the shadowy stairs, and from there she watched the revelry below for half an hour or so, before she spied the infamous Viscount Fairbanks leading his entourage through the crowd. She knew it had to be him, of course. Who else would cut such a broad swath through the guests and leave them fawning over the trailing scent of his perfume?

Viscount Fairbanks, so rumor had it, only ate food prepared by his own chef wherever he went, never wore the same stockings twice, and sent his shirts abroad for laundering. Ever since it was known that this gentleman would attend tonight's party in their father's new London house, Maria had suffered heart palpitations at the prospect of finally being introduced to the man of her dreams.

With great expectations, therefore, Georgiana keenly studied this curiosity as he approached.

He was certainly long and narrow, but then so were toasting forks — which had more purpose. Walking as if his silk knee-breeches were too tight in the rear, and his neck-cloth so stiffly starched that he could not put his chin down, it was a miracle he moved along without trampling anyone underfoot. Although that was wholly due to their speed in getting out of his way, rather than any consideration on his part.

She was unimpressed.

Being in possession of what her stepmother termed a "deliberately contrary disposition", Georgiana had— even into her sixteenth year— retained a stubborn preference for young men of an unlikely sort. She would still much rather choose the company of a boy with an interesting collection of insects in a jar, or a nasty, oozing scar to show off, rather than one with haughty manners and an obsession about keeping his clothes clean. She'd been assured, however, that once she was her sister's age she would learn to appreciate a proper gentleman. Or, in this case, a primped, pretentious oaf.

So tonight the younger sister observed closely as the elder strategically arranged herself on a bench beside the stairs, her bosom heaving rapidly with excitement and her fan making a breeze almost strong enough to move the curling papers in Georgiana's hair so far above. Any moment now Maria would surely give her nerves away with violent hiccups, a malady which always let her down when she was "in love".

Well, even if the man himself was a disappointment, it would still be something, Georgiana supposed, if Maria managed to snare herself the son of an Earl. Their father especially would be pleased. Mr. Hathaway was an upwardly striving fellow who, having recently inherited an unexpected windfall, had uprooted his entire family from their beloved home in the Norfolk countryside and brought them to the great metropolis. Here he meant to expand his printing business, his social status, and apparently the waist of his breeches too— although Georgiana had been sent to her room recently to "consider her wickedness" when she dared mention that last development.

But although his business acumen, and the launch of a successful newspaper, had gained Frederick Hathaway a tentative spot among the "new rich" class, this was not enough for him, or for his extremely ambitious second wife.

He hosted this party tonight in his grand new house to exhibit his eldest daughter before some titled gentlemen of means and, hopefully, form an advantageous connection with one who might take the girl off his hands.

As their stepmother had commented, Maria ought to start earning her keep, for up until now she was naught but an expense and, at one and twenty, headed for a hard seat on the shelf, because she refused to settle for the first man who asked.

But now, at last, Viscount Fairbanks strolled within reach of her sister's charms. His lips were poised in a smirk of condescension, eyelids only half raised, their languid heaviness suggesting his surroundings were not worth the effort it took to raise them fully.

As the tension mounted and a Grand Romance seemed within Maria's hiccupping grasp, Georgiana's mind leapt swiftly to how this opportunity might affect her own life.

Oh, if only she had been a better sister. She should have praised Maria's efforts in watercolor, instead of pointing out that her cows looked like hay bales and all her shadows stretched in the wrong direction. She should have complimented Maria on those carefully constructed Grecian curls, rather than blurting out that the new style drew attention to her protruding ears. And most recently, she should not have requisitioned Maria's evening slippers to run out into the muddy kitchen garden and rescue the cat! But somebody had to take urgent measures. The creature itself was too stupid to find shelter from the rain, and instead had mewled pitifully from the rhubarb patch, waiting for Georgiana to save it. Maria might profess she cared for the cat, but in truth she was far fonder of her slippers— as evidenced by the fuss she made when she discovered them later.

Georgiana made a silent resolution to be a better sister from now on. Just in case there were any treats to be distributed later, once Maria became a Viscountess.

As it turned out, however, her expectations were premature and there would be no wedding clothes ordered.

11

When Fairbanks finally lifted his eyelids long enough to rake the cold prongs of his gaze over Maria's offerings, he did so only once. Then, turning his back to the hopeful young miss, he exclaimed to one of his followers, "You can take the girl out of the countryside, but you cannot take the countryside out of the girl. This upstart newspaperman's daughter should have stayed in Norfolk, with the other fat, slack-jawed and blowsy milkmaids. Why, she's nothing more than a Norfolk Dumpling."

Anyone not near enough to hear his comment was soon apprised of every cruel word by the eager tongues that repeated it swiftly around the party on his behalf.

Georgiana's fingers tightened around the stair railings, and she glared down at his suspiciously stiff and annoyingly tidy white curls.

Fortunately, as she looked around for a weapon, she spied the providential gift of a fishing rod. It must have been abandoned on the landing by one of her careless little brothers, who was forever being told by their stepmama to put his things away and equally as frequently leaving them exactly where they dropped from his hand. Of course, when living in their old home they had all been accustomed to a much messier style of habitation and, in Georgiana's opinion, a much happier one. Now they were transplanted to London, and as Maria had said, things were different here. Everyone and everything was supposed to stay in its place and behave itself according to a strict set of rules.

Well, that might be so, but Georgiana was not about to change her values and standards just to let this insufferable dandy get away with insulting her sister. *She* was the only soul with any right to do that.

Slowly and carefully she lowered the hook and line of her brother's fishing rod between the banister railings until it made contact with a snow white curl of Viscount Fairbanks' wig.

He must not have felt a thing at first, probably because his head was so thick, she reasoned. Only as other guests began to point and gasp, did the peacock finally sense something amiss. Raising a hand to his head, he found wisps of unkempt, thinning hair. Then he looked up, his face crimson with outrage, and saw the wig dangling some distance from his scalp. When he reached for it, cursing wildly, Georgiana began to reel in her prize with more speed, but the violent draft from her sister's fan wafted the luckless wig out of her control. It met with a quick, rather spectacular end when it brushed the edge of a candle flame on its way upward.

The conflagration was immediate and most spectacular. Luckily, due to the hasty thinking of Dead Harry Thrasher, who tossed his coffee at the flames, it caused no further damage.

Burned to a sad and blackened cloud, the coffee-soaked wig began to lose its curls. The wet, malodorous crescents dropped from her hook in a slow pitter-pat, landing on the parquet floor and all over the Viscount's shiny shoe buckles.

As the music stopped and everyone fell silent, apparently not certain how to react, one rebellious voice abruptly rumbled over their heads with thunderous laughter.

Georgiana twisted around to see who it was, and thus her gaze first connected with Dead Harry's warm and curious regard. Candlelight caught in his eyes for just a moment and she felt their comradeship even across that considerable distance. There was a stain on the shoulder of his frock coat, which looked too small and out-dated. And if her eyes did not deceive her, he wore boots from two different pairs on his feet— one with a top band of brown leather, the other solid black.

Perhaps it was only to be expected that the one guest on her side was meant to be a corpse, she mused. Not that he looked like one at all. Far from it. Despite the general disarray of his appearance, this man was very much alive. His presence thrummed with vitality; his eyes, darkly mysterious, were as rich and luxurious as a very fine velvet. His grooming and his garments suggested careless haste, as if he just came directly from a brawl and had borrowed some of his luckless opponent's clothes. Or else he had spent his afternoon wrestling with ladies of a very cheerful disposition— the sport in which bachelors indulged occasionally, as far as she understood it from conversations she overheard between her elder brothers.

Now *he* was far more thrilling to look at.

But, considering his epithet, Georgiana was, naturally, disappointed by the lack of maggots.

* * * *

The next day dawned with the arrival of a letter from Viscount Fairbanks, demanding recompense from her father for the cost of his wig and his dignity. The letter, like the man who penned it, was stretched out and pretentiously decorated, each sentence overreaching for words of four syllables.

But one thing was clearly stated— his lordship expected the issue dealt with promptly. The "issue" being Miss Georgiana Hathaway.

Finally she had her father's attention, a very rare commodity indeed when he had so many other children to manage.

Slap bang in the middle of his brood of seven, Georgiana was the child whose name her father most often forgot. He improvised new labels for her as necessary: Jemima, Jezebel, Gertrude...even Esmerelda occasionally, her personal favorite. And when Mr. Hathaway remarried after the death of his first wife, his demanding new bride soon swept away all chance of the middle child being noticed for much at all by her father.

14

But, unlike the supposed master of the house, the second Mrs. Hathaway was very much aware of Georgiana— her name, the "spiteful, sulky" look upon her face, and her misdeeds. The girl had been a stone in her stepmama's dainty slipper ever since the wedding day and now, at last, that lady saw a chance to remove the inconvenience.

After breakfast that morning, Georgiana passed the door of her father's library just in time to overhear her stepmother's shrill pronouncement.

"She ought to be sent away to school."

"But is that not what gentlemen do for their sons, not their daughters?" Mr. Hathaway replied.

"Not in all cases, my dear. Sometimes the girls are sent away to be polished." Then she added, "You must realize, my sweet, that I say this only for her own good. Georgiana will never find a husband if some effort is not made to curb her difficult nature now, before it is too late. She is naught but a disruption to the discipline and daily running of my household." She paused. "I hear it's quite the *done thing* these days, among the fashionable set, to send their daughters off to finishing-school. All the best people are talking of it." Another pause. "But you must do as you think best, my dearest Freddikins. She is *your* daughter. I'm sure we shall muddle along and somehow manage the embarrassment of her behavior."

Thus, persuaded by his cunning young wife that his wayward daughter could benefit from a ladies academy, Georgiana's father sent her away to school. Having done the best he could to improve her prospects and assure his own peaceful existence, he was promptly enabled to forget about her again.

When the dreadful miscreant was officially informed of her fate, she defiantly declared herself happy to go, proclaiming, "To be sure, the only thing I shall miss is the damnable cat."

Chapter Two

Excerpt from "His Lordship's Trousers" (censored)
Printed in *The Gentleman's Weekly*, May 1817

Yesterday evening's attire: Ivory silk knee breeches. On their return, badly marked with wine and candle wax, three buttons adrift.

This morning's attire: (Eventually) Kerseymere trousers with stirrups and slackly tied gusset laces. Padded seat a necessity.

Today his lordship awoke earlier than usual, before the midday sun had quite reached its zenith. As a regular visitor to this column you will be surprised by the hour of my master's rising, but perhaps not by the curious array in which he was decorated. We shall come to that presently.

The gentleman declared his head to be both vibrating *and* rotating, as he lifted the bulbous mass from its drool-encrusted pillow. There was little to be done to ameliorate his agony until an elixir of raw egg, vinegar and minced garlic, prepared to my own special recipe, was dropped into a mug of ale and swiftly sucked down into his lordship's gullet.

I did my best to reassemble the pieces of his sprawling anatomy, to wipe them down with a wet rag, shave the parts most overgrown and least unsightly, and then hoist him into another new pair of calf-clingers. Throughout this endeavor, he honored me with a tale of his evening spent in the company of a certain lady — whom we shall call 'Loose Garters', on account of the fact that she left hers around his lordship's wrists and bedposts. The lady, it seems, has a preference for trussing my master up like a stuffed goose, and indeed he shall begin to resemble one if he continues to indulge his fondness for

16

treacle tart and marzipan. One cannot retain the well-sprung, racing form of a fine curricle unless one maintains it well with exercise, as I am constantly reminding his lordship.

Alas, his ears are open far less often than his mouth.

"The lady enjoys both the infliction of pain and of pleasure," he informed me between yawns that, if I were of lesser heft, would surely have swept me into the dank abyss beyond his epiglottis. "She performs wonders for a man's filberts, and does enjoy a well hung pair," added the gentleman, congratulating himself on those aforementioned objects in his possession.

Dear reader, during the course of the previous evening, I was occasionally roused from my own light sleep by a loud clapping sound, much like that of a freshly caught pike being wielded with wild force against an empty, round-bellied, iron pot. This morning the cause was clear to me, as I observed the scarlet marks of a riding crop, and possibly a butter paddle, slathered generously across his lordship's posterior.

It was, he confessed to me, Lady Loose Garters' desire to deliver a stern spanking— amongst other punishments— while she had him tied prone to his own bed.

"Ah," said I, "that would explain the clothes peg upon your nose, sir, and the dried candle wax upon your manly nipples. About which I did not like to inquire."

He had, apparently, forgotten these remnants of the lady's passion. Perhaps due to the numbness in those protuberances. His buttocks were not so devoid of feeling, and I fear all his lordship's trousers will require a cushioned seat, should this affair continue long.

As I observed to the gentleman, I do hope his latest amour— in her zest for punitive measures— never procures a pair of nutcrackers for those proud filberts in his possession.

But there was scant time for more warnings. His lordship soon faced the arrival of another lady, rapping at his door in thoroughly unaccountable eagerness for his company.

The necessarily hasty removal of wax from his lordship's chest not only eliminated much of the hair growing upon it, but also elicited from my master a curious noise not unlike the mating call of the great crested grebe...

* * * *

Harry Thrasher was about to laugh out loud, when he noticed the shadowy shape moving about in his peripheral vision. He straightened his lips, rustled the paper and shook his head. The tut-tutting he then exhaled on several terse breaths drew his housekeeper's closer attention as she hovered by the table to be sure he ate his breakfast.

"Not reading that scandalous fiction again, are you?" she demanded.

"It is not fiction, Parkes. It is the true and unabridged diary of a gentleman's valet. A shocking commentary on our times, the sinful, decadent ways of society, and the idiots who abound in it."

"You must realize it's made up— every word— to titillate the masses."

He squinted over the top edge of his newspaper as it wilted toward his chin. "They wouldn't print it, if it wasn't true."

Hands clasped primly, she glowered down at him. "How can you, a Naval Master and Commander, granted a Knighthood for services in war, get the fleece pulled over your eyes by a daft bit of penmanship? Whoever writes that wicked fluff must have a colorful imagination, to be sure." She sighed. "But if the adventures of this imaginary lordship keep you amused and entertained, *they* deserve a medal."

"Parkes, I do not read this for entertainment."

18

"I heard you laughing at it last week. Laughing fit to burst a lung. I thought you must be reading the obituaries again."

Harry closed the paper and tossed it to the breakfast tray. "I read that column to remain informed."

"About what style of pantaloon is favored by this year's dandies?" she scoffed. "Fat lot of good that'll do you since you never go out anywhere, if it can be avoided. You have no interest in fashion or style."

"One cannot turn a blind eye to the horrors of the world, Parkes. This," he jabbed a finger at the paper, "wastrel's misadventures serve to highlight the utter foolishness prevalent in today's society. His behavior is held up for censure, not for amusement."

"And there was I, thinking that you — having shut yourself away in this nowhere place — were simply living vicariously through those wicked stories."

"This is *Surrey*, Parkes. I repeat—*Surrey*. Not the end of the known world."

"It might as well be Timbuctoo. You discourage visitors and you never leave this estate anymore unless your aunt forces you out for an airing in daylight. And then it's not a pretty sight, I can tell you."

"I have everything I need *here*." He banged a fist on the table. "Why would I need to leave this estate, woman? They'll take me out in a box soon enough. And no elm, brass and black velvet, if you please. Plain, worm-holed wood will do me— unlined and undecorated. No cause to waste the coin since it all rots into the ground anyway. In fact, toss me from the mail coach in a winding sheet and have done with it."

"Are you sure even a sheet can be spared?"

"Just being practical. Shed no tears for me, when I finally shuffle off the mortal coil, Parkes. Remember, I've cheated death too many times already." He sighed. "And then you will have this house to yourself without me cluttering the place up, making it all untidy and giving you work to do. That ought to make you and my aunt happy, since you're both constantly conspiring to get me out through the door of my own house for any inane reason. Once I'm truly dead I shan't be able to argue, shall I? Then I'll be the perfect man in the eyes of you two harridans."

Parkes remained unmoved by his insults and unimpressed with what she called his "dramaticals". Of course he had to go out of his house occasionally; they both knew that. But he enjoyed complaining about it nonetheless.

"As for welcoming guests, I've told you before, strangers pry. They make a habit of it. I don't like people knowing my business and so I prefer to lead a very private life. I fail to see the sin in that."

"Ever since you gave up your naval command," she said firmly, "you've retreated into a shell, like a hermit crab. If it wasn't for that good lady, your aunt, you'd never see the light of day."

Ah, but he had not given anything up, had he? His career was taken away from him and he had no say in the matter. But Harry clamped his lips shut rather than correct her. The wound was still raw after two years and he feared what he might say when pushed. Parkes, for all her faults, did not deserve his tirade directed at her.

She now drew his attention to the breakfast tray, pushing the paper aside and pointing to the metal form of a severed hand, poised there like grotesque art. "By the by, I found that hellish thing on the kitchen table this morning." It lay on its back beside the toast, its fingers clawed upward and inward, a gesture of silent anguish. "I assume it fell off one of your unholy creations."

"Ah!" He yawned, scratching his unshaven cheek. "I wondered where that went."

"I wish you'd keep them confined to your study. It does no good for my heart, nor for Brown's, walking into the kitchen half awake in the cold light of morning and finding dismembered joints all over."

"You know I am often restless at night." He grinned slowly, in a manner he'd been assured was suitably menacing. "My creatures take after me it seems. Perhaps they gather in the moonlight and plot mutiny. Take care, Parkes! You'll be the first overboard, since they know you don't like them."

She rolled her eyes. "Whether you slept last night, or sat up working till all hours on those ghastly mechanical contraptions, your aunt expects you at her garden party this afternoon in Mayfair. It's a three-hour ride, need I remind you, and at this rate you'll barely arrive before it's over. No doubt that's your plan."

He pushed the silver lid from a small glass dish on the tray and, ignoring the dainty little spoon provided, collected a blob of sweet, sticky preserves on his fingertip. "How you do enlarge the facts until they enter the realm of pure fiction, Parkes. The journey takes an hour and a half at most." He delivered the jam directly to his tongue via his finger, much to her evident disgust.

"At reckless speed, it may be. If you don't give a thought for anybody else on the road! Or for what poor Lady Bramley will say when they bring your broken, lifeless body to her door."

"I know exactly what she'll say. *How damnably inopportune of the fellow to die a third time, and at the onset of warm weather. Now I must wear mourning again, which does nothing for my complexion and is a great discomfort in summer.*" He paused, sweeping impatient fingers back through his hair. "Kindly refer to my previous statement in regard to the disposal of my corpse and assure the lady not to put herself out."

"Nonsense. You know very well how she worries about you. That's why I'm here to keep you in some semblance of civil order."

"If you wish to maintain that pretense, by all means

do so, but we both know my aunt sent you here to spy upon me, Parkes."

"Somebody has to keep you in order when she cannot. Now, eat your breakfast. Two glasses of brandy and half a cold lamb chop is all I've seen you consume since Wednesday."

"Any other orders for me, Parkes?"

"Yes. For pity's sake brush your hair properly, not just with your fingers— or a fork, as I have witnessed more than once! Now you've got jam in it, I daresay! And put on some decent clothing."

He looked fondly down at his tattered, infinitely comfortable dressing gown and wondered if he might suddenly come up with an illness and send his regrets. But no, the horror of attending one of his aunt's dire social events loomed without possibility of reprieve. Lady Bramley could find vulnerable parts in a man's excuses as effectively as the spikes of an iron maiden could find them in his body. He often thought she would have been quite at home leading the Spanish Inquisition.

"There will be young ladies present from that academy she supports, and she wants you on your best behavior. Not in one of your difficult moods to embarrass her."

Harry winced. "Young ladies? What foul deeds have they been accused of that they must endure such an afternoon?"

"Your aunt says it's their chance to practice their behavior in polite society before they're officially launched upon the world. Don't pull that face! It'll be a good chance for you to practice some manners too. You won't be expected to do anything with a bunch of well-bred girls, but smile and nod without terrifying them too much. Keep the curse words to a minimum and try not to refer to anything that might make a lady blush. You can do that, can't you?"

"I give no guarantees. Lady Bramley surely knows the risks of wheeling me out in public. One of these days, she will see the futility and stop doing it." But he knew why his aunt continually poked and pried him into these awkward situations. The woman was a crazed optimist who thought Harry would, eventually, find a woman desperate enough to marry him.He had a fiancée once, but she moved swiftly on with her own life when she thought him lost at sea forever. When he returned to civilization, Harry felt no inclination to put himself through another courtship. It was all a rather bizarre performance, in his opinion, and he'd always thought how much easier it would be if one could simply find a woman one liked, lift her over one's shoulder and have done with it. Like purchasing a roll of carpet in a souk. But that sort of thing was frowned upon, apparently. People had to complicate matters with bloody silly balls and 'codes of conduct'. Hold her hand only— sometimes don't hold her hand at all— never say damn— don't look at her bosom— don't stamp on her feet— don't scratch yourself— never mention money, flatulence, or the blanket hornpipe. Just a lot of meaningless fluff.

And always use flattery even if it is an outright lie. That, perhaps, was the hardest thing for Harry to manage. For instance, one assumed a lady would like to be informed if her breath was rank, but experience had taught him otherwise.

Now, of course, it was just as well he had no wife. His mind was too unpredictable and sometimes he did not know who he was, where he was, or what he was meant to be doing.

The housekeeper looked grim. "I'm surprised your aunt still makes an effort, since *you* do not. You won't even go to that tailor she recommended. I can't remember the last time you had a new coat made. But your aunt doesn't give up. She's a glutton for punishment, that dear lady."

"Aren't we all rowing against the tide, Parkes? The

good lord sends us challenges daily and yet we bravely continue striving forth. One must look to the sunny side. There are a great many souls in the world worse off than you or I. For instance, meddlesome housekeepers dismissed for impertinence and reduced to the workhouse..."

She muttered under her breath, spun around on her heel and marched out. As soon as her complaints had faded a safe measure into the distance, Harry smiled, put his heels up, unfolded the paper again and opened it back to this week's riveting installment of *His Lordship's Trousers*.

* * * *

"Miss Hathaway! Where have you been? Today of all days!"

The bellowing tones that chased her down the passage like a disgruntled cow overdue for milking, might have halted anyone of lesser determination in their tracks, but Georgiana was not about to pretend she'd heard. Besides, a girl could only hear her name shouted in despair a certain number of times before it became lost in the daily hum-drum racket of her life.

"Her ladyship's carriage calls for us in half an hour, and inspection is in ten minutes. *Ten minutes, Miss Hathaway!*"

The final moos were obscured by Georgiana's footsteps as she took the stairs in her usual graceless clatter.

"I've never known a resident of mine produce so much dust and shake so many nails loose with her *galumphing*," the school proprietress, Mrs. Lightbody, frequently complained. Today, however, she was too busy and flustered to bother with further comment. Instead she lurched back to her private parlor and, very probably, to the gin flask she kept secreted inside a china shepherdess.

One flight of stairs ascended at speed, Georgiana

took the second at a slightly less rapid pace, breathing hard in her excitement and remembering that she could hardly attend a garden party with perspiration stains on her best printed muslin. Especially when it was a wretch to clean and the material cost seven shillings a yard, purchased with money sent by her favorite brother, Guy.

But Georgiana's moment of practical and sentimental concern had already passed again by the time she reached the door at the end of the third floor landing, and dashed in upon her friends to announce grandly, "I have, in my possession, the latest installment of *His Lordship's Trousers*!"

Her two friends, in the midst of dressing for that very proper garden party, immediately abandoned their ribbons and hairbrushes, rushing to devour the latest edition of this naughty, anonymous rake's misadventures. Since his story was banned from the school premises, the popularity of his adventures had only increased.

In order to present her friends with this forbidden entertainment, Georgiana was required to smuggle *The Gentleman's Weekly* into school in a place where it could not be discovered by the eagle-eyed Mrs. Lightbody.

Now, while her friends looked on in deep respect for her daring, she rummaged under her skirt, tugged the folded publication out from the possessive grip of her best garter, and held it aloft with a cry of victory.

Like seagulls finding a broken crab shell, they descended upon the paper, falling together to the nearest bed.

Unlike the other two young women Georgiana already knew what the column contained, but she was obliged to feign ignorance, reading along with them as if discovering each word for the first time. Occasionally, pride and vanity tempted her to spill the secret of authorship to her friends, but with much inner suffering she restrained those demons. There were some secrets a lady had to keep to herself. Even her father didn't yet know that his least significant child was the mysterious author of the most popular feature in his newspaper.

But really, the culprit thought to herself, it was only a little fun. A girl, if she had any brain at all, ought to have some naughty fun or else her world would be a very dull place indeed.

Besides, how much trouble could *His Lordship's Trousers* possibly get her into?

Chapter Three

Years later, whenever Georgiana told the story of what happened next at that disastrous garden party— and it was a tale demanded of her often by a certain group of avid listeners— she did so with a great deal of gravity, building suspense for the benefit of her audience.

"It began," she would say, looking around at their young, eager faces, "as these things generally do, with a murder." Then, once their attention was fixed, she would continue in a hushed tone, "To be exact, the assassination of Lady Bramley's cosseted, prize-worthy marrow. But the marrow was nothing more than the unfortunate casualty of a larger crime."

And so, the story went.

"When my friend, Miss Melinda Goodheart, wildly misaimed the ambitious thrust of her racquet and sent a shuttlecock over the six-foot-tall privet hedge, nobody thought anything unusual of it. The robust young lady was known to be competitive at the expense of grace and decorum, so from Melinda, a returning volley of passion and violence, capable of blacking an eye, was nothing new. The spectators could have no idea that this was the first wicked step decided upon some hours before, when the entire plot to requisition Lady Bramley's magical stuffed owl was carefully laid out. By yours truly."

However, the existence of a glass hothouse on the other side of that tall hedge came as a surprise to the young ladies at the root of this plot. While Melinda was merely supposed to send the shuttlecock out of immediate reach, providing a temporary distraction and requiring the others to search for it over the hedge, a loud shattering of glass proved that worse damage was afoot. A broken pane in Lady Bramley's hothouse had descended upon her most cherished, pampered gourd, and thus a far greater disturbance than the one Georgiana had anticipated was begun.

As the luncheon party turned away from their lemonade and scones to determine the source of that awful splintering, crashing sound, another accomplice, Miss Emma Chance— a small, harmless-looking creature— approached a large pen at the other end of the garden. There, by lifting a wooden latch, she was supposed to set free just one bird to run across the lawn. But instead the timid young lady found herself overcome by a noisy, clattering flock of guinea fowl. They pushed their way excitedly through the gap before she could close it again, and then ran across the grass, scattering all in their path.

Invaded by these chortling beasts, the ladies on the lawn did not know what to do. Adding to the confusion, anyone still left inside the manor house came out to join the panic, for they would not want to miss it. Among them came Lady Bramley's staff, called upon to corral the escaped birds.

Meanwhile, Georgiana— overlooked in all the furor— crept upstairs inside the now silent, unguarded house, and tiptoed along the corridors to find her target. There did seem to be rather more chaos proceeding outside than she had planned, but this was no time to hesitate. She could not return without that stuffed owl, for her name was drawn out of a bonnet that day, putting this mission into her hands, and she would never let it be said that anybody could best her at Reckless Dares. When Georgiana Hathaway was granted a challenge, she set about it with all determination.

The stuffed owl, you see, told fortunes, and because of this fascinating ability it was an object of almost mythological significance at the school. For years it had been tradition — something of a rite of passage—that every senior class make an attempt to "rescue" the stuffed creature from her ladyship's custody. After all, what young

woman of their age didn't want to know the delights, or
horrors, that Fate held in store for her future? Even if, like
Georgiana, they had plans to make their own success, the
mystical lure of an all-seeing fortune teller was irresistible.

Finally locating Lady Bramley's chamber, she looked
around for the stuffed owl and found it staring out at her
through a large glass dome, which was — to her relief and
surprise—easily lifted. With her prize tucked under one
arm, our adventuress was poised to make her merry
escape, when a factor previously not considered suddenly
appeared. Lady Bramley's ill-tempered spaniel, busily
chewing a shoe under the bed, spied the intruder's ankles
and scrambled out to attack them with tremendous spirit.
Clutching the owl under one arm, Georgiana made a run
for it, the angry little dog lusting after her heels as if they
were pork chops, its scrabbling paws gaining ground for
the length of the portrait gallery.

And then the sweeping staircase loomed into view.
She knew of only one way to descend speedily and with
her ankles out of the spaniel's reach. Murmuring a hasty
prayer, she turned and launched herself tail first, down the
shiny, polished banister. Fortunately, she had some
experience of riding banisters, although she had rather
more weight to her at nineteen than she once had at
thirteen and, thanks to the laws of gravity, she hurtled to
the ground much faster than anticipated. Indeed, the slick
speed with which she slid down this polished rail could
have earned applause, if there was anyone to see it.

Anyone, that is, other than the unsuspecting
gentleman standing at the foot of the stairs, apparently
avoiding the party on the lawn and studying a large
landscape painting. Alarmed by the barking dog, he turned
and suddenly encountered Georgiana's backside in a fast
trajectory heading directly at him. Before he could protect
himself from the indignity, the fellow was struck forcefully
by her muslin-wrapped posterior as it shot forth from the

end of the banister, hit him square in the chest, and sent him into a backward sprawl across her ladyship's Italian marble hall tiles.

Georgiana lost her grip on the stuffed bird and her earnest, four-footed pursuer seized upon it without delay. The little dog jauntily dragged his prize out of the house, down the terrace and proudly onto the lawn to show his mistress.

"Well, that was invigorating," said the man, picking himself up off the floor and offering his hand to help her do the same.

Her instinctive response, of course, was to accept his assistance, but in doing so she immediately felt her heart trip over its own thumping pace. Staring in alarm at their joined hands, she realized she had just committed yet another impropriety, and quite unintentionally this time.

Because their hands were naked.

He wore no gloves, and Georgiana had removed her own earlier after accidentally staining them with lemonade. She had planned to put them back on before anybody important noticed their absence, but for now they were drying in the sun outside and she had no choice but to accept his indecently bare hand with her own, equally undressed fingers.

Rough skin to soft. Large to small. Man to woman.

It took her breath away so that she felt lightheaded.

His grip crushed her fingers, not at all hesitant. As if he was unaware of his own strength, and cared naught for propriety. Even less than she did.

If her sister Maria were there to witness the faux pas, she probably would have fainted, only to recover swiftly and give Georgiana a severe chastising, for naturally it would all, somehow, be her fault.

Recovering her tongue, she quickly began to apologize, but he cut her off. "Don't worry about me, madam. I always say it's not a party unless somebody ends up on the floor." His eyes darkened until she, looking up into them, felt quite overheated. Blood raced up and down her body, not knowing where it was most needed. And then he added in his deep, gruff voice, "Or a wig goes up in flames."

Thus, Georgiana learned that she had reintroduced herself to Commander Sir Henry Thrasher. How odd that he had recognized her, she thought. Unfortunate too, for she, feeling wretchedly small and stupid in his presence, had caused yet another ruckus. Here before her was a legend— a man knighted for bravery, and much admired for his valor and steel-spine fortitude. She had eagerly devoured the Commander's heroic Naval exploits in her father's paper, where it was written that even bloodthirsty, lawless pirates held "Dead Harry" in high regard.

The man was a national institution, and she had just felled him with her inconsequential and shamefully airborne buttocks.

For once in her life Georgiana genuinely wished she might have been behaving with decorum, standing in cool, unruffled elegance amid the chaos that somebody else had caused. If this was a Grand Romance, she would be wearing scarlet silk under black lace and with a string of pearls around her neck. That is how they *should* have met. Then she would have extended her hand in a long white glove to let him kiss her languid, discretely-covered fingers, leaving him with a memory of her perfume and a strong urge to write poems about her shoulders.

Instead she had cemented herself in his opinion as a complete and utter ninny.

He had just glanced at her chewed fingernails— exposed in all their guilty awfulness for his perusal. Now his eyes were laughing at her, even if he held his lips in better control.

Her first attempt at tugging her hand free was fruitless, but on the second he relented and his grip released her, but only slowly. The pad of his thumb slid reluctantly over her index finger as she withdrew it.

"Sir..." She pointed with that same finger. "Is that...is that marmalade...in your hair?"

"I believe it's quince jam," he replied, seemingly neither surprised nor concerned about it.

"Shall I help you get it out?" It was the least she could do, she thought.

His lips bent in a sly smile that was quickly curbed, perhaps prevented from progressing further into a full-blown chuckle. "No, that's quite all right. You seem rather busy." He bowed and gestured with the sweep of one arm toward the door through which the dog had scampered. "I would not want to get in your way a second time."

With her heart pounding like muffled hammers against taut piano strings, she slipped out onto the lawn just as Lady Bramley saw the diminutive beast approaching her with something feathery in its jaws. The astonished hostess promptly tripped over her own feet and tumbled to a wicker chaise, taking with her one corner of a tablecloth, a strawberry tart and a jelly molded in the shape of the Roman goddess Britannia.

"All in all, a Good Afternoon's Work," Melinda exclaimed with her usual dry wit, casually resting a racquet over one shoulder as Georgiana arrived, breathless, to stand beside her. Together they watched as Lady Bramley's usually-stoic butler attempted to separate that stuffed owl from the mighty little dog's jaws, cursing like a dock hand throughout. Even Georgiana blushed at the words coloring the air, as did Lady Bramley, who began beating the poor butler around the shoulders with a closed parasol.

Meanwhile, Emma Chance emerged from the nodding sunflowers and joined the other two. "Oh, no!" cried she. "What have we done?"

"Never mind," Georgiana replied. "At least they shan't know it was us."

But of course they would and, really, she did not know why she said otherwise, except perhaps to bolster her own hopes. Or because her mind was still as unsettled as her pulse after recognizing Dead Harry again and feeling that strange rush of warm familiarity. It was, she mused, like being caught in the surprise treat of a sudden summer shower, with an old friend who shared one's delight in the rain.

The Commander had a rather distant, contemplative look in his eyes. As if he was still lost at sea and had yet to get his land legs back. No doubt being knocked off his feet just now had not helped, she thought, chagrinned.

At that moment, the gentleman himself came out of the house and, while exchanging words with their bedraggled hostess, glanced over at Georgiana.

"That must be her nephew, the mysterious Dead Harry," Melinda exclaimed. "He is rarely seen in public these days. They say those years alone on a deserted island quite altered his mind."

"No doubt it would," said Emma, adding pensively, "But he is strangely handsome."

Georgiana, for once, said nothing, although there was a great deal going on inside her head. She was afraid of what might come out if she opened her mouth, and although that gamble did not often bother her— she was a firm believer in "better out than in"— today it did.

Lady Bramley now followed the direction of her nephew's gaze, which had lingered rather noticeably beyond the original glance. Everyone else followed suit, and thrusting its way to the forefront of the crowd, there came one face in particular. With a pair of fiercely narrowed eyes in a flushed, quivering visage.

Mrs. Julia Lightbody, their esteemed headmistress.

* * * *

In general, the students at Mrs. Lightbody's Particular Establishment for the Advantage of Respectable Ladies— or "The Pearl", as some of its wittier residents referred to it— gave the redoubtable proprietress little trouble. Most boarders at this worthy academy were terrified enough to leave her to the enjoyment of her gin flask, a fly smasher and the *Histoire et Vie de L'Aretin* secreted inside a book of sermons. Mrs. Lightbody, in return, saw her pupils graduate through her front door at eighteen and nineteen in much the same intellectual state as they came into it as younger girls. In some cases with an even emptier head, incapable of having a thought or an opinion unless it was put there by her.

The academy was required to provide only a very basic education for thirty guineas a year, and nothing more than an ability to attract husbands was ever expected of those who survived the experience. After all, as Mrs. Lightbody was known to grunt despondently, "There is not much to be done with girls, except teach them sewing, dancing, a little French, and How to Get a Husband."

Although Mrs. Lightbody— probably by mistake— had come into possession of certain educational tools, they were mentioned only in passing, almost as an afterthought, in advertisements placed in periodicals and newspapers such as *La Belle Assemblee, The Gentleman's Weekly* and *The Chronicle*. Within those pages she touted for pupils by relying on three main selling-points: "a separate bed for every lady; brisk, outdoor walks daylly in all whethers, and two compleat, modern globes on the premises".

That advertisement was sufficient assurance to lure in all manner of parent— the lackadaisical wealthy, the ambitious social-climber, and the plain desperate. Glad to escape the responsibility of raising girls and launching them into the world, fathers left their daughters to the care of Julia Lightbody and waited for miracles.

Of course, Georgiana and her two best friends— the young ladies who caused calamity at Lady Bramley's garden party— were not counted among the number of good, undisruptive pupils. They were the troublesome minority, the dissatisfied and unsatisfactory. They would never feature in the annual pamphlet produced by Mrs. Lightbody to announce the engagements and marriages of her former, obedient followers.

Not if these three had their way.

"You addle-pated creatures," the headmistress told them as they stood before her that evening, "will amount to nothing. Her ladyship had to be helped to her bed by a physician and leeches were applied for her headache. We're extremely lucky that she hasn't yet withdrawn her patronage! She is inconsolable over the loss of her great marrow."

"Cut off in its prime," Melinda whispered. "Oh, the tragedy!"

Georgiana made an effort to swallow a chuckle, which only resulted in an unfortunate snort that drew more wrath in her direction.

"Buffoons you are, the lot of you!" Mrs. Lightbody's teeth rattled. "I'm ashamed to have you in this school. At your age you should set an example to the younger ones."

"Yes, Ma'am."

"And you, *Chance!* I would have expected better from you, considering the years of charity I've shown to you!"

Emma colored up and lowered her eyelashes. "I'm sure the marrow might still be eaten and enjoyed, once the glass is removed, madam."

"Eaten? *Eaten?* It wasn't meant to be eaten, witless girl! It was meant to be looked at, polished and admired."

"But, it's a vegetable," said Melinda flatly, "not the Mona Lisa."

"Oh, so there was another girl involved, was there? I might have known you'd try to place the blame elsewhere, madam."

All three young women wheezed helplessly as they tried to restrain their amusement.

The school's proprietress, completely ignorant of her mistake, fanned herself rapidly with a shaking hand and stared through small, hard eyes, her cheeks vibrating slightly with the anger still pulsing through her.

"How do you suppose this behavior reflects upon me?" she bellowed, pausing to swat ineffectually at a fly as it passed her line of sight. "Of all my pupils you three are the very worst. A bad lot. Destined to go down in infamy."

"Well, if one must go down in something," said Georgiana, "it may as well be infamy."

"Of course, you are unrepentant, wicked girl."

But Georgiana was extremely sorry for the massacre of Lady Bramley's marrow and the damage to her stuffed owl. She simply did not see any reason in apologizing to Mrs. Lightbody, when she would rather express her remorse to the lady who suffered these losses. She was not, however, afraid to confess. "I readily admit it was all my fault," she exclaimed. "My friends had no hand in any of it."

"As if I'd believe that for even a moment." Mrs. Lightbody drummed all ten fingers on her desk, itching to reach for that china shepherdess, no doubt. "Wherever you wander, Miss Sharp-Mouth Hathaway, the other two are never far behind. You are three of my most troublesome, unworthy charges and a blot on the reputation of this school." Raising one limp hand she flicked it dismissively in their direction. "One sickly, mousy foundling left to my care and promptly forgotten about; one clumsy, awkward offspring of a scoundrel so-called baronet, who hasn't paid a bill in two years, and then *you*," here she pointed at Georgiana, turning her lip up in a spiteful sneer, "a sly, scheming madam who thinks she can get away with anything, just because her father doesn't pay any attention, and has got himself some new daughters he likes better. Not an accomplishment or talent among you. Not for anything but mischief, that is."

This was not true at all. Emma was an excellent seamstress and played the pianoforte beautifully, although she preferred to play in private. And Melinda had a quick mind when anybody bothered to challenge it— which, in this place, they seldom did. Both her good friends, in Georgiana's proud opinion, were two of the brightest and most promising young ladies in the school, but their talents were overlooked by Mrs. Lightbody because she took a personal dislike to them and could not winkle any more money out of their fathers.

The headmistress took pleasure in the misfortunes of others, liked to lecture at length on subjects about which she knew nothing, and snidely criticized work that she herself could never emulate. She had been known to tear apart finely wrought embroidery or throw it into the fire, simply because the girl who made it once looked at her the wrong way, or her corns were playing up, or she'd been given the cut by someone in the street. All this considered, today's rant was no different to one on any other day. Until she said,

"Since this afternoon's debacle I have decided to seek a governess post for Chance as soon as possible."

In horror, Georgiana looked at her friend, but the girl did her brave best to show no emotion. Unclaimed by either parent— left at the school like lost baggage— Emma had long dreaded the day when she must become a governess to repay Mrs. Lightbody for these "years of charity".

The headmistress continued, "As for Miss Goodheart, she can go home to her father at the first opportunity. I've let that old scoundrel's bills slide long enough and with all the aching she causes my spleen...unless she wants to stay on as an unpaid assistant to work off her debt to me, she can pack her trunk and be gone."

Georgiana wondered which of those options her friend would choose. There was little advantage to either, and Melinda's father had made it clear in every letter he wrote that she was not to come home again, even to visit, until she'd found a rich husband.

The headmistress was not yet done, of course. "And then we come to you, *Miss Hathaway*." Her head twitched with every syllable of the name. "Her ladyship, quite rightly, demands recompense for the destruction you caused today."

"I wish I had the opportunity to apologize to Lady Bramley, but we were removed from the house so swiftly—"

"Do you think she wanted to see your wretched, unsightly face a moment longer, girl?"

"But I might have explained—"

"The less chance you have to speak out loud the better, Miss Hathaway. You are certainly unworthy to address her ladyship directly in any matter. You're a little nothing, no more to her than a speck of dirt on the street."

Georgiana's mind scrambled to calculate the cost of the damaged property. She knew her brother Guy would help if he could, but she did not like to ask him for money and he had already been generous enough. Besides, he was away at sea and her letter might not reach him for months. Her sister Maria, now a married lady, had no patience or sympathy for the "Wickedest Chit", and her other elder brother, Edward, a curate and extremely frugal, would only give her a lecture. Her remaining siblings were all younger and could not help. As for her father, he was too busy to bother with Georgiana, and now he had two new daughters by his second wife — as Mrs. Lightbody had so kindly pointed out— bringing his total offspring to nine, with no sign of abatement.

38

She was, therefore, on her own and at the mercy of Lady Bramley's demands, whatever they might be.

"I shall, of course, repay her ladyship," she said, her mind working frantically on the problem.

"Indeed you shall. I only await Lady Bramley's decision on what the debt shall be. You're a wicked girl. I have never, in all my years, encountered such a graceless...ungrateful..."

Georgiana's gaze drifted to a painting above the mantle in that small parlor. It showed a white-wigged Julia Lightbody from her younger days, when she had a fine complexion and a pert, well-upholstered bosom. Although the eyes in that face remained the same dark crevices, devoid of empathy, little else rendered in paint by the artist was recognizable today. The portrait stood as a chilling testimony to the ravages of time. And gin.

For Georgiana this terrible transformation explained some of that lady's vile moods, even excused the vinegar remarks with which she berated and bullied many of the hapless girls under her roof. A glance at that picture, followed by comparison with the bitter, angry, disappointed woman that image had become, helped cool Georgiana's rising temper and replaced it with pity. If one tried hard enough, one could always find something worthy of sympathy, even in the most trying subjects.

Her brother Guy had once teased her that she had a weakness for troubled souls and a propensity to look for the best in folk, even when their behavior gave her no encouragement. But as a young woman often at the receiving end of an accusatory finger herself, Georgiana believed no one was beyond hope, no one beyond rescue, no one beyond the right of a fair trial. Perhaps this optimism was merely wishful thinking for her own wicked soul— as her sister Maria would remark.

"Now be gone from my sight!" The headmistress reached for her fly squasher again. "Good riddance to the lot of you."

The friends slipped out and as they closed her door, the proprietress hollered, "Mark my words, the three of you will come to no good. You are this academy's biggest failures. By far the most unlikely to make good matches. You'll be three debauched old ladies huddled together, probably living a life of crime, not a decent husband between you."

What exactly would be wrong with that? Georgiana mused. As Melinda often said, who wanted a "decent" husband in any case?

Hmmm. The Ladies Most Unlikely. She rather liked the sound of that.

Chapter Four

"Henry! Wake up, Henry!" His aunt's strident tones broke through his daydream like an axe through his skull. "Pay attention! I didn't invite you to my garden party yesterday so that you would spend the afternoon skulking about inside the house, avoiding my guests. You might have been civil to the young ladies and mingled."

"*Mingled*?" Looking up from his study of the hissing coals in the fireplace, he scratched his temple with one finger. "Madam, had one of them not bowled me over like a skittle, I'm sure I could have attempted conversation, but your list of appropriate subjects dries up rather promptly when one is hurled flat on one's back by a strange young lady's careening nether regions. Forgive me for mentioning that part of her, but I feel now as if I have some familiarity with it."

His aunt stared crossly. "As a gentleman you might still have made an effort, Henry. The mark of good manners is an ability to retain aplomb even in the most uncomfortable of situations."

Harry exhaled a hefty sigh and stretched his legs out until he was almost sliding out of the seat, his frame trying the limits of that dainty chair in which it was constricted. Accustomed to the dark paneling, heavily-leaded windows and sturdy medieval beams of his own house, he felt uncomfortable in these surroundings— airy pastel shades and graceful furnishings. A restlessness had overtaken his limbs that day, but he had nowhere to expend it and this did not improve his mood.

"I fear, madam, that you are destined for disappointment if you continue in this idea of developing and improving me like one of your prize-winning vegetables."

"Don't be foolish, Henry. A champion gourd takes a vast deal more care and trouble to cultivate than a man.

41

Although it is usually a more satisfactory enterprise, I must say."

"Your methods don't seem to have worked with me."

"Henry dear, I haven't even *begun* with you."

As those ominous words echoed around his mind, he heartily regretted bending to the lady's wishes by staying the night in Mayfair as her guest. By now he could have been safely back at Woodbyne Abbey, but with both her sons away and after the terrible events at yesterday's garden party, his aunt had declared herself in want of company. "Even yours, Henry, is better than none," she'd assured him. So he had agreed to stay the night until she was recovered from the atrocity committed against her person and property. Using her knowledge of Harry's soft spots, she had guilted him into it, he realized now. She had cunningly trapped him there as her guest.

Even twenty-four hours later, however, there was no fading of her injuries and no end to her complaints. They moaned onward like a dreary winter wind, reliving again and again the events at the party.

"Every year one of those wretched girls tries to steal my owl. I had Filkins move it upstairs out of the way this time, but even that precaution was not enough."

"I suspect that young woman would have found the object wherever you had it hidden. She seems the resourceful sort." He couldn't help his lips forming a slight smile, as he remembered a fishing rod once put to such unexpected but efficient use, and the horrified expression on the face of that ass, Wardlaw Fairbanks. Couldn't have happened to a more deserving fellow.

His aunt blinked rapidly. "It almost sounds as if you admire the troublemaker, Henry."

"I can appreciate ingenuity," he admitted reluctantly. "Had it not been for that hairy reticule with fangs,"— he glanced over at the dog in her lap— "I daresay Miss Hathaway would have got away with it."

"You know her name? How on earth do you know her name?"

He pushed his heels into her carpet and sat up a few inches, adjusting his pose to reach for a book laid on the nearby table. "I believe I encountered her some years ago. From a distance. Very briefly." Even across the hearth, and with his face now hidden behind that hastily procured book, he could feel his aunt's curiosity stretching like the claws of a cat about to pounce. "We were not formally introduced."

"And yet you remember her name? That's not like you, Henry. You never pay attention to young ladies."

"It was...a memorable occasion."

She huffed. "Whatever her name, she could not possibly have any explanation for her behavior at my party. Hoisting up her petticoats and descending my stairs in that undignified manner! I have never heard of such a thing. Why would you attempt to defend the deplorable actions of that wayward creature?"

Had he tried to defend her? "You know me, madam. One never knows what I might say or do next. Is that not why the Navy retired me at the grand age of twenty-eight and I sit here two years later with a bloody Knighthood that hasn't been any damned use for anything since the days of jousting and long-toed shoes."

Clearly his aunt was too perturbed even to comment on his language. She rambled onward, "That girl is a soul in need of guidance and direction. She was quite dreadfully unrefined in appearance. I have never agreed with so much outdoor exercise as Julia Lightbody advocates, and this girl in her charge is an example of the tragedy that can occur from too much exposure to sun. One seldom sees such a freckled complexion. Surely you agree, Henry."

"She could have been lime green for all I noticed or cared."

"Don't be tiresome, Henry. You are not completely

43

unobservant or you would not have recognized the girl."

"But it was her derriere that greeted me and, I confess," he smirked at his book, "I saw absolutely nothing amiss there."

"Don't be coarse, Henry."

"I was unaware that freckles had become so reviled, in any case."

"Because you have no idea of the standards to which any woman must be held. You live quite in your own world."

"Thank goodness." He remembered, just in time, that he liked being alone in his world. But as he looked down at the book again, the printed words melted away to be replaced by a sensual vision — of her fingers in his, the softest thing he thought he had ever touched. At least, it seemed that way.

He should have worn gloves, of course. But where were hers?

During this discussion, the distant ringing of a bell had evaded his aunt's notice. Too caught up in recounting her troubles, she continued to be unaware of any visitor, or even that the drawing room door was opened, until Filkins, the butler, cleared his throat loudly and attempted an introduction.

"My lady, there is a—"

The very subject of their discussion barreled forth into the drawing room with the flushed cheeks and windblown demeanor of a villain on the run from justice. Stumbling to a brief halt on his aunt's Axminster carpet, she dropped to a curtsey and exclaimed, "I will not bother you long, Lady Bramley, as I am meant to be discharging the tasks for which I was let out— errands at the post office and the haberdasher— but I suffer so under the weight of my guilt that these duties cannot be fulfilled until I have laid my conscience bare before you. I must apologize for the incident of the owl and the marrow."

Lady Bramley's spaniel, formerly curled upon her lap and emitting a steady rhythm of contented snores, now lifted his head, twitched his damp snout and let out a low growl. But the lady herself seemed utterly lost for words and could only comfort the tiny beast with a plump hand on its back.

Meanwhile her butler fussed after the intruder, sputtering in outrage, "How dare you throw yourself at her ladyship! Stop at once and wait to be introduced." He gripped her skirt between his fingers, hauling her backward, away from Lady Bramley.

"Mind my frock, sir. This cost seven shillings a yard! Have an appreciation for good muslin, if you please."

"I wouldn't care if it's spun gold. You cannot confront her ladyship in this manner."

But the sound of ripping stitches caused the butler to release his grip and the young woman dodged nimbly out of his reach. "I must be allowed to plead my case, before judgment is proclaimed. I must have my right to a fair trial."

"Right? *Right*, girl? You have no rights."

"Indeed I do."

Lady Bramley twisted around in her chair, first one way and then the other, raising a lorgnette to inspect the remarkable performance.

Harry closed his book now that he had better entertainment. Probably ought to remove all potential weapons from her reach, he mused. After all, he had witnessed her in action twice now. But at that moment he was too interested in watching her dance circles around the butler and an occasional flash of shapely ankle added to the excitement. Not that he was supposed to notice and if he were a proper gentleman he would have averted his eyes. If.

Miss Hathaway certainly brought a breath of fresh air into that drawing room. He supposed it was her ability to cause a stir with every entrance that made him take note and remember her, for there was nothing otherwise remarkable about her appearance— except for the much-maligned smattering of freckles across her nose, of course. A rare but welcome sight, as far as he was concerned. Whatever his aunt would say of how a lady should groom herself, Harry preferred a natural "imperfection" to an artificial virtue.

"I promise you, madam," the girl continued breathlessly, "yesterday was not meant to turn out the way it did. I am thoroughly, deeply mortified by the disaster I caused."

How, exactly, was it meant to turn out, he wondered wryly, moving his feet before she tripped over them. Clearly she had planned to wreak havoc one way or another yesterday, and liven up an otherwise unbearable afternoon.

Suddenly her eyes met with his. Her color deepened.

It was speckling with rain outside, and she was slightly damp about the edges. This, combined with her yellow straw bonnet, wide eyes and parted lips, gave her the look of a newly hatched chick.

"Well, goodness gracious," his aunt exclaimed finally, gesturing for the butler to halt his pursuit. "I'm quite sure no indiscretion merits this theatrical entrance, girl. Has no one taught you that running is unseemly conduct for a young lady? And speaking before you are spoken to reveals a want of good breeding?"

The girl snapped her lips shut in apparent consternation. Only to open them again a moment later. "Lady Bramley, if I waited to be addressed by anybody of importance, it might be a very long time before I had the chance to speak. I may as well be mute and purely decorative."

"There is nothing objectionable about that idea, young lady."

"Perhaps there would not be if I was, in any way, ornamental."

Harry chuckled at that, and both women glowered at him until he managed to contain his amusement with a series of sputters. "Good lord, look at that," he muttered, pretending to find something amiss with his waistcoat buttons.

"There was a great deal of damage done at the garden party, your ladyship," the intruder soldiered on, "and I, Georgiana Hathaway, am solely to blame. I did not want you to think there was anyone else involved. Nobody else need be punished, no matter what Mrs. Lightbody may tell you. I alone am responsible. I, a wretched, pitiful creature, must throw myself upon your mercy."

Although no longer pursued by an angry Filkins, the young woman still danced from one foot to the other, glancing nervously at the carpet, as if hoping that by balancing on only one set of toes at a time she might ameliorate the mess she made.

His aunt, he saw, was beginning to melt a little inside her stays, not that anyone unfamiliar with the subtlest change in her expression would know it.

"I am solemnly resolved to accept the burden of any punishment you see fit to place upon my unworthy shoulders, Lady Bramley. Although I fear no single act of contrition, however demeaning, will ever fully erase the stain of my wickedness."

"Indeed," his aunt muttered. "I see the enormity of the task before us. How on earth did you get here, girl? Surely not entirely on foot."

"Partly, your ladyship, but for a good distance and only a small sum I managed to procure a seat on the back of a delivery cart."

Apparently a fishmonger's cart. The insidious odor was unmistakable by then, causing his aunt to drop her lorgnette and fumble for a handkerchief to hold against her nose.

It seemed as if Miss Hathaway was something of a magnet to misfortune, even when her intentions were good.

Suddenly Lady Bramley's spaniel escaped her comforting hand, leapt from her lap, bared its teeth, and quivered with excitement.

"But I could not let another hour go by, your ladyship," the young woman continued, eyeing the little dog warily, "without assuring you of my regrets, explaining that my friends are not at all to blame, and expressing my sincerest apology."

"So you rushed into my house like a savage?"

"I felt compelled to take this dire measure, madam, for fear you would not agree to see me if I waited in the hall, and after coming all this way—"

"You might have put your thoughts in a respectable letter, girl."

"I might have done so, madam, but the tone of a letter could be misinterpreted. Do you not agree? I believe that matters of the greatest importance require prompt and face-to-face attention."

"That depends upon the face," Harry muttered dryly, slowly unraveling from that too-small chair and standing before her.

"This is my nephew," said his aunt. "I understand you have not been formally introduced."

"Commander Thrasher." Here she bobbed another curtsey, still teetering on one foot. "To you I also owe an apology, of course, although you would not take one before."

He bowed sharply. "Your eagerness to apologize in person shows some bravery of spirit, Miss Hathaway. However, I'm afraid the odor you brought with you on this occasion has made the greater impression." He knew she was in danger of outstaying her welcome in his aunt's drawing room, for Lady Bramley was best managed with patience— information spooned to her in occasional increments, allowing careful digestion of the facts between each mouthful. But this young lady was a bombardment upon the senses. "My aunt assures me that your unprepossessing appearance alone is a guarantee of villainy. But perhaps a hanging won't be necessary. This time."

Before the penitent could reply, the little dog suddenly launched itself in her direction and Harry's reflexes snapped into action. He caught the beast with one hand under its belly, just in the nick of time— all four of its paws still paddling in mid air.

"Shoo, Miss Hathaway, before any further damage is done. And do try not to break, steal or burn anything on your way out."

She nodded and backed slowly toward the door, squeezing her arms to her sides as if to make herself as narrow and harmless as possible. The butler followed, wafting his hands at her impatiently and muttering under his breath about the lure of a peaceful retirement.

A moment later the door was closed and all that remained of their visitor was a faint trace of fish guts and one damp footprint.

The thwarted animal, now tucked under Harry's arm, growled and writhed in frustration until he was returned to Lady Bramley's custody.

"Well, of all the sauce!" she wheezed, hugging the little dog to her ample bosom. "I begin to think those students learn nothing under Julia Lightbody's care. What is the world coming to?"

"One hesitates to imagine, madam."

Now safely outside the drawing room, their visitor could still be heard pleading her case, even as the butler ushered her swiftly across the hall.

"Fancy, bursting in and demanding to be seen!" his

aunt continued. "And so disheveled! In my day, young ladies did not dash about town on a whim, untended and unchaperoned."

"No indeed. I've always thought the world would be a much safer place in general if young ladies were kept tethered and bridled."

"Now you're just being foolish again."

Harry strode to the window and looked out as the windblown woman was prodded onto the front steps by one stern finger of the butler's white glove. There she stood for several breaths, her face screwed up in frustration, before swiveling on her heels and marching off down the street. Other folk out on the pavement that day passed the unescorted female with questioning glances. Most gave her a wide berth. Wise, on their part.

"What are you going to do about her?" he inquired softly of his aunt.

"She needn't think that by coming here and throwing herself upon my mercy with wide, puppy-dog eyes she can play upon my sympathy."

Returning to his chair and reopening his book at any random page, Harry said calmly, "I quite agree." He sniffed, studying the open page while registering none of the words printed there. "And, as you say, she needs guidance. Someone to put her in order before she turns out completely rotten."

"Hmm. Indeed." When he glanced upward she was brushing stray dog hair from her bosom.

"Since your name is affiliated with that school, madam, you cannot afford to have its students turned out as disastrous young women and released upon an unsuspecting world."

That remark, uttered quietly and casually, caused his aunt to still her fidgeting.

"Someone," he added with a yawn, "with the proper skills, ought to take over her training, where that

Lightbody woman has evidently failed."

Her eyes glimmered. "Why yes! I suppose *I* could."

He feigned surprise. "But would *you* have the time, madam? Your day is so full now—"

"Nonsense. I can always set an hour or two aside for charitable causes."

"Then who better for the task than you, madam?"

"Indeed I ought! Yes. *Yes*, you are quite right, Henry. What a splendid idea."

Hallelujah. Perhaps now his aunt would leave *him* in peace.

* * * *

"Lady Bramley has decreed that you will serve as her companion for the summer," Mrs. Lightbody announced. "I advised her against it, naturally, warning her of your many evils. But she is adamant, and as a member of the school board she must get her way." She sneered. "If the *fine lady* thinks she can do a better job than me on her head be it. I daresay you will put her in a grave." Under her breath she muttered, "The meddling old hag has no idea what she's taking on."

Georgiana had been called into the parlor while the headmistress, suffering one of her infamous "heads" and extremely late rising from bed, was still in her night gown with a ruffled dressing robe thrown over it, and a tattered wig tugged hastily into place. Today there was no other pretense put on and she did not even try to curb the rough, unpolished edge of her real speech— a sharp accent recalling shades of Smithfield Market, rather than the elegant drawing rooms of Belgrave Square.

"If you embarrass me any further, you'll feel the full heat of my wrath!" With one hand holding her hair in place, she stumbled around her desk, bumping her hip into the corner. The odor of gin was rife that morning— a reason, perhaps, for her failure to keep up the facade. "Just you remember, girl, I have a school to run. You ruin my bleedin' reputation and I'll ruin yours, make no mistake."

Ah yes, the school. Georgiana had often wondered how Mrs. Lightbody ever came to open an academy for young ladies. She was not a woman who set a very great example to her pupils. She appeared to have stumbled into this profession by some clerical error, rather than ability or inclination. Most of the time she left her "teaching" duties to the older girls, letting them tutor the younger ones while she remained shut in her parlor with the door bolted.

Julia Lightbody was socially ambitious, but women like Lady Bramley merely tolerated her presence at the school. She had never been one of their "set" and never would reach those heights. But as the headmistress of that school she was able to assure herself that she was, in fact, a "somebody", even if her students— once they achieved a successful match and moved up in society— became completely embarrassed by the old association and would deliberately not recognize her in the street.

Georgiana, who had always loved a good mystery, knew there must be more to Mrs. Lightbody than met the eye. Somehow, somewhere she had influence, of a sort that didn't want to be visible.

A year ago, while being punished and sent to clean the lady's parlor, Georgiana had discovered a thin diary, fallen down the back of a bookcase. According to the cobwebs enclosing its worn leather cover, the palm-sized book had been forgotten there long since, but it contained a vast amount of eyebrow-raising information, penned in tight lines of tiny scribbles across its yellowed pages. And it was this book which inspired Georgiana's wicked imagination and first gave her the idea for *His Lordship's Trousers*.

That little mine of information had actually provided her with a more useful education than anything else she gleaned at the school. Julia Lightbody, meanwhile, had no idea that her least favorite student was now privy to the secrets of her less than proper past.

"I shouldn't be surprised if her high-and-mighty ladyship sends you back by the next post, Miss Sharp-Mouth. Once she realizes what she's gone and got herself into. Don't expect a welcome return here. I've no intention of taking you back."

Mr. Frederick Hathaway, once informed of Lady Bramley's intent to supervise his troublesome daughter's launch into Society, accepted the offer with delight— and probably relief. In his eyes it was a coup, and since he was in no haste to have Georgiana back home again, he raised no opposition to the plan.

"I am to be put 'out' by Lady Bramley," she told her friends with a chuckle. "Presumably like a cat."

Always interested by new people and situations, she did not see this as a punishment at all and was rather surprised that this was the best her ladyship could come up with. But perhaps, like Georgiana herself, Lady Bramley thought no one beyond saving.

Her friends were less optimistic. As the three of them discussed this development the mood was somber. Gathered in their small room high under the eaves of the house they pondered the future while supposedly helping Georgiana pack her trunk. Not that the other two were being much use.

"Lady Bramley seems quite a tyrant, but it might not be so very dreadful for you. You're much braver than I." Emma sat with her elbows on the window sill, her small chin resting in one upturned palm. "We are all to go our separate ways now, I suppose."

"But not for a while yet. I am not going too far, and you two have escaped punishment. Lady Bramley has declared you both innocent of any charge." Georgiana had not told her friends about the daring visit to Mayfair on the back of a fish cart, so they had no idea of her hand in their clemency.

"Nevertheless, the end is coming. This reprieve is only temporary. As soon as Mrs. Lightbody finds a post for me I shall be sent away." Emma followed the wobbly progress of a raindrop down the glass with her fingertip and sighed glumly. "I will miss you both— my greatest and dearest friends."

"Oh, do be a little more cheerful, Em," Georgiana exclaimed, folding a petticoat as neatly as she could and then giving up, cramming it with no further care into a corner of her trunk. "We three will always be friends and that will never change. Wherever we go, we can write and keep each other abreast of our adventures."

"I'm sure I shan't have any adventures. I never did, until you two came along."

As the "natural" daughter of a gentleman who wished to remain anonymous, Emma Chance had been left with Mrs. Lightbody when she was a newly weaned babe. One might think this beginning likely to engender some affection between the woman and the little girl abandoned to her care, but this was not the case. Because no one appeared to want the child and her mysterious father paid only the bare minimum to keep her fed and clothed, Emma was treated at first as just another servant in the house— and frequently punished with a willow switch across her fingers— until Melinda and Georgiana arrived at the school and befriended the poor girl. From that moment onward the three of them were inseparable.

"Whatever else happens, we will always write," Georgiana assured her friends."Certainly," said Melinda. "But Emma is right. Fate will send us all off in different directions eventually, and what can we do about it?" She fell back across her bed in an ungainly flop. "I am to go home to my father, although I am not certain the house has a roof at present. The last I heard he had sold off all the furniture. I know he hoped I'd catch a rich husband to get him out of debt, but that seems impossible." Tucking both arms under her head, Melinda inadvertently exposed a tear in the seam under her sleeve— a gaping hole that proved the frequency of this comfortably unladylike pose. "Unfortunately, I'm not exactly a diamond of the first water and I have no dowry of which to speak. So I must take what I can get for a husband and be grateful." She sighed gustily. "Besides, there's always bonnets."

"Bonnets?"

"Decorating bonnets," Melinda explained. "When all other avenues of pleasure and expression are closed to her, a lady may resort to the comfort of Desperate Millinery. I always rather fancied opening a shop and calling it that. If I ever find a rich husband who is also corrupt enough not to care about the many disgraces of my family. I'll need his money, of course, to fund it."

"Bonnets?" Georgiana repeated flatly. "That is your only idea for the future?"

"What else could there be?"

She felt her temperature rising. Her palms itched, her corset chafed and her feet began a frustrated pacing around the bed. "I have never heard such pitiful resignation. It's very fortunate you have me to keep the two of you off the straight and narrow."

Melinda laughed, but Emma's shoulders sank into further despondency, as if only the palm under her chin was keeping her from sliding down the window along with the raindrops.

"Do you not remember when we studied those globes downstairs and stuck pins in all the places we swore to visit together one day?" Georgiana reminded them. "The three of us made such grand plans to explore the world and have Grand Romances with illicit passion in overgrown Roman ruins. We dreamed of sailing overseas, of riding camels in Egypt and climbing mountains in Austria. Now you're both ready to give up and do whatever you're told, go meekly wherever you're sent and marry the first dull fool who comes along! Some adventurers you are!"

"But we were younger then," Emma replied solemnly.

"It was a mere two years ago!"

"Two years is quite a long time at our age. At sixteen and seventeen we were free to day-dream of exotic places, for the future seemed so far away. Now we must face reality and be prepared for it."

"Well, I say reality should be prepared for us," Georgiana replied grandly.

"You are much too bold, Georgie. In the words of Monsieur de Talleyrand, *The bold defiance of a woman is the certain sign of her shame. When she has once ceased to blush, it is because she has too much to blush for.*"

"And to quote Will Shakespeare, *Thou art pigeon-livered and lack gall.*"

Emma glanced over her shoulder at Georgiana and softly teased in return, "Some of us might be daring enough to ride down a banister, but most prefer the steadier progress of steps to arrive at our destination with a little bit of dignity."

"I can assure you, Miss Chance, that I shall make my own direction. No one is going to tell me what to do, and I shall continue sliding down banisters whenever necessary, even if I am one hundred and eight."

Secretly, of course, Georgiana had already begun carving out her future, writing that anonymous column for her father's paper. What started out a year ago as a daring prank and a way to exercise her lively imagination, had turned into a mission of sorts, her chance to mock the antics of the filthy rich and idle— men like Viscount Fairbanks who once dismissed her sister as a "Norfolk Dumpling".

Since the first chapter, *His Lordship's Trousers* had become a very popular feature in the paper and led to much speculation about the author, as well as the identity of the rake whose life was exposed without mercy in all its awful decadence.

Georgiana's plan, eventually, was to reveal herself to her father as the creator. He would be horrified, no doubt, when he discovered that *His Lordship's Trousers* was penned not only by a woman, but by one of his own daughters. But surely it was time he saw that she was a real person with an able brain and the will to use it.

However, Georgiana realized now that she'd been selfishly preoccupied with her own secret success, when she should have been thinking a great deal more about her friends and how to help them. Clearly suffering a lack of imagination, they needed her to provide them with alternatives. Looking at both young women now, she felt a sad twinge in her heart, followed by the fierce determination to help them somehow.

As the girls embraced, vowing to write often, Georgiana struggled with a great lump in her throat but determinedly fought it back and swallowed it down. This was no time for tears, not with true adventure around the corner at last for all three of them. If they saw *her* downcast, they might lose all hope.

So she cheered the other girls with a smile and a merry reminder, "Once again unto the breach, my Ladies Most Unlikely, and if one must go down in something, it may as well be the good ship Infamy."

Chapter Five

Excerpt from "His Lordship's Trousers" (censored)
Printed in *The Gentleman's Weekly*, May 1817

This evening's attire: Silk pantaloons with buttons the entire length of the leg. An extremely tight garment, apparently meant to provide a shapely silhouette and draw the unsuspecting eye to thighs, calves and any other bulging accoutrement of the gentleman's figure. Best not seen in harsh sunlight. A room lit by one or two candles is perhaps their best venue. If one cannot arrange the welcome relief of complete darkness.

My master has been indulging his sweet-tooth in a great many puddings of late. Perhaps that is all I need tell you, when describing the sweat-and-curse drenched, half hour effort required to squeeze just one of his lordship's limbs into this peculiar atrocity upon the eyeballs.

"Well, good lord," he said to me, puffing out little breaths as he stood before his mirror and examined his appearance. "That took you long enough. I've never known such belaboring of a simple task. What the devil is amiss?"

"I must beg your forgiveness, my lord," I replied. "My mind was not fully on the task at hand. I fear my thoughts wandered to the sausages waiting for me below stairs."

"Sausages?"

"Yes, my lord. They are particularly succulent and bursting out of their skins. My mouth waters at the mere expectation of consuming them later."

"Then you should pull yourself together, man, and stop thinking of your stomach's needs until you have fulfilled your duty to my own."

"Indeed, sir."

Having watched my master attempt three times to retrieve a fallen handkerchief from the carpet while risking the integrity of his pantaloon seams— and my own spleen— I finally gave in and stooped to retrieve it for him. "Allow me, my lord."

He snatched the silk square from me. "I daresay I shall not return until first light. You may consume all the sausages your little heart desires in the meantime."

I bowed deeply. "Thank you, sir."

Moving stiffly with each rigid leg swung round in an arc to engineer the necessary forward progress, he made his way to the door at a glacial pace. "And I think you might have a strong word with the tailor, for his measurements are distinctly off."

"Yes, sir. I am quite sure the fault lies with the tailor and not with your beloved frangipane tarts. He is, it must be said, a despicably smug fellow and not to be trusted."

"Did you not recommend his services to me? No doubt for a share of the takings."

"Indeed not, my lord. I would never participate in such an underhand dealing." Besides which, the tailor had not been forthcoming with the payments promised to me in exchange for my master's patronage. I suspected him of spending my percentage on the new set of teeth he sported about town. Therefore I owed him no loyalty.

"Then you must find me a new man. Someone who understands and appreciates the splendid male form as I embody it."

"I will make inquiries in all haste, my lord." Perhaps Hodson the butcher would be a good choice, I mused. He knows a great deal about squeezing too much meat into a thin skin.

But this, as his lordship would assure me, is what we must suffer for fashion. And on the subject of suffering...

"Will you be seeing Lady Loose Garters this evening, my lord?"

"In all probability the merry trollop will hunt me down." He smoothed a hand over his waistcoat as he took one last survey in the tall looking glass. "And I suppose I shall be obliged to let her."

"I believe I ascertain a certain preference for the lady's company, sir," ventured I.

This immediately removed the smile from his lips. Alarm glimmered through those blood-shot eyes. "Then you are quite wrong, man. I simply find myself suffering a dearth of more interesting companions of late."

"I see, sir. Then I shall amass a good stock of cold compresses, head ache powders and soothing balm for my lordship's buttocks."

As he reached the door handle at last, I thought I heard the pitiful, quiet scream of stitches under duress, but alas there was nothing I could do to help them. Like me, they are prisoners to their duty for his lordship and just as little appreciated.

* * * *

Several drips of water had fallen onto Harry's paper, smudging the ink, before he was forced to stop reading and pay attention to the origins of the leak. Irritated, he looked up to the ceiling of his bedchamber and watched another crystal bead appear before it lengthened, released, and made a direct course for his page.

"Damn and blast."

He reached for the mallet beside his bath and banged it hard into a small Chinese gong. Eventually his housekeeper's steps approached the door.

"What now?" came her surly response to his summons. "Brown has already heaved four pails of heated water up those stairs. Haven't you sat in there long enough?"

Harry tugged on the tasseled rope that led from his bath to the door handle and pulled the door ajar. "Parkes, the leak is back."

"Of course it is," she exclaimed through the widened crack. "Makeshift fixes never last. What do you expect me to do about it now?"

"Kindly cease your warbling and find someone to fetch a ladder, Parkes."

Another splat of rain water dropped to the end of his nose and hung there a moment before it finished its descent to his bath.

In due course, his handyman Brown arrived, bringing a ladder from the east wing where he'd been fixing a fallen chandelier.

"Shall I have a look at the leak for you, sir?"

"No, no! I can manage. Might as well make myself useful. Thank you, Brown."

The old man set the ladder in place for him and then hobbled off.

Parkes returned immediately to chide Harry through the half open door, "I don't know why you can't get a new roof. There's money enough."

"The roof is original to the Abbey, and has sheltered many generations of Thrashers. It is perfectly adequate."

"Until it rains. It's more patched hole than roof by now. You waste time on those fool inventions and pay no attention to the maintenance of this house."

"Thank you, Parkes. Surely I'm keeping you from your work elsewhere."

"Just like that study downstairs, full of papers you refuse to throw out," she went on, ignoring him. "Mice will be nesting in this house, mark my words. Scratching about in the walls, driving me mad."

"As long as the little blighters leave me to my business, Parkes," he replied, "what right do I have to chase them away from theirs? In all likelihood, their ancestors were here first— long before that jolly scoundrel, King Harry Tudor, chased all the monks out with hot iron pokers up their backsides and handed the place off to my family in exchange for a few unsavory favors."

She sputtered irritably. "You're turning that study into a safe haven for spiders too, keeping them around to make sure I stay out of your books and papers, I suppose. So worried about folk prying."

"Spiders perform a service, Parkes. They catch flies. Have you ever studied the construction of a web? It is fascinating! You simply must—"

"I don't have time for that. Some of us have more to do around here than gaze off into the distance for hours on end, like you."

"It's called thinking and somber reflection, Parkes. You, being a female, won't be familiar with those activities."

"Thinking? That's a fine excuse! And nothing ever comes of it but those peculiar inventions of yours."

"Automatons, Parkes. You need not be afraid of the word."

"All they do is sit down there in bits and pieces, collecting dust. Watching me."

"They haven't eyes. How can they watch you?"

"It feels as if they do. Makes the hairs stand up on the back of my neck. It's unholy, that's what it is. Who wants one of those clockwork beasts watching them from a dark corner?"

Harry chuckled. "Sounds as if you're afraid they might catch you doing something you oughtn't. What *do* you get up to behind my back?"

She gave a gasp of exasperation. "How long have you been sat idle in that bath? You ought to be shriveled to a prune by now. I suppose you forgot the time and where you are, as usual."

Parkes frequently complained that the hours in his day were lost before he had even remembered to shave or put on a shirt. He was once so caught up in the elaborate, mechanical design of a bird-scarer to keep crows off a vegetable garden, that two days had passed before he remembered to eat.

"This solitary world of yours, my dear old chap," his cousin Max would say, "is no way for a gentleman to live. You need more household staff to look after you. A valet at the very least."

Harry, however, preferred as few staff as possible. Somehow he had acquired Parkes, and with her came Brown the odd job man, and then Sulley, who looked after the horses. In his cousin Maxwell Bramley's view, this was inadequate. It was incomprehensible to Max that any gentleman could exist without a valet, probably because he couldn't even tie his own neck cloth.

"You'll do yourself an injury one of these days, left to your own devices in this shambles of a house," Max had remarked.

But as far as injuries went, Harry barely gave them a thought. He'd sustained countless wounds in his life, including an encounter with a two-foot oak splinter that almost took him to his maker seven years ago. Since surviving that "fatal" wound and then, a few years later, being declared "lost at sea" and abandoned to his fate on an unchartered island, his life had taken on the rather surreal tenor of one existing on borrowed time.

When a man's obituary has been printed in the newspaper not once but twice, as he'd remarked to his aunt, one had a tendency, if not a duty, to believe it.

"Well, I suggest you get out of the bath and do something about that leak," snapped the housekeeper, about to leave again in another one of her huffs.

"Oh, and by the by, Parkes, I don't like that new soap. It smells like flowers, and I have no desire to attract bees."

"That soap is very fine and used in the best families now, so they say."

"Which means it was outrageously expensive. The quack who sold it to you must have seen you coming a mile off, woman. Yet you call me the gullible one."

"Well, excuse me, for trying to polish coal. I ought to know better by now."

"I'd rather smell like myself, Parkes, than a dandy."

"A savage, that's what you are," she muttered. "And you, a knight of the realm! *Sir* Henry Thrasher indeed!"

"A title I certainly didn't ask for," he bellowed. "You may have noticed, I had to lose half my wits before they granted it, which ought to tell you something about titles in general."

The door slammed shut.

Harry blinked as another drop of water hit him in the eye, shaken loose by the tremor of the housekeeper's wrath. He could well imagine her expression as she stormed across the landing and down the stairs.

Later she'd remind him of how lucky he was to have her around. He would agree and so they'd make their peace again.

And he *was* bloody fortunate, wasn't he? Who would remind him to eat, if Parkes left him too? He supposed it was rather touching, really, that she bothered what he might smell like. Not that he ever got close enough to anyone else these days for it to be a genuine concern.

Well...he only got close by accident, he mused, thinking again of the young lady who recently floored him as violently as a bottle of brandy on an empty stomach. She had a very bright, inquisitive pair of eyes that made it seem as if spring newly flourished each time she looked at him. Life, he mused; she overflowed with it so that he felt her heat warming his own skin. How odd it was that his memory was so unreliable these days and yet he'd recognized her at once as the girl on the stairs at a party some years ago. That event, of course, had ended rather spectacularly, which is probably why he remembered it.

She definitely had a knack for chaos.

This fascination for the inept thief was nothing more than human nature's curiosity for the perverse.

He glanced over at the door again. Assured that he was alone, Harry folded his paper, dropped it to the floor, and reached for his dressing gown, which hung over a nearby chair back. Hidden there, in the depths of a pocket, he kept the little paper token that had fallen from the owl's mechanical beak just before the dog hauled it away from his assailant at the garden party. A "fortune"— the sort of thing, so he understood, that ladies liked to imagine had some significance.

And there upon it was a single phrase, framed by curling scrolls and tiny flowers.

Charm strikes the sight, but merit wins the soul.

Evidently this warning was meant for *her*, not him. Such a wide-eyed, fallible creature was bound to be dreaming of pretty young suitors with silk knee breeches and affected manners.

Well, hopefully the young woman would gain some benefit from his aunt's guidance. Lady Bramley was a formidable adversary, but she could also be a very good ally in a tight spot and Harry had always thought that somebody ought to make use of her munificence. It was energy wasted on him.

He slipped the paper fortune back into the pocket of his robe, sighed deeply and then heaved his body out of the cold water. For a moment he stood by the bath, scratching his damp chest, surveying the ceiling of carved Tudor roses. Water glistened like dew upon the petals of one darkened bloom.

Now what could he use to plug the leak? Better get a better look at it.

As he became absorbed by the problem of that tiny hole in the ceiling, Harry gave no consideration to the ladder being unsteady when he climbed the first rung. His mind already traveling rapidly ahead of his body, he didn't bother looking down, otherwise he might have noticed that when he moved the ladder into position, he set one of the legs on that wet, partially melted cake of soap previously tossed from his bath in contempt.

The tumble came shortly after. His head hit the gong and summoned the housekeeper, who must also have heard the heavy thud of a body hitting the floorboards.

Parkes looked down at him with her head shaking, lips struggling to remain firm.

"You were supposed to be fixing a hole, not making a new one," she muttered. "And you're right— that soap does make you smell like a dandy."

* * * *

"I told you so," his cousin Max announced, barging into Harry's study on a warm summer's afternoon. "You're a danger to yourself, living out here in the midst of nowhere, all alone. Look at you! What a sorry state to be in. Each time I come here I dread what I might find."

With his right wrist badly sprained and his arm tied up in a sling, Harry was at a disadvantage. He couldn't slam or bolt a door as quickly with only one working arm. "As I must constantly remind people, this is Surrey, not the *midst of nowhere*," he grumbled. "Certainly, it isn't far enough from London to stop you venturing into it."

The comment was ignored, as usual.

"I fret about you, old chap, here in this ruin of a house, all alone. Next time it could be more than an arm you break."

"It's not a break. It's a sprain, and I am not alone. I have staff. Adequate staff for an unsociable bachelor "

"What you need is a woman, Harry," his cousin declared, promptly pouring and downing an unoffered glass of brandy. "Here you sit, buried in your books and inventions, getting old before your time. What are you?

66

Eight and thirty?"

Harry sighed. In truth he was only thirty, but he would rather be sixty and then perhaps people would stop asking him impertinent questions, accusing him of hiding like a hermit in the "wilderness" of the Surrey countryside. If only they would leave him to his own business.

"I am perfectly content," he assured his cousin. "I like it here. I like my life the way it is."

Max shook his head. Clutching a refilled glass, he strolled around Harry's study, warily examining the array of mechanical body parts littering the shelves. "Still making these clockwork horrors, I see."

"They are practical devices with many uses."

Much as Henry Thrasher, Master and Commander, had once been, he thought glumly. Before he lost his mind and left half of himself at sea. Now what was he good for?

One of the fingers on a disembodied arm suddenly clicked into action, bending and then pointing, as if it had a life of its own. Of course, Harry knew it was merely the delayed movement of a wheel within the device, but Max jumped and almost spilled his brandy. He stumbled backward, fumbling for a chair.

"It is the future, cousin," Harry continued, hiding his smile. "Machines will one day rule the world. Inventors have created mechanical swans and tigers, an automaton flute-player, even a '*digesting duck*'."

"That's all well and good, Harry. But you cannot pretend these terrible things make good company." Max finally dropped heavily into a chair on the other side of the desk. "You must feel the need for female entertainment. Warm flesh and blood. This," he waved his glass around the cluttered room, "is not normal. You cannot live a chaste dull life just because Amy Milhaven—that unfaithful creature— broke your engagement and married elsewhere the moment your back was turned."

"A year after I was shipwrecked and presumed lost at

sea."

"Twelve months is no time to wait, cousin. It was remarkably cold-hearted of the hussy to write you off so easily."

"Are you suggesting that Amy Milhaven, at the tender age of one and twenty, should have donned a widow's cap, resigned herself to bad sherry because she could afford nothing better, and pined for me ever after?"

"No, but the trollop's eagerness to replace you was unseemly— as my dear mama often says— and her second choice showed a shocking want of taste. You might forgive her for it just to save your pride, but fortunately you will always have me, cousin, to hold a grudge on your behalf."

Harry laughed and shook his head.

"And since you came back, there have been no other women?" Max persisted.

"With good reason, considering the unpredictability of my moods. What woman would put up with me?"

Since he barely knew what he might do from one day to the next, his mind having sudden, unpredictable spasms and memory losses, Harry had decided to avoid Society as much as possible. After the blow to his head at the Battle of Grand Port in 1810, the Naval doctors could not explain how Harry was still alive. The experts all had different theories, but no solid explanations. Once recovered, he had returned to sea and calmly resumed his career with a new command. But two years later he was shipwrecked. Believed gone for good this time, a memorial stone was raised, his house was shut up, and sailors from Plymouth to Botany Bay raised a toast to "Dead Harry".

The world was confounded once again, when it turned out that he had survived twenty-eight months on a tropical island. Rescued, shaved and respectably attired once more, it was expected that he could pick things up as he had before, but Harry was changed. A great many things that had not concerned him in the past, now drew his mind and attention away from those matters considered important by others. After so long alone on that island with nothing but his own company, he had grown accustomed to peace and the tranquility of internal musing. He could sit for hours pondering the arrangement of stars in the sky, or the slow burn of a log in his fire. Worst of all— an even stranger development— he suddenly felt no desire to fire a gun or a cannon at anybody.

So, eight months after his rescue, the Navy suddenly found him more liability than use. He was quietly removed from a once promising career and packed off with the consolation of a knighthood.

But in Max Bramley's eyes, there was nothing wrong with Harry. Nothing that a simple cure could not change. Max generally viewed life through the distorted glass at the bottom of a crystal goblet, of course, and although folk never went to him for advice, it did not stop the blurry-eyed fellow from giving it freely.

"A woman could save you from yourself," he said. "You've already got one arm in a sling, old chap. But breaking one's fall is precisely what a woman is for."

"Then why haven't *you* acquired one?"

That caught his cousin off guard, but only briefly. "We are talking of you, dear coz, not of me. You were in the Navy, Harry, for pity's sake! This chaste life is not what I expect from a sailor."

"Contrary to popular belief, a sailor's life is not all rum and wanton women. I was twelve when I joined the Naval Academy in Portsmouth, fourteen when I became a midshipman and nineteen when I had my first command. How much time do you think I had to spare for the pursuit of entertainment?"

"But I remember a time when you had a spark in your eye and lust for a pretty woman the same as I, or any man.

I remember your love of games too and how, if our eyes turned to the same woman, we competed to win her." Max sighed. "I miss those old days, for now I have no worthy competition to keep me on my toes and, as you see," he ran a hand over his waistcoat, "I am in danger of going to seed."

Harry had a vague recollection of their "competitions", but it all seemed a very long time ago— another world, before the first time he died. The only thing he took seriously back then was his naval career. Women were recreation, briefly had and swiftly forgotten, but then he did not have much of an example to follow. His mother had run off while he was still very young and then his father enjoyed a second bachelorhood with a parade of petticoat. But it never brought the man any contentment. Why he ever continued trying after the first debacle, Harry could not comprehend. He dearly missed his father, who was long since in his grave— and, unlike Harry, had the good grace to stay there, knowing when he was dead— but it must be said that, while living, the fellow had been a fool to himself.

His cousin suddenly leapt out of the chair in which he had previously rooted his backside with sprawling carelessness, and paced around it as if he had nettles down his breeches. "I have an idea in mind, old chap."

Oh, this could only be trouble. "Do treat it gently. It must be lost and afraid in such unfamiliar surroundings."

Max set his brandy glass on a teetering pile of books to refill it again. "I'll find a woman for you. You've been without one for far too long, clearly." He glanced around the messy room with a significant arch of one eyebrow. "It's time I did something about this appalling oversight. You're always helping me out, cousin, and I feel excessively guilty that I have not done the same for you. A creature light of skirt and bereft of virtue is just what you need. A professional to make you feel merry and sociable

70

again. Shouldn't cost too much."

Ah. And there it was. Harry was amused. So money was the real purpose for this concerned visit after all. "If that was what you wanted, Max, you might have just asked, instead of taking this circuitous route."

"What do you mean?" His cousin's face was the very picture of innocence offended.

"To whom do you owe money this time?"

"It is not for me."

"No." Harry chuckled and readied his pen in the inkpot. "It never is."

"Just enough to bring her in a discrete private carriage will do. You wouldn't want her sent on the mail coach, surely. People might talk."

And so, with a hefty sigh of good-natured bemusement, Harry wrote out a cheque, certain this money was going toward another gambling debt. He really didn't mind, as long as it kept Max out of his hair for another six months, and he knew his cousin would never go to Lady Bramley for assistance once he'd spent through his monthly allowance. "Your mama would appreciate a visit," he muttered, handing over the cheque. "She tells me she hasn't seen your face since the new year."

"She always wants to see this face, but as soon as she lays eyes upon it, the good lady is reminded of why she wanted it gone before."

"Even so, it wouldn't be too difficult to drop in. She does seem rather in want of her sons' company."

"Let Mandrake visit her. He is the favored son."

"But your brother, I am told, is much too busy with the country estate. It might be your chance to get back in her favor somewhat, if you spared a little more time for her. I cannot imagine your daylight hours are so very full."

His cousin merely took the cheque, tapped the side of his nose in a curious gesture and then staggered out, whistling a jaunty melody. No doubt on his way back to a game of Faro.

Harry soon put this conversation out of his mind, but later that night he woke abruptly and found that some of Max's warblings remained trapped between his ears, where they echoed back and forth.

Do you not feel the need for female company, Harry?
Getting old before your time.
You cannot live a chaste dull life just because Amy Milhaven—that unfaithful creature— broke your engagement and married elsewhere.

But it was not Miss Milhaven's fault. The fact that he ever became engaged to her in the first place was a surprise— to him as much as anybody else. He was not made for the sport of gentle wooing and had no great interest in marriage. But Amy Milhaven happened to be in need of rescue when they met and Harry, in one of his lighter moments, decided to help her. The lady's desertion later, while he was lost at sea, could certainly not be blamed for his current avoidance of female company. No, it was his own unpredictable mind at fault. Unfortunately, Harry often forgot he was back in the "civilized" world these days and that caused severe problems when he went out into Society, where any properly raised females might be found.

So why not take unpredictability out of the equation, by building for himself a safe "companion"— one he could control? A companion who could not be injured, outraged or offended by anything he said or did. Or by his occasional lapses of memory.

Always up for a challenge when it came to the science of design and invention, Harry went down to his study immediately and got to work.

His creation could sit quietly, listen to his complaints without arguing or lecturing, and, possibly, play the pianoforte to entertain. Most of all, she would stay where she was put and not suddenly decide one day to up and leave him.

Men the world over would thank him for such an invention.

Perhaps he would give this automaton some facial features. A further challenge, for he had never given one of his machines a face before, but he supposed she ought to have something for him to look at. Females were meant to be decorative, if at all possible.

Harry took a fresh sheet of parchment and sketched out the shape of a face, then added the necessary features carefully with charcoal. It took him several attempts before he had what he wanted, but when he was finally satisfied, the face peering up at him from the grey smudges was so realistic that he knew he must have seen her before somewhere. He could imagine those gently bowed lips parting to exhale a hasty apology. Thoughtfully, he placed his charcoal-coated thumb on her cheek and pressed down to leave a shadow. Yes, that completed the image and almost brought it to life.

Miss Hathaway. Who else would haunt his thoughts but that wretched magnet of calamity?

Smirking, he briskly marked three words along the bottom of the paper.

The Wickedest Chit.

Soon consumed with his latest project, Harry did not realize he'd forgotten to get dressed that day, until Parkes entered the study the following morning to see if the fire was lit.

Fortunately she wasn't a screamer.

Chapter Six

"Now, what have we to work with?" Lady Bramley muttered, peering through her lorgnette and once again taking in the awfulness of her young charge. "You've nothing much to recommend, so I've been told." She lowered the lorgnette and tapped it to her cheek. "But there is nothing I enjoy better than a challenge, as my nephew would tell you. It was he who put this idea into my mind, no doubt mischievously hoping I might leave him alone in the meantime. As if I am incapable of putting my thoughts to more than one thing at a time."

Georgiana remembered again the startled face of Commander Thrasher just seconds before she knocked him off his feet at the garden party. He must think she had not grown up much since the incident of Viscount Fairbanks and the burning wig. So this was his idea.

"You ought to act with more decorum," her friend Emma would have said. "You are no longer a dizzy girl."

Of course, nobody could ever accuse Emma Chance of acting like a dizzy girl. She was the most sensible, solemn young woman ever abandoned by her parents, and only drawn into Georgiana's mad schemes because she was too nice to refuse and determined never to let her friends get into trouble without her. It was likely she also hoped to somehow prevent the worst happening.

On the other hand, Melinda Goodheart, the third member of their little band, always went along with anything that promised entertainment and would gladly suffer punishment later as long as she had her fun first. Georgiana had fallen into the role of ringleader most often because she was usually the one who came up with a plan. She grew bored too quickly with no mission at hand and so was always on the lookout for another to undertake.

For Georgiana it was not so simple to do what she "ought", when there was usually nothing worthwhile to gain from it. What she wanted was not a husband, but adventure, and that was not likely to come her way if she went through life afraid of her own shadow, and quietly, politely agreeing with everybody. One had to know what one wanted, even if it was something others believed to be out of the realms of possibility, and one should also know how to make the most of an opportunity, whether it came in the shape of a discarded fishing rod, a passing fishmonger's cart, or a benevolent lady's whim to play Ovid's Pygmalion.

She looked at Lady Bramley. "You and I have something in common then, madam," she said brightly.

The woman drew back, frowning.

Georgiana explained, "We *both* enjoy a challenge."

The little dog, clutched under Lady Bramley's free arm, eyed her across the room, its shiny black nose twitching and ears sharply pricked. Without a doubt, the animal recognized the owner of those juicy ankles that escaped his jaws once before. He licked his snout with a flourish, warning her that he looked forward to their next encounter.

Meanwhile his mistress continued as if Georgiana had never spoken. "You are very fortunate to be taken under my wing."

"Yes, your ladyship."

"I am told you can neither play nor sing."

"I can do both, madam, but not with any degree of skill greater than a very meager average. In the case of singing, people are more likely to ask me to *stop*, rather than entreat me to begin. But I do enjoy it. I always think that if a girl has no chance of pleasing others, she should at least please herself."

"Neither have you much ability with a needle or a paintbrush, and your dancing is only adequate."

"Unfortunately I would rather sew to my own pattern and paint from my own imagination, which tends not to dainty flowers and idyllic scenes. As for the dancing, at least I have plenty of enthusiasm and I do markedly better after a glass or two of wine."

Her ladyship looked askance.

"Miss Melinda Goodheart's father sent her a jug of his homemade wine wrapped up in new woolen stockings every Yuletide," she explained. "It quite enlivened our spirits."

The lady's gaze moved up and down, swift and merciless in its critique. "Your skin is very freckled. Tsk, tsk. Have you no parasol to keep the sun off?" She pointed with her lorgnette. "And stop slouching. Shoulders back. You're not pulling a plow." Finally, her assessment of Georgiana's appearance complete, she turned to the need for other improvements. "A young lady of nineteen has no occasion to slide down a banister. Even if the house is on fire, she should walk with composure and grace, remembering always that her demeanor sets an example for others."

"Madam, I fear in my house such an elegant lady would be trampled in the stampede. With so many children to get out, speed is rather more important than manners in a fire."

The woman across the room peered at her through that little round glass lens again. "Your father owns a newspaper, is that so, young lady?"

She replied that yes, her father ran a publishing house and a newspaper.

Lady Bramley shook her head. "I suppose we'll have to make the best of it."

"Oh, dear." Georgiana chuckled. "I hope not, madam. I don't believe in settling."

"I beg your pardon, girl?"

"It's something of a Hathaway family trait to strive for more and better than that to which society believes us worthy or capable. So we don't believe in making do." She shrugged. "We believe in aiming for more. It makes us restless and, on the whole, a rather disagreeable bunch."

"Then you are a revolutionary."

"Am I? I simply believe there is enough good fortune to be shared and enjoyed by all, your ladyship. And I believe that if one has the will to work hard and earn that good fortune, one should not be held back by the circumstances of birth, or gender. It should be a person's ability that counts and the goodness of their heart, not their sex or the roots of their family tree."

Lady Bramley leaned back, letting her lorgnette fall to the end of its chain. "You believe in a vast deal, for someone not yet twenty."

"Yes." She sighed heavily. "But somebody has to have hope and imagination or we'd all be stuck in place. Nothing would ever change or move forward."

"Good heavens! Who wants anything to change? I certainly do not."

"I think you do, madam, or else you would never have taken me in as a project. It seems you're as big an optimist at heart as I."

Apparently the lady was not accustomed to being debated very often. She studied Georgiana with a mixture of faint alarm and increasing curiosity, while her little dog bared its fangs, grumbling quietly.

Georgiana smiled. "Worry not, your ladyship. I have a feeling that we'll get along tremendously."

* * * *

The letter had arrived at Woodbyne Abbey one dewy morning in early June. Along with Harry's other correspondence, it was laid on a tray and taken in to his study, left there for his perusal when he felt inclined.

"Post has come," Parkes had announced with sarcastic grandeur, sweeping open the window drapes which were still closed from the night before. Too busy with the left-handed sketches of his new invention, Harry had not yet been to bed.

Without looking up, he demanded, "Anything important?"

"How would I know?"

"Could you look? God gave you eyes for a reason."

"Only you know what's pressing to you. I'm sure I don't know how your mind works. No one does. And a good thing too, no doubt." He heard her feet stomping back across the floor, pausing to step over books, wine glasses and plates of uneaten food.

Since Harry had already lost interest in the conversation, whatever the post contained that day — indeed, its very existence—was promptly forgotten.

Consequently, it was almost a week later before Harry, casually reaching across the desk with his good hand, found two letters buried under an inkstand on his desk.

By then it was, once again, too late to stop the disaster he suddenly discovered headed his way. Just like Miss Hathaway's posterior.

Fumbling for his trusty mallet, he hastily struck the gong by his desk. He was still striking it violently, when Parkes finally arrived in answer. She was getting slower, he noticed peevishly, and looking more worn and faded about her edges once she did appear.

"Parkes!" he exclaimed, spitting out paper from where he'd ripped both missives open with his teeth. "What is this about my aunt coming here for an extended visit? Why, by the devil's own arse, is she coming here? What can the woman be thinking?"

"Pretty language indeed from a gentleman and a knight of the realm!" The gaunt, grey woman gingerly took the first letter from his hand as he thrust it at her. "I'm sure I don't know why your aunt is coming here. Why would I know anything that goes on?" she muttered. "I'm always the last to be told."

"Lady Bramley seems to think I require company. That I've been left peaceably alone far too long, so she's coming here to interfere. All because of a wrist sprain? No, no she has some ulterior motive in mind, to be sure." He fell back into the reassuring, well-worn embrace of his father's old leather chair. "She'll just have to be sent away again. What the deuce does she think she's playing at coming here? Inviting herself along just as bold as you please."

"Well, if the mountain won't come to Muhammad, as they say.... She's certainly a determined lady."

Harry looked around in desperation at this gloriously untroubled lair in the center of his easy, bachelor existence. Morning sunlight touched the various tilting piles of blissfully disorganized mess with a fond, indulgent kiss. He thought of his study as a Captain's cabin, his secure retreat in this leaky old hulk known as Woodbyne Abbey.

Parkes read out loud, "*I look forward to a pleasant summer sojourn in the country with my nephew. Pray, do not go to any bother, as I shall stay no longer than a month— or so— and can bring my own entertainment.*" She made the throat scraping sound that meant she was amused. "Just as well, since she won't find anything mildly entertaining here."

"Hmph, that's what you think. Wait until you read the other note."

The housekeeper picked up the second letter, this one much shorter and scrawled in a hasty, unsteady hand.

"*Package ordered and on its way. The name is Mrs. Swanley, an artiste of remarkable skill.*" She put her head on one side to read the signature. "*Yours affectionately, M.B.*"

"Cousin Max is sending me a woman."

"Now there's a thing. What would you want with one of them?"

Snatching the letters back from her, he snapped, "Good God. Max truly meant it when he wanted that money from me. I thought it was just an excuse."

"Money?"

"For the dratted woman. This," he gestured irritably at the note, "Swanley...person."

"You mean you *paid* for her?"

"Apparently, yes. Max thought I was in need of a woman and that he should get her for me. A professional, you understand. A Cyprian. A creature of the demimonde."

"And where would he get that idea?"

"Where does Max get any of his ideas? Somewhere between Brighton and Hell. We must stop the wench at once."

"How do you suppose we stop her? Call up the militia?" Parkes sighed wearily. "This letter is a week old. She'll be well on her way by now."

"She cannot come here."

"But she's coming. And now, so is your aunt. This is a fine farce. Better than a comic opera. I suppose you'll be hiding one or the other in a cupboard or under the bed." There was a definite spark of mischief in her eye before she walked away.

He roared, "I'll turn them both around again at the damnable door and to Hell with 'em!"

In his time with the Navy that voice and tone was enough to bring bold men to their knees. With his housekeeper it barely made a dent. "Clearly a few female guests would teach you better manners. You're not abandoned on your own island anymore. This lonely life is unhealthy. It's time you had company, if you ask me."

"I don't believe I did ask you. And I am *not* lonely."

"No? Then why surround yourself with those frightful automated companions?" She gestured at the sketches laid out across his desk. "You don't want a proper woman about the place, so you say, but you'll make yourself that unsightly bit of clockwork nonsense."

"This is a scientific matter. An experiment enlarging on my earlier work."

"It's another foolish toy, that's what it is. A toy for a grown man. You're afraid, Commander Thrasher. And you *are* lonely. Nobody knows that better than me. I wouldn't be here, would I, if you weren't in need of some company? It's time to face the truth and real life again. It has to be said, young man. If you don't take that plunge now, you never will."

Harry clenched his jaw, anger mounting, a hot flush sweeping his body. But he couldn't find the right words to respond.

"I suggest you get accustomed to wearing a shirt and breeches about the place more often and not just when you remember it," she added. "Your aversion to decent clothing is bad enough for my old eyes, but poor Lady Bramley will have an apoplexy at the sight of your chest hair. Not to mention the other parts occasionally on display."

"Parkes, you are welcome to seek other employment any time, but you will find, I'm sure, that other masters don't allow their housekeepers to address them in such a forward and disrespectful manner."

"And I'm sure other housekeepers don't have to put up with the sight of naked flesh on a grown man. 'Tis no wonder I've got a stomach."

"We've all got a stomach, Parkes."

"Not like mine," she assured him gravely, before hurrying out.

Harry stared at the two missives, turning them in his hands as if that might somehow change the words upon them.

No. Alas, they still declared the same thing.

He didn't know which prospect was worse— the woman of lapsed virtue procured by his cousin Max, or his meddlesome aunt coming to put him in order. Two entirely different ends of the spectrum, both unwanted.

His aunt, of course, was lonely herself, as he'd already observed. Max clearly had not followed his suggestion to visit the lady and now she was at a loose end and itching to meddle in somebody's life. Hadn't that dratted Miss Hathaway creature kept her busy enough to stay out of his hair?

Well, he would let Parkes deal with these unwanted guests. He would pretend to be out. Permanently out. Parkes, being of the same gender, would know how to handle the intruders.

Comforted by this thought, he tossed the letters aside and returned to his work.

Chapter Seven

Excerpt from "His Lordship's Trousers" (censored)
Printed in *The Gentleman's Weekly*, June 1817

Yesterday afternoon's attire: Buckskin breeches
fastened below the knee and worn with riding boots.
Returned grass-stained and considerably mauled.

"I am quite undone," his lordship said to me as he
flopped forth into his room at a quarter to five and
stumbled immediately into the nearest chair, one foot
swung upward in readiness to have its boot removed. "It is
altogether too much, and I may have to become a monk if
it keeps up at this pace."

I felt obliged to reply that I thought monasteries in
general might have rather more stringent rules of
admittance than Whites or Boodles, and that his lordship
could perhaps merely cut down on the number of ladies he
currently entertains. And save us all a vast deal of trouble.

"Excellent idea, my good fellow," replied he. "But
which? I'm fond of 'em all, don't you know? In their own
way, they each hold a special place here." And he laid a
limp hand to a section of his torso which was quite
possibly suffering indigestion at that moment and had—
to my knowledge of the human body— never housed a
heart. "It is entirely with the best of intentions that I keep
so many ladies entertained. After all, what would they do
without me? They would be distraught."

"Some of them might try being entertained by their
husbands," I suggested.

"What wife is ever kept happy by her husband? No,
no, they rely upon me. And so, I 'm quite sure, do their
husbands who have not *my* ingenuity or inclination for the
wilder sport."

"But I fear, sir, that you shall wear yourself out, if you

do not take steps to cut down." Ingenuity and inclination, as I warned him, are worth little without a healthy set of tools with which to practice them.

While my master ruminated at length upon the impossibility of relinquishing one of his "beloveds" merely to give himself— and his trousers— breathing space during the daylight hours, I tackled the mud-encrusted footwear he offered up to me. I could not help noticing that the buckskins in which he had ridden through Hyde Park that afternoon were not only marked with grass stain at the knees— a sadly common occurrence— but that there was a crescent-shaped, jagged tear in the material at his thigh.

"While I took liberties with the lady, her lapdog took umbrage with me," his lordship explained, having noticed my inquiring glance.

"I see, sir. Considering your latest adventures with Lady Loose Garters I could not be sure who or what was responsible for the teeth marks."

As I tugged the first boot free, his lordship muttered, "I quite understand why medieval knights wore so much metal. A suit of armor would be much easier for you to clean."

I was startled, to say the least, that he cared for any convenience of mine. But there was, of course, more to it.

"Could save me from so many injuries too, and I would require you to get me out of it wherever I might be, so you'd have to travel with me...run alongside my horse." His eyes gleamed. "That sort of thing."

I saw he was rather liking the idea of a constant shadow even more at his beck and call than usual. Mindful of what little spare time I currently enjoyed, I swiftly reminded his lordship of the squeaking and rattling that would forestall any attempts at secretive nocturnal exploits up and down the corridors of country estates.

"The amount of oil required to keep your lordship in

smooth and silent working order, should you don such a suit, would certainly be prohibitive. And on a warm day like today it would leave you with the odor of Lancashire Hotpot. A pleasant enough fragrance on most occasions, sir, but perhaps not when one's intention is to discourage the interest of dogs."

"Good lord yes! I wouldn't want my tender parts cooked."

Thus we quickly discounted the idea.

"Do you think it will grow back?" his lordship asked abruptly.

"I beg your pardon, sir?"

Lifting his shirt to show the bald spots where we had earlier removed the spilled wax, he explained, "My chest hair."

"Oh yes, sir. More abundantly than ever, as befits such a splendid specimen of manhood."

And so with nothing more trying to challenge his lordship's mind than his chest hair, the number and varying savagery of his female conquests, and the relevant tightness of his breeches, we went about our day.

* * * *

"What the devil is that?" Parkes exclaimed, stumbling to a halt in the door of his study.

Harry glanced up from the newspaper to see what she was looking at. On that afternoon heavy storm clouds lowered from the sky, causing a premature darkness inside the house, casting eerie shadows from every corner. Only the fire in his hearth and a lamp on his desk gave out any light, and it was this flicking amber color that had drawn her attention to a new part of his female automaton, where it rested on the seat of a chair.

"It's a head, of course," he muttered. "What does it look like?"

The housekeeper stared, one hand to her throat.

"Something from the bowels of hell."

Harry leapt up, moved around his desk and, with his good hand, proudly lifted the half finished orb he'd constructed mostly of dented scrap metal.

"See?" A sudden flash of lightning speared through his gothic arched window and lit up the horror. Well, perhaps "horror" was too strong of a word, but Harry had to admit it was no beauty. It was, however, his creation and as such he was already fond of it.

"You've been stealing tools from my kitchen again," Parkes exclaimed crossly. "Is that one of my copper jelly moulds?"

"It is indeed." He had topped it off with a chimney-sweep's brush just to add "hair". Smirking, he warned the housekeeper, "I suggest you look about you, Parkes. By the time I am done with this, she will be serving tea and turning down the bed. You may be out of a post."

"Good. I'd happily turn you over to someone else. I hope she doesn't get overheated or lose a spring rushing from one end of this house to the other, trying to obey all your commands."

"She certainly won't be talking back to me." He hadn't given her a tongue since it was utterly unnecessary.

Parkes had already made her feelings clear about his "mechanical wench", muttering under her breath whenever she came upon the pieces.

"Despicable thing!" She lifted her shoulders in an overly-dramatic shudder. "Whatever next?"

Thunder rumbled and bumped overhead. The sky darkened further.

"You've got soot all over your shirt," the housekeeper grumbled, "and all over the hall tiles out there. As if I have nothing else to do but clean up after your experiments."

"I make this automaton for the benefit of men the world over. A female companion with none of the usual shortcomings. She won't require feeding, grooming, good manners… or clothes."

The housekeeper gasped irritably.

"And you will kindly refer to her as Miss...Petticoat." The name came to him quite suddenly as he thought of Max again.

"Dare I ask what you're intending to do with this *Miss Petticoat* exactly? I suppose she'll end up in parts all over the house, when she frustrates you, just like the others."

Another vivid spike of lightning illuminated the room with a quaking silver flare. "She has no purpose but to entertain. I shall teach her to play the pianoforte," he paused, squinting, "or possibly the harp."

"That'll be useful," Parkes replied scornfully. "Something else to collect cobwebs and dust."

Thunder bounced across the roof, the storm moving closer.

"Go about your business, Parkes. Don't let me stop you."

Once she was gone again, he set the head back upon the seat by the fire and patted its sooty spikes of hair. "Good girl." He smirked as he thought of Parkes and her appalled expression. She was a woman seldom rattled, except by his inventions, and she certainly jumped tonight when she saw that makeshift head. There was still a thrill to be had in terrifying Parkes, he must admit.

Standing back to admire his handiwork, he thought it seemed almost to come alive with the firelight flickering over its misshapen visage. The sooner he made her a proper face the better. But this was proving a far more demanding process than he could have imagined.

He looked down at his soot-blackened left hand and wiped the fingers clean on his shirt and the sling, so he wouldn't get marks on his important drawings.

Rain pelted the windows in the hard, rough patter of gunfire and a quick glance outside showed gusty wind dragging ashy clouds across the sky. Any storm that blew

up this time of year hung relentlessly over Woodbyne
Abbey for hours, as if the clouds, while on their breezy
way across the county, suddenly encountered those
chimneys and became snagged upon them, forced to hover
there, torn like the sails of a battle-scarred frigate.

The storm that afternoon was definitely in no haste to
move on, but Harry was soon deeply engrossed in his
design and had forgotten the weather entirely before the
next rumble commenced.

* * * *

Howling wind blew cold spikes of rain almost
horizontal. Georgiana stepped down from the carriage and
tried to hold her head up high enough to take in the grim,
bulky shape of the house before her.

There was no sign of life, no one to greet them.

"I thought your nephew was expecting us, Lady
Bramley," she cried against the wind, one hand on her
bonnet.

"Yes, he certainly is," the lady replied irritably. "And I
hope he has not forgotten! Sometimes things just go right
out of his head."

They'd suffered a dismal five-hour journey in this
weather, made all the worse by a finding a tree down
across the road at one point and then suffering a broken
wheel that required waiting while the coachman went for
aid. Neither passenger was in a very good mood by the
time of their arrival. The coachman was even less happy.

As he dropped another trunk at their feet, he
mumbled crossly, "Good luck to ye," before climbing back
up onto the box seat. Georgiana was almost certain she
heard him add, "You'll need it with yon madman."

A moment later she and her chaperone were
abandoned in the storm, the coachman having been sent
back again the sixteen miles to Mayfair for the retrieval of
a lady's maid and several other trunks that would not fit on

his first journey.

As Lady Bramley pulled hard at the bell chord beside the front door, a great, discordant clattering could be heard echoing through the house. But no one came to let them in.

Lightning flashed around the chimneys, revealing ivy-strewn slabs of the ugly stone structure and wildly overgrown bushes flanking the steps. Thunder followed immediately, trembling through the soles of Georgiana's boots.

She looked around for signs of life. If Commander Thrasher knew his aunt was coming, where the devil was he?

Aha! There. Candlelight pooled like melted butter around the corner of a crumbling buttress.

Battling the wind, Georgiana set off for that light at once, determined to rouse someone to their aid.

* * * *

Harry felt a tickle against his spine, a frisson that traveled up to the nape of his neck.

What the devil—?

He looked up. Firelight and shadow dodged and darted about the room. It almost made his book shelves and that dead, brown potted plant in the corner come to life.

Thunder growled above, and rain rattled at his windows. He ought to get up, close the curtains and light another candle since it was suddenly so dark out.

Instead, he fumbled, dropping his pen as a very loud bang shook the walls of the house and the stone under his feet. Slowly, with unsteady fingers, he scratched the back of his neck where some sense of great unease had made itself felt by pricking his skin with little bumps like those on the belly of a plucked goose.

"Sir. Hello, sir?"

It was a woman's voice. And definitely not Parkes.

His gaze went immediately toward the chair where he had set his automaton's grotesque head.

Did that voice come from Miss Petticoat's bodiless appendage?

Harry laughed uneasily at his own foolishness. It was the storm, of course, making the commonplace eerie and menacing.

Another flash of lightning tore through his windows and lit Miss Petticoat's head so that the dented metal seemed suddenly to move, forming features among the bolts.

"*Sir! I see you!*"

His pulse quickened, his heart thumping away against his ribs like a brutal fist trying to break out through his chest.

"*I see you sitting there!*" the woman's voice howled in a ghostly pitch.

Good God. He had finally gone insane, lost his last grip on reality. He knew it must happen one day, naturally.

Now his heart was beating so hard it echoed around the study, even rapped against the window, louder than the rain.

He stood, staring unblinking at the automaton's head while it stared back from the chair. Leered might be a better description of that expression, he thought, chilled to the bone.

"*Let us in!*"

Suddenly he caught the movement of something at the window. Finally he tore his gaze from the chair and saw a real, moving, agitated woman leaping about in the rain, trying to get his attention.

His heart slowed to a more manageable pace. For the first time in his thirty years he was actually relieved by the sight of a woman. Although it was but a brief sensation.

Miss Hathaway? She of the burning wig and the flying

buttocks?

What the devil was she doing outside his window?

She gestured wildly, reminding him of a dancing monkey he once observed in a bazaar. Good lord, she was soaked through, her bonnet drooping, her face pink with cold and shining wet. Why on earth would anyone be out on a wild, windswept, dark afternoon like this?Eventually, with great caution, he sidled up to the gong. Keeping his wary gaze on the creature through the window, he banged the mallet hard into the copper disk. "*Parkes,*" he yelled for good measure, in case she failed to hear the urgency, or decided to drag her feet. "*Parkes! The door!*"

The woman outside his window stopped bouncing and scowled, rain dripping off the brim of her hat and the end of her nose.

"Parkes!" he cried again, his temperature rising. "Something at the door!" Armed with the mallet still in his left hand, Harry walked slowly to the window.

The vision on the other side looked hopeful, her lips opened to speak, her eyes gleaming brightly. He placed the mallet between his teeth and, with his one good arm, drew first the left curtain and then the right one shut. Let Parkes deal with this. He was in no fit state to manage a woman—everybody said so. "Everybody" being the voices in his head.

What would she be doing outside his house, on an afternoon of premature darkness and violent storm? But then she did rather seem to make a habit of appearing where and when she was not expected.

With horror he concluded that his aunt had arrived. And not alone.

Chapter Eight

A stout fellow with graying hair and a hooked nose finally let them in.

"Brown! Thank heavens. I began to think nobody was in," Lady Bramley swept over the threshold, gesturing for Georgiana to follow.

"I am sorry, Ma'am. Didn't hear a carriage in all this thunder."

"And I see my nephew still has no footman to answer his door."

"No, your ladyship. He says the fewer staff the better."

"But how is your rheumatism?"

"Not too bad, your ladyship. I rub a bit of horse liniment on it from time to time, and that does wonders. Puts the spring back in my step." He stopped and squinted, apparently just realizing there was another figure huddled in the doorway. Lifting a candelabra in one shaky hand, he muttered, "You brought a guest, Lady Bramley. Oh dear, we weren't expecting another."

"My companion, Miss Hathaway, requires nothing beyond the very simplest of rooms. I had already made a commitment to take her on before I heard of Henry's mishap, so I had to bring her with me. She will not get in anybody's way. She is here to observe and learn."

The old man muttered doubtfully, "To learn, Ma'am?"

"How to disport herself in a proper manner. Here in my nephew's house she can put some of her lessons into practice without embarrassing anybody too badly. The nearby villages of Upper and Little Flaxhill are just far enough away from London to prevent any disastrous public mishaps among finer society, yet there is surely some little bit of local culture, a few good families upon which she might hone her skills. People who aren't as particular."

"I see, Ma'am." He blinked at Georgiana in a worried way and she gave him one of her best smiles, but it didn't seem to reassure the fellow.

Lady Bramley continued, "Since I am always promising my nephew to visit for the summer, I thought this would be as good a time as any— now that he's hurt himself again with a nasty fall. He needs me here to get him in order, clearly."

"Yes, Ma'am."

"And while we're here he can learn to entertain guests graciously and stop being this curiously unsociable wretch he's become."

The old man winced, and a small sigh of despair oozed forth from his chewing lips.

"How do you do, Mr. Brown," Georgiana said politely, again hoping to enliven his spirits. "I promise I shall not cause you any trouble."

His puzzled regard drifted back to her face, taking in her features with greater interest. Until then his grey eyes had seemed rather weary— fogged over like the carriage windows through which Georgiana had spent the last several hours trying to see her surroundings. But now, as the old man closely studied Georgiana's face, that misty apathy cleared, as if he had just rubbed sleep out of his eyes.

"I don't know what the master will think of this one...Miss Hathaway, is it? If she were a horse, I wouldn't buy her. Not with that wildness in her eye. Looks like mischief to me."

Before Georgiana could submit a word in her defense, Lady Bramley concurred matter-of-factly with his assessment, "Yes, I'm afraid she's a revolutionary, Brown my good man. Be warned. Miss Hathaway does not hesitate to speak her mind, as I have already discovered.

And she has a great deal of mind to bespeak."

He chuckled. "That'll go down well around here then." Leading them into the hall, he set his candelabra down on a narrow table beneath a rather ugly portrait of Queen Elizabeth. "You get those wet coats and bonnets off, Ma'am, and I'll get a bit of dinner together in the dining room."

"That is very good of you, Brown. Nothing fancy, of course."

"Aye, your ladyship. There's no other choice but plain."

"Still no cook either, eh?"

"No, Ma'am. I do what I can, but the master prefers to throw a tray together himself and hasn't had a hot meal in weeks. Not for want of my trying. My sister came to cook for him, but she gave up. Says it's insulting to see so much good food sent back uneaten. He won't keep to regular hours, of course, so three meals a day means naught to the master. He'll eat when he feels the need — even if 'tis the middle of the night—and not until."

Having swept a gloved finger along the console table upon which he'd set the candelabra, Lady Bramley tut-tutted at the thick grey layer of dust she found there. "No maids, I see."

"No, Ma'am."

"This won't do at all, Brown. I did not expect to find the place so untended. I must send for some of my staff until a few can be hired from the village. It seems I must extend my stay beyond my original scheme."

His shoulders sank. "Yes, Ma'am." And then he muttered under his breath, "I feared you might."

Untying her sopping wet bonnet ribbons, Georgiana looked around at the impressively large hall and the other gloomy portraits hung along the wood-paneled walls. These must be the Thrasher family, she thought, for there was a resemblance in all of them— that strong jaw

94

changing little through the generations.

"Is the Commander quite well?" she ventured. "He looked a little...startled... when I saw him through the window."

"Aye, Miss, that's the way he is. Perpetually startled. Poor feller. Something ought to be done—"

"Yes, thank you, Brown," Lady Bramley quickly interjected. "That's why we're here. Now you needn't worry a moment longer about your master. I shall set everything to rights."

He sighed. "Yes, Ma'am."

"I suppose we must see Henry at once," Lady Bramley said, shifting her little dog under her other arm. "Best get all the protesting over with. Just like bathing a recalcitrant pup, getting a man in order must be done periodically for their own good and despite the growling."

* * * *

He stood with his back to the fire, assuming a pose of authority in readiness to deal with these guests. Best to let them know right away that he was in charge. Unfortunately tonight, because of his wounded wrist and the sling, he couldn't stand with both hands behind his back, only one, but he made the best of it, head up and feet shoulder-width apart so that he might rock on his heels as required. Yes, that was better. Normal, was it not? As "normal" as he could be.

It had been his intention to let Parkes handle the matter of his unwanted guests, but she was nowhere to be found tonight, of course— practicing that typical feminine skill of vanishing at the most inopportune moment.

So he was left alone to handle his aunt when she swept into his study with her voice already raised to soprano pitch. "Well, Henry, I have arrived, no thanks to the state of the roads around here."

The damp and drooping Miss Hathaway followed

close behind her. Harry drew a deep breath and was about to speak when Lady Bramley exclaimed, "Henry, what *are* you wearing? For goodness sake, put some clothes on."

But he had clothes on, didn't he? Yes. He looked down to be sure. Breeches, shirt. Not as tidy as it should be, however—

"You will remember my companion, perhaps," she added, too impatient to wait for Harry to adjust his garments. "This is Miss Georgiana Hathaway of the Particular Establishment for the Advantage of Respectable Ladies."

"How could I fail to remember?" he muttered, looking again at the young woman beside his aunt. She was, in fact, impossible to forget, although he had suffered a momentary confusion at seeing her suddenly appear outside his window. "The Wickedest Chit that ever breathed air."

Her eyes, he noted today, were fringed with such a preponderance of ebony lashes that they looked heavy. *Centipedinous* eye lashes, he mused, inventing the word on the spot, as was his tendency when nothing in existence suited.

"Henry."

Who? What?

"*Henry!*"

His gaze swept left and slightly downward to take in the sight of his aunt's round face. "Madam?"

"Henry, tuck your shirt in and put on a jacket. We're going to eat dinner."

"Not hungry." He looked around the room again, wishing Parkes might reappear and manage the situation in her usual way. *Where the devil was she?* "You can't stay," he blurted. Deliberately not looking at the woman with all the eyelashes again, he finally remembered to rock on his heels as previously planned. Ah, that was better. He regained command over his own vessel, no matter how distracting this stowaway's eyelashes.

"There's been a mistake, you see. I haven't anywhere suitable to put you. The house isn't equipped for females, we're infested with mice and the roof leaks like a colander. Sorry, but there it is."

Parkes abruptly whispered in his ear, "Surely your aunt can take your mother's old bedchamber— which is the least drafty and most comfortable for her health— and her companion can make use of your father's room in the east wing, until something else might be arranged. A fire can be lit in there now that Brown took that old nest out of the chimney. And it's got a pleasant view across the park. I daresay the young lady would like the sunrise when she wakes in the morning."

Suddenly Parkes wanted to be helpful? She certainly picked her moments. He glared over his shoulder. "Don't you have other duties to tend?"

She was all smiles. A very rare occurrence and indicative of mischief afoot. "Oh, it won't take long to air the beds and knock down a few cobwebs."

"Henry!" His aunt's voice drew his attention back to her again. "What's the matter with you? What are you looking at? Where are your manners?"

Did he ever have any manners? He couldn't remember.

But as he turned back to his guests, he noticed that a few drops of rainwater had fallen off Miss Hathaway and landed in fat splotches on his drawings, which were spread out across the floor. She was smudging the charcoal, he thought anxiously. Ten minutes after her arrival and his work was endangered already.

"Are you quite all right, Commander?" the young menace inquired.

"All right?" he sputtered. "Of course, I'm all right. Not that it's any of your damned business."

"Henry!"

"I won't get in your way, sir. I am eager to learn under your aunt's tutelage and to make recompense for all the destruction I caused at her garden party. To make amends for anything I did to you also, of course, sir."

Anything she did to him? What had she done to him now? Harry ran a quick mental assessment of all his body parts and was relieved to find them intact. Stirring, in fact, with vigor.

"Your aunt intends to make me into a lady," she added, a slightly mischievous spark under her lashes. "I am not to slide down banisters anymore."

"Excellent," he muttered. "That should be a relief to gentlemen everywhere. The fewer flying backsides there are about the place the better."

"Henry, be polite," his aunt exclaimed. "We're here now, and we're staying for a month. Perhaps longer. Now that I see the state of the house, I have a better idea of all the work to be done. I shall send for some staff tomorrow. I suggest you acclimate yourself to the idea of ladies in the house. I know you haven't had one about for many years. But it's time, Henry."

He looked down at the wet footprints left by Miss Hathaway's walking boots. Then his perusal ascended slowly over her muslin frock, only to be delayed in its progress by her softly rounded bosom— never to be mentioned, of course— until his gaze fumbled its way upward to that dimple in her cheek. He found her lips pursed up like a tight rosebud. Her eyes squinted hard under those abundant lashes. Trying to puzzle him out, perhaps. He wished her luck with that.

She would not be the first to try and fail.

A drop of rainwater had fallen from her chin to her bosom and dampened the lace chemisette, making it stick to her skin, enticingly transparent. There was a tiny mole at the base of her throat, visible beneath the ivory lace. In the old days, folk used to call them witches marks, he thought darkly. Could that be why freckles were now considered an unforgiveable flaw?

Reaching for the mantle behind him with his left hand, he missed, knocking a small china figurine to the hearth rug. He ignored it and his fingers, fumbling blind, finally found the ledge they sought.

"Do as you wish then," he said tersely, back in control. "But you stay at your own risk and don't assume I'll change the way I do things just for the two of you."

Miss Hathaway still watched him quizzically, her eyes a warm chestnut shade with just a twinkle of bronze. Her broom-like lashes looked wet. Perhaps that was why he was drawn to staring at them. It was as if they'd been dusted with tiny crystals and each time she blinked the firelight was caught there, reflected in miniature prisms of rainwater.

Harry wanted, very badly, to brush those lashes with his fingertip. Just to see how soft they were. To feel them move.

He remembered the touch of her hand in his. The shock of it sparking through him. Flesh to flesh. How long was it since he touched a woman?

Another drip of rainwater, having meandered along her jaw line, now reached the point of her small chin and wobbled there, before it fell. The drop trickled between those two panels of her lace chemisette and took a trembling course downward into dangerous territory, out of his sight.

Harry had begun to suffer the tickling of sweat under his clothes. It felt as if he was back on that tropical island, under the midday heat of a bright sun. Hooking a finger around his neck-cloth, which was already partly undone, he tugged it looser still.

"You *are* ill," his aunt declared. "You look hot, Henry." She stepped forward and tried to reach his forehead, but he slipped smartly aside and, having a good two feet on her in height, he escaped her questing hand. "You're breathing very hard."

"Breathing? How dare I breathe. I shall stop at once."

"And perspiring in a most uncivilized manner."

"I am perfectly well. I have an excellent constitution. I wouldn't be alive now if I didn't, would I? Breathing helps with that, perhaps you have not noticed."

Parkes coughed, once again interrupting. "We'll see to the rooms then, shall we?"

"If we must," he grunted.

"If we must what?" his aunt demanded.

"Good afternoon to you both. Please enjoy your dinner without me. As you see, I'm busy." He'd looked at Miss Hathaway and her dangerous eyelashes long enough, he decided. He wanted her out of his study, and himself out of this sticky shirt, as soon as possible. "Shoo."

With his good hand he flung the door open and waited for the unwanted guests to leave him in peace again. A welcome draft of cooling air swept in from the passage, and he felt his pulse ease to a steadier trot.

"Dear Henry." His aunt paused to pat his cheek on the way out. "Lovely to see you, as always. Now I am here and all will be well. I told you I'd bring my own entertainment, didn't I? But do let Brown give you a shave, won't you? There is something of the Norse pirate about your appearance and that will not do for a Thrasher. We're not rampaging, ravaging pagan raiders."

"Perhaps not now," he muttered darkly.

* * * *

Georgiana and Lady Bramley dined in a long narrow room that smelled as if it had not been aired out in a great many months. Or years. Fortunately the journey had given them both an appetite so they ignored the dust and the musty odor to eagerly consume a hasty dinner assembled by Brown.

"Is he really the only servant?" Georgiana asked, after the elderly fellow had hobbled out again. "This is a very large house for one to manage."

"Indeed. And as you can see, he barely manages it. All very worrying, but my nephew can be extremely stubborn."

Yes, she saw that in his hard, proud jaw and the stormy demands of his searching gaze. But it was more than a stubborn nature that left his house in disrepair, clearly.

"Henry is very fond of Woodbyne Abbey," Lady Bramley continued. "He was born here and enjoyed a very happy youth on this estate until his mama left."

There was a pause. The lady suddenly looked annoyed and hurriedly forked another cold, boiled potato into her mouth.

"His mama left? You mean she died?" Georgiana thought with sadness of her own mother, taken too soon from life, and the effect it had on *her* when she was a child.

But his aunt swallowed, coughed into her napkin and shook her head. "It would have been better if she did, but no." She paused, sighing gustily. "I suppose it does no harm now to tell you. The wretched woman left Henry and his father— my dear brother— without so much as a letter of explanation. There was a scandal, of course." She cut into a slice of ham with one ruthless saw of her knife. "Henry went away to the Naval Academy in Portsmouth soon after and that was that. Until he retired two years ago. Since then he has kept himself busy here with his work."

"What sort of work?"

"Something...of a scientific nature. He has little time to socialize, but I mean to bring him out of himself." Lady Bramley spooned a large dollop of pickle onto her plate. "Henry has been left alone for far too long. Alas, I've been much too caught up in my own concerns, but now I can see things have been let go," —she cast melancholy eyes around the room— "far beyond what I had been told."

"Perhaps the Commander likes being alone."

"It is not about what he *thinks* he likes, but about what I *know* he needs."

Georgiana mulled over that for a moment and then asked, "What happened to his arm? The one in the sling."

"Haste and thoughtlessness."

"Oh."

"It is merely a sprained wrist, and it must be healed by now, but like all men he makes more of it than is necessary."

"Poor fellow. He does seem to be suffering from some malady however."

"You refer to his display of ill manners just now, and his careless attire, no doubt? That is only due to all this solitude. He is not often out in company and luring him away from Woodbyne Abbey is a trial. After this latest accident I decided it was time *I* came to *him*. I shall soon put him back together again."

"Does he wish to be put together?"

"Whether he wishes for it or not signifies little, Miss Hathaway. He must be brought back into the land of the living, and I will brook no opposition. Nobody knows, so well as I, how to manage these matters. Brisk and sharp, Miss Hathaway." She gestured with her fork pointed upward like Britannia's trident. "*Brisk and sharp*, that is the way of it. One must sweep in with ruthless determination and take the reins of the chariot."

There followed a long pause while they ate their cold repast and listened to the soft click of the mantle clock. The walls around them seemed full of creaks and groans, but while she liked to imagine the presence of ghosts, Georgiana supposed this noise to be caused by the wind that afternoon. It was indeed harsh and had almost swept their carriage over several times on the journey.

She thought again of Dead Harry's expression when

he saw her at his window. Clearly he was not happy to have them there, but this did not bother his aunt in the least. Lady Bramley was a woman who always thought she knew best, of course.

"It must have been very hard for the Commander, when his mother left," Georgiana ventured thoughtfully. "I'm sure it had a lasting effect. I've found that people are often shaped by their experiences in youth."

"Another one of your beliefs, eh? You make a study of such things, do you, Miss Hathaway?"

"Yes. You see, my friend, Miss Emma Chance, was treated cruelly as a very young girl. She was looked down upon dreadfully and never encouraged to trust in her abilities, so now she is diffident about her own skills and seldom puts herself forward, because she thinks she's unworthy. As for my other dear friend, Miss Melinda Goodheart, she lives precariously and for the moment, enjoying herself as much as she can and facing the consequences later, because she follows the example she saw all her youth, of her father— a man who lives a life his bank account cannot support. Yet somehow he always seems to get away with it, despite the wretched state of his finances."

The lady touched her lips with the corner of a folded napkin. "It is not proper to speak of finances."

"That's unfortunate, since the world revolves around the subject, does it not?"

"You're very shrewd for one so young."

"I shall be twenty in December. Age is surely less important than one's experiences."

"And your experiences have taught you to slide down banisters and cause a ruckus? To win attention perhaps. You mentioned a large family at home."

Georgiana felt her cheeks warm.

"I see you don't study yourself, Miss Hathaway. You spare little time on introspection."

"Other people are generally more interesting," she agreed with chagrin. "Less apt to disappoint."

The lady's brows arched high and then she drawled, "I suppose that makes a pleasing change. Young folk are most often self-involved and care little for the needs of others. You, it seems, are different."

For a while they ate in silence and Georgiana expected no further information to come her way in regard to the Commander's unwelcoming behavior and his family history. Lady Bramley was of a class that did not discuss family secrets— such as runaway wives and mothers— in public. Or even in private. In fact, it was a surprise that she'd told her companion as much as she did already. Perhaps she was tired after her journey and had let down her guard temporarily.

But Georgiana's ideas about youthful experiences making their mark must have stuck with Lady Bramley, for quite suddenly she added, "I wonder...no...I cannot imagine that the departure of Henry's mother affected him greatly. She had little influence in his childhood, even when she was here. As a boy he had a nanny, of course. A very good, reliable sort of woman who thought the world of him and he of her. Sadly she died soon after he got his first command." Lady Bramley shook her head at the last piece of ham on her plate. "Poor Henry, he was closer to Parkes, the nanny, than he was to his mother. But that is often the way of things. It is a pity she is not still here. Sometimes I think Henry's forgotten that she isn't."

Chapter Nine

After dinner, Lady Bramley— exhausted from the trials and setbacks of their journey— retired early to bed. Since the master of the house remained locked away in his study and the storm still raged outside, Georgiana decided she may as well go to bed too despite the early hour. Brown showed her to a room in the east wing.

"It's not the best of rooms, being on this side of the house," he mumbled, glancing around worriedly. "But the master says for tonight it must do. If I'd known Lady Bramley meant to bring a guest I could have sorted out something more suited. A chamber in the other wing would be better for a young lady like yourself, although most of the rooms are beyond repair at this point, I reckon. I'd be ashamed to put you in one of them, until it can be made comfortable."

Her trunk had already been carried up and left at the foot of the large four-poster bed. A fire lit in the hearth helped warm the room. It was, all things considered, quite cozy and the bed looked welcoming. "I'm sure this is more than adequate for me, Mr. Brown." She smiled.

"Aye, well...I'd advise you, Miss, to stay in your room and lock this door until morning." It came out in a low rush of breathless words, as if he hadn't decided whether to say it until that very moment.

"Why?"

"It's just... for the best, Miss. I'll get you moved to the other wing as soon as I can."

Georgiana was intrigued. Did the manservant infer that she might encounter a ghost? Such hapless beings must be frequent wanderers at night in a house like this.

But no, it was not the supernatural she must fear, apparently.

"Sometimes," Brown added in a hasty whisper, "the

master of the house goes wandering at night. Just a habit since he came home. The doctor says he'll settle down eventually and start to sleep peacefully again."

"I see. I suppose it is understandable since he has been through a great ordeal."

"More than one, Miss."

As the man turned to leave, she stopped him. "Have you worked here long?"

"Since the master were a young lad, before he went away to Portsmouth."

"Commander Thrasher was wounded some years ago in battle, was he not?"

"Aye, Miss. Lucky to be alive, he is. It's a brave man that goes into the Navy."

She nodded solemnly. Even before her brother Guy joined that brave corps of men she'd had great respect for the profession. "If I were born a man I would have been a sailor. It is a most admirable career."

The fellow's brow unfolded from its tense lines and his jowls lifted. "Commander Thrasher were a very fine seaman," he said proudly. "Destined for great things and in command of his own ship before he were twenty." The candle he held fluttered wildly as he sighed. "All that ended after ...well, when he were rescued from that island after being so long alone. Such a thing changes a man. So he came back here and shut himself away."

"How very sad."

"Yes. 'Tis a great shame. A terrible waste of a good man. You mustn't mind some of the things he says and does, Miss. He gets confused at times." He passed her the candle. "I'll leave you to your bed then, Miss. Good night to you. And remember what I said about keeping this door locked."

"Oh, I shall," Georgiana assured him. "Thank you." She slowly closed the door, her head still full of questions about her host.

106

The Commander was every bit as fascinating as he seemed at first glance. But today he was curt, ill-tempered, inhospitable. Confused.

Well, if he walked around the abbey at night in his sleep, it was no wonder he didn't care for houseguests.

* * * *

Harry lurked in the passage with a candle until he saw Parkes walking briskly along. He stepped out into her path.

"Well? What did they say? What are they doing?" he demanded in a low whisper.

"The young lady has retired for the evening and so has your aunt. What else would they be doing after a long journey?"

He wasn't sure about that. The young one might go creeping about his house. He had not felt so unsettled and on edge since he was a ten year-old Eton boy, forced to conjugate a Latin verb in front of a very angry professor who had just discovered him doodling naughty pictures in the margins of his book.

"The dark-haired creature has far too much to say for herself," he grumbled. "I thought young ladies were meant to be seen and not heard."

"What did she say that got you so upset? You thought her amusing before."

"That was when she was on someone else's territory. Now she's here, invading *my* ship. I must be on my guard."

"And who are you most worried for? Miss Hathaway or yourself?"

"Dripping all over my sketches and asking me if I'm quite *all right*! The gall of it. A girl of nineteen, asking me such a question!"

"I take it you refer to the young lady's polite inquiry into your health." Parkes didn't stop, but walked on, leaving him to follow. Which he did, tripping over his own boots, stubbing a toe against a console table and almost

107

sending a Wedgewood vase to its demise.

"What did she tell Brown just now? Why is she here asking questions? What did she say about me?"

"Nothing of any consequence." Parkes had turned back just in time to steady the rocking vase with one hand and then she walked on. "I daresay she's not very interested in you. Why should she be, a pleasant, quick-minded, lively young girl like that? What would she want with the likes of you— a man with an aversion to good manners and sensible clothing, and who can't string more than six words together these days without a curse for punctuation?"

He clamped his lips tight. Parkes was right, of course. With ladies in the house, he must try to moderate his language. Damn and blast it.

"She's a bold, amusing creature though, just as you said she was," she added, a smile evident in her tone.

"I never said that. I never told you anything about the woman."

"You didn't have to. I'm inside your mind, aren't I? I know it all."

Harry frowned and ran fingertips over the wrinkles of his forehead. Yes, there were times of clarity when he understood Parkes was not really there with him in person. But on other occasions she seemed very real. He always knew, of course, exactly what she would say to him if she *was* there, so she might as well be at his side every day, whispering in his ear, chiding him to get dressed, reminding Harry to eat. His memories of her many kindnesses far outweighed any recall of his mother, who had passed in and promptly out of his life like a fragrant leaf in the wind.

"She speaks boldly for herself, too," the construct of his mind added with unusual jauntiness. "I can see why Lady Bramley has taken to her."

Oh, he didn't like that idea at all.

"My aunt needn't think she can come here and turn me and my house inside out, using that girl to do so. This had better not be one of her matchmaking schemes. As if I'd take any interest in that girl. She's far too young and silly. And nothing much to look at either."

The housekeeper did not reply, but quickened her steps.

"Hmph. Something is amiss with that dark-haired creature and her centipedinous eyelashes," he grumbled, still following. "Something is definitely adrift."

"She's come to the right place then, hasn't she?" Parkes replied drolly. "Ought to be right at home."

* * * *

It sounded as if the storm had died down now. Only a sulky sort of rain remained to spatter against the window, and her fire sputtered and danced whenever a draft blew down the chimney. But the rest of the house was quiet, with just the occasional slow creak within its walls and beams. Very different to life at school, where the sounds of whispers, quarrels, and footsteps charging up and down the stairs never seemed to cease for long. The same with life at home.

Yawning, she let her gaze wander to the writing box beside her. A few moments ago she'd taken out her pens and ink, but she was having a hard time focusing her thoughts. She ought to write to Melinda and Emma, for they must wonder whether she had driven Lady Bramley to an act of desperation yet, as Mrs. Lightbody predicted. But she also had her next episode to write for *His Lordship's Trousers*.

Not certain where to start, she procrastinated, staring into the fire, parts of her body feeling as if they still traveled in that bumpy carriage over bad roads.

Perhaps she should write a letter to her brother Guy too. He at least would be interested to know what was happening to her, even if the other members of her family couldn't care less.

Both Guy and Edward, her two elder brothers, wrote to her more frequently than their father did. Guy's letters made her laugh, although his spelling was truly atrocious, his writing almost entirely full of exclamation points. He always smudged his ink, being too impatient to wait for it to dry. Edward, on the other hand, labored over his rigid, orderly script and let the sentences run on so long that it was a trial to read. One frequently forgot the gist of a sentence— and certainly lost all will to care about it— by the time the full stop was reached.

But both brothers had a certain amount of rebellion in their veins. Guy had joined the Navy against their father's wishes, while Edward had disappointed their father by choosing a quiet life and returning to the country, avoiding London society. Edward now had the living of a small, tranquil parish back in Norfolk and was apparently very content there. Staying out of their father's way.

Georgiana, like her brothers, planned to carve out her own life, regardless of her father's ideas of what a woman could, or should, do. She would begin as a newspaper journalist. Many respected novelists had begun by writing for newspapers— Fielding, Defoe and Swift, to name just a few— and Georgiana hoped to follow their lead. But her writing would have a twist, for she would reveal the truths about society from a woman's point of view. She would open folks' eyes to the injustices—

A loud bang somewhere deep in the house made her start, woke her from those airy dreams, and reminded her that she had yet to inform her father of these plans, or even to let him know that she was the author behind *His Lordship's Trousers*. That was quite a fence to leap before she could get any farther.

But for now here she was, a guest in the house of

Commander Sir Henry Thrasher— a man of whom so
little was known in recent years, a man who had withdrawn
from life to become something of an enigma. Here before
her was another opportunity, for with his experiences and
adventures, the Commander had much to share with the
world. If he could be persuaded to do so. This could be
her chance, she realized excitedly, to pen something more
serious than *His Lordship's Trousers.*

Spending his days in isolation here, he clearly lived as
he pleased, a bachelor who greeted ladies in his
shirtsleeves, with his neck-cloth undone, his hair tousled
and his shirt half-untucked. A man who stared at
Georgiana, not only as if he'd never seen anything
remotely like her, but that he might possibly decide to eat
her with a bit of bread and some butter.

Naturally, if this was a Grand Romance, she would be
very beautiful with long hair the color of honey and wheat,
and a neck like a swan, while he would be a tortured,
brooding soul who pounded his chest while reciting
poetry. And they would fall in love. At least, until she
tumbled to her death from some tall place and her skull
was, quite tragically, crushed.

She yawned loudly.

Enough pondering about her eccentric host and their
unlikely Grand Romance, she thought scornfully. She had
a column to write.

Finally she readied her pen and took out a small
square of paper. But before even a page was complete,
Georgiana fell asleep on the paper and woke some time
later to a renewed burst of thunder.

That temporary lull before must have been the eye of
the storm, for now it was back full force. The candles had
almost burned out, wax hanging like icicles from the
holders, the wicks sizzling and smoking. She snuffed them
both, set the guard over her fire and crawled into bed, but
only a few breaths later a loud thump out in the hall made

her start, a sleepy yawn stalled half way up her throat.

She lay still, every nerve in her body on high alert. Rain flung itself hard at her window and spat down the chimney. Wind howled and whistled as it cut around the corners of the house.

Thump.

There it went again. She had not imagined it.

Thump. The sound moved closer.

Georgiana sat up. Remembering what Brown had warned her about, she turned her anxious gaze to the door. Alas, she had forgotten to bolt it.

Oh, lord! Did she have time to run from the bed to the door and slide the bolt across? What if he got there first? The bolt might be rusty and stiff.

What was he doing out there? It sounded as if he dragged a dead body along, letting its head bump into the wall every few steps.

She scrambled from the bed and ran across the cold floor to the door, but her fingers paused on the old iron bolt. If she never knew what that noise was, she reasoned, it would haunt her imagination with gory thoughts— possibly much worse than the reality. Therefore, she may as well know what was causing the noise.

Georgiana Hathaway, queen of Reckless Dares, refused to cower under her bedcover like a frightened rabbit. She had always suspected that she was born with a duty to venture where no other woman would dare go. Therefore, rather than secure herself behind a locked door, she threw maidenly caution—and Brown's well-meant warnings— to the four winds. And opened that door to look out.

Chapter Ten

Lightning pulsed through a narrow, arched window at the far end of the passage. Those torn, flickering silver rags of light provided the only color in that dark space, but it was just enough to outline the profile of a man seated on the floor, his back against one wall, his feet against the other.

The thump was made by a cricket ball, which he bounced at the wall every so often and caught with the hand that was supposed to be sprained. He seemed almost in a dream-like state, quite calm, despite the storm raging outside.

Georgiana thought about going back to bed, but quickly dismissed the idea. If she turned her back and huddled under the bedclothes, that would make her no better than any cowardly person who put their blinkers on rather than face trouble directly. A problem could never be fixed by simply ignoring it.

Besides, since she was here, she could try to help this man— and not necessarily in the forceful, bossy way favored by his aunt.

On the practical side, she was hardly likely to get any sleep with that irregular thumping against the wall to keep her nerves on edge.

So, with all these reassurances in mind, she took a woolen shawl from the chair by the door, threw it around her shoulders for some additional modesty over her nightgown, and stepped out into the hall.

Again the warnings of that good fellow Brown sizzled in a fraught rush through her mind. *I'd advise you, Miss, to stay in your room and lock this door until morning.*

Brown, of course, couldn't know yet that Georgiana was a young lady of stout bravery. She had an inquiring mind, and was not a timid, easily shocked creature afraid of her own shadow. Again she thought of how she had always felt destined to go where other women would not dare. This was clearly a test of that resolve.

As she walked slowly down the passage, the man stopped throwing his ball and turned to watch her. His features were not clear, hidden in the shifting shadows.

"Sir?" she whispered. "Is something amiss?" She glanced at the wall and, in another flicker of lightning, saw a worn, scratched spot on the Tudor paneling. Evidence of frequent, similar misuse.

He slowly stood, pushing his back up the wall as if he needed that to help him rise. Another immediate pulse of brighter lightning gilded his full length in shimmering, rain-spangled silver.

Good lord.

He was stark naked and made no gentlemanly effort to cover himself.

Thunder shook the floorboards under her bare feet.

Raising her startled gaze hastily to his face, she saw his expression— something fierce and hard, carving sharp lines into his face like the marks of an axe blade in steel. How tall he seemed now, much larger than when they met in his study earlier. Slowly his height kept unfurling until he appeared to be running out of space and would soon have to bend his neck or else hit the roof beams with his head. There was a difference now, not only in his countenance but also in his demeanor. The man she'd spoken to earlier that evening was impatient, wary and nervous, reminding her of a boy caught in mischief and searching for excuses; this man— even in his nude state— had the commanding presence of one who would never feel the need to hide his wicked thoughts. His features, although the same as earlier, took on a harder bite.

She might have imagined she encountered an identical twin, had she not already been warned about the master of the house and his nocturnal wanderings.

"Who goes there?" he growled.

Georgiana did her best not to look below his shoulders again, but the temptation was great. Destined to go where no other would dare...and all that.

"I am Miss Hathaway, sir." Somehow she kept her voice steady. "Do you not remember?"

He leaned over and sniffed the air above her head. "But are you friend?" he demanded huskily. "Or foe?"

Her heart was beating so hard in her bosom that it seemed to vibrate through the curls on her head. "Friend, of course."

His left hand came up and fingers, long and sensual, wrapped around the braid that hung over her shoulder. "There is no *of course*, about it, woman. A foe is more likely than a friend these days, so Harry has found."

More lightning fizzled down the side of his face and hooked under his firm chin.

Gathering her courage, Georgiana looked deep into his angry, suspicious eyes. "You should go to bed, sir. It is late. Are you...are you not cold?" He was just a man, not a beast. Nothing to fear. Nothing to—

"Why aren't *you* abed?" he said. His long fingers wound their way through her braid, loosening the strands of hair. Despite his supposedly sprained wrist, he was remarkably dexterous, she noted. He tugged upon her braid, moving her closer. "Why are you creeping about my ship, in the dark, stowaway?"

Thunder banged hard across the roof.

"I couldn't sleep because you were keeping me awake. Sir."

Again he leaned over her and she felt his warm breath on her temple. "Keeping you awake?" he muttered.

"Yes, sir. The noise kept me from falling asleep."

Suddenly the tip of his wet tongue touched her brow. His heat surrounded her, a powerful aura more dangerous, she suspected, than the vivid lightning that split the sky outside that window. "Falling awake," he murmured.

"Falling asleep, sir."

She felt his lips move against her skin as he whispered. "In my bed."

"In yours? No, sir. In my—"

He moved swiftly closing in and backing her to the wall. Her heart jumped under her skin, that ambitious Hathaway nerve being tested by something equally strong, terribly menacing. And wickedly tempting.

The fingers of his left hand traced a path down her cheek to her chin. Suddenly, to her astonishment, his tongue followed suit, but in the reverse direction.

Georgiana was frozen to the spot while this eccentric fellow slowly and deliberately licked her face.

"I like the taste of you, woman," he muttered, running a thumb along her lower lip. "I will take another spoonful."

He applied just enough pressure to part her lips and then his mouth found hers. That wayward tongue slipped inside and he leaned forward, with a hand pressed to the wall on either side of her. She had never been kissed like this in her life. Even the angry thunder was suddenly muffled beneath the too-rapid thump of her pulse.

"Take care, sir," she gasped out at the first opportunity. "Your wrist—"

"Quiet, perfumed hussy. Still your lips so I can kiss them. If you stowaway on my ship, you must pay a price for safe passage."

Oh, lord! Why could she not have listened to that poor, over-worked man Brown and bolted the bedchamber door?

"When will you listen to the advice of others, Georgie?" her brother Edward used to say to her. *"You seem determined to make mistakes for yourself, when the experience of others could lead you more wisely."*

Ah, but she didn't want to go through life being protected and cosseted by others. That would hardly be living at all, would it?

Her strange host pressed his mouth to hers again, stealing the startled breath out of her, his tongue thrusting against her own, forcing its way in. Clearly he mistook her for somebody else rather than the maidenly companion of his very proper aunt.

Trapped between his body and the wall, she had nowhere to put her hands unless she held them to his chest, and before she could do that, he closed the last little bit of space between them. Now she felt the taut, hard muscle of his torso with only the linen of her nightgown and the thin wool of her shawl between them. His thigh stroked her hip, moving the soft material of her nightgown. It was a caress that felt more improper even than his kiss.

"You must be sorry you came to this house of madness," he murmured. "I feel you tremble. You are afraid."

"It is just the cold, sir." That seemed a plausible excuse, but in truth she did feel fear. At least, she thought that must be the name for it. Her shawl had fallen to her feet at some point, and she dare not bend to retrieve it, aware of what she would encounter on her way down.

"I will warm you." His left arm slipped around her waist, holding her firmer. "I will set you afire. Come with me now."

She could even feel the beat of his heart. It pulsed across her skin. Now she knew for sure her trembling was nothing to do with the chill temperature of the air in the house, shawl or not, for even with his heat and strength enveloping her, she still quivered like a jelly. "Sir, come with you where?"

No reply. At least, not with words. He kissed her yet again, his not-so wounded hand fumbling with her nightgown, tugging it upward, his knuckles brushing her bared thigh.

She gasped, turning her face away so that his lips caught the corner of her mouth and his lusty tongue dampened her cheek again. "Stop, sir!" She wriggled, desperately restraining a very foolish giggle as his breath tickled her ear. Oh, dear! That was, apparently, a vulnerable spot— there, just below.... his teasing was in danger of leaving her weak and utterly ruined. "What do you think I am?" she managed, breathless.

He paused, his hungry mouth now pressed to the side of her neck. "What do *you* think you are?" he repeated in a low, needful moan. "I do not know...I do not know what *I* am." His voice broke on the words as he took his lips off her skin. For a moment there was raw grief in his tone and it connected to something deep in her own heart. He bowed his head and in a flare of lightning she observed a drop of water hovering from a lock of hair that hung over his brow.

Had he been outside, naked, in the storm? The heat emanating from his body suggested not, but the little crystal tears now visible running down the side of his neck and over the broad planes of his chest must have come from somewhere.

"How do you know you're not falling awake instead of asleep?" he muttered, his eyes closed. "Sleep could be our normal state. Awake we could be dreaming. Which am I?"

Pounding thunder rumbled across the roof of the house and surely made the slate tremble. But Georgiana no longer felt the same vibration. She was calmer now. He was a wounded man, scarred beyond what the eye could see, and she would not walk away from a wounded man in the street, would she? Not even if he was a stranger.

He opened his eyes, and they were filled with something she had never before seen in any man's regard when they looked at her.

"You should be sleeping, sir. Please go to bed," she

whispered, moving to push him back gently. She meant only to touch him with her fingertips, but he was too solid for that light gesture to make any difference, so she placed both hands on his upper arms— on those taut, well-hewn muscles. They were damp too. "You must get some rest. You are not yourself."

"How do you know?" he muttered, staring down at her lips. "How do you know what myself is? Do you know what Harry is?"

Georgiana struggled for a reply, very much aware of his hot, moist skin and all that flexing power under her small palms and inexperienced fingers. "I know Commander Sir Henry Thrasher is a gentleman."

"But *Dead Harry* is not." His lips toyed with a cocky smile as they hovered closer to the tip of her nose. "Harry is a rampaging, ravaging raider. Harry answers to none. He lives on his own island by his own rules." He whispered, "Harry likes to play. And he wants to play... with you."

She studied the sensual curve of his lips, the thin line of his fine nose, and again the wrath of lightning in those eyes. How easily he could sweep her up over his wide shoulder and carry her off somewhere. If she shouted for help in this wing of the house, would anyone hear? And who would come? Brown who hobbled at the pace of a snail, or Lady Bramley with her flimsy parasol to fight off any villain she encountered? They might think her cries were merely the hapless wails of ghosts and thus hide under their bedcovers.

Georgiana saw she would have to save herself. But she could manage this. She'd dealt with her naughty little brothers before.

"Well, *Dead Harry* had better be a gentleman for Miss Georgiana Hathaway," she said sharply. "Or Dead Harry might wake to discover certain parts of his anatomy bouncing off the walls like that cricket ball."

He blinked slowly, lazily. "Not very ladylike, woman."

119

His right hand— the one meant to be in a sling—ventured to the slender laces that fastened the front of her nightgown. "You said you were friend, not foe." One finger slipped under the knot and touched her skin, the pad of his fingertip gently tickling the hollow at the base of her throat. A touch that felt just as intimate as his kiss. "Did you change your mind now? Women do that, don't they?"

"Do what?" She was finding it difficult to concentrate with his fingers gently caressing her throat. So much shocking tenderness in his touch and she almost did not want it to stop, although she knew it must.

"Change their minds. Abandon him. And everyone tells the boy that she simply died, but he knows what really happened. He finds out that she left them. Not even a goodbye to the boy she birthed." His lips moved closer again, but Georgiana felt no urge to flee. The warning whispers were silent in her head now. She imagined her reckless, daring spirit holding those cowardly doubters at sword point. "His father fills the space she left with as many women as he can find, but the boy chooses escape and goes to sea."

"Until he has to come home?"

"No. He is still at sea. All at sea."

Yes, she had seen that in his eyes. "Then he needs rescue." It slipped out of her on a thin breath of desperation, "I want to help you, sir."

"So help me," he whispered, his fingers straying under the laces of her nightgown.

"But not this way." She placed her hand over his. "I shall not let you take advantage of me, sir." Not that she didn't want to. Oh, lord, she had never felt quite like this. Surely it was very wrong to enjoy the kisses of a man she barely knew. Yet Georgiana remembered that sensation of comradeship, palpable from their very first sight of each other. An impossible impression of having known him forever.

He squinted, looking bewildered. "Take advantage? It is you who has the advantage. You know who you are." Moving his thumb to her chin, he pressed down until her lips were parted again and then he tipped her face up toward his. "You are stronger than Harry. Inside. Harry has not the strength to restrain his needs." She felt certain he was about to take another improper kiss. One that would perhaps be even deeper, fiercer. But he could not hide the shadow of sadness in his eyes and it appealed to that softness in Georgiana's heart, that willingness to see the good in a person no matter what.

The sudden whirring clunk of the long-case clock in the hall below, warned of an imminent strike. That sound apparently shook the man out of his moment of sorrow and he forgot the kiss.

"We will discuss your fee for safe passage on my ship tomorrow, stowaway. Try to stay out of further trouble until then."

While he turned away from her, distracted by the stern chime of the clock, Georgiana took her chance and slipped away, ducking under his arm.

She ran back to her room and this time she bolted her door. Perhaps she was not quite as brave as she thought, but fortunately neither of her friends were there to witness her lapse.

On further reflection, lying in the bed and stretching out her oddly excitable limbs, she decided that this sensation rippling through her was not fear. It was very much like the precarious exhilaration caused by Melinda's father's wine at Yuletide. Hopefully this too would be temporary, but would not leave her with a headache in the morning.

Chapter Eleven

It was still raining the day after their arrival, but in a sullen manner as if the clouds could barely be bothered—as if they'd stop entirely, if not for the inconvenience they liked to cause.

Georgiana found her way to the kitchen that first morning by following the strident tones of Lady Bramley giving orders to Brown and explaining how she meant to put her nephew, and his house, in order.

"Afraid you'll have to wait a few days for the post, Miss Hathaway," Brown said when he saw the sealed papers in Georgiana's hand. "The creek overflowed bad last night and flooded part of the road to Little Flaxhill. There's only the one road unless a horse takes to the fields, but they'll be under water after that storm and anyone who tries to pass through will be a right mess at best and stuck in the mud at worst."

This was not good news for the next installment of *His Lordship's Trousers,* which would now be delayed.

"I'll take the letters for you next time I can get out," Brown added. "The water will recede in a day or two and even if the road isn't fixed, the fields should be more passable then."

"Thank you, Mr. Brown."

"There's breakfast in the dining room," Lady Bramley informed her crisply, without looking up from a list she prepared for the handyman. "You can help yourself, of course. I have much to do."

"Yes, your ladyship."

Just as she turned to leave in search of food, their host suddenly appeared in the kitchen doorway, bellowing, "And another thing—"

It looked as if he might have forgotten the arrival of another guest, for he jerked to a halt when he saw Georgiana standing there. He paused with mouth open, left hand raised, index finger pointing at the ceiling.

For a few expectant moments, the only sound was that of the fire crackling and the distant pit-pat-ping of rain leaking into a row of vessels assembled on the landing.

Georgiana remembered to curtsey, trying not to think immediately about what she had seen last night. "Good morning, sir." Alas, it was quite impossible not to recall the sight of his beautiful, strong physique under those clothes. He was magnificent. She may not know a vast deal about the naked male body, but she had that little book she'd found in Mrs. Lightbody's parlor for reference. She had also suffered several lessons on art appreciation, not to mention a disastrous attempt at sculpting with clay herself— an attempt that was immediately smashed with a hammer by Mrs. Lightbody who called it "obscene". Ha! The hypocrisy in that woman knew no bounds. So, yes, Georgiana could recognize a well-made form when she saw it.

His upward thrusting finger now changed into a horizontal arrow and pointed directly at her. "Ink. On face."

Thus, she learned the consequence of falling asleep on her writing last night and having no mirror in her room. Brown must not have noticed, and Lady Bramley had barely spared her a glance.

While Georgiana licked her palm and rubbed her cheek, checking her reflection in one of the copper pans hanging from the rack above, Lady Bramley admonished her nephew sternly, "*Miss Hathaway. Good morning, Miss Hathaway.* That's what you're supposed to say. Have we lost our last few good manners in the storm, as well as more slates from the roof?"

He scowled, his head tilted slightly forward to avoid knocking his brow on the lintel. "I know not. Best ask Brown. He is in charge of these matters."

"Brown manages your manners too, does he?"

"Why not? He knows as much about manners as I do."

The lady finally raised her gaze from the list in her hand, but she looked only as far as Georgiana's dress. "Miss Hathaway, what do you have on?"

"It is one of my best frocks, madam. Why? Is something amiss?"

"It is far too fancy for a day gown. What could you be thinking?"

She looked fretfully down at herself. "Unfortunately my trunk leaked on the journey and this was the only dry frock when I looked this morning. I hung the others up by the fire." The dye had washed out of some too, giving a few of her gowns a sad, mottled appearance. She dreaded Lady Bramley's reaction when she saw them.

"I see. Then you will have to manage in that this morning. Ball gowns at breakfast, whatever next?" She shook her head and made a clicking sound with her tongue.

"Will civilization survive?" her nephew remarked drily. His eyes, Georgiana noted, were at their darkest today. Last night they had reflected the brilliant flashes of lightning and seemed almost wild. But now they were more guarded when they looked at her.

He was still unshaven, however. His sun-tickled hair flopped about until he ran fingers through the mess, and then spikes of it stood on end. In the same way that another part of him had stood brazenly upright last night, as he held her to the wall and warmed her with kisses.

She simply must stop thinking about that. About his masterful touch that seemed as powerful and dangerous as the lightning itself.

Georgiana exhaled a small sound of despair that, hopefully, nobody else had heard. "What does Miss Hathaway have to smile about this morning?" he demanded, those searching eyes narrowed. "What wickedness has she perpetrated now?"

Hastily she sought an excuse, guilty heat flooding her face. "I was just thinking, sir, that I am feeling very rested after my journey and had an excellent night's sleep. My thoughts were extinguished as quickly as a snuffed candle as soon as my head hit the pillow. Despite the storm that raged."

He stared coldly and blankly at her, either remembering nothing about their encounter in the passage, or hiding it very skillfully. "How fortunate for you. Still, I daresay an empty head is often less troubled."

She decided not to take offence. Allowances must be made for a Naval hero and he could hardly know that her head was far from empty. Yet. So she said politely, "I wondered if the storm last night kept anybody else awake."

Lady Bramley replied sharply that storms never kept her from sleep. Her tone suggested that they wouldn't dare try. But Georgiana looked at the master of the house, waiting to see what he would say.

"I suppose I bloody-well slept. What does it matter to you?"

"Henry!" his aunt cried. "Language!"

Today he had tucked in his shirt and tied his neck cloth, but there was still no waistcoat or jacket. Perhaps the sling made it too difficult, she thought. The sling which he, interestingly enough, didn't appear to need last night.

"Why don't you escort Miss Hathaway to the dining room for breakfast, Henry?" his aunt demanded. "Light a fire in there too. It's bitterly cold."

"Can't Brown do it?"

"Brown is too busy here with me. There is much to do until my staff can get here through the floods. You know how to light a fire, surely."

"It's June," he grumbled.

"You may not have looked out of a window yet this morning, or even raised your head far out of your books, but it's cold as a Scotsman's kneecaps in this house. Summer or not, I could see my breath this morning when I came downstairs."

"Oh....blast!" His eyes swept briefly back to Georgiana, before he swiveled around and disappeared behind the door frame.

She hesitated, not knowing if she ought to follow.

Suddenly his head ducked back to look at her. "Bestir your stumps, Miss Hathaway! I have other things to do today, you know."

Georgiana hurried after him.

* * * *

He heard her feet tapping along the corridor behind his own long stride, but he didn't slow down to wait for her. When women ventured into places where they were not welcomed — like his ship, for instance— they could fend for themselves.

"Your aunt said you don't often have houseguests, sir." She caught up with him as he reached the dining room door.

He shot her his most menacing glare. "I try not to."

"Don't you like company?"

"Company has a tendency to complicate a man's simple life. At the very least, it demands that he get dressed."

Undaunted by his cross tone, the girl nodded somberly. "I daresay, since you managed on that deserted island, you are accustomed to being alone. But that doesn't mean other folk should not have the pleasure of your company. You must have many fascinating stories to tell."

"Most not fit for mixed company, Miss Hathaway."

"That makes them all the more intriguing. We ladies are not nearly as delicate as you've been led to believe."

He was still thinking about that, and assessing her mischievous smile, when she glanced at his sling and said,

"Does it hurt very much?"

He clutched his elbow. "Sometimes worse than others."

"May I look at it?"

"Certainly not."

"The doctor at home used to say he'd never known a girl so unmoved by the sight of blood and broken bones. I helped him set my little brother's arm once, when he fell out of a tree. He was protesting, you see, because he did not want to leave our home in the country and move to London. The poor child thought that if he hid no one would be able to leave until he was found again. But as I told him later, he was lucky anybody noticed he was gone, because if it was me they would not have cared. My elder sister fainted at the sight of that misshapen limb when they carried him in to the parlor and my stepmother was reduced to hysterics, but I retained my full capacities to be useful."

"A fascinating story. May I ask why you felt compelled to relay it to me?"

"To show I have experience in these matters, that I am not squeamish and I can help you."

"Isn't that nice? Fortunately for me I am not reduced to the care of young girls who can barely manage themselves. The doctor here in the village tends my maladies quite sufficiently."

"All of them?"

Harry stared down at her impertinent face. "I am in good health. He is not greatly taxed with my care."

She nodded, lips pressed tight.

As he turned to reach for the door handle, she abruptly exclaimed, "Last night your wrist did not seem to hurt you at all."

The door handle turned, but there was no opening movement. It was stuck. "Last night?"

"Don't you remember?" she said.

His hand slipped from the handle. He spun around and scowled his hardest, but she stood there looking up at him, her face innocent.

"I came out of my room last night and found you in the passage, sir."

"I think you must have been dreaming, Miss Hathaway."

"No, sir. I believe *you* were dreaming."

See, he thought angrily, *this is what happens when you let people in. You're not fit for female company.*

Frustrated, he resumed pushing at the door to open it. The damp, warped wood required several hearty thumps of his shoulder before it finally opened, accompanied by a sound like a cracking whip. A small chunk of plaster fell to the floor and shattered on impact. As he stepped over the mess, he saw that Brown had set some cold toast, cake, butter, and jam out on the dining table, along with a pot of chocolate kept warm over a little candle.

"Well, there you are," he exclaimed gruffly, waving a hand loosely in that direction, "breakfast. I trust you can manage to feed yourself."

But as he spoke, his words formed quick puffs of cloud before his face. It was, as his aunt had said, rather chilly that day. In the cozy surroundings of his study he had not noticed the cold temperature, but once he ventured out of his sanctuary he found the rest of the house definitely in need of warmth. He supposed he ought to make that fire for the girl, especially since she was reduced to wearing a gown that looked paper thin.

Before he could take another step, however, his guest went directly to the hearth, professing herself capable of making a fire without his help.

"Although your aunt calls me a revolutionary," she smiled, "I am not going to burn your house down." Then she put her chin higher. "Unless you make me very angry. I do have quite a temper when roused."

"Indeed. So I witnessed once before."

As she stood at the hearth, grey, rain-streaked daylight slipped through the window and sought her out with tentative fingers. Lit by this moving, shifting pattern of shadow and light, she might have been a ghost standing there in her inappropriate ball gown— some impish spirit sent from the past to cause trouble. Behind her one of the old curtains had, at some point in its history, been torn from its hooks and left to hang dejectedly, that twisted, frayed shape moving in the draft, adding to the impression of a haunting, otherworldly vision.

What happened last night when he met her in the darkened corridor? He wished he could remember. Damn!

Harry rubbed his creased brow with two fingers, trying to ease the dull ache that lurked there— sign of a sleepless night, alas. Dimly he remembered a vision in a white nightgown, dark hair in a loose braid over her shoulder. Laces tied in a knot. A smooth thigh slipping under his palm, soft as satin.

Increasingly alarmed by the possibilities, Harry studied her slyly from beneath his fingers and with a safe distance of several feet between them. The woman did not appear harmed by the encounter, fortunately.

She was cheerful and had mentioned the meeting quite casually, not with any tone of accusation. Now she hummed a nonchalant tune and stood before the cold hearth, pretending— most unconvincingly— that she knew how to light a fire. In a ball gown as dainty and fragile as a butterfly's wing. Her strange attire was actually not so out of place in his surreal existence, he mused.

"Better close the door to keep the heat in," she said.

Ah, but it was not entirely proper to be in that room with her, behind a closed door, was it? Parkes would remind him, if she was there. Hesitating for a few moments, he finally decided to err on the side of caution and leave it slightly ajar. Wouldn't want it getting stuck again while they were inside together.

Or was that part of her scheme?

It might have been a number of years since Harry ventured out into society, but he remembered the ruthless and mercenary business of husband hunting, and how some young girls would stop at nothing to bag their prey.

In his experience, these things were best nipped in the bud immediately. It saved everybody a vast amount of time and trouble.

He cleared his throat loudly and then announced, "You may as well know this from the start, Miss Hathaway— I am not disposed to acquire a wife. Whatever you may have been advised, I do not need one, nor do I want one. I am quite content. So please do not form any romantic fancies about me while you're here. If you do, you are destined for crushing disappointment."

She looked over her shoulder, eyes wide, lips parted.

"My memory might be unreliable at times, but I do remember well what young women are like," he added. "And it has been my aunt's oft-expressed desire to see me married for some time now. I'm afraid she may have brought you here with misguided intentions."

After a lengthy pause, the young woman finally moved her lips. "I appreciate the candid statement, sir, but I doubt your aunt brought me here for that purpose. I'm hardly the sort of woman she'd want for her only nephew. My accomplishments are not the right kind, neither are my looks, and she says I talk too much."

"Yes, well, true as all that is, she could be verging on desperate by now and ready to lower her standards. My aunt is very determined when she has a bee in her bonnet."

"As am I. And I am not looking for a husband, sir." She gave a short, dry chuckle. "I would only misplace him, or forget to feed him, or something equally dire. So... now we have got all that straight from the beginning and we can be quite at ease with each other. Perhaps, if you are staying to eat, you can stop hovering by the door. I promise not to cause you any bodily harm."

After a moment's hesitation, Harry cautiously approached the fireplace. "I thought matrimony was the aim on every young woman's mind at that school," he muttered. "Especially when she reaches a certain age. Indeed, I understand there is not much room for any other idea in such a young lady's mind. I've never found evidence of one."

"Then it will surprise you to learn that young women often have other plans for their future. Not every girl seeks the bother of a husband. Men, as I have observed, are most often in the way."

"In the way?" he repeated, bemused.

"I mean to have all manner of adventures, to travel extensively and explore, not to be told where I can and cannot go. I will take charge of my own life, be answerable only to myself, and not live in fear of disappointing or displeasing anybody." She took a quick breath. "Your aunt says you're very busy with your work."

How swiftly she diverted the subject.

"Yes," he replied, rasping fingers over his unshaven cheek. "My work."

"What sort of work?"

"Naught of interest to you."

Her left eyebrow quirked. "How do you know what would interest me? We've already ascertained that you know little to nothing about young women." She added smugly, "Particularly this one."

Since her gown was already marked with coal dust and ashes, and fire had yet to appear, Harry decided he'd better help. She was too stubborn to ask for assistance. "Apparently I know as much about young ladies as you know about lighting a fire." Lowering quickly to one knee beside her, he fumbled to open the flue with his good hand. His other wrist was throbbing.

Now, where was the bloody tinder box?

She passed it down to him before he asked for it. Then, quite suddenly, she dropped to her knees at his side. Very close. It seemed quite casual, unconsciously done.

But he almost dropped the tinderbox.

Last night Parkes had wryly asked for whom he was most afraid— Miss Hathaway or himself. He did not yet have an answer.

"This is a lovely room," she was saying, as he laid kindling wood over the grate, "or it could be, with a little tender, loving care. What a pity you have not used it often. It's been wasted for several years it seems. Abandoned to spiders and woodworm."

"There is little point in making Brown bring food all the way from the kitchen and light a fire in here, merely so that I can eat at the grand table in solitary splendor."

"No, I suppose not. Such a great shame however— all this lovely old house with only you and Mr. Brown rattling around inside. I grew up in a much smaller house and there were nine of us in it."

When Harry stole a quick glance at her face again, her attention was absorbed by the task ahead of them and she seemed quite unaware of anything unusual or discomforting about her proximity. He took the sly opportunity to study the stubborn upward tilt of her nose and that dent in her cheek, above which some faded ink markings yet remained.

"*Sretrag esool ydaL,*" he said.

She sat back on her heels. "Is that Latin?"

"You tell me." Harry pointed with a scrap of kindling wood at her right cheek where, despite her frenzied rubbing, the remnants of ink had left this curious message. Unfortunately for her he was adept at reading backwards. "Lady Loose Garters?"

She was silent, but he could almost hear the cogwheels of her mind turning as she sought for an answer. Those lengthy lashes blinked several times in quick succession. "It was a letter to a dear friend," she muttered eventually, blushing pink and snatching the strip of kindling from his hand. "Let's get on with the fire. It's awfully cold."

"You don't look cold," he observed.

Her cheeks flushed with even brighter color. She grabbed a shovel of coal and tossed it onto the wood kindling with such savagery that several lumps scattered across the hearth.

Harry was intrigued. "With what sort of friend would you discuss loose garters, Miss Hathaway? I doubt my aunt would approve. Such a subject is surely not within the bounds of her rules for young ladies."

"Why should I not discuss stocking garters, loose or otherwise, with my dear friend? Besides, what do you care about the rules?" she replied archly. "I rather got the impression that you didn't. You said that Mr. Brown knew more about them than you do."

He gave a gruff laugh. "That was manners."

"Is it not the same thing?" As she licked her lips, drawing his attention to her mouth, he imagined suddenly that he could taste it, could feel that softness yielding under his kiss.

His pulse was very rapid, his thigh too warm where she knelt near him. It was hot enough to ignite the tinder before he even struck the steel with the flint.

"Miss Hathaway, *if* anything... untoward... occurred last night—"

"Such as?"

He did not answer that, but said firmly, "You should not be wandering about the house in the dark. Brown should have told you. Perhaps, from now on, you will stay in your bed at night."

"Will you stay in yours?"

Again he did not reply, but turned his full attention to

the fire until a flame leapt among the kindling wood and then caught upon the coals. Once satisfied, Harry quickly got up, brushed down his knee and took a seat at the table, where he began scooping jam onto his plate in a lavish heap. He hadn't meant to eat breakfast and had only brought her to the room on his aunt's orders, but now, suddenly, he had an appetite. And a sweet tooth.

It was unsettling, of course, to have a new person in his house. She disturbed the dust— of which there was plenty— and his routine, which, until then, he had not known existed. He thought his life was unbalanced before, so how was it possible that she upset the equilibrium?

Anxious to forget the presence of this young woman, her questioning eyes, distracting eyelashes, and ink-smudged cheek, Harry tried fixing his mind elsewhere. But his thoughts were muddled, spinning in circles.

What the devil did happen last night?

In desperation, his gaze swept the dining room again, searching for a memory of the last meal he'd enjoyed there. Faded images floated through the stale air—of his restless father seeking satisfaction, but never finding it with the many women he brought to that table. A fleet of them, all much the same in looks and temperament, now that Harry thought of it. They had all been very similar to his mother. But they did not fill the space she had left in their life. If that was his father's intention with those other women, it failed miserably.

Miss Hathaway was nothing like them. She did not wait to be spoken to, or hide her thoughts behind a false smile. She did not watch fearfully from the corner of her eye and cringe when he spoke curtly.

She was now shaking dust out of that drooping curtain and sneezing violently in the subsequent fog cloud.

Where the devil was Parkes this morning? The woman had not appeared yet to make any comment about him eating breakfast, or reminding him to dress decently now that he had guests in the house.

"There's a terrible draft through this window, sir. You ought to have somebody fix it."

Ah. Miss Hathaway, it seemed, was here to nag him since Parkes was not.

"Goodness, will this rain never let up," she added with a sigh, turning her back to him and rubbing her arms while she looked out of the window. Now she had soot on her sleeves too. Didn't seem to notice. Another thing that made her different to other women who had dined in that room.

He should get back to work. A gloomy, damp day like this was perfect for reading or working in his cozy study. But, instead, he found himself reaching for another piece of toast and venturing into the realms of proper conversation. "How did you enjoy your time at the ladies academy, Miss Hathaway?"

"Since your aunt is a patron of the school, I had better decline from answering, sir."

"It failed to turn you into a lady."

"It failed on every count, or rather the headmistress failed. The school itself might have been a pleasant experience, if not for her."

"Explain."

She hesitated.

"I am trying to understand, Miss Hathaway, how the school could have turned out somebody quite like you."

So then it poured out of her, as if her frustration had too long been held back by a flimsy dam. "Mrs. Lightbody has no liking for intelligence in other women. She feels threatened by it and so she crushes it at every opportunity. As a result, her students, rather than graduate with a sound education and allowed to reach their full potential, are shaped only for one purpose in life— marriage. I have tried to pity her, but even my desire to find good in anybody is severely tested in her case."

As she passed the tall windows, daylight touched her with a brighter glare, reaching through the thin, summery fabric of her gown, and granting Harry a teasing, temporary glimpse of her figure. How could he keep himself from looking? He was not dead, after all; that was just a rumor.

"Mrs. Lightbody takes apples of all shapes and sizes, sir, and insists upon making them into an Apple Fool. The same Apple Fool, made to a recipe that has not changed in a hundred years at least. She has no imagination, no fancy to try a pie, or a crumble, or a pudding. No chunks of apple can be tolerated. The fruit must be pulped down until it is the texture of cream, has very little taste, and takes no trouble to eat."

What was she talking about? "Hmmm. Apples." He licked his fingers. "I like apples. Sweet, juicy apples."

She groaned softly. "I do not know why I bothered. It does no earthly good explaining to a man." She walked around the table, running her fingers along the dusty chair-backs. "But if you had to have a wife, would you rather not have one with some intelligence?"

Depends upon the size of the apples, he mused wickedly. But having considered her question a little longer, he finally said, "No," and ripped savagely into his toast.

"No? But—"

Through a full mouth, he added, "Wouldn't want her to outwit me, would I? Besides," he gave a little grin, "the entire world knows that women should be seen and not heard, certainly not taken seriously." Carefully, he kept his eyes on his plate, somehow restraining the urge to laugh.

She made a small, frustrated sound and then snapped, "Well, I made two very good friends there at least, and we would never have met had we not gone to that school. Miss Melinda Goodheart and Miss Emma Chance are two of the loveliest young ladies that ever lived."

"And I assume one of these friends would be the

136

correspondent to whom you wrote your letter about this...Lady Loose Garters."

"Yes. That is so." From the pert expression on her face, and the weighty silence that followed— not to mention the fingers clenched tightly around the chair in front of her, Miss Hathaway fully expected him to doubt her word. She waited to argue. To defend what was evidently a lie.

How did he know she lied? Because the confident gleam left her eyes for the first time when he questioned her about it. The young lady had been caught out. In his experience, a woman never fought harder to make a man believe her than when she fibbed.

But he said none of this. Instead he calmly shrugged and looked down at the crumbs on his plate.

Uh oh. Slowly she had resumed her progress around his table and she had a habit of humming under her breath as she did so. Harry was terribly aware of every move she made, every tap of her finger or lick of her lips. Every blink.

Part of him was amused and interested to see what she might do next, the other half was certain no good could come of having her in his house. He felt as if he could not put his full foot down on the ground, but hovered on the balls of his feet, unsure whether to stay or flee. What an odd feeling it was.

But she was just a woman, after all. Why would he flee? What was the worst she could do to him?

"So you are an apple that declines to be pulped." He paused. "But you are, no doubt, just as eager to be in love as any other addled girl of nineteen. Perhaps you simply haven't had the opportunity. Your plans for adventure will vanish then soon enough, after one agreeable smile from a dashing young buck with a smooth, pretty face, elegant manners and a fancy-embroidered waistcoat."

"Well, *you* need not worry then." She snorted with

laughter.

He scowled.

"Are you disappointed that I didn't come here to seduce you and make you fall in love with me?" she demanded saucily. "That I have other plans?"

Harry had just taken another bite and almost choked on his toast. "Devastated."

"Did you expect me to swoon before you? Perhaps you said all that about not wanting a wife, just to set me a challenge."

He shook his head. "Miss Hathaway, I do not play games with words. I say what I mean, precisely as I mean it. Occasionally my brutal honesty gets me into trouble. So I can assure you that when I say I don't want a wife, that is exactly the case."

"And so it is with me," she replied smugly. "We both say exactly what we mean. Just as you know what you want, I know what I want. Why should my choice be questioned, if yours is not? To me, a husband would be as much of an inconvenience as a houseguest is to you, sir."

His aunt was right— the girl did talk too much. And she did not honey her words any more than Harry did. No doubt it got her into trouble from time to time, too.

Now he watched while she examined the Staffordshire spaniels on the mantel. The fire light glowed through that flimsy bit of gown and revealed the curve of her hip. Or did he imagine he saw it? Such diaphanous fabric was created to mislead a man as the pleats moved and the thin layers shifted. And that gown was designed for dancing in candlelight, of course, to make the transparency even more subtle.

A few stray curls rested on the nape of her neck— shiny little coils of mahogany. Deceptively innocent little curls.

sretrag esool ydal.

Lips pursed, he shook his head. Young, unwed

138

women should not be reading *His Lordship's Trousers* and discussing it with their friends.

That serial was not meant for maidenly eyes.

Good thing she wasn't his female to worry about, or he'd have something to say about her choice of reading material.

And her choice of fabric too.

Chapter Twelve

The daylight version of Sir Henry Thrasher did not have the arrogant swagger of his nighttime twin; he was tied up in his thoughts, cautious of every word he spoke.

Georgiana studied the frowning fellow as he sat at the table, shaking his head— probably at something she'd said— and slathering an abundance of apricot jam all over another thick slice of toast. He had almost emptied the entire pot.

There was no charm in his manner, no warmth today. None on the surface, at least. He seemed almost afraid of being physically close to her while they made the fire together. But the way he kissed her last night suggested a man capable of making fire without kindling and a tinder box. A man accustomed to getting his own way and laying waste to anyone who tried stopping him.

What a pair they were— he in his eccentric state of dishabille and she in her party frock.

He wore boots from two different pairs on his feet again, one with a brown top, one solid black. She'd never heard of a gentleman without a valet, but her host was unique in many ways. Here he lived as a recluse, apparently determined and content in his isolation, probably because he didn't want anybody else to know there were two sides to his personality.

I am not disposed to acquire a wife.

As if she was likely to fling herself at him, she mused.

But last night, in the storm-lit corridor, "Harry" had told her he was lonely and wanted to play.

Poor Harry. If only the different sides of his personality could be put back together, he might feel better able to confront life and society. Somehow he'd been split into two. One half was lost, wandering— "Still at sea", as he'd put it.

"Miss Hathaway, you're not eating," he observed

from the table.

"I'm not terribly hungry, sir."

"Have some chocolate at least. I thought all young ladies liked— ah, you will tell me again that I know nothing about young ladies."

But she was much too excitable this morning to think of breakfast. There were many things she would like to know about her strange host, and she puzzled over the problem of where to begin.

Gripping the back of a dining chair again, she watched the man eat for a moment and then said, "What are all those sketches on the floor of your study?"

After a pause and a huff, he replied, "Part of my work."

"And you won't tell me anything about it?"

His eyes narrowed. "Why would *you* want to know?"

"Because I'm interested. Despite being only a woman, I have a very active curiosity."

He was silent, still scowling.

"Your aunt said you could show me the house this morning," she said. "Since this weather confines us indoors, you might as well—"

"Hush, woman. Must you chatter quite so much? A man cannot get his thoughts in order while you're throwing more words at him."

Yes, she could see the daytime man did a lot of thinking. So much of it that he did not get anything done. The house was falling around his ears.

Georgiana waited as patiently as she could before exclaiming, "I'm not a spy who might take your secrets to the enemy. I am the soul of discretion."

He looked as if he might laugh. And he seemed surprised by it. Alarmed even. Taking another bite of toast, he chewed slowly, watching her.

What had Brown said of his master? "*A terrible waste of a good man.*" Solid, steady and overworked, the manservant, she suspected, did not give out praise very often. But the Commander wanted to hide his pleasant side from her, it seemed. He did not mean to let her close. Why? What did he fear? She'd assured him that she was not there to catch a husband.

Perhaps a little teasing would help lower his guard.

Georgiana added wryly, "Perhaps my sheer beauty has enchanted you, Commander, and you fret that I might endanger your bachelor's resolve? I suppose showing me your work is the first step to sure ruin and before we know it, you'll be falling hapless at my feet."

A new expression had passed over his face, almost as if another man briefly stepped into his skin and looked out at her through those same eyes. Same but different. Wilder. Like last night, when naked Harry kissed her savagely and told her, without words, that he wanted much more.

But that was last night and today he was unsociable Commander Thrasher again, trying to be stern and gruff with her. Intent on keeping his distance.

"It is quite sweet really, sir."

"What is?"

"Your attempt at a menacing glare."

Georgiana Hathaway was not about to be frightened off by a man who couldn't even find a matching pair of boots.

Finally he said, "Very well, Miss Hathaway, I will show you my study. Since you are currently at a loose end and I can see I'll get no peace until you are occupied."

Oh. Excitement fluttered through her. "Exactly," she agreed fervently. "And you never know what I might get up to when left to my own devices."

* * * *

What else could he do? His damnable aunt had brought this creature into his house and then apparently left her to his management when she found something more pressing demanding her attention. Someone would have to watch over the creature.

Harry entered his study, and the young woman followed close on his heels again, having a distressing disregard for respectable and comfortable distance. He felt like a ram being herded by an overly-eager sheepdog.

"I know what these are," she exclaimed. "They're automatons."

He nodded, surprised she knew the word.

Where the Devil was Parkes today? She'd been absent all morning, not coming to offer a single word of advice.

The intruder walked around his desk with her head high, as if she was mistress of the house. "Wouldn't it be more practical to put your talents to mending the leaking roof?" she demanded.

Harry drew himself up, squared his shoulders. "I'm getting around to that."

A sudden renewed gust of rain blew hard at the windows, reminding him why he couldn't put her out of his house today. She had invaded his world and he was helpless.

Now she picked up the head of Miss Petticoat and held it at arm's length. "She's a sad-looking creature."

He snatched it away from her, tucking it under his left arm. "Kindly don't interfere."

"Is it a sort of doll for you to play with?"

Harry carefully set the head on a shelf between books. "My work is important, Miss Hathaway. I do not make toys."

"It looks like a toy."

"Well, she is not one." He felt his temperature rising. She blinked, shrugged, then resumed her thorough appraisal of his study. "Do mind my sketches, Miss Hathaway!"

She grabbed one of them before he could get to it,

and her eyes shone with amusement as she held it up to the light through the window. "This looks like me...a little."

"Indeed it does not," he muttered, busying himself with a pile of books on the desk. "Why would it?"

"But it does. Look." She held the drawing up to her face.

"Pure coincidence." He snatched it from her, before she might read the words he'd marked across the bottom.

"If you do not mind me giving you some advice, sir, I think you would be happier with a real woman, rather than one made of hard metal bits and pieces."

He glared. "Is that what you *think*? Thank you for your counsel, Miss Hathaway of nineteen sheltered years and lately of the Particular Establishment for the Advancement of Rampant Lunacy."

She laughed good-naturedly, but did not retreat. "I believe you'll find a real woman much more satisfying, even if she is not the ideal you have in your mind. I mean to say, sir, no man or woman is without fault, and even this creature may have imperfections. Even she might disappoint you."

"Miss Hathaway, I would prefer it if you did not pry into my business. That is precisely why I did not want to show you my work. As for women of the flesh and blood variety, I find that they are *most often in the way*." He gestured impatiently for her to move aside so that he could walk around his desk. "Much as you have found the male species."

She had the grace to look sorry then. "Oh, I didn't mean to make you angry."

"You had better mind your own business then. But since we are giving out advice where it is not welcomed, now it is my turn. You may think you have clever plans, Miss Hathaway. You may have some whimsical scheme for your future, but I would advise you to forget all that and marry. Conform with convention. Quickly, before you get your prying nose and fingers— and any other part— into greater trouble. My aunt assures me that matrimony is the only obstacle to sin, for a young lady such as yourself."

She looked quizzical. "A young lady such as myself? What is that supposed to mean?"

"Well-spoken... has all her teeth...mostly symmetrical features...sober."

"Sober? Only for want of opportunity." A sharp chuckle shot out of her and was instantly curbed, although he saw it trembling through her shoulders.

Harry eyed her dubiously. "Such a young lady ought to be respectably married and not running about strange men's corridors at night."

"Well, I am the adventurous sort, sir, and when I hear noises at night I tend to investigate, rather than hide under the covers."

He dropped to his chair and began shuffling papers frantically. "You know what they say about curiosity and the cat, Miss Hathaway."

She began tracing a pattern on his desk with her fingertip. "You think I have symmetrical features? Is that *flattery*, Commander Thrasher? Take care or it might go to my head and make me insufferably vain."

"It was merely an honest assessment of the items on your face, which are all in their place. Mostly. No need for excitement."

"Then you do not find me completely unattractive."

"I've seen worse faces," he murmured, shoving a pile of papers into his desk drawer. "I suppose."

Miss Hathaway abruptly overflowed with bubbles of laughter that she could apparently not restrain another moment. "I believe that is indeed the closest I've ever had to a compliment, sir."

He got up out of his chair again, trying to think of some way to remove her from his room. If he had a ball at hand he'd throw it and see if she chased it. "You are not misshapen, madam, that I will admit. Your features have some favorable qualities. They are not grotesque. And you have a lively disposition, which is likely to attract the worst sort of rogue. Until you do marry."

"Oh stop! I pray you, stop! Before I am overcome by too much unaccustomed adulation."

He made his way around the desk toward her. "I daresay, if you were not covered in ink stains, mischief and soot, you might be more presentable, but my aunt has not yet begun her work on you, has she?"

"Poor Lady Bramley. What has she taken on? She is a great optimist."

"Clearly. One must admire her fortitude."

She laughed up at him, her eyes shining. It was a very long time since he'd heard feminine laughter in his house.

He was still absorbed in studying the naughty curve of her lips when she spun away and picked up Miss Petticoat's head again to examine it. "Are you going to give her my face? My not-entirely-grotesque and mostly symmetrical face?"

"Good God, no." He moved to take it from her again, but she walked away and set the head on his windowsill where there was better light. "One of you is surely enough, Miss Hathaway."

"What's she for then? What are you going to do with her?"

"I will teach her to play the pianoforte."

"I suppose you think she'll be less trouble than the real thing. She will do exactly what you want and never question. I see she has no tongue."

He joined her at the window. "Precisely so." His knuckles of his good hand accidentally brushed the pleats of her gown and he quickly put it behind his back. It was too late, however. That slight kiss of rough and soft sent a frisson of pleasure through his veins, unstoppable as it was startling. "How very insightful of you, Miss Hathaway."

146

"I have brothers, sir." She smiled broadly. "Five of them. Thus, I know what goes on inside the male mind."

He sincerely doubted she knew what sometimes went on in *his* mind. Certainly, he hoped she wouldn't.

"What do you need that for?" She pointed at his Chinese gong.

"The bells don't work."

"So poor Mr. Brown has to run around to the summons of that thing? Why do you not fix the bells?"

"I'm getting around to it."

"Like the roof and the windows too?"

"Yes. And Brown does not run anywhere, I assure you."

"Well, I would never answer to the rude crash of a gong either. I would ignore it."

"Yes, well I doubt I'll be summoning your presence with any sense of urgency."

"I suppose you miss the Navy and sailing," she said suddenly.

Another jolt of surprise ripped through him. Her conversation swerved about like a runaway cart, and he began to feel bruised from getting in the way of her wheels.

"It must be awfully difficult," she added, her face solemn, "to be forced into giving up a promising career and then trying to find something worthwhile and fulfilling to occupy your days and your mind. But you are not *so* old and decrepit. Don't you ever want to go out into society? The Navy men I've met are all very jolly and lively, even gentlemen older than you."

"The Navy men you've met?"

"Through my eldest brother, Captain Guy Hathaway, of His Majesty's Navy," she said proudly.

"Ah."

"Men are fortunate that they can have careers."

"I was led to understand that marriage and

motherhood are fulfilling pursuits for most women."

"I'm sure they are for some. They have to be, do they not? Since we aren't given any other choice."

"What else are women good for?" He waited for her anger, but none came. Or she hid it smoothly.

"You must feel somewhat adrift after leaving the Navy," she persisted, studying his face with those sparkling, impertinent eyes.

"Well, I—"

"Just imagine how it would feel if you had never been allowed to have a career in the first place. If you were expected to sit around on your posterior and do nothing but look pretty?"

Harry looked at that shadow of an ink smudge on her cheek. And thought about trying to wipe the mark off for her. With his tongue.

"If you continue to look at me so crossly, Commander, I shall assume that, despite your proclamation to the contrary, you're desperately in love with me and trying not to be. That is, of course, how all romances begin. The grand ones. In books and such."

"I wouldn't know, Miss Hathaway. I prefer factual books, of course. Not nonsense about unlikely ladies and their even more unlikely gentlemen."

Again she turned away and took another stroll around the study, examining his books and then exclaiming in joyful surprise when she discovered his aunt's owl perched on a shelf.

"Please don't touch that, Miss Hathaway." He groaned. "I've just mended it after the poor creature's last encounter with you."

She sprang back from the shelf and knitted her fingers together under her chin, as if to keep them out of temptation. "I'm glad the owl could be fixed. Has he told you your fortune?"

"Don't believe in it." He thought of the little slip of

148

decorated paper still hidden in his dressing-gown pocket. *Charm strikes the sight, but merit wins the soul.*

"Neither do I really," she agreed with a sigh. "It's just a little fun, and everyone has to have some of that, don't they?"

"What for?"

"To lighten their spirits. Laughter is a powerful restorative, sir. I suppose that's why your aunt brought me here. Entertainment to cure you."

"Miss Hathaway the only ailment you might cure is a fear of silence."

The woman was still considering her reply to that, when Parkes appeared in the doorway. "So this is where you are! Why is there a fire in the dining room and all the dust shaken up?"

"It's her fault," he grumbled. "She wanted to see all my bits and pieces."

The housekeeper grimaced. "I've no doubt she will, sooner or later. Better be careful what she wishes for."

"Yes, thank you, Parkes," he muttered, stepping away from the window and fussing, one-handed, with his neck-cloth.

Miss Hathaway looked startled. "Parkes?"

His head and his world felt crowded now. Why on earth was he indulging this girl in conversation? Letting her pry into his work and give her opinion.

He didn't want her poking around in his papers and books, asking more questions. Being nosy and dismissive of his work. Getting in his way.

"She's not in your way," Parkes whispered in his ear. "She doesn't take up *that* much room."

True. "Although a constantly moving object uses up more space than a still one," he murmured.

"Are you talking to me?" Miss Hathaway exclaimed, brows arched high.

"No. I was thinking aloud. Now, if you are finished—

149

But while he steered her toward the door, she resisted, taking small steps in a circular motion. "I could be of help to you in your work," she said. "I could be an assistant."

"In what way?"

"Sir, if you're making a woman you ought to refer to a real one, don't you think? For research purposes."

"Madam, how do you mean to help me complete my project when you are not yet complete yourself?"

"And you are, sir? I think you're quite undone."

He groaned deeply. "*I think* you had better find my aunt and annoy her instead. Were you not supposed to be *her* companion?"

"But is anyone ever complete, sir?" she persisted. "Surely life's lessons are never ending."

"Miss Hathaway, this conversation begins to feel never ending." Finally Harry picked up a book from his desk and used it to urge her toward the door. "Kindly keep out of my study in future and find something else to do. If you don't care to sit around on your posterior, looking pretty— which is probably beyond your abilities on the best of days— at least make yourself useful. I'm sure my aunt has plenty to keep you busy. Shoo."

Her expression was now so comical that he turned away quickly, because the very worrisome sensation of a laugh had sprung up out of his stomach and into his throat, and he wouldn't want to let it out in her presence. Who knew what else might follow it? Because suddenly he knew what that strange, unsettled feeling was. Life. This is what it felt like to be alive.

He had almost forgotten.

Chapter Thirteen

His aunt's piercing tones could be heard up and down the corridors of his house all day, from sunrise to sunset. Poor Brown did his best to keep up with her, but the odd-job man, like Parkes, had a knack for hiding when he needed a moment to himself. Lady Bramley's greatest and most constant ally, therefore, was the young woman she'd brought with her. Astonishingly, Miss Hathaway appeared to tolerate his aunt, even to enjoy her company. They butted horns on occasion— both being hard-headed— but no lasting harm was done.

Together they commandeered Harry's ship, or thought they did. His aunt was full of ideas for refurbishment of his house, but he stubbornly resisted every one. He knew she had sent for some staff from her own house and he might have to put up with that, but when it came to larger issues he was firmly resolved to make no changes. Her visit would not last forever, he kept reassuring himself. Soon he would be back to normal. Or as normal as he could be.

In the meantime, he supposed Miss Hathaway was entertaining. In a small way.

Yes, it was somewhat amusing to observe his aunt's attempts at coaching the menace on the finer points of elegant behavior.

"One does not dash into a room, fly across it and drop into a chair like a sack of potatoes, Miss Hathaway. One enters with one's head high and shoulders back. One proceeds in a gentle glide, neither too fast nor too slowly. And one lowers oneself onto the seat with poise and balance, ankles crossed, knees to the side, hands still and placed calmly in one's lap."

Harry's formerly quiet evenings were now shattered by the discordant sounds of Miss Hathaway "playing" at the old pianoforte in the drawing room. Her singing was no better than her playing, but it did not appear to cause her any embarrassment. She sang lustily and without the slightest deference to a tune, but so persuasively that if one listened long enough one could be convinced that her version was the original. She erased all memory of any other.

He listened with interest as she debated his aunt on a variety of subjects, always standing her ground where others — strong men— would have fallen under the barrage of Lady Bramley's weaponry. In her tender years of life, Miss Hathaway, so it seemed, had formed opinions on everything and she held fast to her beliefs. It would, he suspected, make her a formidable enemy once she took against a person. But it would, in the same way, make her a loyal friend. Indeed, she spoke often of her two closest friends, Miss Chance and Miss Goodheart, with so much warmth of feeling that he was almost envious of them.

Slowly he grew accustomed to having her in his house. He was forced into it, he assured himself. What else could he do but adapt?

If only the flood did not recede, for once the route was clear, his aunt's reinforcements would arrive to further destroy his precious calm. But the water would drain, of course, and the road would then be passable again for more than ducks and geese.

"Where shall we put them all, sir?" Brown asked worriedly. "The top floor of the house, where the servants used to sleep in the old days, is in a very bad state, sir, with peeling walls, holes in the ceiling and a few missing floorboards."

"Indeed, we cannot, in good conscience, house anybody there. Perhaps it would be best to put them in the west wing with Lady Bramley. After all, it was her idea to bring them here." There would be a ladies maid, two footmen, a cook, a kitchen maid and two housemaids. Filkins had been left behind to hold the fort in Mayfair. He was, probably, soaking his feet in salt water and drinking his employer's brandy.

"Very good, sir. We'll find space in the west wing. And what about Miss Hathaway, sir?"

"What about her?"

"She's in the east wing, sir, since we put her there that first night— it was the only other room furnished and in habitable condition. But I wondered if that was suitable."

"Has she complained?"

"No, sir, not at all. In fact she said what a pretty view it had and when I asked her if she wanted to move she insisted on staying put."

He was pleased. Yes, he had thought she would like that view. Not everything about his house was falling down. "Then I fail to see the problem."

"Don't you, sir?" the old man replied, brows lowered and squeezed into a knot.

If Brown alluded to the fact that Harry tended to wander in the east wing when he was restless at night, he should just say so, he thought crossly. But he knew the handyman was the only soul cognizant of his moonlight journeys, and Brown would never raise that subject to anybody. Not even to Harry. They were men. Men did not talk of things like that. Instead they skimmed over and around anything uncomfortable.

Only Miss Hathaway had dared tell him to his face that he was "undone". A bold creature who thought she knew it all. Youth: groan. Women: even bigger groan.

"I'll get to work, sir, on preparing those other rooms for her ladyship's staff."

"Good man, Brown. Chin up. It won't last forever. Get Sulley to help you. Remember, there is a silver lining. With more staff in the house, you'll have less to do."

"Yes, sir." But the poor man looked very bleak. "You seem cheerful, sir," he added woefully, as if no good could come of it.

Harry sighed. "No cause for alarm, Brown. I daresay it will not last."

But he understood the man's concern. Everything was much simpler when it was just the two of them inside the house. And Parkes, of course.

The housekeeper, however, had rarely appeared over the course of the last few days. He had observed her becoming faded about the edges before his aunt and her companion came to Woodbyne. Now she left him to manage alone, as if she thought this was her chance to take a holiday. Like Filkins, his aunt's butler, Parkes must be making the most of it and soaking her corns somewhere in a corner.

When she came back, he would certainly have a few severe words for that woman.

In the meantime, she left him at the mercy of Miss Hathaway who, when she was not busy with his aunt, trailed after Harry around his house, poking at him with her questions and endless, unwanted opinions.

"What was it like on that island?" she wanted to know. "Did you feel abandoned? You must have been afraid that you would never see England again."

"Miss Hathaway, I am never afraid. Men do not have the luxury of fear."

"I know men do not like to confess a weakness, but—"

"Madam, my only weakness is my temper, and you are trying it severely."

"I only wanted to know about your experiences. Do you not think people are curious to know all about your time as a castaway?"

"Why would they? It's no business of theirs."

She looked astonished. "Why, because it was an adventure most people will never have, sir. I think they would be enthralled to know how you survived, what thoughts went through your mind and how you passed the days all alone."

He stopped walking and she almost tumbled into him. "I thought of all the irritating folk I would like to eat if they were stranded with me, Miss Hathaway. I thought of which parts I would eat first and how I would cook them for the best flavor. Is that what you want to hear? Is that enough lurid detail?"

Rather than back away clutching her petticoats, like any other decent young lady, she exclaimed, "See? That's exceedingly interesting. Most people would be captivated by—"

"Who are these *most people* whose curiosity you continually want to appease by destroying every last shred of my privacy?"

"The general public, sir. The everyday man and woman. In my opinion they would very much enjoy reading about your experiences. It might be good for you too. Get anything that might be troubling you, off your chest." She licked her lips. "So to speak."

"Miss Hathaway, in *my* opinion, when *most people* push their noses where they do not belong, they ought to be prepared to get them—" he reached for hers and pretended to twist it between his fingers, "snipped off."

"Only trying to help."

"Are they not hiring apprentice rack-handlers at the Tower this week? Surely there are traitors to the crown that require interrogation."

She pointed at his hand. "Your wrist is better, sir?"

"Yes. Much." He hadn't worn his sling for a few days and he barely felt a twinge now.

"I am glad."

"Are you? Why? What difference does it make to you?"

She looked up at him, clearly vexed at last. "Well, goodness, apparently none, since it has not improved your mood at all."

155

"I am not in a bad mood, Miss Hathaway. I simply do not care to answer your wretched, nosy questions. To have you meddling and poking around my house, and my life. Such as it is."

She wrinkled her nose and then laughed, a sudden spark of naughtiness dancing under her lashes. "I must watch out, I suppose, because now you have two good hands in complete working order."

He narrowed his gaze. "Explain."

"You might see fit to punish me for these many and terrible misdemeanors of which I am accused. You might decide to eat *me*."

Quite unable to answer that, Harry walked on, shaking his head. For a moment he thought she would not follow. Good.

He slowed his pace. It sounded odd not to have her step shadowing his. Ah, she must have found something more interesting to do. He knew that would happen sooner or later. Surely she must grow tired of him eventually.

But then he heard her steps tripping after him again. Seemed as if he would have to put up with it a while longer. He began to whistle cheerily and turned his course to take the corridor that passed outside to a covered, paved walkway with open arches along the side. He knew she enjoyed the scents of the herb garden and the gentle trickle of the old fountain. If she was intent on following him about, she might at least have something pleasant to look at while doing so.

* * * *

One day, Miss Hathaway dashed up to Harry in the hall and backed him against a suit of armor. "Commander Thrasher, I require your assistance and you cannot say no, or I shall be obliged to take desperate measures and ask Brown, who is quite busy enough and should not be troubled."

"And I should?" he muttered, perplexed.

"I tried her dratted dog, but it wouldn't sit still for me, of course, peevish creature. Then I thought of a bowl of cherries, but before I knew what I had done they were all eaten, but for a sad few." She sighed heavily, tugging hard on his sleeve. "Once I had one, you see, I couldn't stop. They were very succulent and quite delicious, but now I have stomach ache. That's when I thought of you. You're all long, hard parts—"

"I beg your pardon?"

"And straight lines. I can do you."

He squinted, trying to follow her winding trail of chatter. Almost afraid of where it might lead. "Me?"

"You don't have as many round parts, and I'm much better at straight lines and sharp angles."

"Miss Hathaway, what exactly do you want from me?"

"Your aunt insists on seeing a sample of my sketching ability."

Slowly and carefully he extracted her pinching fingers from his shirt sleeve. "I am gratified, Miss Hathaway, to be considered a suitable subject, somewhere *after* an angry little dog and a bowl of cherries. And Brown, who is apparently not to be disturbed, but I am."

"*Were* you doing anything important?" she asked, chin in the air, eyes bright and searching. Sometimes, when she looked up at him in this manner, he forgot entirely what he was meant to be doing.

This was one such occasion. "Oh, for pity's sake, I suppose I can set my work aside and spare a half hour."

In fact, it took almost two hours, at the end of which time she was still only satisfied with his left ear. Her discontent was expressed in such a way that Harry began to feel it was his fault— or the fault of his face. She constantly abandoned her charcoal to rush over and reposition his limbs, his head, his fingers. He suspected she was trying to make him look like her sketch, instead of the other way about, but each brazen touch of her hands caused him to breathe a little faster, made his pulse a little more unsteady. Too caught up in her project, she did not seem to notice. Perhaps she mistook him for one of those many brothers she'd mentioned. Her actions were quite casually bossy.

"Are all young ladies as forward and demanding as you these days, Miss Hathaway?"

"Only when obliged to be. You are the most difficult shape I ever encountered," she exclaimed, pouting with cherry-stained lips as she gazed angrily at her effort. "There is too much of you for the dratted paper, and each time I look up at you there seems to be more. How am I supposed to fit you all in? Can you not make yourself smaller and less stiff?"

"I'm afraid that is an impossibility." Never had complaints before, he mused.

"Gah!" She tossed her charcoal aside. "Why do men have to be so difficult?"

"Are you finished then, madam?"

"Oh yes, I am quite done with you." With a wave of her fingers, she gave him his leave. "Off you go, back to your burrow."

Harry did not envy the man that would become her husband one day. It would happen, of course, whatever her plans. It must. She would fall in love eventually, with some fool who couldn't get out of her way fast enough. Then she would boss her husband about for a few years until she managed him completely into a grave.

For the poor fellow's sake, he had better be hard of hearing. And exceedingly patient.

"Madam," he said to his aunt one morning, "Is it not the business of that ladies academy you patronize to turn out perfectly suitable brides? Surely you must wonder at the efficacy of the place if it's turning out restless, unaccomplished troublemakers, resistant to matrimony, like Miss Hathaway."

"The Particular Establishment for the Advantage of Respectable Ladies does very well, Henry. Several of last year's graduates are now married to peers of the realm. One of them is soon to be a duchess." She sighed. "Miss Georgiana Hathaway, I fear, is not destined for those heights, but we must do the best we can with the materials at hand. I have been assembling a list of potential suitors, although it is not vast."

"But she declares herself in no haste to marry," he muttered, watching through the window as she ran by in a desperate flash of ankles with his aunt's dog chasing her. "She means to have colorful adventures. I suspect, of an unsavory kind."

"She's nineteen, Henry. Few girls of that age know what is good for them."

"Did you, madam?"

"Of course, I knew my duty. I was born and raised knowing it."

"You never wanted to do anything else with your life but marry?"

She hesitated. "There might have been a time in youth when I thought I could try my hand at one or two other things, but that folly passed and I saw reason." She quickly picked up her usual stern tone. "My father decided Lord Bramley would do for me and so I set about improving his life immediately, putting all my energies into that. By the age of nineteen I was not only a wife, but a mother. I was sensible of my responsibilities in life. But the same cannot be said of young girls these days." He heard her moving closer, her gown rustling. "And when, pray tell, did you speak to Miss Hathaway of her marital prospects? I do hope you're not going to interfere in matters of which you know nothing, Henry. Leave that side of things to me, if you please. I know something of marriage, and you do not."

"I merely thought you should know of her intention to remain unwed. She seems steadfast in that opinion, as she is in all of them. If marriage is your ultimate scheme for her, you may find your efforts are in vain. She tells me that sometimes young ladies have *other plans*. And she utters the phrase with such perilous gravity, that I dare not ask what these plans may entail, for a I fear the images conjured by her reply could scar me for life."

"Nonsense. She is not a stupid girl, and she will see the advantage of a good, settled marriage. Once I find her a suitable match. Just as one was found for me."

Harry scowled, remembering wistfully the days when he commanded a ship and people actually paid heed to what he said. "I think I agree with her opinion that your school should provide lessons in subjects other than dancing and how to fool a man into marrying them."

"Then don't think, Henry. It seldom comes to any good when a man thinks too much. And what on earth are you doing, agreeing with her opinions? Since when did you agree with any marked opinion but your own?"

"I suppose you include my name on your list of potential suitors," he grumbled, hands clasped behind his back.

"Good lord no." She stood with him at the window to see what he was looking at, just as Miss Hathaway dashed by in the other direction, still being chased by the determined little beast. "She's only the daughter of a newspaper publisher. She'd never do for you, Henry."

"A newspaper publisher?" Interesting. "Which paper?"

"*The Gentleman's Weekly*, I believe. Frederick Hathaway is new wealth. A parvenu. An ambitious grasper who thinks breeding may be bought, no doubt. She's a funny little thing though, don't you think?"

"Hilarious," he replied flatly.

"Of course," said his aunt, following a short pause, "I knew you were in danger after the garden party, when you knew her name already. I cannot recall the last time you remembered a young lady's name, Henry."

He turned his frown upon her. "In danger of being assassinated by her, you mean?"

"Don't be tiresome. In danger of falling in love, Henry."

But that, in his mind, equated to the same thing. Returning his gaze to the woman on the lawn outside, he said, "I am quite safe, madam. It was merely by chance that I knew her name."

"That's as may be. As I said, she is entirely unsuitable for you." She moved away from the window. "It would, of course, be just like you to take such a contrary fancy, especially when you have been warned against it by me."

He huffed loudly, but did not turn to watch her leave— too busy watching Georgiana's ankles. "I have taken no fancy, madam."

"Just as well, for your sake." He heard her open the door. "Miss Hathaway is highly unlikely to fall in love with an unsociable, unfashionable curmudgeon like you, Henry. I told you, she's not a foolish girl at all. You need somebody far stupider."

He smiled grimly at his reflection in the glass. "What did you make of my portrait? Does her sketching pass your test?"

"What portrait? What are you talking about, Henry?"

"She said you wanted a sample of her drawing ability and forced me into posing for her due to a lack of suitable subjects. Two entire blasted hours of my day wasted."

"Well, she didn't do it for me. I did not leave her any such instruction. Perhaps she wanted it for archery practice."

He heard the door shut loudly soon after.

161

As a cloud slipped by, a sudden harsh glare of sunlight bounced off the glass and made his eye smart. At that same moment, Miss Hathaway saw him watching and waved with one hand, while trying to wrestle the hem of her skirt from the little dog with the other. He squinted against the sun, cursed his sore eye, and finally turned away from the view.

What the devil was that stowaway up to on his ship?

Chapter Fourteen

For several nights there was no repetition of "Dead Harry's" midnight adventure. Georgiana sat up late, reading or writing by the fire and listening, in case she heard his steps, but there was no sound other than the usual creaks and moans of the old house. She was rather disappointed.

Then, at last, she heard him again.

Creeping out of her room, she followed the Commander barefoot down the corridor quite a way before he realized she was there. It gave her an opportunity to admire the muscular contours of his back and the shocking sight of his firm buttocks as he moved along, stroked by starlight through the windows. She shouldn't admire any of it, of course. She shouldn't even look. But she did, and she sincerely doubted that any other young lady, finding herself in the same extraordinary circumstances, and in full command of her senses, would *not* look.

When he finally turned and noticed her there, she was glad of the dim light so he would not see her blush.

"You again!" he exclaimed. "My stowaway."

"Yes. Sir, you should go back to bed. Are you not cold...without clothes?"

"No. I'm hot. Feel me."

Before she could argue he took her hand and placed it on his chest. Really, she mused, how could one debate propriety with a naked man? It seemed altogether too late for that.

"I am always hot," he said. "I do not care for clothes. They restrict me, and I have much to do."

"Much to do?"

"I must hunt food and smoke it over the fire. I must build a shelter."

She realized he was still a castaway on his island,

planning for his survival. Under her palm she felt his heart beating, strong and fast. So much power throbbing within his body, waiting to be unleashed. As she took her hand away from his chest, his strong fingers were still wrapped tightly around her wrist, slowing her progress and causing her fingertips to accidentally trailed across the sandy hairs that curled there.

Until she first saw naked Harry, Georgiana had never imagined there to be hair growing on a man's body, under his clothes. In so many curious places.

Marble statues and grand frescoes did not show men with hair on their bodies and her elder brothers had never been in a state of undress around her.

It was still a shock now that she saw her host a second time completely uncovered. Her throat went dry quite suddenly and she could not swallow.

"You do not want to touch me?" he muttered, his voice low and hoarse.

"I do not think it wise, sir."

Abruptly he placed his hand over her right breast. The weight of his caress caused her own body to react instantly in a manner that seemed to please him. And encourage him. "Not wise, eh?" he whispered.

Oh lord, definitely not. But she couldn't speak.

A slim breath of teasing laughter blew against her temple as he leaned over her. "I think you are wrong. I think you know you are wrong. I think you want what I want."

"No, sir." She placed her hand over his. "It is just not right for us...this way."

"Women only board my ship for one reason," he said, sounding puzzled. "They have no other purpose on a ship, but sometimes the crew deserves a reward."

"Yes, I...I see that, sir. But I am not that sort of woman." *Why wasn't she?* The angry question darted through her mind. She wanted adventure, did she not? She felt no great desperation for a husband, who would likely curtail any hope she had of achieving something beyond what society expected of a woman.

And he was tempting. Everybody knew she was a wicked chit, so what stopped her?

Georgiana looked up into his hungry, wild gaze and felt sadness cool her own eager blood.

He did not know who or where he was at that moment. He needed help. For once she would get it right and not leave disaster in her wake.

"Let me take you back to your room, sir. You will be safe there."

"I need you."

"Yes, of course. You need me to help you. Now come back to bed." She spoke firmly, as she would to one of her little brothers if he misbehaved and she'd been sent to corral him.

And to her surprise, he let her take his arm and lead him back to his bed chamber. At the door he stopped and bent toward her.

"A kiss, my stowaway, before I retire. One kiss and then I shall sleep." His eyes were hidden in shadow.

"Do you promise to sleep then?"

He nodded, waiting. She would have to trust his word, of course; he was a war hero, even if he did have an aversion to decent clothing.

So she rose on tip toe and pressed a small, shy kiss to the corner of his mouth. Much to her relief this seemed to satisfy him and he went slowly into his room. Georgiana waited a moment to be sure he did not come out again and then returned to her own room.

A wonderful feeling of having accomplished something powerful made her light on her feet, and she knew she was smiling when she lay down in her bed. All because Dead Harry appeared to like her. He certainly listened to her. She knew how to manage him and that was no small feat with a man of his size.

The same routine happened the next night, and the next. Each time he wanted a kiss and she gave it as gently as she could. Each time he let her take his arm and lead him back to the safety of his room.

"You must regret stowing away on my vessel now, woman," he said. "Now we are shipwrecked and it is just you and I left in this savage place. Like Adam and his mate, Eve."

"I do not regret being here with you at all," she replied softly, "for you would be quite alone without me."

It was a strange parade— the tall naked man and the girl in her maidenly nightgown— wandering together down the moonlit passage, but it soon became almost normal to her. The night turned into another world, another state of being, and there was just the two of them in it.

She would keep this to herself, for she knew the proud man would be mortified if anybody else should learn of his nightly wandering in the nude. The Commander was a very private man who did not even want to talk about his previous life at sea. During the day he treated her as if she was an irritating fly buzzing around his head.

So this was a secret she shared only with Dead Harry.

When he let her take her arm and lead him along, she felt a thrill like nothing she'd ever experienced. Gone was the "dizzy girl" and in her place there was a woman who finally had an important purpose, and somebody who needed her.

By her bed Georgiana kept his picture— the sketch she had persuaded the Commander to sit for. She had pretended to burn it out of frustration, but instead had folded it carefully and smuggled it up to her room inside a book. Every night she whispered, "Goodnight, Harry", in his ear before she blew out her candle.

She felt a little guilty about keeping the portrait to herself, actually, because her first intention had been to send it, along with a letter, to Emma and Melinda. Perhaps she might encourage one of her friends to fall in love with him and then she could play matchmaker, but in the end she decided it was unfair of her to undertake such a project when he told her from the start that he did not want a wife. She would be most annoyed if anybody meddled in her life the same way.

Besides, it was not a very good sketch, was it? She was not a good enough artist to capture the intriguing nuances of his expression.

The more she considered it, the more reasons she came up with to keep his picture to herself. At least she would have this souvenir of her adventure at Woodbyne Abbey.

One day, she mused sleepily, the paper upon which he was drawn would be very worn and yellowed with age, and one of her nieces would find it among her treasures when she was dead. They would all speculate on the identity of the sitter and imagine he was once her lover.

That was the way tragic, Grand Romances usually went, of course.

Luckily she was far too clever to fall in love. She had too many adventures ahead of her and an entire world to put to rights, without the complication of love to get in her way.

* * * *

The weather slowly improved and sun shone down on the sodden fields again. At last it seemed as if summer was truly upon them. An abundance of honeysuckle blossomed outside her window— perhaps the reason for the name of the house— and the view across the lawn was breathtaking. A great improvement on the bustling, noisy street outside The Pearl.

167

One day, when she woke early and looked out, she caught a glimpse of the Commander galloping his horse across the grass, leaping hedges and ditches with a fearless, powerful grace. When he came to breakfast later he still wore the same mud-spattered breeches and boots, much to his aunt's loud despair and his own quiet indifference. When he passed Georgiana's chair, muttering a gruff "Good morning", it seemed as if he bristled with energy and fresh air. It was no surprise to her anymore that his clothing gave up on the struggle to restrain it all. In fact, she would have been shocked if he ever came to the table with all his clothes intact and his hair brushed.

He resisted any attempt to improve his manners and watched the steady invasion of his house with a sort of morbid fascination. Whenever he could, he stole away to his study and stayed there for hours behind a locked door.

With the roads now passable again, Lady Bramley's coachman returned, bringing more luggage and some household staff. Georgiana saw how this new influx of people caused the master of the house to withdraw even more often into his study, but his aunt still insisted that this storming of his fortress was the proper method of cure and she was not a lady accustomed to being wrong. In frustration she barged about his house, shouting at the staff and thumping on his study door, but she achieved little more than the stirring of dust.

"Do you not think a little gentleness might be more effective at drawing him out, madam?" Georgiana inquired politely, thinking of how she managed to get him back to his bedchamber at night. Admittedly, he was a different man in the daylight, but perhaps the same method might work then too.

"*Gentleness*? Gracious, girl, I have neither the time nor the patience for that nonsense. Brisk and sharp is the way of it. The British Empire was won with cannon and rifle, not with a tickling feather."

Georgiana chuckled. "The world would be a far better place if it had been though, don't you think?"

Lady Bramley was not amused. At least, not so that it showed.

Her war campaign of "Brisk and Sharp" continued.

"Today I have arranged to pay a visit to Parson Darrowby and his wife," she announced at breakfast one morning. "You will come too, Henry."

He was in a grim mood that day, rustling the newspaper and muttering under his breath as he searched within the pages for something of interest.

"I understand they have not long been married and Mrs. Darrowby is a young, genteel lady, the daughter of a magistrate." She turned to Georgiana and said, "This will be a good chance for you to practice your manners, but perhaps it would be best if you say as little as possible for now." Lady Bramley had not yet managed to curb her student of wandering off into subjects deemed unsuitable. Apparently she was to talk only of meaningless things— to compliment the carpet in a room without veering off into a speech about the terrible working conditions in the textile mill where it was made, for instance.

"Miss Hathaway's opinions might liven up the visit," the Commander muttered from behind his paper. "They would certainly ensure we don't get invited back again."

"Henry, it is ill-mannered to read at the table. How many times must you be told?"

"Clearly once a day at least."

"There can be nothing in that newspaper more interesting than my conversation."

With a great heaving sigh, he closed and folded it. "Not today, it would seem."

Georgiana had noticed he was reading her father's paper. For the first time in a year *His Lordship's Trousers* would not be printed in it since the floods had kept her from posting her installment on time.

169

"How is your latest invention progressing, sir?" she asked.

His gaze skimmed Georgiana's face above the rim of his coffee cup. "As well as might be expected with a distraction following me about all over my house, demanding my time, asking me endless questions."

"I thought she would be finished by now. I looked forward to hearing her play."

"Good heavens, I am glad that dreadful thing is not finished," exclaimed Lady Bramley. The mere mention of her nephew's work caused her countenance to become hard as stone. "The less said about *that* in front of the Darrowbys the better. What will they think of you, Henry?"

"I'm sure what the parson and his wife think of me matters as much as what I think of them."

"What has got you in such a churlish temper today?" his aunt demanded.

"A column I like to read seems to have been temporarily discontinued. I don't like my routine meddled with, and I usually start my week by reading it."

Georgiana's pulse skipped.

"Do you refer to that scandalous *His Lordship's Pantaloons*?" Lady Bramley exclaimed, setting her cup down so hard she nearly chipped the saucer.

"*Trousers*," Georgiana corrected, before she could stop herself. "The name of it is *His Lordship's Trousers*." Then she looked down, drawing a breath. "I heard something of it." She felt the Commander's gaze watching her closely above his own cup and decided to keep her hands busy by sweeping crumbs into her napkin.

"*The Gentleman's Weekly* is your father's paper, is it not?" he asked.

She nodded.

"Yes, yes," his aunt said, "whatever the thing is called. But you must have heard, Henry, there's been such a ruckus about it— although I suppose you are so seldom out and about you may not know."

"Know what, madam?"

"Wardlaw Fairbanks insists that column is written about him. He has threatened to bring a suit of libel against the paper if it is not stopped. I daresay that is why there is no episode this week."

Georgiana stared in horror. Of course, her father would not tell her this news— he had no idea she was the author, and this was a business matter, not something he would share in one of his short, formal letters, dutifully penned to his least favorite child.

The Commander gave a harsh laugh. "How typical of Fairbanks to assume it's all about him." He paused and then laughed again. "And he is so incredibly stupid that he would actually let the world know that buffoonish character has any resemblance to him. The man is oblivious to his own pomposity."

"Well, they say he is most irate about that newspaper column, and he is a powerful man." Lady Bramley glanced at Georgiana. "Your father would do well to keep the peace and print an apology if he wants to save his paper, young lady."

"Why should he?" she blurted. "Why should he not print whatever he wants to print, and whatever people want to read, just because one awful excuse for a man decides it offends him?"

The Lady popped her eyes, as she often did when her "companion" boldly refused to agree with her.

"And I'm sure it isn't about Viscount Fairbanks, in any case, madam," Georgiana added in a more civil tone. "How can he prove it is?"

"There is no need for raised voices and immoderate tones, Miss Hathaway. You are talking to me, not dealing with errant tradesmen. Well, if your father has a similar temperament to your own," she added with a wry chortle, "we shan't be seeing any apology printed."

She hoped not. Her father had a tendency to bow a little too much to the nobility, however, and he might not wish to earn the wrath of Viscount Fairbanks. Not a second time.

An awful thought came to her then, as she twisted her napkin into a tight knot: was the incident with the burning wig still smarting in that wretched fellow's pride and now he took it out on her father's paper, using *His Lordship's Trousers* as a reason? Surely a grown man would not continue a vindictive campaign against their family, even years later, for such a small incident.

Or would he? Perhaps it was not so small an incident to have one's vanity and pride trampled by a sixteen-year old girl, in front of a room full of people. She had heard that it was still an event much talked about and even enlarged upon by subsequent retellings. But since she was far more concerned by the effect it had on her relationship with her sister— who never forgave her— Georgiana had given scant thought to the owner of the charred wig and whether or not he recovered from it.

"Viscount Fairbanks demands to know the identity of the author," Lady Bramley added, signaling to the footman for more coffee. "I daresay it is somebody with an axe to grind."

"Then the author could be anybody," the Commander replied. "Wardlaw Fairbanks is not nearly as well liked as he assumes he is, and with good reason."

"Surely you're not still bearing animosity toward him. That scandal with Amy Milhaven was so long ago, Henry."

Georgiana's ears pricked and she glanced over at him, temporarily forgetting her own worries.

"That trollop is certainly not worth you sparing another thought for her," Lady Bramley continued. "Not after she betrayed you. Good riddance is what I said then, and I say it now."

The Commander's eyes were warmly bemused as he looked down the table at his aunt. "Miss Milhaven is not a trollop, madam. Nor did she betray me. That is an exaggeration, to say the least."

"But she—"

"My dislike of Wardlaw Fairbanks was ingrained long before he attempted to ruin Miss Milhaven. I had observed his behavior on several occasions and found his attitude quite repugnant. He is a vacuous waste of breathable air, if you want my opinion, and whether or not he is the subject of that column, he *deserves* to be lampooned. He is, as Miss Hathaway said, *an awful excuse for a man.*"

Georgiana felt her heart lift and the beat quicken. That explained the comradeship she'd felt on the night their eyes first met. Neither of them could tolerate falseness and hypocrisy.

Lady Bramley now continued with her instructions for their social visits that afternoon. Henry was to speak more and Georgiana to speak less. Henry was to pay attention and make an attempt to move the conversation along, while Georgiana was meant to sit quietly and smile benignly.

But Henry always did what he wanted, and Georgiana was finding it hard to listen, far too distracted, her mind spinning with thoughts.

Despite the good lady's best intentions, this foray into Little Flaxhill society was obviously destined to fail, but she was the only one who didn't see it.

Chapter Fifteen

Henry sat stiffly, his clothes irritating him, his foot tapping, arms folded. Although aware of his aunt looking over with a meaningful glare, he allowed his foot to continue its steady rhythm, ticking the seconds away.

"Do you mean to stay long in Surrey, Lady Bramley?" the parson's wife inquired softly.

"Just for the summer. I have many commitments in Town, but a visit to my nephew was overdue."

A short pause followed, before the parson said, "We see so little of Sir Henry Thrasher. I must confess, for a long time I did not know he was in residence. I had often ridden by Woodbyne Abbey and thought such a pity that it was deserted." The small fellow laughed uneasily. "I would have called in, had I known you were home, sir."

Harry said nothing.

Lady Bramley exclaimed, "You have not been attending church, Henry?"

In truth he rarely knew what day it was unless Brown mentioned it, so Sundays slipped by unnoticed. "No."

"Henry!"

"I made my peace with the Almighty seven years ago on the deck of a battle ship. He and I have nothing more to discuss. We both know where we stand. Since the wound that should have killed me left me alive instead, drifting in a state of purgatory with a memory as ephemeral as the morning mist, I decided that God must have no use for me yet. And a very dark sense of humor. He would, therefore, surely not object to me doing things my own way."

"Henry!"

"What?" He blinked. "You told me to speak up more."

Flustered, his aunt said, "You must excuse my nephew. He can be dreadfully stubborn."

"It runs in the family," he added tartly.

Another pause followed and then Miss Hathaway said, "That is a very pretty carpet. I'm sure not many people were harmed in the making of it."

Harry choked on a gust of laughter and leaned his head back so far back he almost tipped out of the chair.

"Miss Hathaway," his aunt explained apologetically, "is my companion for the summer. I have taken her under my wing."

"I see," the parson's wife smiled, surprisingly undaunted. "How do you like Surrey, Miss Hathaway?"

"I have not seen much of it yet, but I look forward to exploring now that the weather has improved."

The conversation turned to the best paths for walking and the prettiest groves for an afternoon's wander. It was evident that Miss Hathaway's cheerfulness — even slightly subdued under his aunt's hand, as it was today— appealed to the young Mrs. Darrowby. As his aunt had said, the Darrowbys were not long married and the young wife gravitated toward that spirit of youth brightening her parlor. Understandable, since she was not much older than Georgiana and had married a man of gentle, but somber demeanor, ten years her senior, and whose interests lay in studying ancient texts.

The imbalance was one Harry had observed before in marriages. An age difference of ten years or more was not rare in a couple, and from the business-like way most marriages were conducted, it was not necessary that a husband and wife should share anything more than a toast rack. But today something unsettled Harry, as he watched the Darrowbys being dreadfully polite to each other in the rather grim parlor, which still contained the decorating choices of a bachelor and had yet to make way for anything feminine except for a bowl of roses on the windowsill.

They were more like teacher and pupil in the way they

acted— the parson often correcting his wife if she mispronounced a local place name or got a direction wrong in her description. And if this habit annoyed her, she managed to keep a respectful tone in her voice when she thanked him continually for setting her straight.

Harry sighed and shook his head. The marriage was a mistake, of course. Darrowby had been a happy bachelor for a long time and was set in his ways. Must have been hard for him to clear space for a wife. The fellow did appear rather bewildered by it, as if he did not know what he had done. Or why.

Well sometimes there could be no explanation for the thoughts and ideas that crept into a man's mind— and Harry knew that only too well. Parkes had often said that reaching thirty was just as difficult for a man, as it was when he arrived at the age of two. It may be that she was right and he must take care not to slip into the same mistake as poor Parson Darrowby— get some foolish idea in his head and let everybody convince him he was lonely.

He looked over at Miss Hathaway, who without any particular beauty or remarkable skill, had begun to dominate his thoughts and his attention.

He may be, as she had said, *undone*, but he was not incapacitated. Harry was fine the way he was, wasn't he? He told everybody, all the time, that he was quite content.

She had considerable sauce, in fact, to give him her unwanted, uninvited diagnosis. Few people he knew would dare talk to him as she did. He was a Naval Commander and a war hero, for pity's sake. What was she?

He did not yet have an answer for that.

Harry narrowed his gaze upon her face as she nodded and smiled at the parson's wife. The very picture of innocence, if one did not look too closely for the ever-smoldering perceptiveness beneath those thick lashes, or observe the meandering trail of freckles that seemed to have been placed there solely to distract a man's thoughts when she stood near.

Now she had tricked him into posing for a sketch—her purpose yet to be discovered. He did not know how he felt about that. What prank would she try next?

His aunt seemed convinced that a husband was the best thing for her young charge, but any man who attempted to keep Miss Hathaway's curiosity to himself was destined for trouble. She would quickly become bored, resentful and unhappy. A woman who wanted company and new experiences, she was not afraid of life. Rather, she rushed at it without due thought given to the possible consequences. That too would be something any man willing to take her on must consider. He would never have a moment's respite.

"And you," Parkes whispered in his ear, "want only to hide from life."

Yes, exactly.

His gaze roamed the room again and landed on Parson Darrowby, who now prepared to correct his wife again, on some issue that mattered to nobody else, while she clenched her jaw in a pained smile for her guests.

But then, as he watched, the young Mrs. Darrowby turned and put her hand upon her husband's, where it rested on the arm of his chair, and the Parson briefly raised a finger to brush against her palm before she took it back again. It was a slight gesture that might easily have been missed in the blink of an eye— if Harry was not so absorbed in watching, and the sort of man who took in every detail.

It occurred to him then that perhaps the Darrowbys were awkward in front of guests because they had not expected callers to interrupt their afternoon. Perhaps they were as eager to be left alone as he was to leave.

Feeling ashamed of studying them so closely, Harry returned his gaze to Miss Hathaway. Their eyes caught and she smiled, as was her habit. The damn woman was too affable for her own good. But something about her smile suggested a shared secret, in the same way that the gesture between the Parson and his wife had revealed a warm connection.

Damn! Surely she was not forming some attachment despite all his efforts to put her off? He thought he had made his position clear.

Suddenly Harry felt stifled, slowly suffocating. He needed to get home again, to get out of his clothes and back behind the sanctuary of his locked study door.

He checked his fob watch yet again, trying to ignore the sweat that made the lines on his palm glisten. Almost eleven minutes had passed since they arrived. That meant four more at least must be spent to be "polite".

"Henry, do not forget to invite the Darrowby's to the party you have planned," his aunt urged between gritted teeth.

"What party? I'm not planning any party."

She ignored him and told the parson's wife, "Just a small gathering with cards and some music. On Wednesday. I hope you will attend."

"That sounds delightful, Lady Bramley. Thank you."

Harry was horrified. The sooner his aunt bored of this project the better. He looked again at his watch and muttered, "Three minutes."

"Thank goodness the weather has improved," Miss Hathaway exclaimed so loudly that Parson Darrowby almost leapt out of his chair. "I thought the rain would never end."

"Of course it would end," said Harry with a sniff. "Everything ends sooner or later. Thankfully." He stood. "Well, that's it. Time's up."

* * * *

Other visits paid that day were no less painful and ended with an equally abrupt lack of finesse. Two local widows and the village doctor all suffered calls and did their best not to look too shocked by the Commander's temper. At last, this wretched experiment with Little Foxhill's "most consequential" society behind them, Lady Bramley's carriage took the trio back to Woodbyne Abbey at a brisk trot.

"Well, really, Henry!" his aunt grumbled every few yards.

He had tugged down the sash window as soon as the carriage pulled away from the last visit and was already loosening his neck cloth. "I did as you wanted, madam," he replied eventually. "I made an effort. As you see it's entirely pointless. Perhaps now I might be left alone and you can concentrate your efforts on Miss Hathaway, who is far more worthy of your attention. She did very well today, I thought. The parson's wife seemed especially taken with her."

"Yes, Miss Hathaway has shown much improvement."

"There you are then. She's much more likely to do you credit. I'm too old. With Miss Hathaway and her bright, inquiring mind, you have scope."

Georgiana caught his eye and received a very quick, sly grin. Oh yes, he would very much like his aunt to focus all that attention upon *her*. But Lady Bramley had known that from the start. Her nephew underestimated her, as he did all women apparently.

He looked intolerably handsome today and she wondered if he knew it. With a woman one could always tell if she knew she looked well, but men were more difficult to read. Or at least, he was. She often had cause to wonder how much he was aware of, for she could not be exactly sure that he had no memory of his nightly encounters with her. Occasionally she caught a look, or a devious smile suggestive of his amusement at her expense.

"You have more chance of getting Miss Hathaway

179

well shackled to some unsuspecting chap," he added, "than you have of making me presentable to good company."

"If you expect to put me off by that truculent display, young man," Lady Bramley exclaimed, "you can think again. Today's little performance has only reassured me of the absolute necessity of getting you out of that study and among good people who are not run by cogwheels and levers, before it is too late and you are quite lost to civilized behavior."

He turned his head to look out of the carriage window, but Georgiana could still see his lips smirking, even if his aunt could not.

Once they got back to the house, the Commander returned to his work, impatiently stripping off his coat as he strode across the hall and tossing it, along with his hat, into the air as if there was somebody waiting to catch it. There was nobody, of course, and both items fell to the floor. Did he think his old nanny, "Parkes", would pick them up for him, Georgiana wondered. At least she had not heard him banging that dreadful gong lately. That must be a great relief to poor Brown too.

As he disappeared behind his study door, Georgiana had hoped to slip away and compose a letter to her father, but instead she was applied to for a stroll around the grounds with Lady Bramley who, having much to get off her chest and no one else's ear to bend, was obliged to make do with her as a suitable confidant.

"I thought I was done raising boys after my two were grown. I never thought Henry would be left to my care too. He should have been married by now."

"Although I suppose a man has to feel inclined to marriage, just as a woman must, in order for it to be successful."

"Inclination comes second to duty, Miss Hathaway. What a man wants, or thinks he wants, is quite beside the point. It is Henry's duty to find a wife and create heirs.

After all, if he has no sons, who will inherit Woodbyne?"
She waved her parasol at the crumbling facade of the
ancient, grey stone abbey. "It cannot be allowed to fall out
of the family's hands. My dear brother, foolish though he
was in many ways, adored this place, as did our father."

"But the Commander has cousins. Your own sons.
Won't they—"

"My eldest—Mandrake, Lord Bramley— has
inherited my husband's estate in Shropshire and, of course,
the Baronetcy. He has no interest in this place, and if it fell
to him he would only sell it. He may be my son, but I can
admit he is dreadfully mercenary. Then there is Maxwell."
Here she paused beside a blossoming bush resplendent
with scarlet roses. As her fingers worked ruthlessly among
the branches, tearing off dead heads, she continued,
"Maxwell would wager all this away on a horse race, or
some other bet. So you see, it is imperative that Henry
produce a strong son and heir, or Woodbyne will be lost to
another family."

Georgiana began to have the idea that perhaps the
Commander was right to suspect his aunt's motives in
bringing her there. But no, in the next moment she was
reassured of the lady's disinterest in making *her* into a
prospective wife for Henry.

"I have a number of eligible young ladies in mind, and
I intend to persuade my nephew to hold a summer ball
here at Woodbyne, to which I shall invite them all. You
will assist me. Let us see if he can turn his back on
matrimony when he is presented with a garden of fair
blooms from which to take his pick." She looked over the
bush, checking for any other unsightly brown heads of
shattered roses. "Yes, indeed. I shall not leave Woodbyne
until I am satisfied that I have seen to this matter for the
future good of this estate. My brother— God rest his
soul— would expect it. As a Thrasher by blood, it is *my*
duty to be sure that Henry fulfills *his*."

181

Georgiana could not help but feel sympathy for the Commander, to have such a responsibility resting on his shoulders. As an only child he must feel keenly the expectations of his ancestors.

Lady Bramley now returned her attention to the lessons for which she'd taken her young charge under her wing.

"As I observed today, much has improved, but your conversation still leaves something to be desired, Miss Hathaway. Now, as we come to each shrub along this path, you must start a *new* subject. And make it interesting."

Alarmed, Georgiana looked down the gravel path ahead of them and counted ten tall boxwood cones. Brown was currently up a ladder trimming one of them with shears, for they were all overgrown and sprouting stray branches, which had caused Lady Bramley great upset.

"A new subject at each one, your ladyship?"

"That is correct. A woman should be capable of steering a conversation and keeping it flowing smoothly, even if the gentleman at her side has all the personality and good sense of a garden shrub."

So they turned and proceeded down the new path, bright sun beaming down upon them.

"Suggested approved subjects are the theatre, fashion, books— some of them, music, gardening and food. Stay away from politics, religion and your opinions."

But Georgiana decided to plunge bravely in with her first subject, which belonged to none of those categories. It had been burning in her mind like a cliff-top beacon all morning. "Who was Miss Milhaven?" She slowed her steps to give this conversation plenty of time before they reached the next bush.

To her surprise, Lady Bramley answered without hesitation. "Amy Milhaven was once betrothed to Henry.

182

He was young and so was she. I always knew it was a mistake, but he was set upon it."

Suddenly the sun felt much too hot and it made her head ache. "I see. But she married elsewhere?" The Commander had not made it seem as if he was hurt by his fiancée's desertion, but the phrase "*he was set upon it*" hung in her mind, a heavy weight.

Suddenly she thought of his little glances, the touch of his hand on hers, that sense of recognition at first glimpse. Of the way he tried not to smile at her, and how, if she caught him doing so, he always looked away. She swallowed hard and felt a pinch of something she could not identify. Or perhaps she did not wish to.

He did not even remember the evening walks they shared.

You are not misshapen, Miss Hathaway, that I will admit. Your features have some favorable qualities. They are not grotesque.

That was stern Commander Thrasher's assessment of her slight charms. But Dead Harry saw something else in her. Something more. He had kissed her with passion, startled her with his desire.

Perhaps, at night, in the shadows and moonlight, Dead Harry didn't see her face well enough to know that her looks were only plain to mediocre.

Miss Milhaven, on the other hand, was probably very beautiful and accomplished. She must have been something quite special for the Commander to take notice, not to dismiss her as he did other people.

"When my nephew was lost at sea in 1812," Lady Bramley continued, "Amy Milhaven wasted no time sailing onward and putting him out of her mind. She married Admiral Shaftesbury within a year."

"And what happened with Viscount Fairbanks? What did he have to do with it?"

"There was a rumor about him seducing and then abandoning the girl. That was before Henry's engagement to her. I warned my nephew she was a trollop, but would he listen? No. He took it upon himself to rescue that girl from scandal. She was never grateful, never appreciated the sacrifice he was willing to make, and the length to which he would go for a girl he barely knew. It wasn't a love match, but Henry was willing to do it all for her, just out of the goodness in his heart. That's always been his way. He is terribly contrary, and I should have known better than to warn him against it, for that only made him more determined. When he gets an idea in his head he can rarely be prevailed upon to change it. He pretends to be careless, but he is far from that. Indeed, I begin to think he cares rather too much and has so many thoughts in his head that he cannot move forward."

Georgiana nodded slowly. *It wasn't a love match. He took it upon himself to rescue that girl from scandal.*

"And above all else," the lady added, "he believes in standing up for what is right, instead of what is proper or suitable. It can be so very tiresome."

A terrible waste of a good man, Brown had said.

They were already at the second shrub. Lady Bramley put up her parasol to shade them both.

"Next conversation, Miss Hathaway, if you please."

Conversation? On such a glorious day, who cared about conversation? How could she think of anything else but him? Her heart thumped in a reckless rhythm.

Lady Bramley could not have encouraged her into this giddy state any more proficiently had she set out deliberately to paint her nephew in a saintly light, but this was all uttered quite casually, even wearily, as if Harry's kind heart was a great nuisance and would always get in his way.

Now here came the man himself, striding toward them down the gravel path, coatless, hatless and all too handsome in the sunlight. Even from a distance the intensity in his dark eyes was startling. She felt it all the way to her toes.

Today she looked at Dead Harry in the daylight, as if properly taking him all in, for the first time.

"Brown, you missed a bit," Lady Bramley was calling out. "Give the shears to me! I'll show you how it should be done." She thrust her parasol and her dog at Georgiana. Fortunately, the sly theft of several rashers of bacon and two sausages from the kitchen had, over the past few days, granted the ill-tempered lapdog a greater appreciation for the fingers of its previously despised enemy and they had formed a partial, tentative truce.

With his hands behind his back, Harry passed the ladies at some speed, whistling. He nodded his head toward them. Just once. Then he was gone, sweeping by, gravel crunching under his boots, which were, today, a complete pair.

And Georgiana Hathaway suddenly had the hiccups.

The little dog gave her a questioning growl, its furry head on one side, ears pricked.

In horror she remembered how and when this affliction used to come upon her sister.

This was the very worst thing that could have happened to an ambitious girl like her. But it wouldn't last, she reassured herself— that was the good thing about hiccups. She had temporarily fallen foul of a silly, girlish fancy and that was all. She had never had one of these, and at nineteen it was probably overdue.

Her heart faltered pitifully, unable to find a steady pace. Gripping the parasol handle and the little dog with all her might, she firmly resolved not to look over her shoulder. Under no circumstances could she let him see any difference in her. For sure he would tease her mercilessly if he ever suspected. As he had said to her once, "*You are, no doubt, just as eager to be in love as any other addled girl of nineteen.*" And she had denied it fervently, because at the time she had no such intention.

She did not want any preposterous fixation in her way, particularly not one formed for the most impossible, inflexible and truculent of men. Oh, this was a disaster.

* * * *

That evening before dinner he found her at the little writing table in the parlor, bent over a letter and earnestly concentrating. She didn't even look up when he came in. Usually she would commence chattering immediately, asking questions and meddling, giving her opinion on all and sundry.

But today— nothing.

Harry walked by her several times and noticed how she hunched further over her paper, hiding it from his eyes. One moment he had all her attention and the next none. Perhaps he had been mistaken to worry about the girl forming any unwanted attraction to him. It could be that they were all like her these days— back and forth like a flame in a draft— and he was simply out of practice with women.

In that case he should leave her to her writing and be glad.

Instead he paused, turned on his heel and passed her again.

"Are you writing your nefarious thoughts in a wicked diary, Miss Hathaway, or is this another letter to your *friend?*"

Whatever it was, she blotted and folded it swiftly. "I ran out of paper from my own writing box, sir, and have not yet had the chance to get more. I hope you don't mind me using yours." She looked up worriedly. "Lady Bramley said you would not mind, but you were in your study and I did not want to disturb you just to ask about paper."

Suddenly she worried about disturbing him? It had not bothered her until now.

"Of course, I do not mind." He frowned. "Why

would I mind?" Did she truly think him so curmudgeonly, as his aunt had said? "Somebody might as well make use of my writing paper," he added, trying to use a softer tone. "I have nobody to whom I would write a letter, in any case. You may as well use the bloody stuff."

As he walked by the desk again, she turned to watch him. "Sir, do you think Viscount Fairbanks really would bring a libel suit against my father's paper, because of *His Lordship's Trousers*?"

He huffed. "Wardlaw Fairbanks is all hot air. He likes to make a lot of noise. But I very much doubt he would put himself to the trouble of a law suit. Unless he has true cause to do so." He stopped and looked down at her. "Does he have cause? Can he prove that character bears more than a passing resemblance to himself?"

She scowled at his waistcoat, for some reason avoiding looking any higher. "Of course not. I'm quite sure that *His Lordship's Trousers* is not about him at all. It's a satire. I believe that's what they call it, is it not?"

"Yes." He ran a hand over his stomach, and wondered when was the last time he had a new waistcoat. "But Fairbanks is not clever enough to know what that is."

Her eyes remained concerned, her lips tense. She was definitely not her usual spirited self. "Do you remember, sir, when he called my sister a Norfolk Dumpling?"

"I do indeed. You rather ingeniously found a way to wreak your revenge that evening, as I recall." He thought of her sitting on that staircase, holding the Viscount's wig victoriously aloft at the end of a fishing line.

She looked up at him. "You were there to put the fire out, fortunately, or the damage might have been far worse."

Harry scratched his chin, hastily finding use for fingers that wanted suddenly, and unaccountably, to touch her shoulder and reassure her. "Another social event that my aunt insisted I attend. But I must say, it was the most enjoyment I'd had since they rescued me and brought me back to England."

Even this did not raise a smile from her lips.

"Fairbanks did want some sort of recompense after the wig toasting, I assume?" he asked.

She sighed heavily. "That's why I was sent away to school. To be taught the error of my ways. My father paid him too, for the cost of the wig. My poor sister, Maria, suffered most of all. The Viscount snubbed her, so after the party all his sycophantic friends did the same. We were very lucky she ever found anybody to marry her after that. Our stepmother is convinced Maria could have done much better than a solicitor, if not for all that business. Entirely my fault, of course. Neither lady has forgiven me."

He was much too distracted looking at her and could barely pay attention to what she said. So Harry walked to the cold fireplace and back again while she sealed her letter, giving her words time to sink in and make sense. Eventually he said, "Fairbanks could, therefore, plausibly imagine your father prints *His Lordship's Trousers* in retaliation. Even if it is not so."

"But it is *not* about him," she replied crossly. Jumping to her feet, she exclaimed, "The world does not revolve around *him*, whatever he thinks. If he sees his own faults in that character, he has nobody to blame but himself."

"Well, then," Harry said smoothly. "Nothing to worry about, is there?" He had never seen her concerned like this before, and he did not like to think of her worrying over that ass Fairbanks. Nobody should ever fret about that idiot. Least of all Miss Hathaway. In fact he did not like to think of her being afraid about anything and he would prevent it, if he could. It was the clearest, most certain thought he'd had for a long time.

His aunt had told him before that his "gallant heart" was his downfall, but he didn't think his heart had much to do with it. Surely his potent dislike of Wardlaw Fairbanks

188

served as a large part of his interest in this matter.

"Thank you, sir, for the reassurance." An odd, strained look had come over her face and then a hiccup popped out. Apparently covered in mortification, she made a hasty, head-down course for the door.

"What's the matter with Miss Hathaway?" Parkes exclaimed, passing the young lady in the doorway. "What have you done to her?"

"Me?" he grumbled. "I have done nothing to her." Not that he wouldn't like to. Damn and blast.

"She seems upset. Have you been rude again?"

"Parkes, I take umbrage at the suggestion that I cannot spend ten minutes in the company of a woman without offending her."

"Umbrage? Do you, indeed? I always thought you took pride in it," she replied smugly. "*Lady Bramley surely knows the risks of wheeling me out in public,* as you said to me in May. *One of these days, she will see the futility and stop doing it.* That was your plan, was it not? Be as difficult as you could and scare everybody away?"

"I have no inkling of what you might mean." He reached down and turned the scrap of blotting paper Miss Hathaway had used.

gel eht guh ot tuc snoolatnap eremyesreK :eritta s'gninrom sihT

Ah.

Harry quickly folded the scrap and put it away in his waistcoat pocket.

"What did you say, Parkes?" Spinning around, he found himself alone in the room.

Chapter Sixteen

Georgiana requested a bath in her room that evening, using this as an excuse to leave the dinner table early. Now that she was painfully aware of her attraction to their host, she felt awkward and clumsy. She was certain she might eventually do or say something terribly embarrassing in his presence. This fear eventually led to her falling completely silent, which even Lady Bramley commented upon.

"I hope you are not coming down with a summer cold, Miss Hathaway. You look rather pale, even with all those freckles, you have hardly tasted a morsel of Brown's rabbit, and we have not had a single opinion from you all evening."

So she leapt at the chance to say that she was not feeling well, and then retreated to her bed chamber.

Once relaxing in the bath she felt calmer, better able to put her thoughts in sensible order. This foolish calf-love would pass sooner or later. As for the trouble about *His Lordship's Trousers,* that could all be nothing more than rumor. Lady Bramley may have misunderstood, or made a mountain from a molehill. As the Commander said, Fairbanks was all hot air.

Despite what anybody else thought, the latest edition of *The Gentleman's Weekly* had not contained her column simply because she was unable to send it during the bad weather, but nobody except Georgiana herself knew that, naturally.

Within a few days her father should receive the episode Brown had finally posted for her, and tomorrow she would ensure the chapter she wrote today was also sent off. According to how her father reacted, she would know whether the Viscount's threat really had led him to end the column. If he published his paper next week without *His Lordship's Trousers* it would prove he had given in to fear. On the other hand, if he decided to print both

190

her new chapters— the extra one to make up for the lost week— she would know all was well.

Writing to her father directly and asking him about a law suit was impossible, so she had found. After attempting several drafts, she had given up, wasting her paper in the process. She knew her father would never discuss such a matter with his disappointing daughter and she did not know how to approach the subject either. Usually bold and to the point, seldom reluctant to express herself, Georgiana was at a loss when it came to her father. Sometimes it felt as if they were complete strangers. Any letters he had sent her over the last two and a half years consisted of a few formal inquiries into the general state of her health, how she progressed in her lessons, and whether or not she handled her allowance wisely.

So, no, she mused— studying her pink toes where they peeked out of the bath water and rested against the edge of the tub— she could not expect her father to confide in her about his troubles any more than she could tell him she was falling in love with Commander Thrasher.

Falling in love. What a dreadful expression.

Good lord, she must pull herself together, before she made a complete and utter ass of herself in that man's presence. Yet again.

But Georgiana had just rubbed her body dry and slipped into her nightgown, when she heard steps in the passage outside, which meant that Dead Harry was off on his travels again tonight.

Considering the terrible realization that had hit her today, she ought to leave him to it and never lay a hand on his naked arm again.

She could not, however, leave him alone out there, lost at sea.

Grabbing her shawl and one candle, she opened her door and looked out. There he was, walking along with his shoulder against the wall, as if his eyes were closed. Again he was naked. How strange, she mused, that the sight had become familiar to her.

But what if one of Lady Bramley's servants should see him? As the house filled with more people, there was always a greater chance that his secret would be exposed. *Their* secret. After all, he had inadvertently let her in on it.

Hastily, Georgiana left her room, closed the door and hurried after him. Her breath pummeled the candle flame as she whispered his name and bade him stop.

Harry turned. His eyes were open after all, but glazed, confused.

Oh don't look at his body, you fool, she chided herself. *It's not fair to look when he doesn't even know what he's doing, where he is, or who he is.*

But he knew her. A mischievous grin moved his lips. "My stowaway. You are still here."

"Yes. You ought to be abed, sir. There are more people on our island now, and you might be seen."

His eyes blinked and then their gaze sharpened, less puzzled now. Fiercer. "Why do you worry about Harry?" he murmured. "Why do you care?"

"Why shouldn't I?" she replied impatiently. The way she felt about him was something that frustrated her because she'd always thought herself immune to this sort of attraction. She refused to become like her sister Maria, hiccuping and blushing pitifully over a man.

And what would Commander Sir Henry Thrasher ever see in her when he was awake? Her host was not unkind to her. Especially considering the way her company had been forced upon him. She might have expected the fellow to be vastly more ill-tempered toward her than he had been. But he clearly saw her still as "The Wickedest Chit". He had even written it under his sketch of her face. Yes, the one he said was not meant to look like her at all.

Well, Dead Harry, was different; he did see something in her. She simply did not know how she should feel about *his* attention. It was very physical and not at all gentlemanly.

He took a step toward her and gripped her left wrist, his long fingers circling her pulse. The feral light was back in his eyes. "Harry wants to play," he said.

"I cannot play with you, sir." The candle in her other hand trembled, the flame dancing fitfully.

"Harry wants to play."

Georgiana glanced around nervously, but the house was quiet and once again they might have been the only two souls in the world. Outside too was peaceful and calm tonight. She could hear her heart beat pounding in her ears. "Let go of my hand, sir."

But he did not. Instead he raised it to his mouth and kissed her knuckles. She stretched out her fingers as if that might make him stop. He smiled and kissed her fingertips. Slowly, one by one, his eyes watching her face.

"It is late," she gasped.

"And we are all alone."

"Sir—"

"The name is Harry."

"Yes, and—"

"I have urges like any man and you are here with me on my island. My flesh and blood companion. My woman. My mate."

He blew out that struggling flame in her other hand and tugged her up against his body.

"I need you," he whispered urgently, lips brushing her cheek. "Stay with me."

She dropped her candle as he kissed her hungrily, his arms holding her tightly, squeezing her as if he meant to crush the breath out of her lungs. Once again her shawl slipped from her shoulders and before Georgiana knew what was happening she was returning his kiss with equal fervor. Her fingers stroked his rough, unshaven cheek and then slid around his broad neck. She'd never touched a man's neck, never felt that pulse under his skin, wild and passionate. All of this was new to her. New territory to explore.

"I want you, my mate," he whispered.

And she wanted him too. But which side of Harry did she want?

He was a beautiful man— physically— but there was so much more to him than that, if only he would let himself be rescued from his island, brought home, and put back together again.

She knew then that it was all of him she wanted, not just one part. She was greedy. Always had been.

But what came next? Marriage was out of the question for either of them. They had both made their feelings clear on that regard. She did not want a husband to rule over her, stand in her way and keep her trapped. To birth a child a year, see only half survive, and then die herself, to be replaced as if she was an old coat that wore out her use. To be remembered, like her mama, in a few sad words on a small, weather-beaten stone in the graveyard.

Mercy Hathaway, devoted wife and beloved mother 1772-1811.

Besides, she was getting ahead of herself. He might be eccentric, but he was not mad enough to look at her with a view to marriage. At that moment, to Dead Harry, she was a potential plaything. He wanted nothing more complicated than that.

As their lips parted, he groaned softly. "Come play with me, Stowaway. You have a fee to pay for the safe passage I gave you on my vessel."

"If we are shipwrecked, sir, it does not seem to have been a very safe passage."

"Impudent, as well as insubordinate, eh?" She saw a flash of white teeth as he grinned down at her. "I was warned. 'Tis lucky for you I have no other woman on my island." He raised a hand to her face and his fingertips tenderly grazed her cheek. She caught her breath, that touch as intimate as if he had caressed under her nightgown.

Suddenly she felt a little conceited. It was his fault, she decided. The intense way he looked at her, made her feel special, cosseted. Even beautiful for the first time in her life. Dead Harry, the castaway, did not see her as a foolish girl who talked too much and left chaos in her wake. He saw her as a woman of value. A desirable woman, a fact made very clear by the way his naked body reacted to her.

Commander Sir Henry Thrasher might be able to hide such things from her, just as he locked his study door and jealously guarded his automatons from her "prying". But Dead Harry— his other side— had nothing to hide behind, not even clothes.

Harry answers to none. He lives on his own island by his own rules.

She ran a fingertip over the prickles on his cheek. "I am lucky to be the only woman on your island."

"Yes," he said with a sigh. "I have no other choice for my mate, do I? Therefore you'll have to do." He sounded more like the Commander then, more like his daylight self.

Georgiana withdrew her finger and frowned. "You would not be playing a trick upon me, would you, sir?"

His strong arm did not release her. If anything the muscles tightened, as if he thought she might try to escape his embrace. "Trick? What trick?"

She sighed. "I believe you would choose me, even if there were other women here." Why not be bold in this matter, as she would be in any other? Seize her opportunity for adventure. "Because we are both rebels, Harry, trying to be happy, as we want to be, not as the rest of society wants us to be. Because I understand you and I don't want you to change. I only want you to be whole again."

He appeared to think about this for a moment and then said, "You must be mad, like me."

"Indeed," she replied with a sigh.

It *was* madness. She should never have left her bedchamber on that first evening; should never have continued these nighttime walks with a naked man and tempted fate. But there they were.

Dead Harry and the Wickedest Chit tangled up together.

Before she came to Woodbyne Abbey, she imagined she could manage anything, get herself out of any trouble, fix anything. After all, she had experience.

But now she knew differently.

Georgiana knew differently now about many things.

She was powerless to resist when Harry swept her off her feet and carried her over his shoulder like a roll of carpet, even though she had always promised herself that she would never let a man take control of her. It was happening, and there was absolutely nothing she wanted to do about it.

He carried her along the dark corridor, his shoulder skimming the wall again, guiding his steps.

"Harry," she whispered, her eyes closed as she dangled in the dark, entrusting herself to him entirely. *I am mad. Madly in love.*

But not mad enough to say it out loud.

Her sister would be proud of her, she mused, for finally learning to hold her tongue and keep some of her thoughts inside.

He stopped at a door, kicked it open and took her inside.

Too late now to come to her senses. Emma Chance would despair of her, but Melinda Goodheart would excitedly want to know every detail of her ruination. Later she would write them a letter and try to explain what had become of her in this house. She must, because the three of them had pledged to always share their adventures.

However, while she fully expected to find herself tossed onto a bed, she was, instead, set down on her feet.

"Here we will play," he said, pointing to a board made of scrap wood, marked by lines scratched into it, and with a few shells and pebbles scattered across the surface. "Be seated, woman. You can be the shells, and I shall be the stones. I have waited a long time to find somebody to play with me. It is not so much fun playing alone."

This was what he meant by *playing*? She wanted to laugh and was not sure whether it was out of relief, or something else. She had expected wrestling, at the very least. Suddenly she realized he was staring heatedly at the front of her nightgown, where her wet hair dripped over her shoulder and made a blossoming transparent patch over one breast. Quickly she covered it with one hand and then his gaze swept upward to her face.

"We can converse while we play, if you would like to," he added. "Usually I play alone, but now I have you for company. Worry not. I shall teach you how to play my game, woman."

His room was not large and it was sparsely furnished, but warmed by a roaring fire, in front of which several blankets and furs were laid out. This, it seemed, was where he slept, for the bed had been stripped of linens and pillows.

Her host gestured again for her to sit by the fire. He handed her the shawl he must have rescued from the floor. "You are cold?" he demanded, sounding cross about it.

"No. I'm much too hot in here," she said. The temperature in his room was almost tropical.

"Then take off your gown." He grinned, standing tall and proud, his hands making a sweeping gesture down his body. "I, as you see, prefer to be as my creator intended." The rough line of a scar that traveled from his left side,

197

under his arm, and ended just below his ribs was clearly visible tonight. There were other marks too— souvenirs of battle, she supposed.

It reminded her of how many times he'd escaped death, how lucky she was that he still lived. She might never have known him.

"Yes. I mean, no. Thank you. I'll keep my nightgown, if it's all the same to you."

"Are you certain? We do not need clothes to play my game."

"I can see that." She looked at him, squinting so as not to let her eyes stray too far.

"Or to converse. Women like to converse a vast deal, I know."

But if he sat cross-legged before her on the blankets, Georgiana knew she absolutely could not "converse" sensibly with him in that state. She handed him her shawl. "Please...put this...around...that."

But he rested his knuckles on his hips and glared. "Why? I am not ashamed."

And he had absolutely no reason to be, she thought wryly.

"Why do you fuss, woman? You are my mate. There is nothing here with which you will not soon be familiar. You may as well befriend it now."

Oh, Good Lord. "Humor me, Harry, if you will, and just tie this around yourself. Otherwise I cannot stay and will have to go back to my room."

That appeared to confuse him, but when she tossed her shawl across the short distance, he caught it instinctively. She demonstrated with her own hands how he should wrap and tie it, and after a moment he finally complied.

Thank goodness. She could breathe again and look at him without having to see parts he would, in the daylight, keep respectably out of her sight. Really, Georgiana assured herself, she did it for the Commander's modesty, as much as for her own sake.

Alas, in his cross-legged pose, that shawl did not do quite as good a service as she had hoped. It was, at least, a little better than before. For now it was the best she could do.

"Now pay attention, my mate," he said. "I will teach you my game and we will play." He looked up. "Why do you smile?"

She shrugged and shook her head. How could she explain the strangeness of all this...and what she had expected when he first carried her to his room? What she had thought he meant by "playing".

"You have been alone on your island a long time," she said gently.

His chest heaved with a great sigh. "Yes. But now you are here. So pay attention and I will teach you my game."

Georgiana nodded and lowered herself to the furs. Lady Bramley would say a guest should comply with her host's wishes, would she not?

Earnestly she tried to concentrate as he taught her this game he had invented of shells and pebbles, but a naked man— even one with a shawl tied around his groin— was powerfully distracting. He didn't seem to realize this fact. Adamant that she learn the rules of his game, he chastised her firmly if he thought her attention wandered. But just when she thought she understood the rules, he changed them. She might have been annoyed, if it was anyone else but him. How could she be annoyed with Harry? This time alone with him, when he was talkative and wanted her company, felt like a priceless treasure accidentally put into her hands for safe-keeping.

He won, of course, since he made the game rules up as he went along. Not that she minded at all. In fact, it was the only game she had ever enjoyed losing and she knew she was in danger of letting the winner take all.

And then what? Tomorrow he would not even remember this.

"Now to bed," he said suddenly, pushing the wooden board aside.

Recovering quickly, Georgiana stood. "Yes, Harry," she said. "Me to mine and you to yours." She was much too hot in that room and needed air to clear her mind, before she made a mistake they might both regret. Thank goodness for his game of shells and pebbles, she mused. It had stopped her from leaping in with both feet and letting her passion for adventure carry her away.

"But you must stay with me," he said crossly.

"I cannot stay with you tonight, Harry. It would not be wise." A Reckless Dare was one thing she had never turned her back upon before, but she was not a "dizzy girl" any longer. She knew the consequences she would face if she gave in to her desires now. It would not be fair to either of them, especially while this half of him was still lost at sea. "Goodnight, Harry."

"You defy me?"

"I must. If I gave you my heart tonight, tomorrow you might break it by not remembering."

"Your heart?"

"I would never give the rest of myself without giving that too."

He looked at her with his head on one side, eyes narrowed. Finally he took her hand and kissed it, showing that Dead Harry did know something of manners after all. "Goodnight then, if we must...Georgiana."

And he also knew her name.

She studied his face, wishing she was a better artist and able to capture it more accurately than she had in her sketch. But was such a complex man ever to be captured?

It was, by no means, easy to leave his room and close the door behind her, to walk slowly back to her own chamber with the air cooling her over-heated skin as she came back to reality. Back to sleep or to awake? As he had said, sometimes it was hard to know which was which.

That night her dreams carried her to a strange tropical paradise, where she enjoyed the sensation of his hands on her body. Their firm caress following the curve from hip to bosom, and then his lips following the same path. She dreamed of warm air, humidity making her perspire in a manner that would cause one of Lady Bramley's stern reprimands. She even felt sand beneath her, in her hair and under her fingernails. Exotic birds called out from the twisty branches of the mangroves, where they perched watching. She could hear the rush and sizzle of waves lazily lapping at the shore.

There with Harry she was happy as she had never been, in a way she had never thought possible for herself.

He raised his hand and she pressed her palm to his. How much larger he was than she. Against the sun their hands made a dark ink blot, and when he spread their fingers, rich, buttery rays dripped down her arm, tickling her skin.

It all seemed very real, every sense fully enthralled.

When he enfolded her in his arms she was absorbed by him; she became another part of Harry. She might lose herself completely in the process, but at that moment she was too blissfully relaxed to care.

His fingertips kissed her thigh like a naughty whisper, seductive and teasing, and when he kissed her she felt the urgency spark between them, the desperate yearning about to be sated.

"*Georgiana*," he groaned.

But her imagination, lively as it was, took her no further.

She woke, twisted up in her blankets, damp with perspiration, covered in goose feathers. The only wrestling that night had been with her pillow, and she had won.

Chapter Seventeen

When Harry approached the drawing room door the following day, he heard his aunt in mid-shriek,

"Miss Hathaway, you are not a sack of grain. Lightly, Miss Hathaway, with your weight upon your toes, not your heels. And why are your shoulders hunched about your ears again, girl?"

By now his aunt should have been hoarse, but no such luck.

"You move like a dazed ghost, Miss Hathaway. Did you sleep ill last night?"

He opened the door and looked in. Neither lady noticed him for a moment, too caught up in the dancing lesson, so he had an opportunity to admire Miss Hathaway's figure through the white, gossamer material of her gown again as she moved back and forth before the sun-lit windows. His furniture had been moved aside to make space, but the pupil still managed to crash into it occasionally, much to his amusement. His aunt's dog ran around her ankles, trying to nip her petticoat, but when he saw Harry he stopped and barked.

"Ah, there you are, Henry, and just in time!" his aunt bellowed above the music she was thumping out at the pianoforte. "We need a partner for Miss Hathaway. I was about to resort to using Brown or one of the footmen, but now you can be of use. Stop skulking there and come in."

He cleared his throat, entered the room and looked at his young guest. "Miss Hathaway, I found this...I believe it belongs to you." Stretching out one arm, he showed her the shawl which he'd found wrapped around his loins when he woke that morning.

"Oh." The young woman stumbled to a halt, and her hands dropped to her sides.

"It is yours, is it not?"

"Yes. Yes, of course." She hurried over and reached

to take it from him.

Harry kept a grip on one corner. "Do you remember where you left it?"

Those centipedinous eyelashes wafted upward and her eyes widened. "Yes." She added with a whisper, "But do you?"

He did not. Although his mind simply did not want to let him remember, some part of him had been misbehaving with her. There were certain signs when he woke that morning which assured him of it.

When she gave another tug, he released the shawl to her custody. "Thank you, sir, for returning it safely."

As the fringe fell through his fingers like a soft, teasing kiss, he saw her sitting before him in her nightgown, wet hair over her shoulder, teeth biting her lip as she leaned over to examine something on the floor between them.

When she bathed last night she must have used that soap he thought he didn't like.

He liked it now. Very much.

Suddenly he was unable to resist touching her eyelashes where they fluttered against her cheek. He heard her take a sharp intake of breath, felt her eyelid twitch as his fingertip brushed over it, but she did not move away or mutter any objection.

His aunt, sorting through music at the pianoforte, paid no attention to what they were doing. "You will partner Miss Hathaway, Henry. A minuet will do to start."

He did not like dancing, but it would be an excuse to hold her hand. Her fingers, light and hesitant, hovered over his like a tentative bird. "You do not mind, sir?"

"Why would I?" He gripped her fingers firmly.

"I'm sure you have more important things to do."

When he looked into her eyes he read the question there, asking if he remembered what had happened last night. If only he did.

This was very bad, dangerous for her.

Well, today it was only a dance. There could be no harm in that. Later he would discuss this business of nightly encounters with her, because they could not continue. Absolutely could not.

"I'm not a very good dancer," she whispered.

"Excellent." He managed a tight smile. "Neither am I, so we can muddle along together. A perfect partnership."

But as Lady Bramley struck the first keys on the pianoforte, a loud voice interrupted the lesson before it had begun.

"A minuet? Who dares dance a minuet without us?"

And Harry's pleasant thoughts about soap, eyelashes and wet bodies were shattered when the drawing room door burst open and there stood Maxwell Bramley looking pleased with himself and probably drunk, teetering in the doorway and beaming as if his face might split in two.

Until he saw his mama.

* * * *

It was a most uncomfortable luncheon. Through her trusty lorgnette, his aunt stared at Max and the woman he'd brought with him, assessing them both as if they were the last items left on a market stall.

"Well, this is a surprise, Maxwell." Her tone left no doubt that it was an unwelcome one too. "And who is this...Mrs. Swan?"

"Swanley," he corrected, his lips turned down as the footman— obeying one of Lady Bramley's stern looks— only half filled his glass before moving on to the next. "Mrs. Swanley is a..." he glanced over at Harry, "a friend. An old friend."

Lady Bramley then raised her voice, as if the woman across the table might not understand. "Are you one of the Canterbury Swanleys?"

Maxwell's companion looked startled to be addressed

204

directly, but that turned quickly to coy amusement. "No, madam," she replied with a sideways glance at Max and a little smile. "I am of the Bethnal Green Swanleys."

"Oh." The lorgnette was dropped and the soup spoon retrieved. "You are nobody then."

Harry cleared his throat. "You are just passing through, I assume, cousin." Max surely would not linger now that he knew his mother was in residence.

But his cousin eyed Georgiana across the soup tureen and grinned broadly. "I suppose I can stay a day or two, Harry old chap. If it won't put you out." He swigged his wine and held the empty glass aloft for the footman. "It has been a hellish journey, I must say, and you ought to take pity on us. We would have been here days ago but for the dratted weather." When the wine decanter did not return promptly, he tapped his glass with a knife blade and finally his mother relented with a nod to the footman.

While Harry watched, Georgiana smiled back at his cousin and he was sure her eyes held a new sultriness he had not seen before. Since when had she begun wearing her hair off her forehead and pinned back? It was a more sophisticated style and he did not recall the moment she'd changed the way she wore her dark curls. And she should have changed out of that gown after her dancing lesson, for it was not suitable daytime attire for a young lady. The color was the only thing innocent about it when it was worn over curves like hers.

She ought to be taken out of it immediately. He imagined his own hands completing that task with haste and efficiency.

As the bread basket passed his line of sight, Harry took a roll and ripped it apart quickly and ruthlessly, crumbs flying all over. "We're stretched for space at the moment, Max. Perhaps you and Mrs. Swanley would be more comfortable at the inn in Little Flaxhill."

"Would we?" Max still studied Georgiana with

increased curiosity. "I doubt it." He glanced at Harry and then back again to the prettier face. "I think I'd rather stay here, even if it is suddenly an inconvenience."

Harry felt his temperature rising. "The accommodations in the village would suit you both better."

But Mrs. Swanley abruptly exclaimed, "I came all this way for you, Sir Henry. You paid for my services. I cannot be any use to you at an inn, can I?"

There was a short silence while everybody ceased moving their spoons and looked at Harry. Max grinned, stuffing his face with bread, soup dribbling down his chin. His aunt raised her lorgnette again, and Miss Hathaway looked confused. And much too attractive for her own good suddenly. What the devil was she playing at, looking that way?

He had to think quickly, something he hadn't been required to do for the past few years, while he was alone in that house and had no one to bother him. This was the sort of difficulty that arose from having other people around and opening one's life to their messes and problems. As if he didn't have enough of his own.

"Mrs. Swanley is an artist," he said, reaching for his wine glass. "I hired her, Lady Bramley...to paint the house."

"To paint the house?"

"In watercolor" he explained. "I thought the place ought to be recorded in paint. For posterity."

Perfect! By sheer accident he had stumbled upon the ideal lie.

His aunt was delighted. "My dear brother always planned to have Woodbyne Abbey painted and he never got around to it."

No, thought Harry dryly, his father was too busy with the legion of women he brought home to the house. That had kept him far too occupied in the last years of his life and he never gave another thought to the state of the

206

house, or the idea of having it memorialized in paint. After Harry's mother left, his father had not bothered fixing anything as it broke around him. Instead he sank with it, decayed slowly and let the ivy cover everything. Hence the state of the place today.

Perhaps it was time he got that roof replaced and had somebody look at those drafty windows, as Miss Hathaway had suggested.

Already, in secret, he had begun tidying his study. When he was behind that locked door they all thought he was at work on his inventions, but Harry had lately lost interest in his automated woman and instead spent his mornings sorting through his books and papers, gradually clearing space on the floor and shelves, shaking up the dust and shattering the cobwebs. It was only one room, but it was a start.

As he looked around his dining room he realized that his aunt had supervised the sewing of new curtains— or were they the old ones cleaned and re-hung? Perhaps it was merely the gleam of the summer sun through those newly washed windows that brought everything to life. He knew Brown had been put to work clearing overgrown ivy from the front of the house and that let in more light too.

And when his roving perusal settled again on Miss Hathaway, the cider-tinted glow seemed to make her curls shine with a richer luster. Her eyes sparkled beneath those thick lashes like sunlight tickling the surface of a deep still lake.

She caught his eye and smiled. As he knew she would. As she always did now. It was pleasant, he realized, to look up and see her there at his table. For as long as she stayed, of course. Nothing permanent.

But it was time to wake up that slumbering house and chase out the ghosts. He felt an ardent desire to show Woodbyne off at its best, while she was in residence.

"Better pray that Swanley person can paint," Parkes

whispered in his ear.

He smirked into his wine. They'd deal with that problem once they came to it. In fact he was feeling as if he could cope with anything now. More like his old self.

* * * *

"That was quick thinking on your part, coz." Max laughed. "At luncheon."

"You might have warned me you were bringing that woman."

"I did. I sent you a letter, old chap."

"Yes, but so much time has elapsed between the letter and your arrival, I assumed plans had changed. As yours often do."

"I told you, the weather held us up or I would have been here last week."

The two men rode side by side, a chance for them to talk alone while the ladies stayed behind in the house.

"I hope your Mrs. Swanley can be discreet," Harry muttered.

"Of course she can. It's important in her profession." Max tapped the side of his nose in that gesture he had used before when taking a cheque from his cousin's hand. Now Harry understood what it meant, of course.

"It did not seem so at luncheon," said Harry. "She could not wait to say I had hired her services."

Max laughed so hard he almost toppled sideways from his saddle. "She was offended by your eagerness to be rid of us so hastily the moment we arrived. You were not very gentlemanly, it must be said."

"I was being honest. You know the Abbey has few habitable rooms and they are all full, thanks to your mama and her need for a battalion of servants."

"But Mrs. Swanley, dear chap," Max lowered his voice to a harsh whisper, leaning closer, "is meant to share your room and your bed, isn't she?"

208

"That is out of the question. I told you I don't need a woman." Not that one, in any case.

They turned the horses, moving into the leafy shade of a small coppice. Here, out of the sun's glare, it was cooler, the gentle breeze ruffling the canopy of leaves overhead.

"So what about that funny little piece, Miss Georgiana Hathaway. What are you doing with her, coz?"

He replied crisply, "Miss Hathaway is very young and not your sort."

"Not my sort? She's a woman, is she not?" Max grinned.

"She is here as a companion to your mama, apparently to learn how to behave herself. That means she does not need any of your charming words of *wisdom* blown into her ears to distract her."

"Sakes, coz, you sound rather protective of the young petticoat."

"You will find her capable of protecting herself. I merely tried to save you the trouble.""Well, that's very sweet, Harry, but all's fair in love and war."

"Explain?"

"I can hardly help it if she prefers me and my handsome face. I'm the sort girls fall in love with. You're not. I have charm. You don't. I have good looks. You don't."

"You believe she would prefer you to me? Is there anything about Miss Hathaway that makes you think she has forfeited her wits?"

"You intrigue me further, cousin. That almost sounded like the old Harry, and I see a bit of that long lost spark of competition in your eye again. No doubt you will warn her against me as soon as you get her alone."

"That caution will not be necessary. Miss Hathaway may be young and virtuous, but she has eyes, ears and intelligence enough to make her own sound judgment.

And she seeks adventures...without men, who, she assures me, only get in her way."

Max laughed again, the sound disturbing blackbirds from the trees so that they rose up in a dark cloud, before scattering into the clear sky. "You can be as protective of your little house guest as you like. It is rather touching. But the fact is, all young ladies will look wherever they fancy and, sometimes, the more you warn them against a fellow, the more they run after him."

This was true of certain ladies, he knew, but Miss Hathaway— Georgiana— was different. She did not strike him as the sort to have the wool pulled over her eyes.

And speaking of covering certain things...again he thought of waking to find her shawl tied around his loins, the fringe tickling his thigh as he rolled over, emerging from a deep, and for once gratifying, sleep. She must have given it to him last night, or else he took it from her.

Max was right, he was most definitely feeling a spark.

"It's not very sporting of you, Harry old chap, to keep Miss Hathaway all to yourself!"

"I was unaware Miss Hathaway had become a sport."

"Dear coz, you may not have competed for a woman before, so perhaps you don't recognize it now, but that is exactly what you are doing. Competing with your own cousin. I know not what has come over you. It's disgraceful, and you should stop at once."

"And let you win?"

"Precisely." Max winked. "You know I'm better for her. You have no idea how to manage such a creature. She's not one of your automatons, you know."

Oh, he was very much aware of that. "Max, I'm not going to let you annoy Miss Hathaway and that's all there is to it. I suggest you stick to the Mrs. Swanleys of the world and we'll all be happy."

"Tsk tsk. Anyone would think you're in love, Harry."

"Don't be ridiculous."

210

Hell and damnation, he wished he could remember what had happened last night.

He closed his eyes, turned his face upward, and felt the sun-dappled shadow slip across it. Never had an elusive memory haunted him so with so much seductive promise of what he might be missing.

If he had been ungentlemanly with a young lady, he should at least remember it.

* * * *

Georgiana expected the arrival of two new guests to keep the Commander behind his study door even more often. She thought he might even return to avoiding meals in the dining room, but to her surprise it had the opposite effect. She found him popping up frequently, no matter where she was or what she was doing. Especially if his cousin Max was nearby. She concluded that he must be more fond of his cousin's company than he would ever want to admit.

Mr. Maxwell Bramley was an amiable fellow, but a little too full of himself. Although he had his mother's forceful ways, he had none of her insight.

It was interesting to see mother and son together— the heavy glare of disapproval on one side and the studied carelessness on the other. Lady Bramley's loaded remarks about wasting one's life and her son's determined pursuit of frivolous distractions. This habit of closing his ears to advice reminded her of Harry, but Max was far more concerned with keeping up an appearance. He was also much more gregarious— sometimes a little too affable if he had unrestricted access to the decanters for an afternoon— and not nearly as forthright, or, she suspected, as trustworthy. He was the sort of fellow who would agree to a plan one day and forget it by the next. Where the Commander kept too many things in his mind and became confused by the clutter, Max Bramley was ruthless at sweeping his thoughts aside to keep only one at a time. Usually something trivial.

His traveling companion, Mrs. Swanley, was a very fashionable lady with an elegant, studied poise to her every move, but Lady Bramley could not be deceived.

"There is something hard beneath all that Brussels lace and ruffled silk," she confided in Georgiana. "She is not what she pretends to be, of that I am sure. My son continually entangles himself with the wrong sort. I quite despair of him."

"Oh, do not despair, Lady Bramley. Nobody is beyond saving, you know. Where is your love of a good challenge?"

The lady winced. "I believe it is trapped under my ribcage, Miss Hathaway." And then she sent her maid for some stomach powders. After her son's arrival she relied upon their soothing qualities more than usual.

Georgiana was curious about Mrs. Swanley too. After the lady's loudly stated objection to staying at an inn near Little Flaxhill, she stayed quiet and watchful. Very beautifully maintained, she seemed, at first glance, content to be mostly ornamental. But her eyes were much too wily, revealing that the lady paid close attention to every word uttered. She assessed her surroundings cautiously and thoroughly, while seldom moving a finger. In her eerie stillness she reminded Georgiana of an automaton in the Commander's study.

Harry would probably like that, she mused glumly.

But when she glanced over at him, he seemed to be avoiding Mrs. Swanley. Instead his merciless gaze was occupied throwing sharp daggers at his cousin. Not that Maxwell Bramley was at all wounded by the assault. The fellow seemed vastly amused and kept looking at Georgiana as if she was in on the joke.

Eventually Lady Bramley said, "Miss Hathaway, why do you not take Mrs. Swanley for a tour of the herb garden in the courtyard. I am sure she would like to hear the history of the place."

While there was nothing about Mrs. Swanley that suggested an interest in history or herb gardens, Georgiana was glad to get out into the fresh air. The sunny courtyard, with its large, moss-covered, gently-trickling fountain was one of her favorite places to sit and ponder, so she was quite capable of proudly showing it off and reciting the history she had learned from the master of the house.

"This is part of the building that dates from the medieval period, when it really was an abbey and monks grew their medicinal herbs here," she explained as they strolled along the covered walkway and through the old stone arches. "As you can see, the—"

"Let's sit in the shade, Miss Hathaway. That bench over there looks comfortable enough and the sun is giving me a rotten bleedin' headache. To tell you the truth, young lady, we walked the last two miles to get here when the dratted carriage broke down— and Max didn't have the money to get it fixed or to hire another— and the last thing I want is another bleedin' walk."

"Oh." What did one say to that? Lady Bramley's lessons had not prepared her for this eventuality.

So Mrs. Swanley was, as she'd suspected, not much of a history student, nor a fan of walking, but Georgiana need not have worried about finding interesting subjects to keep the conversation flowing. The lady was eager to exercise her tongue, even if her legs were tired. Once out of the drawing room and away from Lady Bramley's demanding glare, she clearly felt more at her ease and could relax her stiff poise.

"I heard you say that you recently left finishing-school, Miss Hathaway."

"Yes. I was a student for two years at The Particular Establishment for the Advantage of Respectable Ladies."

"Crikey, that's a mouthful."

"Some of us referred to it as The Pearl. But I'm afraid we needed far more polishing than we received there. We remain specks of insignificant sand rather than the pearls we were meant to become."

"You didn't like the place?"

"The headmistress, Mrs. Lightbody, did not like *me*, and the feeling was reciprocated. We had a clash of personalities, you might say. That made my life there challenging."

"A tartar, was she?"

"And very cruel to some of the other girls who did not, or could not, stand up to her." She thought of the red marks on Emma Chance's knuckles— a discovery she had made soon after her arrival at the school, and her first knowledge of Mrs. Lightbody's liberal use of corporal punishment upon those girls whose parents were especially lacking in vigilance. Lately she had been thinking about that more than ever and struggling to find some way to rescue her friends.

"The world is full of her sort. The best we can do is hope they get their comeuppance in time. And we get our vengeance by finding fortune and success."

Georgiana nodded. "Did you train as an artist abroad, Mrs. Swanley?"

She chortled. "No, deary. I learned my art in the streets of London. Dragged myself out of the rookeries and I've done well, make no mistake. There's a few people I wish could see me now."

"I greatly admire your success, madam. It cannot be easy as a woman to be appreciated in the world of art."

Mrs. Swanley looked askance and then chuckled dourly. "Well, sometimes it 'elps to be a woman in my line of work."

"It does? I've always found it rather trying to be a female."

The lady made her face solemn again. "Ah, well, a

girl's got to know how to make the most of the talent God gave her."

"I always thought that way myself, but the rest of the world thinks I ought to marry and be done with it. That is, in their eyes, my only option."

Mrs. Swanley swished her feet in the fountain and squinted at her for a moment. "If you've got plenty of talent, young miss, then you should use it. What do you care about the rest of them? I suppose it was all embroidery and flower arranging at that school of yours."

"I'm afraid so."

"That is meant to prepare you for a husband, is it?" The woman gave a little snort. "I pity you young girls who must go blind-folded to the marriage bed. 'Tis no wonder it's a shock to most of you."

Sitting straighter, Georgiana tried to remember her lessons about her posture. "I am not completely ignorant of those things. I grew up in the country." And she had learned a few interesting points from the little book she found in Mrs. Lightbody's parlor, but she knew better than to mention that. Let the entire world think her a naive miss.

Mrs. Swanley leaned closer. "Well, you might know what it is and what it does, but you wait until you find out where he means to put it. Not always where you'd expect either." She took a small silver flask from her reticule. "Here...looks like you could do with a drop." She held it out for Georgiana.

"What is it?"

"Gin."

"Oh, no thank you." She shuddered. "It reminds me too much of Mrs. Lightbody, my old headmistress. That was her favorite tipple."

The other lady laughed and took a swig from the flask herself. "Just for my aching head and feet, you understand," she muttered. "This is *my* medicinal herb. A sip a day keeps the quack away."

Georgiana decided the new guest was rather more amusing than she had first appeared. Her fashionable manners had made her seem rather dull and smug before, but now her shoulders relaxed and she lost her pretentious accent. She made herself even more appealing when she removed her walking boots without ceremony and dangled her aching feet in the fountain.

"What did you say that headmistress of yours was called?"

"Mrs. Julia Lightbody."

"Lightbody." Her eyes glistened with new interest. "That's not a common name, is it?"

"No."

"Fancy that. Well, I—" She looked away for a moment and gave a tight, scratchy laugh. "Spiteful sort, was she? And fond of gin you say?"

"Yes."

"By chance, was she a bit too keen on the willow switch too?"

Georgiana looked at her in surprise. "Yes. Do you know her?"

The other woman held her lips pinched for a moment and then replied, "A long time ago, in another lifetime, I knew a fellow named Bill Lightbody and his... partner, who called herself Salome Flambeau. We worked together once in a house, in Bethnal Green." Then she shook her head. "May not be the same person, of course. Lot of folks fond of gin. Meself included." She winked.

"Mrs. Lightbody said her husband was a musician of some sort, but she has been widowed fifteen years or more. She kept his silhouette above her mantel, beside a much larger and grander painting of herself."

At this, Mrs. Swanley's eyes flared again. Those plump, suspiciously pink lips twisted slightly in a disdainful smirk. "The Bill Lightbody I knew played the fiddle, but he

216

only knew three songs. I'd hardly call him a musician." She lifted her feet out of the water and reached down to remove a long green weed from her ankle. "Still, I daresay Salome of the Seven Veils would make up something better. She always had a taste for the finer things and fancied herself worth more. Ambitious she was, thought she would leave us all behind one day and fit herself in with the higher-ups somehow."

"And your Salome was married to the man called Lightbody?"

"Lord no, they weren't never married." After another gust of laughter, she remembered her accent again and clipped it back into place. "Not the two persons I knew. He had all the advantages of a husband, however, if you get my drift, Miss Hathaway."

"I believe I do."

"But Salome always had an eye out for a better chance and would never tie herself permanently to a penniless old scoundrel like Bill. They rubbed along together, getting what they could out of each other. That's what folk do, ain't it?"

"Yes, I suppose so."

Salome? Georgiana thought of that elegant portrait above Mrs. Lightbody's mantle. All that ivory, powdered bosom on abundant display, hoisted upward and decorated with a beauty spot that drew the eye, even when one would much rather not look. Could this be the same woman? A fondness for gin and the "finer things" certainly seemed familiar. There was also the little matter of that slender leather volume of explicit notes that Georgiana had found tucked down behind the woman's bookshelf when sent to clean out her parlor— the book that had, in part, inspired the character of Lady Loose Garters in her column.

"You worked in a house, Mrs. Swanley? What sort of house? You mean, you were in service there together?"

"Service?" The lady laughed again. "You might call it that."

"Before you became an artist?"

"That's right. Before I went out on my own and became...an artiste." Mrs. Swanley rearranged the pleats of her gown over her knees and added proudly. "I am the best in the business and do very well for myself, but one has to know the right clientele. Where the money is. I don't waste my time for a paltry sum. A woman's got to know her worth."

"Yes. I suppose so." Georgiana saw no point in reminding Mrs. Swanley that a lady never discussed finances. Let Lady Bramley tell her that, she mused. "When was it that you worked with your friend Salome?"

"Ha! She weren't no friend of mine." Then she stopped, readjusted her poise again and continued in her studied, more-refined tone, "Turn of the century it must have been, my dear. Nearly twenty years ago, I'd say. Lord, I was a young thing when I started! No more than sixteen or seventeen. So yes, twenty years or thereabouts."

"When you began in service?"

"Hmmm. Service. That's right." Suddenly the woman nudged her hard in the side. "So tell me about this Sir Henry. I hear he's rather eccentric. Not all there in the head, so they say."

Georgiana smiled. "Oh, is anybody all there in the head?" He was certainly all there in body, she thought with a wistful sigh.

Mrs. Swanley considered this for a while, as birds chirped overhead and water dripped lazily over the stone brim of the fountain. "He's younger than I expected. A looker too. I'm surprised he needs a woman brought in," she murmured. "Ought to be able to get one for himself well enough."

If, before then, Georgiana had been in any doubt about Mrs. Swanley's purpose there on the arm of Max

218

Bramley, she did not now.

But the other woman, realizing her slip, hastily added, "His lady aunt brought you here for that, did she? Wants him married off, no doubt, and you're in the running now you're out of that finishing school."

"Me? No, I am only here as a companion for Lady Bramley. I am not in any race." She managed a smile. "The field is quite clear, as far as I know."

Mrs. Swanley looked pleased then, folding her hands together in her lap, a cat anticipating a large dish of cream. "Well, I'm sure I can put the fellow in a better mood than he seems to be. Max warned me I'd have my hands full, but no man resists my charms once I get to work. I'll dust him off and put him straight soon enough." She chuckled throatily at her own jest, probably thinking that Georgiana would not understand it.

Poor Harry, she thought. All these people full of good intentions, blundering about in his house. First came his aunt, marching in like an Army Major, then his cousin with a different idea— using Mrs. Swanley to dust off Harry's cobwebs.

It must be heart-warming to know one had people who cared, she thought. But Harry did not want the attention and shrank away from it. She supposed it might be possible to have too much notice from one's relatives, just as it was to have too little.

Chapter Eighteen

Before retiring to bed that evening she sought out Brown in the kitchen, and quietly suggested he might want to lock his master's bed chamber door from the outside.

"There are now, as you know, a great many more people in the house," she said.

He looked at her as if she had two heads.

"Brown, you do know the matter of which I speak. You warned me of it on my first evening here and I—"

"Why, yes, Miss, of course I know."

"Then why—"

"But I *have* been locking his door," the big man whispered fretfully, grey eyebrows writhing in concern. "I didn't know he was still getting out."

Her eyes must have been as large as his then. "Well, he is," she muttered. "Somehow."

"Miss," Brown set down his pipe and rested both hands on his thighs. "I did tell you to bolt your own door, did I not?"

She hiccupped and nodded.

He stared at her steadily, lips pursed. Slowly he heaved a deep sigh and shook his head. "He must be getting out of his window and climbing around to the next room."

"No. He manages to unlock his door somehow. I have taken him back to his room and he walks in so the door is unlocked."

"Then he must have another key I didn't know about." The old man cursed under his breath and then added a curt, "Sorry, miss."

"That's quite all right, Brown. I'm feeling rather desperate myself and anything could come out of my mouth at such a time. We must try to stop him."

"Short of tying him up in ropes, miss, what would you suggest? Nailing the fellow's feet to the floor?"

"There's no need for sarcasm, my good man."

But Brown was evidently very tired, worn out by all these additional guests and the renovations to the house. In no mood to worry about anything else today, he had been looking forward to a late-night pipe, a porkpie and a large tankard of cider in his peaceful corner of the kitchen.

"Why not give me the key," she said casually, "and let me manage the Commander this evening?"

He paused, pie half way to his lips, mouth already open.

Georgiana held out her hand, palm up. "You might as well. I'm the one he wakes up. Why should you be bothered too? And since I already know the secret, who better than me to stand guard?"

Adding to her sense of urgency, she had overheard Maxwell Bramley advising Mrs. Swanley on the location of his cousin's bed chamber and suggesting she "take the bull by the horns". Under no circumstances did Georgiana want that eager lady discovering Harry in his altogether. Her concern was purely for Harry, of course, and nothing to do with her own confused thoughts.

But her hiccups intensified as she clutched that key in her sweaty hand and took it upstairs that evening.

* * * *

On his way to bed, Harry stopped at the door of Georgiana's room. He listened a moment but there was no sound within, so he assumed she was asleep already. Good. Safely abed. He didn't want her wandering tonight and encountering Cousin Max, who was also something of a nocturnal creature. And who knew what Mrs. Swanley might get up to? These corridors could be busier than a promenade in Vauxhall Gardens this evening.

Harry had stayed up later than usual, drinking brandy with Max in his study, for as long as he knew where his cousin was, the man couldn't be pursuing anybody and making an ass of himself. But as a result of this delay he was feeling rather worse for wear. Trying to keep up with Max's drinking was always a mistake and he should have known better.

However, he made the sacrifice for Miss Hathaway, did he not? Any sore head in the morning was worth it to keep her out of Max's clutches. The girl did not deserve that.

He entered his own room and found the fire cheerfully burning, just as he liked it, even in summer. The heat replenished him somehow and he always woke refreshed. But tonight he was still too restless to sleep, so he poured yet another brandy night-cap from the tray by his bed and then paced— or rather staggered—back and forth before his fire, trying to make order out of the chaos in his brain.

Having watched Max flirting with Georgiana all evening, he had a great deal of pent up anger and frustration to dispel before he could lay down and close his eyes. He didn't really know why it bothered him to such a degree. It was not as if he wanted her for himself, was it? He simply thought she could do better than Max. Not that she wanted anybody, or so she claimed.

"I am not looking for a husband, sir. I would only misplace him, or forget to feed him, or something equally dire... young women often have other plans for their future. Not every girl seeks the bother of a husband. Men, as I have observed, are most often in the way."

Finally he set his glass on the mantle to begin undressing. He flung off his jacket and then his waistcoat, tossing them across the room. Aiming for an old chaise in the corner, he missed by several feet. Who moved the bloody chaise?

Harry groped along the mantle for his brandy glass and tripped, stubbing his toe on the fender and splashing brandy over his fingers. "Oh, ballocks!" And then he tapped his wrist and mimicked his aunt's voice, *"Henry!*

Language!" He snorted.

Ouch, but his damnable toe hurt. Everything hurt.

This being alive business was much more trying than he remembered.

Glass half way to his lips, he paused.

What was that sound? A mouse?

More like a bird chirping somewhere in his room. Or a cricket— which was, of course, not native to this country and so must be utterly lost.

Perhaps it was his imagination. Perhaps it was the drink. He took another sip of brandy, just to be sure. Silence.

Harry set his glass on the mantle and began removing his shirt, almost ripping the neck-cloth in his haste to be free of it.

There it was again. An odd chirp, a little bubble of air.

Harry looked around his room. In the light of a few candles and the glowing fire, everything seemed the same as usual. Nothing out of place.

He briskly finished removing his shirt and threw it at the chaise, missing again. Next came his boots. For that he lowered his buttocks to the leather-padded fender seat around the hearth, and tugged them off, somehow managing not to tip backward into the fire despite a distinct lack of good balance this evening. The boots were a little muddy still from his ride with Max and his aunt had spent half an hour that evening reprimanding him for wearing riding boots to dinner. But this was still his house, was it not? He would wear whatever he wanted to dinner and they could all go —

There it was again! He knew he was not imagining it now.

Barefoot, he stood in his breeches and approached his bed.

"Miss Hathaway." He rested his hands on his hips. "What, by the devil's own arse, are you up to now?"

223

* * * *

She groaned. Her hiccups had given her away. Once he began removing his clothes there was nothing she could do to stop them escaping her mouth with greater alacrity.

"Would you be so good as to come out from under my bed, Miss Hathaway?"

"How did you know it was me?" she managed meekly.

She might not be able to see him roll his eyes, but she heard it in his voice clear enough. "Who else might it be, madam? I told you I have nothing worth stealing, but I knew you'd have to see for yourself."

"I had no bad intentions, Commander," she exclaimed anxiously from her dusty hiding place. "You must believe me."

"Must I? Sometimes I wonder if you think your schemes through thoroughly before proceeding. Do you never consider the possible consequences? Out you come, madam, and explain yourself."

Oh lord, how could she do that? How to explain that she meant to wait there until he slept and then lock him in, as well as take away any other key he might have. She had to hide in his room in order to see how he got out, if it was true that Brown had been locking him in at night.

Harry had begun to pace again and she watched his feet stumble back and forth by the bed. "Even for you, Miss Hathaway, this is remarkable behavior."

"I was worried, sir, about—"

Suddenly he stopped. Fingernails were scraping at his door.

"Sir Henry," a sing-song voice floated through the key hole. "I know you are still awake. Do let me in."

"Damn it," he murmured, "Parkes was right, this is becoming a fine farce."

With desperation racing through her, Georgiana tried

to remain still, but every ounce of her wanted to crawl out, run at that door and slide her key in the lock. She would flatten herself to the door, she thought, and stop him from letting the other woman in. He'd have to pry her cold, dead hands off the door handle!

But in her agitation she banged her head under the bed and then, while rubbing it with her hand, could only watch as his feet stomped the door. A cooling draft blew across her face as he opened it.

"Mrs. Swanley? Is anything amiss?"

"I don't know, sir. Is there? I am here to cure you, if there is."

Georgiana screwed herself into a knot, trying to stay hidden, even though she desperately wanted to see what the other woman was doing.

"I regret, madam, that I cannot entertain you this evening."

"But I can entertain you," the persistent woman replied. "That's what I'm here for, ain't it?"

"I would advise you to seek out Maxwell Bramley's room, madam. I believe he is far more in need of a cure than I."

"But he said—"

"Mrs. Swanley, I appreciate your devotion to your work. It is admirable. But I am not the one who requires servicing this evening."

"Dear old Max can shift for himself. I'm here for you. He says you've had difficulties."

"*Dear Old Max* wouldn't know a true difficulty if it bit him on the hindquarters. If you have no liking to share his bed, I would pocket the money and enjoy this brief sojourn in the country. Take a few walks with the parson's wife. Enjoy yourself. Let the fresh air give your cheeks a natural blush, Mrs. Swanley, and you'll save a fortune on carmine rouge."

Georgiana could not help smiling at that. She could

well imagine Mrs. Swanley's face as that door began to close.

"Good evening, madam." Having disposed of that lady, he paced back across the room. "Well, Stowaway, I keenly await your explanation. Must I poke you out with a stick?"

Slowly she crawled out from under the bed. "I was just looking...for something I—." Oh, what was the point? "I was concerned for you, sir," it came out in a rushed whisper, "and wanted to be sure you were secure in your room...with so many other folk about."

"You don't think I can manage, madam? You think I require the assistance of —"

"A nineteen year-old girl, sir? Yes, I do. And I am heartily tired of being told my age as if I might forget it. Would you like me to remind you of yours?"

He glowered at her, hands on his hips. "What do you think you can do for me? Do you not have your own troubles? A certain newspaper column, for instance, that faces a libel suit from a man about whom it may, or may not, have been written?"

She tried to swallow, but found her throat dry. "I do not know what you mean."

"No. Of course not."

"And even if I had troubles, it would not stop me from helping you with yours."

"Putting the world to rights, eh, my little meddlesome miss?" Harry finished his brandy in one swig and then bent for the coal shovel. "So you want to help me. Like Mrs. Swanley?"

Although he hid his face, she heard the smirk in his voice. Georgiana remained undaunted. He had caught her again in another embarrassing position so she might as well plow onward and get everything out into the open. They had tip-toed around each other and the matter of his problem for long enough. She refused to be like everybody

226

else, who ignored it, hid it like a shameful sin and dare not raise the subject to him.

"Mrs. Swanley wants to help one part of you. I want to help the whole man." She took a breath to steady her nerves. "If you would let me."

"Rather brave of you. My crosses are heavy enough for *me* to bear." He dropped into a chair and stretched out his long legs, his pose careless. "What can you do? A girl who has barely been out in the world yet. How can you know what I have been through?"

"I would know if you shared anything, but you insist on keeping it all inside. Hiding from me and the world." She paused. "If I were in trouble, would you not seek to offer me assistance?"

"That's different."

"Why?"

"You're a woman." He frowned up at her, evidently annoyed. She wondered why he had not yet tossed her out of his room. But even as she thought that, here it came— "And you should not be in my room, Miss Hathaway."

Of course, he relied on what was proper only when it suited him.

"Last night you wanted me to stay here with you," she exclaimed.

She watched his fingers curl tighter around that empty glass as if he might throw it. "Last night?"

"When you called me Georgiana."

* * * *

Sprawled in his chair, clutching the empty brandy glass to his bare chest, he eyed her thoughtfully.

"You called me Georgiana," she repeated. "And you said you needed me."

"Why would I say that?"

"These past few nights I have walked with you up and down that passage and tried to keep you out of trouble," she confessed reluctantly.

Alarm rattled through him, but he kept his expression calm. Harry knew he must deal with this one step at a time or else his head would become too crowded and the rage would set in. The frustration at a failed memory; the anger at so much of his life stolen by fate. The fury of being put out to pasture before he was ready, before he had done all the things he planned.

But this girl did not deserve his wrath, any more than the ghost of poor Parkes.

"So I asked you to stay last night. Did you?" he demanded softly.

"No."

He should have felt relief, but he did not know what to call this emotion careening recklessly through him. Harry looked at his empty glass. "Then why come back tonight?"

"I hoped to keep you in your room and out of Mrs. Swanley's grasp. Sometimes, at night, you are not completely yourself, and unfortunately you have no control over it. But you know all that, of course."

She put it so simply and easily, as if it was nothing to be ashamed of.

"Shall I pour you another brandy?" she asked.

He sat forward, arms resting on his thighs. "No. I'd better not. I think I've had enough."

"The truth is, sir, you are still lost at sea. Part of you, seems to be. You have floated all alone for a long time and then you ran aground here, with no hope of rescue."

"That's your theory, is it?"

"Yes. I have given your predicament a great deal of thought."

In truth, he was touched that she cared enough to help, but she had no idea what she would be taking on. If he let her.

He had his masculine pride still, despite his

228

"predicament".

Harry set his empty glass on the floor. "You had better go to your own room."

"I'm not going anywhere unless you let me lock you in and give me your key. Brown says he's been locking your door at night, so you must have another key somewhere."

Forearms resting on his thighs, he squinted up at her, bemused. "What do you think Mrs. Swanley might do to me? You don't believe I can manage her myself?"

"*Now* you can," came the brisk reply. "But later, when you are not yourself, you might want her company. You might welcome it."

"That would save you some trouble then, would it not? Let her take me off your hands at night. Clearly I've been a great concern, making you keep me company all these nights."

She scowled fiercely. "I didn't say I minded."

Other thoughts clicked slowly into place. "Wait...you have discussed me...and this... with Brown?" he demanded tightly.

"I would not say we discussed it. I asked him to give me your key, that's all."

"But you talked together, gossiped about me wandering about at night." He got up, too angry now to sit still. "That damn fellow should know better."

"It was not his fault," she exclaimed. "He was concerned about you, just as I am. It was not gossiping at all. Nobody else knows."

"What about your dear friends? You have not shared all this with them in your letters?"

"Of course not, sir. This is our secret."

"Bloody women!" He took a step toward her, swaying slightly. "This is precisely why I didn't want you here!"

"Do not raise your voice to me."

"I shall do as I like. This is my damned house, my

229

damned room. My damned everything!"

She started for the door, but he caught her by the sleeve.

"I may not have invited you here, but *I* shall say when you leave my presence, woman!"

The rage was glowing hot now, as if he were wrought iron heated in a blacksmith's forge, ready to be bent into a new shape. He felt the hammer coming down, heard the clang echoing inside his head.

"They may have taken my life and career away from me, but here is where I am in control," he hissed. "This is my island. I say how it is."

Her eyes were wide, the long lashes still, unblinking.

"I rule this place. I, Dead Harry, take charge here. Do you comprehend me, woman? This is my world. I made it. I decide who stays and who leaves. You will *not* leave me until I am done with you."

His blood was pumping too fast, it made him light-headed for a moment. But when he closed his fingers around her arms and held her tight, his world stopped tipping and he saw clearer.

Why was he still wearing his breeches? He felt too constricted and uncomfortable in these clothes forced upon him by the rigid demands of civilization.

Ah, but *she* was here. And his nakedness made her anxious. Which was foolish, since he was in a better mood without clothes and so she should welcome it.

Her lips were slightly parted, her cheeks flushed. Harry could see his face reflected in the satiny darkness of her eyes. "When you are quite done shouting at me," she said softly. "May I speak? I know I'm supposed to hold my tongue until I'm asked, but these are unique circumstances. And I shall have bruises on my arms, if you do not stop squeezing them."

The clanging hammer stopped.

He glared down at her.

"I told nobody about our secret." She faced him bravely, chin up, hands curled into little fists at her side. She still had on the dress she'd worn at dinner, but now the front of it was covered in dust from under his bed. The woman was hard on her gowns, he mused. "Why else would I go to these extreme lengths to try and keep you in your room, if I didn't care to help you keep this secret? And you can glower at me and shout at me all you like, I am not afraid of you. I've dealt with the temper tantrums of little boys before, sir."

He narrowed his gaze and relaxed his fingers— but not enough to release her arms completely. "Should you not call me Harry by now?"

He saw her swallow and then she bent her lips in a shy smile. "Your aunt would never approve."

"She's not here." His gaze traveled down her throat to that little mole at the base— her "witch's mark".

"Why would you want me to call you Harry, when you have made it clear you do not trust me and in the daylight I am an inconvenience?"

"If I have made you feel so unwelcome, why did you come to save me tonight? Why do you care?"

She had no answer for that, apparently.

Harry bent his head and pressed his lips to that tiny mole on her skin, just as he'd wanted to on her first evening in his house. He heard her gasp, felt her shudder. Slowly he trailed the tip of his tongue all the way up her neck to her chin, her cheek, and then her ear. "It is just you and I," he whispered, "everybody is in bed now. Whether their own or somebody else's. That leaves you and me."

No response. Her eyes had turned dewy, her lashes looked heavy now and she struggled to keep them lifted.

"If you want the other key to my room, you'll have to find it," he added, mischief awakening in his veins. "Before Mrs. Swanley does."

231

Her lips parted again and then snapped shut. Apparently he had rendered her speechless. No small feat.

"Harry likes to play." He grinned.

Her brow ruffled in a frustrated frown, but she could not keep the expression for long, far too curious and amused, he suspected.

Stepping back, he spread out his arms. "Look for it. Harry will tell you when you are cold or hot."

She licked her lips, her gaze wandering down over his bared chest and then hastily looking away around his room. Harry took two more steps away from her.

"Now you are cold, Georgiana."

With one deep breath she began her search for the key.

Chapter Nineteen

Harry was different tonight. His eyes were more alive than they had been on previous nightly adventures and he seemed aware of who she was, why she was there. Was it possible that the two sides of his personality were slowly melding back together?

Excitement lifted her heart and made it beat out a new rhythm. She did not mind playing this game if it helped him recover his lost self again.

And kept Mrs. Swanley out of his bed too, of course. That was motivation enough.

So Georgiana began her hunt for his key. She checked the mantle above that roaring fire, only to be assured she was almost freezing with the cold. Next she looked in the pockets of his dressing-gown, under his chair, even inside his discarded boots— shaking them by the heel. As she moved around his room, Harry walked behind her, always keeping a distance of two or three steps.

It occurred to her, finally, that the only thing she had not searched was the man himself. She spun around to face him.

Harry stood there looking smug, hands behind his back, wearing only one garment.

The one thing left to explore.

"It's in your breeches," she said.

He arched an eyebrow. "Is it? To what do you refer, woman?"

"The key." Georgiana held out her hand. "Give it to me."

But he pursed his lips in an idle whistle and shook his head.

The wretched man did love his games. And winning them.

She took a step toward him.

233

He paused his whistle to say, "Getting warmer."

Naturally he would not make it easy for her, but in truth she rather liked that about him. Harry Thrasher was a mystery that challenged, intrigued, and fascinated her.

"Very warm now," he added as she came right up to where he stood.

Well, she had always felt quite certain that she was destined to go where no other woman dared. Gathering her courage, Georgiana reached into the fall of his buckskin breeches.

There was his fob watch. She brought that out and gave it to him, then returned her hand to the search.

"Warmer still," he muttered, sounding a little hoarse.

Her questing fingers had discovered a bulge. She knew what it was, of course, having met it before when he was naked.

"Hot," he groaned."Very hot."

"I happen to know that's not a key. It doesn't open any doors."

"Not true. I can show you what it's for, if you like. All the doors it does open."

She caressed the arching ridge and heard his breathing deepen. "I refuse to be shocked. Where's the key, Harry?"

"Impatient, aren't you? Keep looking, woman."

With a gasp of frustration, she moved her fingers to the buttons at his waist and quickly slid them open.

"Getting hotter!"

She had to pause for a moment, just to appreciate the tightness of his stomach and the splendid, powerful way all those hard muscles worked in perfect unison. There was even a kind of beauty about those scars crisscrossing his torso. A slender trail of dark curls led her gaze, and her fingertips, downward, under the opened waist of his breeches. Plunging bravely in, she tugged the buckskin from his hips.

"Thank you," he muttered wryly. "I thought you'd never get there."

"Harry Thrasher! There is no key! Did you do this just to get me to take your breeches down?"

"Well, they are very constricting and I find it easier to think without my clothes."

"Where is the key?" she demanded.

"You must keep searching. You are getting hotter. Do not give up, woman."

"I suppose this gave you a devious thrill!"

"Perhaps." He smirked. "What about you?"

She couldn't resist smiling in return. "I must admit you are not boring company."

"But I am not charming, eh?"

"Charming? No, that is not your skill. You're too rumpled... and honest."

He scowled and grabbed her hands, holding both in his. "Do you find my cousin charming?"

Georgiana chuckled. "Only in the manner of a blundering, overgrown pup. Endearing in small doses, if one does not mind the occasional puddle or torn bonnet ribbon."

This seemed to appease him. He brought her hands to his mouth and then released them. She slipped her fingers around his warm neck again. "This is where we usually kiss, Harry."

"Is it?"

"Before I say goodnight and leave you at your door."

"But I might go wandering when you leave tonight. Have you given up searching for the key that will keep me safely in my chamber?"

"I do not know where else it might be." There was surely nothing left to search.

"You found it, Georgiana," he murmured. "You found it already."

* * * *

He knew it was wrong, but he wanted her to stay and he was in a selfish mood. Had he not suffered all these guests as politely as he could? Surely he was due a reward.

On that night he was ready to give in to his raw desire, the side of Harry that did as he pleased and answered to no one. The side of Harry that still lived on that island and had begun to think like primitive man. To yearn for a mate. She had put herself there in his way, why should he not take his pleasure?

Sliding fingers through her hair he loosened the pins until a long, thick braid tumbled over her shoulder and curls framed her small face.

"I told you before that I cannot stay the night with you here," she said, her sentence punctuated by a hiccup. "I would not be satisfied with only a part of Harry, but I do not believe you can give all of yourself, and neither of us wants to marry. That much has already been decided."

True. He did not want marriage, did he? Had he not, only yesterday, assured himself that he was a danger to this young woman? She had mysterious plans for her future and they did not include marriage. But if she spent the night with him, Harry would be obliged to marry her. He was, despite everything, a gentleman. And she was not a hussy— a light-skirt chasing after a brief thrill and nothing more— but a young woman of good family, respectable.

Tonight he felt calmer, his mind moved at a regular pace and no longer felt overcrowded, or over-stimulated. The touch of her gentle hands possessed a very soothing quality and he wanted her to keep stroking him until he fell asleep. Well, on second thought, perhaps "soothing" was not exactly the right word for what she did to him. But he liked it.

As he'd said to her, his aunt was not there. Why did they care about proper?

Christ, he was drunk. Should never have tried to keep up with Max when he was so out of practice.

"Then lay with me until I sleep," he urged, coming to a compromise. Or as near as he could get to one in his current state of warm arousal and intoxication.

"Lay with you?" Georgiana cast him a skeptical look and he smiled.

"Is that too much to ask?" His fingers worked quickly to separate the strands of her braid and leave those thick brown locks cascading free, all the way to her waist. "You said you wanted to help me."

Did she know how much pain he'd been in? How much he'd lived through, and died through? If she did she would take pity, he thought with a sharp burst of drunken sulkiness.

"Lay with me," he growled. "That is all I ask."

* * * *

There was a key somewhere. There must be. He had been using something to get out of this room after Brown locked his door from the outside, but he was not going to tell her apparently. Then she would just have to find out for herself and search again once he slept.

Staying with him was a risk, of course— she would be a fool not to know that. But even in his state of undress she trusted Harry. He had always told her what he thought and what he wanted; he was never sly.

"This is all you ask?" She looked up at him, her hands resting on his shoulders.

"All I ask," he vowed solemnly.

With her fingers, she traced his lips slowly, felt their curve as if she meant to hold it in her memory. "Just one more kiss then," she murmured, wondering whether she would be able to resist more.

Suddenly he lifted her off her feet, not waiting any longer, and lowered her to the assortment of furs and blankets beside the fire.

"No more of your games?" She caught her breath as he kissed the side of her neck and she felt that thudding pulse begin again. The man seemed to know exactly how and where to touch her and make her forget herself. He wound her up like one of his clockwork creatures.

"No more games tonight," he murmured throatily, almost purring. "We'll be together, but very still and on our best behavior."

"Hmm." There was nothing more she could say for his lips were on hers, kissing hungrily, urgently. His hands swept her body, exploring every curve with tenderness, the material of her gown shifting under his palm but never lifted. When he moved his lips to her jaw, nibbling playfully, she groaned. "This is not lying still, Harry. Or behaving!"

"Just one more kiss you said."

"Harry!"

"Georgiana," he groaned, nuzzling beneath her air, burying his face in her loose hair. "I am still kissing you. I am not yet done. I might never be done. Resign yourself to it, for I am very thorough."

She laughed breathlessly because his words tickled her neck, and his fingers did the same to her nipple where it rose in a taut peak against the front of her gown.

Thus, for the next few minutes he made his "kiss" linger. With his lips and hands he worshipped her, petted her, covered her in adulation— any part of her skin that was bared for his caress. Georgiana had never imagined how a man might trace the vein in her wrist with his damp tongue and leave her in a state of heated sensual anticipation of something more. She could never have guessed that the gentlest nibble upon her earlobe would leave her squirming with restless, breathless delight.

He knew all these things, however, and diligently saw to it that her eyes were opened to all these teasing pleasures. She might have been an exotic princess being tended to by her gorgeous, naked slave.

The thought amused her, made her blush and close her eyes.

He made no move to go further than the top of her stockings and, just there, on the trembling flesh of her inner thigh, inches from her garter, he placed the most tender of all his kisses. At least, it began that way. But when she gasped out his name again and clasped a handful of his hair, he opened his lips to suck upon the damp skin, nibbling there as he had done with her ear, leaving her panting, melting into the furs upon which she lay sprawled. And then, as she pushed her gown down over her thighs, he made a small, low sound of frustration, but did not try to prevent her.

Finally, with one hand on her waist, the other arm beneath her head, he held her close, saying nothing. They lay together before his fire, the air hot and moist now, shimmering with need and a palpable desire, barely restrained.

It was as if he had struck the flint inside her, started a spark that now smoldered keenly and impatiently. When he moved his left leg and rested it over hers, his nakedness was even harder to ignore, but Georgiana soon heard his breathing fall to a more regular pace and she knew he was close to sleep. In the heat of that room, she too felt her eyelids grow heavy, her body relaxed under his. But she did not sleep.

He, of course, had downed several glasses of brandy that night before he came to bed, which helped lull him into his dreams.

How strange it was to lie there with him beside the crackling fire. As her senses took it all in, her thoughts came in bubbles, floating and popping in the air, like those hiccups that had betrayed her.

His breath blew steadily into a curl of Georgiana's

hair, moving it against her neck. His skin held its own heat, releasing his scent into the air— leather, brandy and something spicy. The weight of his hand on her waist, and his broad thigh across her hips, did not make her feel trapped, as she might have expected, but comforted and needed.

It was peaceful, almost like her dream of lying under mangroves with the ocean waves sizzling over sand nearby. If only life could be that uncomplicated— just a man and a woman enjoying themselves, taking pleasure as and when they wanted it.

But real life was not that way, of course. In real life there were consequences, customs and conventions.

Their island was different.

Shockingly, he had nibbled her thigh. She could still feel the mark he must have left there and it seemed likely she would never be the same again.

Curiously enough, her hiccups had ceased.

When she whispered his name and there was no reply, Georgiana felt safe to investigate, but as he felt her move he tightened his hold to prevent her leaving.

"Thank you for saving me from Mrs. Swanley," he said sleepily.

Oh yes, she heard the amusement in his tone.

But he did not open his eyes.

* * * *

Harry woke a few hours later. His fire had died down and his mate still lay within his arms— sadly fully clothed, but for her slippers. Her sweet scent surrounded him. He inhaled a great breath of it and watched the dark curl dance beside her cheek when he blew upon it. Those lush lashes fluttered against pale freckles and he smiled, remembering how they had first bewildered him, made him want to touch her.

For once he could remember the events of the

evening before. Every kiss was held in his memory, tied up like a bundle of love letters— ugh what a dreadfully sappy, romantic thought. Must be drunk still.

As he lay there, letting the pleasure wash over him again, every part of his body, inside and out, tingled with anticipation. There was an excitement, an eagerness to greet the day that he had not felt in a long time.

Somehow she had broken the spell in which he'd been held for the past two years. Perhaps the two Harrys finally had a reason to join forces again. Georgiana Hathaway was a formidable, slippery creature and far too much for one man to handle.

Look how she had tricked him into falling asleep, instead of seducing her.

Max would despair. *You were in the Navy, Harry, for pity's sake! This chaste life is not what I expect from a sailor.*

Georgiana's determination to keep him away from that other woman, while pretending it was all for his own good, amused Harry greatly. Did she really think he could not defend himself from a woman like Mrs. Swanley? That was easy, compared to fighting against the temptation *she* brought him.

He ran his thumb across her lips and felt her sigh as she nestled closer.

His gallant protector. Where had she been all his life?

* * * *

Georgiana woke as dawn light broke in blush streaks across the sky outside her window. Yes, *her* window.

She sat up and found that she was back in her own room. Was it all another dream?

Her gown had been removed and her corset, but she still wore her petticoat, chemise and stockings. Surely she must have slept deeply not to feel herself being disrobed. But there was her dress from last night, laid neatly over the brass railing at the foot of her bed.

241

If it was not a dream, Harry must have carried her back to her room.

She could smell his scent on her still, as if she had bathed in him.

And then, as another thought came to her, she hurriedly pulled up her petticoat to examine her inner thigh just above her garters.

Thus she learned for sure it was not a dream.

Last night she had slept with a man while there was no intention, or expectation, of marriage on either side.

She fell back to her pillow with an enormous sigh and a smile on her face. It all felt very naughty, although it could have been a great deal worse. Especially considering her record for burgeoning disaster.

She could manage this perfectly well, she decided, arms stretching over her head. It was just a little attraction and that was all. He was a man and she was a woman. These things happened.

That wicked smile still twitching over her lips, Georgiana wriggled deeper under the covers, hiding her hot cheeks even though there was nobody to see them.

Chapter Twenty

Mrs. Swanley was set up on the lawn with an easel and all the tools she needed for her watercolor masterpiece of Woodbyne Abbey.

"What am I supposed to do with this?" she whispered to Georgiana.

"I'm sure you'll manage perfectly. Splash the paint about and frown a lot. I have found that even if you do not really know what you are doing, as long as you look confident nobody notices. When it comes down to it, we're all just pretending to know what we're doing."

The supposed artiste gave her a strange look. "You're not quite the naive little miss I took you for, are you?"

"I hope not, Mrs. Swanley."

Lady Bramley was so pleased by the idea of this painting that it could not now be got out of. She was already cleaning a space in the hall where it would hang.

"I cannot let anybody see it until it is finished," Mrs. Swanley explained at dinner, after facing a fleet of questions about the progress of her work. "And I would rather not discuss it at this stage. I hope you understand, your ladyship, but I do my best work in private."

"The artistic mind must have its quirks," said Georgiana jauntily.

"Oh, of course," Lady Bramley agreed, trying to look as if she knew a vast number of artists and had familiarity with their work methods.

"You and Mrs. Swanley have formed a friendship, it seems," Harry muttered, standing behind her in the hall while they all admired the clean area on the paneling where his aunt planned to hang the completed art.

Max had proceeded to quarrel with his mother about the direction of the wind that day, or something similar as was their habit, and Mrs. Swanley attempted to keep the peace. Nobody, therefore, paid attention to *them*.

"Why would we not? We are both women of a similar type."

He arched an eyebrow. "You are?"

"We are both resourceful and believe in a lady making the most of her gifts, not being held back by convention."

"I see. So I have two revolutionaries in my house."

"Precisely." She grinned over her shoulder and whispered. "Now you understand the necessity of locking your door at night."

"On the contrary. If you're going to burn my house down and riot on the lawns, I need to be able to get out and save myself." He paused and she felt his breath tickle the edge of her ear. "Unless you mean to save me, before you wreck the place."

He still had not told her how he managed to escape his locked room, much to her irritation. The night she stayed with him, he could have used her key, of course, but that did not explain all the other times he managed to go wandering.

"Georgiana," he had said solemnly to her the morning after, "do you honestly think I would be tempted by Mrs. Swanley? Can you not credit me with some sense, despite the various holes in my brain?"

"She said her charms are hard to resist. She's the best in the business."

"Hmm." He placed a finger to his chin. "Perhaps I made a mistake then and should have let her in." Then, seeing her expression, he had laughed. "Even slightly intoxicated I knew better, Georgiana. You are far more tempting to me than she is."

He picked up his book immediately after, still smiling and shaking his head, apparently unaware of the devastating effect such a comment would make upon a girl who had never been found attractive by anybody — except Dickon Moone, the blacksmith's son, who, when

244

they were ten, offered to marry her. Of course, his motivation was entirely due to the new bow and quiver of rubber-tipped arrows she'd received for her birthday. When Georgiana made it clear that she would not share her splendid weapon with him, Dickon's mercenary interest in marriage quickly waned.

Commander Sir Henry Thrasher did not give out flattery for the sake of it and he was not after her bow and arrows. Nevertheless, she had apparently gone from being merely "not grotesque" and "mostly symmetrical", to being a creature of temptation. A woman whose thigh he kissed and left branded with a very tiny bruise.

This conversation was the only one they had in regard to the events of that steamy evening in his chamber. Words were not always necessary, however. A look, a slight brush of the fingertips, a shared smile— all were sufficient to bring that memory back and conjure with it every gloriously naughty sensation.

She knew now that she did not need to worry about him wandering into Mrs. Swanley's arms one night for he no longer took nighttime trips as Dead Harry. He was, however, still in the mood to play.

After dinner the foursome of herself, Harry, Mrs. Swanley, and Max Bramley often sat down to cards. The Commander proved himself adept and seldom lost a game, much to his cousin's annoyance. He also brought Lady Bramley's owl out of his study one evening and they all had the chance to ask it their fortune.

Georgiana was astonished by the remarkable foresight of that stuffed bird, for each paper slip that fired from its mended beak contained a Shakespearean quote seemed tailor-made for the person who sat before it.

For Harry, the wise bird had this to say, ***The fool doth think himself to be wise, but a wise man knows himself to be a fool.***

All at the table agreed, laughing heartily. Even Harry

gave an amused shrug of acceptance to the truth of this.

Next came Mrs. Swanley, who, unable to wait, grabbed the owl before it could be passed around the table. A moment later she received unexpected encouragement for her artistic endeavors when the owl assured her that, *We know what we are, but not what we may be.*

And for Mr. Maxwell Bramley there was only a teasing slight. *I would challenge you to a battle of wits, but I see you are unarmed.*

"Mine is not even a fortune," he complained, tossing the little scrap of paper aside and reaching for his port. "I shouldn't be surprised if you made these up yourself, Harry."

"I certainly did not. This owl is far cleverer than me."

Finally it was Georgiana's turn. With baited breath she waited until the little tube of paper shot forth into her palm. Then, slowly she unrolled it and read,

'Tis one thing to be tempted, another thing to fall.

"Do read it out loud," Mrs. Swanley exclaimed. "We must know what it says for you."

But she hid it quickly and laughed it off, not meeting Harry's eye. She had no doubt that he had made these fortunes himself and set them inside his aunt's owl to entertain his guests.

But was this "fortune" a polite warning for her, or did her blushes amuse him?

* * * *

"There you are, Miss Hathaway," his cousin bellowed upon seeing her enter the dining room for breakfast one morning. "We are going boating on the lake, and I insist you ride with me. My cousin has quite suddenly decided to open the summerhouse."

She glanced over at Harry, who wore all the proper garments today— shirt, waistcoat, neck-cloth and coat.

Only his hair remained in its usual disheveled state. For once he was not reading at the table, but paying attention to the conversation of his guests.

"I thought it was time I aired the place out," he said. "Mrs. Swanley can get a better feel for the house if she views it from the lake." And he looked down at his plate, deliberately, Georgiana sensed, not meeting her eye. Why suddenly did he avoid looking at her again? "It is a perfect day for boating and fun. As you say, Miss Hathaway, everybody needs some of that. One never knows when the English summer weather might change for the worse."

The summerhouse, Georgiana knew, was a small building with arched windows on all four sides and a weathervane on the top. It sat on its own grassy island in the middle of the lake and, according to Brown, was full of mildew for it had not been used, or aired out, in years— since Harry was a boy.

At that moment the dining room door opened and Lady Bramley swept in, holding an opened letter.

"Are you coming boating too, Lady Bramley?" Georgiana asked.

"No. I must oversee arrangements for the card party tonight. Indeed I have a hundred things to do."

"Perhaps I should stay and help you."

"No, no. You go and enjoy yourself on the lake, while you still can. The summer will not last forever and you'll be going home soon enough to Allerton Square." Lady Bramley waved her letter. "I received correspondence from your father this morning and he is in some haste for you to return home. It seems your mother has taken to her confinement earlier than expected and two of your younger siblings have fallen ill. He is quite overwhelmed by the household chaos and requests that you return to be of assistance. Apparently you are useful in such situations and are known to have a calm head when nursing the sick. He suggests sending a carriage for you at the end of the week, but you may take mine, of course."

Georgiana felt as if the floor dropped away beneath her feet. The room spun and then came to an abrupt halt. She had been so caught up in her games with Harry that she had barely noticed the summer slipping by. She might have known these happy days could not last.

"But what about the ball?" she managed at last.

"Yes. That is a pity, but I daresay we shall manage without you. You are needed at home, and I can hardly keep you from your father just for a ball."

Had somebody stuck a pin in her and let all the air out? Just like that the rest of that summer was wrenched away from her.

"But do take care not to fall into the lake today," the lady continued. "My son rows a boat just as he dances—with his eyes closed and trusting to fate."

"Nonsense, mama, I shall be on my very best behavior with such precious cargo on my little boat," Max Bramley gushed, beaming across the table at Georgiana, whose own lips had gone numb. "And I shall most certainly keep my eyes open to train them upon this lovely lady while we still have her."

* * * *

Max Bramley was one of those men who thought the way to impress a woman was to scare her half to death.

The moment she was in that little rowboat with him he began foolishly rocking it about, pretending he would capsize the thing if she did not smile at him. He could not possibly be drunk as it was too early in the day, so Georgiana could only conclude he imagined this irritating behavior to be entertaining.

Perhaps there was a time when she would have shrieked at the thrill of it and slapped at him with her bonnet, but she was much too mature for these childish antics now. She sat rigidly in her end of the boat, gripped

Lady Bramley's parasol over her shoulder, and advised Mr. Bramley to conserve his energy for the exercise of rowing the boat there and back. In the heat of the day he was already perspiring heavily and the exertions of performing for her would surely cause him to melt away entirely.

"Miss Hathaway, you must tell me all about your time at that ladies academy," he exclaimed with a sly grin. "I long to know what goes on in such places." He pulled back jerkily and unevenly on the oars, splashing more water onto her skirt as the rowboat lurched across the surface of the lake with absolutely none of the smooth, graceful motion for which it was built.

"I doubt it would be of much interest to you, Mr. Bramley." She was really not in the mood for this jaunt across the lake, especially not since it had been pointed out to her that the summer would be over for her soon enough. Sooner than expected. A week from now she would be back in her father's house, on Allerton Square, and all this would seem very far away. She would be sewing by the fire, listening to her little siblings squabbling and rain tapping at the windows, being nagged by her stepmother for some minor indiscretion. No doubt the second Mrs. Hathaway would be even shorter-tempered and harder to please when she was in this condition.

Woodbyne Abbey would seem like a different world.

"No interest in your school, Miss Hathaway? On the contrary. That ladies academy is of great interest. One should always attempt to uncover the secrets of the enemy camp."

"Enemy camp?"

"They teach you strategy against gentlemen like me at that school, do they not? They teach you cunning measures by which to capture my heart and throw me in irons."

He said a lot more, but she was looking across at the other boat and wondering what Harry could find to talk about with Mrs. Swanley. There appeared to be a great deal of parasol twirling and laughter going on. "I'm sorry, what?"

"It is all about hoodwinking the unsuspecting male into marriage."

"Hoodwinking?" She had never heard that word before.

"To blind by covering the eyes, Miss Hathaway. The female animal, intent on courtship, enlists many rotten methods to mislead the male and leave him completely befuddled."

"I would never want to hoodwink anybody, Mr. Bramley."

"But you are looking for a husband, are you not?"

She gave an exasperated sigh. "No, I am not."

"All single ladies are seeking an eligible bachelor, Miss Hathaway." He jerked on the oars again and the boat rocked. "I know all your battle plans to scupper us."

"Goodness," she exclaimed, "I'm surprised you want to spend any time with ladies if we are so very devious. It cannot be good for your health to always be on your guard against us."

He laughed. "You have me there. I simply cannot stay away. Like strong drink, Faro and horse races, the ladies are bad for me and yet here I am, constantly drawn in by their beguiling methods of distraction."

"Perhaps you let yourself be drawn in because you enjoy it. I know few men who are forced to enjoy themselves, not many who do not do exactly what they want to do."

Again she looked over at the other boat. Sunlight, dancing on the water, leapt up and dazzled her sight, making her eyes water. Quickly she adjusted Lady Bramley's parasol to shade her face from the glare. The last thing she needed was another freckle.

"I do enjoy it when I have such pretty company as I

have today," he said.

"Yes," she murmured, "Mrs. Swanley is very beautiful."

"And I do love it when I have a lady's full attention."

"I suppose she has more sophisticated conversation and knows all the right things to say."

The boat drifted and bobbed as he lifted his oars out of the water and leaned forward. "Miss Hathaway, you really must try to hide your feelings a little better. It won't do to let him see you're smitten."

"I beg your pardon?"

Max shook his head. "It seems they didn't teach you how to be aloof at that school, eh?"

Aloof? It was too late for that, she thought, chagrinned.

"The trouble with Harry is that he's been alone too long. He's out of practice with women, as I warned him weeks ago." He pulled back on the oars again. "Don't let him break your heart, Miss Hathaway. Remember he doesn't know what he's doing. Doesn't know his own strength. It is best not to take anything he says or does to heart."

Yes, she had been warned by everybody. Even Harry had referred to the holes in his brain and told her she stayed there at her own risk. Yet she had cast all those warnings aside and taken the banister. Would she land, yet again, without dignity? It was too late now. Already sliding down, she could not be stopped without injury.

He had said nothing about the news that came that morning. Did not seem to have any opinion about her leaving his house. Why would he? And why should it matter so to her? She would move on to another adventure.

Or not.

Her father's letter seemed to suggest he expected her to go home and play nursemaid to her young siblings, to attend her stepmother in the months of confinement, and to manage the house for him. It might be that she never had another chance to escape again, and she would be trapped there taking care of the children that his second wife continually produced.

With this glum thought on her mind, she let Max Bramley take her hand and help her out of the boat. The summerhouse doors were all open and vases filled with roses helped sweeten the fusty air inside. A mildewed sofa had been covered with a silk embroidered blanket and a silver dish of strawberries sat waiting on a small table. Clearly Harry had prepared the place for their visit.

He must really want to impress his guests with the view, but did they have to come all the way out here to see it, she thought churlishly. Her feet and gown were now wet thanks to Max Bramley's clumsy rowing and the boat had been so ill-managed on the journey across the lake that Georgiana felt certain she had thrice come close to falling in and drowning.

Perhaps she did not like boats and water so much after all and would have been a very poor sailor, had she been born male and therefore given the opportunity.

Chapter Twenty-One

It was warm inside, sunlight beaming down through the many glass panels, and Georgiana thought it the prettiest place on the grounds, despite its damp and neglected state. With a little care the summerhouse could be quite beautiful, but the same could be said of everything on the estate. With only the aging Brown and part-time Sulley to maintain the place it had been sinking slowly in the past few years.

Hopefully, since Harry was ready to open the summerhouse again, he felt the same about the rest of his house. There was definitely a brighter, more cheerful air inside the Abbey these days.

He now stood with Mrs. Swanley, pointing out the house from this view. The pride in his stance made it clear he loved the place, however much of a burden others might think it.

"Do have a strawberry, Miss Hathaway." Mr. Bramley stood beside her with the silver dish of juicy crimson berries. So she took one and sat upon the sofa. "I hope I have not deflated your mood," he added, hovering beside her. "I meant it only for your own good."

"Yes, of course."

"I have known my cousin thirty years, faults and all," he whispered. "Since he returned from sea he's been rather difficult to deal with, hence my mother's concern, I suppose."

"And yours, Mr. Bramley."

"Mine?"

"When you brought Mrs. Swanley here."

He took out a handkerchief and wiped his glistening neck. Evidently he was not a man used to the exertion of rowing across a lake.

"I am not so naive, Mr. Bramley, that I do not know her original purpose here and it was not to paint the house."

He sneezed and blew his nose, muttering about the summer air being filled with "floating things".

"I am sure both you and Lady Bramley had the best of intentions and your own ideas for getting him out of his study," she added.

"Quite. You are something new and lively, of course. Something to shake up the dust. My mother knew that when she brought you here."

That was not what Georgiana meant. She was thinking of the lady's idea for a ball to reintroduce her nephew to society and find him a wife. But Max Bramley apparently had much to get off his chest and he gave her no chance to speak just then.

"The truth is, Miss Hathaway, I know a little more about what makes a man happy and I wisely chose a professional to help Harry out of his doldrums. I knew Mrs. Swanley would be in no danger of losing her way, or expecting something from my cousin that he is not able to give." He said all this in a kindly voice, as if she was a little girl to whom he had to explain a hard truth. "My mother, on the other hand, has chosen an amateur, a novice for this task. I fear she did not give due consideration to the wounds you might suffer in the process. She gave no thought to the fact that you will, inevitably, be set adrift again. Sadly my mother thinks of people like you to be dispensable. You must not despise her for it. She cannot help the way she sees the world, and she is too old to learn anything new." He paused to rip a fat strawberry from its emerald stem and swallow it so quickly she could not believe he tasted it. "Your heart is vulnerable, but she did not think of that when she brought you here. Your every thought and feeling is apparent on your face, my dear girl. As I said, they didn't school you on the art of being aloof, did they?"

She stared out across the still lake. On this little island

they were surrounded by water that shone in all directions like a polished mirror reflecting the midday sun. It should have been beautiful, but the day was spoiled now by a shadow which, although unseen, was nonetheless pervasive. "People like me? You said she thinks of people like me to be dispensable?"

"You must not mind me, Miss Hathaway. Nobody ever does mind me, as Harry would tell you." With quick fingers he searched through the silver bowl for one of the plumpest, most succulent offerings, clumsily squashing a few smaller berries in the process. "I would not blame you for trying to win my cousin over while you are here. For a newspaperman's daughter it would be quite a coup. You landed on your feet the moment you caught my mama's notice and she is eager for Harry to produce those long-awaited heirs to Woodbyne. I suppose you seized your opportunity as any clever girl would."

What Bramley meant, of course, was that she was not of their class. Whether he tried to be kind and helpful, or simply to insult her and put her in her place, she could not decide

"But life with my dear cousin Harry— despite all this," he gestured across the lake, so that anyone watching would think him harmlessly pointing out the scenery, "would not be smooth sailing. You would both be desperate to get out within a year. Even *if* you managed to get him to the altar in the first place." He laughed emptily. "Surely he has told you his thoughts on marriage— how he is not fit for it. The little Milhaven hussy dug her nails in the moment he let down his guard, and I daresay he never recovered from that travesty."

A moment later the Commander left Mrs. Swanley and, with both hands behind his back, strode over to where they sat. This cut off their conversation, much to her intense relief.

"What do *you* think of the view, Miss Hathaway?"

255

"Breathtaking, sir." But her head was hurting, her thoughts racing.

"It was worth coming all this way across the lake in the company of my irritating cousin?"

"Certainly." She did not want to smile at him too much. Suddenly she was very self-conscious as she realized her growing admiration for Harry must have been so easy to read upon her face. If Mr. Bramley noticed it, even in his frequent state of intoxication, she must have made herself dreadfully obvious. Restraint had never been one of her assets.

No wonder Harry kept referring to her youth in a mocking fashion. He would never take her seriously. And Lady Bramley, who usually thought she knew best about everything and insisted upon getting her own way, gave no opposition when her father wanted her home? Perhaps they were all eager to be rid of her now. Perhaps the lady feared she had ambitions above her station in life, as Maxwell Bramley suggested. Had he whispered in his mother's ear too?

"Offer the strawberries to Mrs. Swanley, will you, Max?" Harry muttered.

"You take them."

But Harry stood firm and glowered down at his cousin so fiercely that Max eventually got up with a groan, grabbed the silver dish and stormed off to where the other lady waited by the bulrushes at the edge of the little island.

Harry promptly dropped to the empty seat beside Georgiana. "What were you and my cousin conversing about so deeply? You looked enthralled."

"Did I?" If she had a fan she would have fluttered it.

He scowled, leaning forward, resting his arms on his thighs and with hands clasped together. "He's trying his arts upon you, no doubt."

"Like you with Mrs. Swanley, sir, I can look after myself. It is all just silly games, is it not?"

"Sir? Now we are back to that?"

"I think it's for the best, don't you?" She took a deep breath. "At the end of this week I'll be gone, the game will be over, and we'll both have other things to think about."

Harry turned his head. Hair flopped over the creases in his brow. "What prompted this change?"

"It is not a change, sir, merely an observation of how quickly time passes and how we are destined to take separate paths." He was a man far above her in consequence, but she had allowed herself to forget that, too stupidly flattered by his attention and by Lady Bramley taking her in as a charity case. Even that little dog was in on it— letting her think she was a friend at last.

And where would it all lead? To her ruin.

There could be nothing else awaiting her at the end of this slippery banister. No one to catch her.

"This was all for you, you know," he said quietly. "The trip out here. I thought you would like the summerhouse and the strawberries. I would have brought you here alone, had my cousin not decided to join us."

"I do like the summerhouse. Very much." He had done this for *her*? Why? Sudden panic ripped claws through her heart. Why would he bring her out here to an island in the middle of the lake? She was trapped here, surrounded on all sides by water. How ironic— she had rescued him from his deserted island, and now he brought her out here.

Harry rubbed his thigh with one hand. "I thought it was the sort of thing a young lady would like, but then, as you have observed before, I do not know a vast deal about young ladies. Not anymore."

Her heart ached where those panicked-cat claws had rendered slashes through it.

Today should have been such a beautiful, sunny summer day. But sunlight, of course, was not only warm and bright, it also had a tendency to catch things in its glare that one might otherwise wish not to see.

"I'm sure you know plenty about ladies really, sir." After all, he had known exactly how to steal her heart, had he not?

"I thought I did. Before you came."

He looked lost again and confused, as he stared off through the open doors and across the still surface of the lake. Once more he rubbed his thigh, before clasping his hands together.

"What are you thinking now, Georgiana? Usually you are full of questions and opinions. You are being strangely quiet and, while I never thought to hear these words upon my lips, I miss your chatter. I can only assume something is wrong, but it is not like you to keep it inside, unexpressed at the first opportunity."

She sighed and looked around at all the glittering windows of his summerhouse. "I was just thinking it's a jolly good thing my friend Miss Melinda Goodheart is not here or something would break all this glass, sooner or later. She is extremely heavy-handed."

"Ah, yes. I remember." He fidgeted, cleared his throat. "I also remember you promised me that you are always truthful and always say exactly what you mean. *Just as you know what you want, I know what I want.* Those were your words. So I must ask you—"

"I have enjoyed my stay at Woodbyne," she blurted. "It was kind of you to put up with me so long and you have—"

"To marry me, Georgiana."

At the bank side, his cousin was feeding strawberries to Mrs. Swanley and they were both laughing, paying no attention to the two people inside the summerhouse. It seemed to her as if time stopped, even the geese on the water were still and silent.

Again she looked desperately around at all that water surrounding them, stopping her from fleeing this conversation. The boats were tied up and one could not make a hasty exit in a rowboat, especially when one's rowing skills were questionable.

The summerhouse on its isolated little island, suddenly seemed menacing, a pretty prison.

* * * *

He had made up his mind somewhere half way across that lake, with Mrs. Swanley's high-pitched, empty laughter ringing in his ears — too much laughter over some unfunny remark he'd made. When he knew his cousin was rowing especially slowly to spend time alone with Georgiana, and the sun was beating down on his head, making it throb.

Somehow he had to make her stay at Woodbyne. He was not certain how it could be achieved, but he'd find a way.

He did not think of marriage until he sat beside her on that mildewed sofa and she reminded him of the fact that she would soon be leaving. Then it felt like that moment— the moment when he should give the signal to fire the guns.

She had not replied, but was looking at him in mild horror.

"It seems the right thing to do," he said somberly.

"The right thing to do?" Her words fell heavily, with a tint of sarcasm.

"After what happened between us. I must do the gentlemanly thing."

A deep groan came out of her and she sagged in the chair for a moment, before straightening her spine again, shaking her head and looking out across the lake. "It is absolutely not necessary. Please never speak of it again."

This was not how it was supposed to go. He scowled. "You dismiss my offer, as if it is nothing more than a dandelion seed landing on your shoulder."

"I know you always want to do the right thing and would propose to a woman even if she is unsuited. That you would sacrifice yourself to save a lady's reputation."

"Then why do you not—"

"It is only your perception that my reputation is endangered. It is not. Nobody knows about our evenings together."

Frustrated, he whispered angrily, "*I* know."

"But I do not want to marry you, Harry." She finally looked at him again. "I do not want to marry anybody. Not yet, in any case. I might never want to marry. I do not know. As you keep saying, I am too young." She smiled, but her eyes were sad. "Thank you for the offer. I am honored and flattered. But we both know you don't want a wife any more than I want a husband. And to be perfectly honest, I would never marry a man who thinks it is his *duty*."

"I see." His jaw hurt from grinding.

"I hope you do not think I came here with an intent to catch a husband. To *hoodwink* you into marriage."

"Of course not. You told me that from the start."

"Then you should understand."

His innards had gone cold, despite the sunny day. "So you would chose writing that foolish column for your father's paper over marriage to me?"

She blinked, her face paled under the freckles and her mouth tightened.

"Has the sun gone to your head?" he demanded. "I offer you all this, everything I have, and you reject me because of this wretched idea of adventure you seem to have stuck in your addled head. You think the world out there is waiting for you, Georgiana Hathaway, to set it to rights? All by yourself?" She had wounded him with her flat refusal and he could not stop himself from wanting to wound her in return.

Her lips popped open. "Yes, I have an ambition to

260

write. I want to do many things with my life, other than marry and birth a battalion of children. All this I told you before, just as you told me you do not want a wife. Now you change your mind, because you think you have to marry me. Out of charity, or pity, or whatever you wish to call it. What foundation for a good marriage would that be?" She paused. "You must know I am right, Harry."

He briefly covered his face with his hands, trying to calm his anger and whatever other emotion currently whirled around inside his mind. Then he scraped fingers back through his hair and let out a tense breath.

"We are still friends, are we not?" She put her head on one side.

Harry sniffed and looked away. "I don't know." Then he felt her hand reaching for his clenched fingers and he relented. A little. "I suppose so."

"Good." She sighed deeply.

But, unable to sit still another moment, he released her hand and got up.

* * * *

Georgiana's heart was pounding. An odd tightness in her throat made it necessary to say nothing more just then. As he left her on the sofa, she put her hands together in her lap and looked over at his cousin and Mrs. Swanley to be sure they were still busy— which they were. She closed her eyes, desperately fighting back the tears that challenged her resolve.

She had made her decision.

It was for the best and she could not regret it. Ever.

A husband was the worst thing for her future. The Commander, a knight of the realm, a war hero, would not appreciate a wife who wrote scandalous columns in the newspaper. He had just admitted as much. She would have to give all that up, if she accepted his proposal. It would forever be a matter of contention between them. One of many, including the differences in their status and upbringing. Georgiana would argue her point for hours, and he— if he disagreed— would simply walk off and hide behind a locked door. Then she would have no recourse. He, the man and master of the house, would have all the power.

There would go every chance for adventure and travel.

Wherever they went— if she could ever get him out of his study— people would look at her in disdain as an "opportunist" and they would wonder what the Commander ever saw in her.

She could hear the spiteful gossip already.

She threw herself at him, and the poor man had to marry her. Her father is nothing but new money. Don't you know who she is? Why, that wicked chit who set fire to the wig of Viscount Fairbanks and dragged her family into scandal. Dead Harry Thrasher only married her to save her reputation.

Her decision, therefore, was sound.

If only her insides were not in turmoil.

Chapter Twenty-Two

The trip to the summerhouse was brought to a brisk halt, as Harry stormed to the edge of the island and began untying the boats.

"Going back already, old chap?" his cousin exclaimed.

"I have work to do and wasted my time long enough," came the terse reply. "You can stay if you wish."

But nobody wanted to stay longer. Mrs. Swanley declared herself inspired to get on with her painting, and Georgiana simply walked toward the boats, saying nothing. Since the ladies were leaving and the strawberries were all eaten, Max Bramley had nothing to stay for.

Soon they were all on their way back across the lake, in the same boats as before. If Mr. Bramley spoke to her, she did not know it, her mind was too full.

If only her friends were there and she could discuss all this with them. Melinda would tell her she was mad to reject a proposal of marriage from a handsome man of consequence. Emma would urge her to follow her heart.

Whatever that meant.

She felt sick and overheated. The parasol seemed to give her no shade.

Suddenly Lady Bramley's little dog came running down the slope at full gallop, chasing geese and causing a ruckus that drew everybody's notice. Somehow the creature had escaped his owner to go exploring, and he was so excited that he could not stop at the edge. With a plop he landed, surprised, among the squawking, disgruntled geese and sank directly. He came up again, panting and paddling frantically with his short legs, but he drifted away from the grass instead of toward it and quickly began to lose strength. Clearly the little beast was no swimmer.

Georgiana dropped the parasol and leapt overboard without another thought. Their boat was closest, and she did not wait to see if anyone else had observed the dog's plight.

"Miss Hathaway! Good lord! Do take care!"

Fortunately her happy youth in the countryside had given her the opportunity to swim, although it was an exercise forbidden to her. She had never, however, swum in a gown and petticoats. The fabric, she rapidly discovered, hindered her legs as she tried to kick, but in a series of ungainly splashes and sputterings she made her way to where the Lady Bramley's uncivil pet had got itself tangled in some weeds and barely kept his snout above water.

With ears flat to its head, the dog allowed her to scoop him out of danger.

No sooner had Georgiana saved the wriggling wet lump of fur than she herself was likewise in need of rescue, but the Commander had already dived in after her and he swam with a much stronger, faster stroke to reach them.

What happened next was all a blur.

* * * *

"Miss Hathaway! Henry! What have you been up to? I told you all to take care today on that lake." Lady Bramley dashed across the hall as the bedraggled party returned from their outing. Only as she drew nearer did she notice her baby clutched in Georgiana's arms. "Horatio! My darling Horatio! What has happened to you? What have they done to you?"

"The rotten little thing fell in, and Miss Hathaway dashed dramatically to the rescue," her son replied. "She is quite the heroine."

Immediately the lady took her rescued pooch to her breast, fussing and cooing, largely forgetting the people involved. But she did remember Georgiana eventually — once she had ascertained that her dog was unharmed.

"Miss Hathaway, you must go upstairs at once and get

out of those wet things, before our guests arrive. We cannot send you back to your father with a cold. Good lord, you are pale as a ghost and quite limp!"

"And Sir Henry saved Miss Hathaway," Mrs. Swanley told her eagerly. "It was very exciting. Quite livened up the trip."

But Harry was already on his way back to his study leaving a wet stream in his wake. He did not wait to be thanked by anybody or fussed over by his aunt. Shoulders hunched and head down he disappeared behind his door without a word.

"He only jumped in to save the dog," Max was quick to add. "It just so happened that Miss Hathaway got there first and then he was obliged to save her instead."

Georgiana hurried upstairs to change, to be alone with her thoughts, and her apparently transparent expressions.

* * * *

He sat at his desk for a while with his eyes closed, running over the events of the day, trying to find where it all went wrong.

Finally he opened his eyes and saw the bodiless head of his automaton *Miss Petticoat*, where it sat upon his shelf, staring emptily back at him. How ridiculous it seemed to him now, that he had ever thought he could build himself a female companion.

Pitiful.

"So you're going to sit here, feeling sorry for yourself?"

"Go away, Parkes. Surely you have work to do elsewhere."

She walked around his desk, slowly moving into view. "Yes, I do have work elsewhere, now that you mention it, but someone's got to look after you, haven't they? I hoped by now you'd find another woman for the job, so I can go and get some rest."

"Well, it doesn't look as if I shall, does it?"

"What's amiss? Miss Hathaway wounded your abominable pride, did she?"

"Yes," he replied sulkily. "It was unforgiveable. The woman knows nothing. She is utterly ungrateful for the honor I offered her, and has her silly head in the clouds, thinking she can find something better to do with her life. I begin to think she only came here to study me and that she means to put me into one of her wicked satires. I am nothing more to her than a curiosity. Poking at me with her damn questions."

"Good riddance to her then. If she cannot appreciate you, what do you want with her? Sounds like nothing but trouble to me."

"Yes," he growled. "Precisely."

But it was not that easy and straightforward, was it? Women never were. He rested his elbow on the desk, one fist holding up his head, while the fingers of his other hand drummed upon the blotter.

"I probably said a few things I shouldn't have," he confessed begrudgingly. "My temper ran away with me somewhat."

Was it possible that he had misread her actions and seen more than she meant by them? Perhaps it really was just the kindness of a good woman that made her want to help Harry in some way, that made her sacrifice her own sleep at night to walk up and down those corridors with him. And when she stayed the night in his room, had he persuaded her into it for his own selfish needs and desires? Had he seen in her behavior only what he wanted to see?

"What are you going to do now, then?" Parkes demanded.

"Just get on with my life," he muttered. "What else?"

"Well, at least you know you have a life now. You weren't so sure about that before she came."

"Indeed."

She had changed a great many things for Harry and he would never be the same again. Neither would his house.

"You'll have to make it up to her, if you said some bad things in that summerhouse." Parkes turned way and the sunlight seemed to flow right through her until she was almost absorbed into the light itself. "If she's leaving you don't want to part with anything unresolved between you. There's nothing worse than leaving something undone and regretting it later, when it's too late. I should know."

* * * *

Georgiana stood in her room, dripping steadily onto the carpet. Her pulse would not settle and her heart beat was so hard and fast that it made her head ache. She could hardly breathe.

How quiet the house was now. Or was it the thud of her heart that drowned everything else out?

The sun had gone in, clouds gathering, shadows darkening the carpet pattern at her feet.

Any moment now it would rain. And she would give anything to be inside that summerhouse, to hear the rain pitter-pat on the glass panels and to be sheltered there, while she watched the lake dance.

Ironically, now would be the perfect time. But all that was gone.

She would probably never go out there again to that little island.

Bringing both hands to her face, she began to weep then. It was the shock, she supposed. She had started that day with no idea of what was about to happen. In just a few hours she had turned down a proposal of marriage and then had her life saved by the man she rejected.

As those long, thick, slippery fronds captured her legs, wound around them, and pulled her down into the lake, Harry's arms were there. Strong and determined, they tugged her free with what seemed like remarkable, magical ease. When they reached the side of the lake and could stand in the shallower water, he was barely out of breath, but just as wet as she.

No words were exchanged. None that she could remember now. Perhaps she said something. She should have thanked him!

But it all happened so fast and she was shattered inside.

Georgiana's legs crumpled and sank slowly to the carpet. It was not like her to cry. Not since her mother died had she felt this way. Six years ago. Ever since then she'd too busy proving her resilience in the face of obstacles, showing her independence.

Suddenly she missed the family cat. She missed that silly creature who never knew when to get out of the rain.

So that was why she let herself sob into her hands. The cat was as good a reason as any. A safer reason than any other that might have crept in.

* * * *

The "evening of cards" his aunt had organized for that evening was, for Harry, everything horrific, and his feelings could only be intensified by the anguish he suffered inside after the events of the day. He had made up his mind to be civil and, when he had the opportunity, to apologize to Georgiana for the things he'd said. He kept seeing her face, so pale, puzzled and then angry. His proposal had clearly taken her by surprise. Hopefully they could put it behind them and forget the embarrassment.

When she appeared in the drawing room to greet the guests, Harry was relieved to see her smiling, the color back in her cheeks. She had changed into a very pretty blue dress covered in flowers and her pleasant scent quickly awakened in him that warmth of feeling that made him forget anything else on his mind at that moment.

She would not have sat next to him, had he not slyly apprehended the lace cuff of her sleeve as she tried to pass.

"Miss Hathaway, there is a chair beside me and I believe I may need your help this evening."

She licked her lips and looked down at his fingers. "You always win at cards. What help could I give you?"

"I always win in your presence because you are my lucky charm." He smiled, wanting her to know he held no grudge. "Please sit with me."

So she did, looking nervously around at the other guests. "I did not have the chance to thank you today for saving me," she whispered.

"It is not necessary to thank me. I only did what any man would have done."

She looked at him. "Not every man. Your cousin did not jump in after me."

"Probably just as well, or I would have had to save him too. Max cannot swim."

"Oh." Her eyes seemed larger than ever tonight, the lashes even thicker and longer. Harry had to look down at his cards to prevent being sucked in by her gaze. Didn't want to make a fool of himself again. "That's why I suggested rowing out to the summerhouse today," he added wryly, "I assumed he wouldn't want to join us. Alas, I reckoned without his fancy for... my guests."

"Yes."

Harry sensed there was more she wanted to say, but she held her tongue and looked at the cards she'd been dealt.

The other guests around the card table seemed very excited to be there. In Little Flaxhill there was not much in the way of entertaining society and an evening at Woodbyne Abbey was, for many of them, an unexpected highlight. The Parson and his wife were there, along with the village doctor, the two wealthy widows whose names Harry could never remember, and the son of one of them— a tall, slim, nervous fellow. They had all arrived promptly, no doubt exceedingly curious to traipse about inside his house, he mused. But, determined to be on his best behavior, he kept a polite tone when answering their questions.

He wanted Miss Georgiana Hathaway to see that he was calm again and had accepted her choice without ill-feeling.

She was quiet this evening and pretended not to notice his cousin Max's attempts to catch her eye across the table. Studying her cards, she took the game seriously, smiling only occasionally, talking mostly to the parson's wife.

Max eventually grew irritated— it must have been strange for him to find a young lady oblivious to his charms. He then began to talk loudly of a conversation he had shared earlier with Georgiana.

"I asked Miss Hathaway to tell me what sort of things she learned at that ladies academy," he bellowed above all other conversations. "She was taught to ensnare unsuspecting males, I daresay. But she would not admit it."

Harry was about to silence his cousin, when Georgiana spoke up. "I fear, Mr. Bramley, as I told you today, the only thing *I* learned is that a lady disappointed with the way her life has turned out can become very bitter and vindictive. But I daresay that can be said of some men, as well as ladies I have known."

Max squinted, his jowls trembled slightly and he quickly raised a hand for the footman with the wine.

"What lady was this?" the parson's wife inquired with concern.

"The headmistress. Mrs. Lightbody. She should probably not be given the responsibility of looking after young girls, who need their confidence lifted, not torn to shreds."

Lady Bramley exclaimed, "Julia Lightbody has had great success with many of her students, and they are now well married to prove it. You are in the minority, Miss Hathaway."

Harry felt his young guest fidget restlessly beside him. Clearly she struggled between the need to be polite— like him on her best behavior— and her usual instinct to express a deeply felt opinion and hold nothing back. The latter won, as it most often did.

"That is true, madam. But can one measure success in those terms? The girls I knew at school were all desperately unhappy, their good spirits and self-assurance trampled by the woman meant to be guiding and guarding them. Their talents were belittled, even ridiculed, unless they knew how to flatter her. If they made *good* marriages, one has to wonder by whose measure are they good? Many of those girls married men they did not love, but they had been taught to please everybody else. All the spark of life had been snuffed out of them by the time they left Mrs. Lightbody's custody. Is that success? Not in my eyes, but, as you say, I am too opinionated and not slow to show it. She could not flatten my spark. One of the reasons why I am in that disgraced minority."

She fell silent then and looked down. He heard her breathing hard.

The other guests had listened to all this in various stages of amazement. They were probably not accustomed to a young lady expressing her opinion so soundly. Parson Darrowby looked uncomfortable, but his wife drank in every word with great sympathy on her face."Goodness," she ventured, "it does sound like a frightful place."

Lady Bramley flushed scarlet. "I'm sure it was not that bad, Miss Hathaway. You exaggerate."

"Well, she was there," said Harry, joining the conversation suddenly. "Miss Hathaway ought to know.

And perhaps we ought to listen to some of her opinions. Even if there *are* a great many, it does not make them any less valid."

His aunt gave him a very strange look, but was oddly silent. She stared hard at the girl who caused all this trouble and then back at Harry again. He hurriedly returned his own gaze to the cards in his hand.

Chapter Twenty-Three

Grateful to Harry for stepping in and taking her side, Georgiana did not know where to look. She had not meant to offend Lady Bramley, but she was tired of hearing about the "successes" produced by that school. In her mind they were not successes at all, but miserable ends for girls who could have been, and done, so much more.

Later, when she went to get herself a glass of punch, she was joined by Mrs. Swanley, who sidled up to her with some hastily whispered advice.

"If I were you, Miss Hathaway, I would take great care to mind what I say in public about that woman. If your Mrs. Lightbody is the person I knew, she has fingers in many a pie, and ears in many a corner. I know these are only folk from the village here tonight, but I warn you now, for your own good, to be more circumspect. You do not know how far her dangerous influence can reach."

Georgiana was annoyed, at first, that even Mrs. Swanley was now telling her to curb her tongue. But after a little more consideration, her temper cooled. She may be out of Mrs. Lightbody's reach now, however, her two good friends were not. It might be wise, therefore, to tread cautiously until they were safe from her retaliation.

Mrs. Swanley added, "If your Julia Lightbody is the same Salome of the Seven Veils that I knew, just be glad she has nothing to hold over *you*."

She had often wondered how The Pearl continually managed to get pupils from among the upper echelons of society, and how so many supposedly "good" matches were made, when Mrs. Lightbody remained such a vulgar creature. Did Mrs. Swanley infer something like blackmail was afoot at that school?

Georgiana had no chance to ask, for the Commander suddenly appeared at their side, ending Mrs. Swanley's interest in that subject, or in her.

273

"Sir Henry, you have had much good fortune again this evening at cards." The lady simpered up at him, flapping her lashes and sticking out her bosom. "I think you must be a scoundrel with slight of hand talent," she teased.

"Not at all, madam, I simply pay attention to the game and I concentrate. It is not difficult when one has had the pleasure of spending twenty-eight months as a castaway, entirely alone."

"Your poor thing," she cooed, placing an elegant hand on his arm. "You must tell me all about it."

"The Commander does not like to talk about that," said Georgiana firmly. "He is a very private man, and that should be respected."

"Of course," Mrs. Swanley agreed, her lips sliding wide apart again. "I can be very discreet."

Georgiana took a large gulp of punch and stared at those fingers on his jacket sleeve. Why did he not move his arm away? She knew he did not like being fussed over, but tonight he tolerated it.

Well, who was she to question the company he chose? She held no rights over him. Not now. She had given that up.

A short while later she was relieved, however, when he bowed to them both and walked away to speak with the Parson.

"I cannot get to the bottom of that man," sighed Mrs. Swanley, her smiled fading as she shook her head and those gold ringlets shone in the candlelight. "Never met anyone quite like him."

"Me neither," Georgiana agreed, feeling it more so than ever.

Did he really propose to her because he thought he had compromised her reputation? Even when nobody else was aware of it? Why could he not have given her some warning? Perhaps it was a spur of the moment proposal, and he would have regretted it immediately if she accepted him.

She had done the right thing. Surely.

"If I were you, Mrs. Swanley," she said, "I would use my skills to cheer up poor Mr. Tipton, who is here with his mother and seems quite afraid to do anything without her nod to encourage him. I daresay he would benefit most from your talented artistry."

Instantly the lady looked over to see who Georgiana talked of. "He does look a little sad and shy."

"Indeed. Who better than you to cheer his spirits? His mother is a very wealthy widow, by the way, although she lives quietly, and her only interest is her son now. He will inherit everything one day quite soon I suppose."

Mrs. Swanley quickly rearranged her curls, adjusted the shoulders of her gown, set down her punch cup and sailed off to enchant Mr. Tipton.

Seeing Max Bramley heading directly for the punch bowl, Georgiana made a hasty exit of her own and sought out the pleasant company of the Parson's wife.

* * * *

That night, unable to sleep, she took her candle and went out into the passage. Gentle moonlight fell through the windows and patterned the scratched Tudor paneling with diamonds of silver. All was quiet.

She patrolled for a while, like a night-watchman, making certain nobody else was restless that night.

About to return to her room, she suddenly stumbled upon Brown, the handyman, who was sat on the floor at the end of the passage, half asleep himself. When Georgiana's foot tripped over his leg, he woke fully and cursed.

"Oh, I am sorry, Mr. Brown," she whispered, bending down with her candle to see if he was all right.

"Miss Hathaway! What are you doing out here?"

"Just making sure everybody is asleep. What are you doing?"

"What you said about the master got me worried, Miss. Thought I'd best keep an eye on things while the guests are here."

"That's very good of you."

"Aye, well, he's the best of men. I wouldn't do it for just anybody."

"No. Quite." She knew entirely how he felt.

"But you go to bed, Miss. You shouldn't be up, fretting. You leave that to me."

Instead she sat beside him on the floor with her candle. "I fear I cannot sleep, Mr. Brown, not tonight. When a person has narrowly escaped death among the grasping weeds of a treacherous lake, one's mind tends not to peaceful sleep."

He looked at her. "You do know, Miss, the spot where you jumped in were no more than four feet deep."

Her candle flame fluttered. "Well goodness, Mr. Brown, do not lessen the exquisite terror of my adventure, or the bravery of your master in saving me!" To her it had seemed like twenty feet or more.

He gave a lopsided grin. "Sorry, Miss."

"Oh, never mind," she replied gloomily. "It has cured me of my fancy that I might have been a sailor."

"Aye. Best stick to dry land in them petticoats."

"I could wear breeches."

The old man eyed her warily. "You're a woman. Don't talk daft, Miss."

For a while they sat together in silence, the house creaking softly around them. Then she said, "Tell me what he was like as a boy. Did he always want to go to sea?"

Brown rubbed the curve of his big nose and thought for a bit. "He were a playful lad. Mischievous. Always in scrapes of one sort or another."

"Like me." She sighed.

"When his mother left...that changed the lad."

"Lady Bramley told me his mother ran off and was never heard from again."

"Aye. Took off with some fellow from London. He used to come sniffin' around here— were supposed to be a master landscape designer, or some such. Meant to be improving the grounds. The mistress wanted a fancy maze and all sorts. Me and Parkes never trusted him."

"Parkes was the nanny, was she not?"

"She was a good woman, plain-spoken, didn't suffer fools. Cared more for the boy than his mother did, I reckon. Anyway, the mistress of the house took off one night— just left the master and her own son." Brown rubbed his nose again and she saw his eye glisten in the light of her candle. "For hours the boy would sit out in that summerhouse, playing with his soldiers, waiting for his mother to come back. That used to be her favorite place, you see. She rowed out there to get away from the master of the house, I reckon. Or to meet her lover." He sniffed. "The boy just sat there waitin' in all weathers. Finally I suppose he realized she weren't comin' back, and that's when he asked to go to the Naval Academy. After that he came home once in a while, when he were on leave, and each time he came we saw how much he were grown. Such a fine young man he became. Did us all proud. He never went back out to that summerhouse, until today."

Georgiana's heart pinched as she imagined Harry— the boy— waiting for his mother and eventually realizing he'd been abandoned. The lake and the summerhouse had more significance to him than she could have known about.

"And Parkes died."

"Aye, she passed away one winter just before he were due home on leave. She tried to hang on, to see him one last time, but...well...the Good Lord couldn't wait any

277

longer and even Elsie Parkes couldn't win a quarrel with Him."

"I'm very sorry."

"The lad were distraught that he did not get home in time. We all said the house were not the same without Parkes, but he grieved for her more than anybody. Not that you'd know it. He were never the sort to talk about his worries."

"No. I have seen that."

The old man sighed heavily. "He's been more cheerful though, miss, since you came."

She nodded, her throat tight again. "I'm glad."

"We'll all be sorry to see you go."

Again she nodded, her candle trembling.

"But you go to bed now, Miss, and leave him to me. He'll be my charge again now."

Afraid she might dissolve into silly tears and embarrass Brown if she stayed, Georgiana said goodnight and returned to her chamber.

Chapter Twenty-Four

Excerpt from "His Lordship's Trousers" (censored)
Printed in *The Gentleman's Weekly*, July 1817

Yesterday evening's attire (which was also this morning's attire): Striped silk pantaloons somewhat resonant of a gypsy tent. Complete with gold-dyed tassels at the waist, and possibly more than one gypsy still in residence— with his rusty squeeze-box.

As his lordship prepares for the hunting season next month, saying 'adieu' to the Town with his own inimitable style, I must spend many hours organizing his garments for the forthcoming country house parties. One can never be too well-dressed to shoot at poor, startled grouse, of course, but this season his lordship has a particular reason to look his best while dodging misaimed bullets in the field. It is with great trepidation that I announce my master's imminent engagement to a filly very soon to be finished off at certain Mrs. X's institution for young ladies.

It has become a matter of importance to impress this young lady with everything in my master's possession, because her dowry is apparently as plump as her behind, and his lordship requires an influx of filthy lucre to pay the tailor's bills. And my wages. Believe me, dear reader, I would not be so concerned that this engagement be fulfilled— indeed I should do everything to stop it— if not for my own desire to finally be paid what I was promised when first hired.

But you must be as shocked as I was to hear that the master has decided to take a wife at last. He strolled in this morning as daylight broke over the dome of St. Paul's, and informed me — amidst gales of laughter—of his plans, which have not, it would appear, been shared with this particular lady's family. His lordship assures me she is eager however, and has accepted his proposal with great warmth. And, I would suspect, some urgent necessity.

How this has all been arranged while the young, hapless maiden remains under the supposed guardianship of the trusted 'Mrs. X', I shudder to imagine. Not that I dare suggest some wicked deceit and seduction has taken place under that lady's purview. Surely such things never happen.

Once I had recovered from shock at this news, I congratulated the gentleman, although— as I pointed out— the belles of London Society will be quite bereft to learn that such a popular perennial bachelor is taken off the market.

"Good lord, have you lost your wits?" said he, striding back and forth like a striped, slightly effeminate cockerel in his new pantaloons. "I shall certainly not change my habits just for one little chit. She'll learn her place."

"Ah, I see. Then Lady Loose Garters will continue to visit?"

"Naturally! Why would I give up that saucy minx?"

"And your new wife will not object, sir?"

He rolled his eyes so hard I expected to see them fall from his head. I even went so far as to imagine eager pigeons swooping in through the open window to steal the bloodshot orbs away. But alas, it was not to be. "These young girls turned out of Mrs. X's academy are well-trained to do as they are told and never to question their lord and master. My little wife has been specially selected for me, and I have put in a vast deal of effort to win her over."

"You have, my lord? Effort? Are you certain you are using the right word?" There were, after all, certain other "eff" words with which he was more familiar.

But he merely shook a finger at me and laughed again, too delighted with his plan of marriage for money and mayhem on the side for his pleasures.

It is, he assures me, quite how things are done.

* * * *

Excerpt from "His Lordship's Trousers" (censored)
Printed in *The Gentleman's Weekly*, July 1817

This morning's attire: Kerseymere pantaloons cut to hug the leg. And a slapped scarlet face.

Dear reader, much has occurred since last I wrote. It would seem the young lady about to be "finished" by an academy here in town, accidentally came upon her beloved betrothed— my master— in a state of *flagrante delicto* with his favored inflictor of pain, Lady Loose Garters.

This unhappy circumstance did not go well for his lordship, as one might imagine. It proceeded downhill at a rapid pace, when Lady Loose Garters learned from this "innocent" miss that his lordship is soon to be wed.

It seems neither lady was so willing to share as his lordship had planned.

Now, at the center of this debate, he did not know which way to turn and thus received a prolonged and well-deserved slapping from all directions. With his arms bound in their usual fashion by his liveliest paramour, my master was powerless to fight back.

Although he claims he called out for me— in some urgency— I did not hear anything other than a shriek from some drunkard I presumed to be stumbling by in the street below. By the time I had put my book aside and left the comfort of my fire to seek out the cause of the ruckus, both ladies were leaving and I discovered his lordship still bound to his bed, utterly bereft of hair again. All of it, this time.

Lady Loose Garters had put her hot wax to liberal use, aided, I suspect by the young lady to whom my master was engaged.

So my master is now as bald as a babe and just as wrathful as one whose teeth have yet to emerge from its smarting gums.

You will know him if you should see him.

Will he make amends first to his lover, or to his betrothed? How shall this be resolved?

One thing is certain, his lordship will require a cooling compress and a loose pair of galligaskins for quite some time.

* * * *

Harry looked up from the paper. "It would seem, Miss Hathaway, as if your father has decided to publish and be damned."

"Henry!" his aunt admonished, "Language!"

He laughed. "My dear Aunt, it is a very good thing you will never have cause to venture onto the deck of a ship."

"But I should soon have the crew in good order and the decks polished."

"*Swabbed,* madam. The decks are swabbed. That is the term. If they were polished we'd all be swept overboard at the first rough seas."

"You knew very well what I meant, Henry."

While they argued, Georgiana jumped out of her chair and ran around to read over his shoulder. Thank goodness her father had not succumbed to the Viscount's threats— had there been any. Where Lady Bramley had come by her rumor was anybody's guess and she could not seem to remember the origins of it herself.

But later that same day they had a surprise visitor at Woodbyne Abbey. And she came to see Georgiana.

282

* * * *

Mrs. Lightbody stood in the drawing room in her best hat and coat, her face twitching with anger before she even spoke. Her flushed demeanor suggested she had bolstered her spirits with gin prior to arrival.

"I hope you're happy now, Miss Sharp-Mouth Hathaway. I've had to drag myself all this way to see to this business."

"Business, madam?" Her first thought was that that headmistress had come to check on her progress with Lady Bramley. This, however, was not the case.

"I want that book back." Mrs. Lightbody held out her gloved hand. "At once, if you please."

"Book? I do not understand, madam."

"Oh yes, you do. I might have known it was you that took it. Didn't know it was missing for quite a while and then I thought I must just have mislaid it. But now I know what became of it. You've been creating mischief with it, haven't you? Using your father's paper. Who else would be behind that newspaper column."

"I'm sorry, madam. I am still—"

"Viscount Fairbanks brought it to my attention when he first read the piece. Certain details made him suspicious. He accused me of taking his secrets to the paper, but it was you who stole that book out of my parlor, was it not? Oh, I put it all together when I realized whose paper it all came out in. Now hand it over, or the Viscount can make things very difficult for your father. And for you."

Georgiana folded her hands together calmly. "Mrs. Lightbody, nothing in that column is meant to identify any particular person. It is a satire. I know this, because I know the author."

"Of course you do, brat. It's you, isn't it? I'm not slow in the brain, whatever you think."

"If Viscount Fairbanks sees himself in some way

within that story, perhaps it is his own guilty conscience."

"Don't think you can get away with this, Missy. I've known him a long time, and he's a very powerful man."

"So I keep hearing. If that is true why is he so bothered by one little newspaper story?"

"He told me you're already on his bad side. Do you really want to make it worse?"

"I won't be threatened, madam. If there is nothing else, you must excuse me as I am busy packing my trunk to go home."

"Sick of you here already, are they? I thought it wouldn't take long for her fine and fancy ladyship to give up. That meddling old cow should have listened to me. Ever since she wheedled her way onto the school board she's been looking over my shoulder at every turn."

Georgiana spun around, heading for the door, but the other woman shouted at her,

"Don't you show your back to me, Miss Hathaway. We can ruin you and any prospect you might have for the future. We can bankrupt your father."

"We?"

"That's right." The woman looked smug. "The Viscount and me are very old, very dear friends, like I said. If you don't give me that book back, be aware that you defy not only me, but him too."

"But it's not *your* book, is it?" She knew it was not written in Mrs. Lightbody's hand.

"It happened to come into my possession years ago when the owner died suddenly. It's certainly not yours, girl."

"If the Viscount sent you here to get that book back, how did he know about it?"

"That's none of your concern. Hand it over, you wretched little bitch, or I'll—"

A low growl stopped them both.

"Mrs. Lightbody!" Lady Bramley stood in the open

doorway that led out to the terrace, her dog under one arm. Neither Georgiana nor her accuser had heard steps approaching, but she had been there long enough to hear plenty. "What can be the meaning of this? How dare you speak in such a manner to this young lady?"

The headmistress was apparently at the end of her tether, too far out by now to reel her temper back in. "Young lady, indeed. She's a rotten apple, a troublemaker, a wicked creature who cannot be trusted. And a thief, what's more!"

"And I, according to you, am a *meddling old cow*, who *wheedled* my way onto the school board." Her dog bared his teeth and growled again.

Mrs. Lightbody had nothing to say in her defense, of course. The words had been said and heard. Her eyes turned black with fury, her lips trembling.

Lady Bramley came into the room. "It seems my predecessor on the school board hired you under some false impression of your suitability, but I have lately come to realize that changes are overdue."

"Changes? What changes?"

"I suggest, Mrs. Lightbody, that you go back to the school, pack your things and leave the premises immediately. I entrusted you to manage those students, and I see now that I should have been more vigilant."

"You wouldn't dare cast me off."

"Oh, but I would. And I shall. Good day to you, Mrs. Lightbody. Your services are no longer required, by this meddling old cow."

"That school will be ruined without me to run it. And you cannot send me off without the rest of the board's agreement."

"I can assure you they will not want to keep you when I have spoken to them. Viscount Fairbanks is not the only soul with power in Mayfair. *Good day*, Mrs. Lightbody."

Grumbling wildly, the woman marched out, shoving

past Georgiana with another curse.

Through the open door into the hall, they watched as the former headmistress encountered Mrs. Swanley, who happened to be on her way to the drawing room. Both women stopped sharply. The raging color drained from Mrs. Lightbody's face. The other lady feigned shock.

"Fancy seeing you here, Salome. I thought you were dead. Or in the Fleet."

The visitor said nothing, but held her head up, her hat slipping part way off her head, and quickened her exit without looking back.

* * * *

Georgiana said her own goodbyes the next day. She left early, when only Harry and his aunt were up to see her off.

"You must write, my dear," said Lady Bramley, "and let me know how you get on at home."

"I shall, your ladyship," she replied, scratching the little dog behind its ears. "Take care, Horatio, and do not chase any more geese. Or lady's ankles."

Then there was only Harry left.

With her heart in her throat she thanked him and said she hoped her presence had not been too great a nuisance.

"Not too great," he agreed solemnly.

He said nothing about her writing to *him*.

"Good luck with your automated woman, sir. I wished I could have seen her working."

"Alas, she is being very difficult to put together. I cannot seem to get her parts in order. I fear that she will always be contrary and defy me. As you warned me once."

"I did not say that. I said she might turn out to be less than perfect. Like a real woman, she might disappoint you. It does not mean she seeks deliberately to defy you."

"Hmm." He looked down at her, his eyes warm, questioning. "I'll survive the disappointment, somehow.

286

Make the best of it."

"We Hathaways don't believe in only making the best of things. We don't believe in settling. We are a restless bunch and always want more than that to which some think we are entitled."

He slowly took her hand to his lips and kissed it. "Yes. So I see. I wish you every good fortune in your adventures, Georgiana."

As she stepped into the carriage and he closed the door for her, his eyes narrowed and he murmured very softly, so that only she would hear, "I suppose, just as I tried to create a female to my specifications, you created a man to yours."

"How so?"

"I had my woman I could control as I required, and you have your strangely charismatic lord rake and his many trousers."

Georgiana bit her lip and winced. "You make it sound as if I am fond of him. He is a dreadful scoundrel without morals of any kind."

"Yet you control his every move with your pen." He smirked. "And you enjoy his wickedness tremendously."

There was one last look and then the carriage jolted forward.

One hand gripping the edge of the sash window she leaned out a little, his name poised on her lips.

But he already walked away with his long stride, his back to her and his boots crunching on the gravel as the horses pulled her carriage away from the steps of Woodbyne Abbey. What would she have said anyway?

She was going home.

Chapter Twenty-Five

Allerton Square
August 1817

Her stepmother spent most of the day in her bed, although she was still five months away from birthing her child. Apparently taking care of her other children and running the household was too much for her delicate health, and so she reclined in that sort of graceful disarray that some women managed to perfection. Mr. Hathaway fussed over her as if she was a china doll, although there was nothing fragile about his wife other than her nerves and her tolerance for noise. Which was a pity since she'd married a man with so many children already.

Meanwhile the twin daughters of their union, Cassie and Isabella, just two years of age, gave Georgiana plenty to keep her busy. Surely she was never so naughty a child, she complained to her father, who merely shook his head and briefly looked at her over his spectacles to assure her she was doing an excellent job.

Her younger brothers had all grown up in the time she'd spent away. Thomas and Jonathan were merely boys when she was sent off to school, but in the two years and three quarters since, they had become young men. Little Nicholas, now eight, was still a child, however. She would always think of him as the baby of the family, no matter how many children their stepmother produced. Nicholas had ruddy cheeks, golden curls and the wide, blue eyes of an angel— although that was deceptive. Perhaps it was because he was so young when their mother died, but Georgiana had always treated him as if he was her child.

She feared that during her time away he would have forgotten her, but he did not. As soon as she arrived home and before she could remove her coat, he ran to her legs and clung to them, much to the disgust of his brothers.

Soon she was caught up again in the life of her family. It was apparent that she had been missed, more so than she could have expected. Everybody had something they needed from her or had desperately to tell her about. There was little time to think about her days at Woodbyne, except at night, when she lay in her narrow bed and listened to her brothers quarrelling in the next room, or her little stepsisters squealing for attention across the hall.

The maid told her one morning that her father had received a letter from Viscount Fairbanks, and that he took it directly to his library. If he was worried about anything the letter contained, he gave no sign when she saw him later, but then her father had always been a stoic gentleman.

Georgiana sought him out in his library after the children were put to bed that evening, and confessed that she was the author of *His Lordship's Trousers*. May as well get it over with, she thought.

For a long moment he simply stared at her, but when she, thinking he might not have heard, began to repeat her statement, he held up his hand for silence.

"*My daughter* has penned this story of scandal?"

"Yes, papa. I wanted to show you that I can write."

He dropped to his chair. "And where...might I ask...do you come by your dreadful ideas?"

"Mostly from my imagination, although I have had some inspiration for the character of Lady Loose Garters, from this book." She showed him the slender volume she'd found behind Mrs. Lightbody's bookcase. "It seems to be a series of brief notes taken by a courtesan. Notations about her various lovers...likes and dislikes, their...attributes and measurements and such." She cleared her throat as he took it from her and leafed through it, his eyes gradually widening in horror. "When I first discovered it, I did not think they were real people. I suppose I should have realized, but I kept my own details general enough so that nobody might be identified. As you see, the author of the book uses no names herself, only what may be initials."

"Where did you find this book?"

She told him and then explained that Mrs. Lightbody had come to find her at Woodbyne, demanding the return of it.

"You should never have taken it, Georgiana," he said sternly. "This does not belong to you.

"But, papa, I have reason to believe that Mrs. Lightbody has been using the notes in this book for blackmail."

"Blackmail? That is a heavy accusation, daughter."

"There is no reason why that school, under her leadership, should continue to receive new pupils, when anybody leaving the place would never want to send their daughters there."

"Georgiana, just because your experience at the school was not—"

"I recently learned that her true background is nothing like the one she pretends to have known, and I believe she knows the identity of some of these men whose fancies and foibles are described in that book. She is exactly the sort of woman who would use that information to her advantage and hold it over their heads."

But her father took off his spectacles to polish them— an old gesture she remembered as one which meant she was about to be dismissed from his library.

"How is it that you learned about her school, papa? Who recommended it to you?" she demanded.

He squinted up at her. "Why, my wife suggested a school for you."

"Yes, but who came up with Mrs. Lightbody's establishment?"

After a pause, he muttered, "Viscount Fairbanks. When I told him of my intention to send you away, he suggested that place."

"Of course." She was triumphant, but her father still refused to see the connection. He put his glasses back on and prepared to stand, which would mean their conversation was over.

In desperation, she cried, "I also believe she arranged forced marriages for some of her pupils. I know of at least two girls my age— girls who had inherited large dowries— who were seduced while they were still in her 'care'. Now they are married to men who were in gambling debt, or needed a fortune to restore their family homes."

His dismissed that concern easily. "But that sort of arrangement happens all the time."

"Without the girl's parents approving of a courtship, until her ruined state is known to them and Mrs. Lightbody threatens to expose the poor girl's condition and cast her out of school?"

Her father now looked at the little books again, turning it over in his hands. He sank back to his seat, her dismissal postponed for now. "But how do you know this was her doing? That she arranged it?"

"If you knew her, papa, you would see how she is capable of any method to secure her own comforts. She has no interest in her pupils, other than their monetary worth, and she wants very badly to move herself up in society. The information in that book has given her access to the secrets of many gentleman of the upper crust. It has made a bitter woman privy to the intimate details of a social class to which she yearns to belong. Can you imagine what such a person would do with that power?"

"Yes, you have a great imagination, daughter, but this is all conjecture. One cannot make such an accusation without certain proof."

Her frustration mounted, but she kept her temper. "She boasted to me of her long relationship with Viscount Fairbanks and eluded to the fact that he sent her to get the book back from me. Why would it be so important if it was all nothing? This book is their lightning rod, papa. It is the root of all their evil power."

"Evil power?" her father raised his eyebrows and leaned back in his chair.

"What else would you call it, when one woman sits, like a big, ugly spider in the midst of a web, and waits to catch any helpless fly that lands near her, and a man as shamelessly repugnant as Fairbanks continually receives invites to every ball and party?"

He shook his head. "So what can be Mrs. Lightbody's connection to Viscount Fairbanks? They seem an unlikely pair."

"I do not know all his part in this." Georgiana took the book back from his hands. "Since he claims that *His Lordship's Trousers* bears some resemblance to his private life, he must be one of the men written about in this book. I suspect he was one of this courtesan's customers and Mrs. Lightbody recognized him in the book when it came into her possession. Perhaps he was once *her* lover too and so there were details she found familiar. When the column came out, he saw himself in it and accused her of spilling his secrets. That's why she came to get the book back from me."

Her father got up. "Lovers, seductions, courtesans, scandals...I never thought to see the day I must discuss such matters with my daughter."

She sighed. "I am a female, father, not a fool, and I have long known how the world turns. It is the year of our Lord, eighteen seventeen, papa. You should move with the times."

"Should I, indeed?" he grumbled.

"I never intended my character to be a complete reflection of Viscount Fairbanks— only to lampoon the figure of the aristocratic rake in general. It just so happened that it struck a nerve and he recognized himself in that buffoon. It seems they share certain... amorous tastes."

"Yes, yes, daughter," he scowled, "I think I understand that much, despite this being eighteen seventeen and myself stuck in the last century."

Georgiana searched through the thin book with quick fingers. "And there is more, papa. This may be the most important reason why he wanted her to get the book back." Having found the short passage, she turned it to show him.

He read it, and his face became tense. Snapping the book shut he dropped it into a drawer in his desk.

"You had better leave this to me now."

"But you will continue to print *His Lordship's Trousers*?"

"I must decide. In the meantime, for your sake, Georgiana, find something else to do with your imagination and your pen."

"But papa—"

"Enough, Georgiana! Go now and see to the little ones. That is the work a woman should enjoy. That is what should bring a gleam of pleasure to her eye, not this unwholesome business."

As she left his office, it occurred to her that at least now he remembered her name. She might even miss being called "Esmerelda".

* * * *

The sweating horses clattered down the street at speed and came to a snorting halt, the carriage creaking and heaving behind them. Harry Thrasher leapt down from his carriage without waiting for the step to be lowered. Head down, he charged his way through a crowd of people passing along the pavement and rushed into the building. Inside, he demanded of the first man he saw, "Hathaway's office!"

293

The bewildered fellow hesitated, until Harry bellowed again, "I am Commander Sir Henry Thrasher, and I am here to call upon Mr. Frederick Hathaway."

Almost dropping the papers he'd been carrying, the man hurriedly took Harry down a short, bustling corridor, knocked upon a door and then opened it. "Mr.—"

Harry did not wait to be introduced, but shoved his escort aside and strode in. "Mr. Hathaway, I have come to see you about *His Lordship's Trousers*."

Fortunately Hathaway knew him by sight and immediately gestured for him to take a seat, but Harry chose to stand.

"I insist that you do not cease publishing that column, sir."

"Really? I ...in truth I had not yet decided—"

"The author deserves the chance to bring her story to an end. If it must end."

"Her?" Hathaway looked worried as he pushed a pair of spectacles up his nose.

"I know it is your daughter's handiwork. Let us not waste time debating that." He had come all the way into London to speak his piece and he did not like being here, where the streets were so crowded that he could not walk at his usual stride without tripping over some idle fool who did not get out of his way fast enough. "The foul air of this town makes me short-tempered and very disinclined to brook any argument. So kindly keep the column running. If you have problems and pressures from any other quarter, let me deal with them."

"That is...most—"

"In fact, I want you to hire Miss Georgiana Hathaway as one of your permanent writers. If you need further enticement to do so, in addition to her obvious talent and the readership she already brings to your paper, I will offer you an exclusive to my own personal story of life as a castaway. A story of which she, and she alone, will be the author."

The other man looked as if he might topple backward. "Commander, that is a tremendous offer. I thought your story would never be told. I know you to be a gentleman of great natural reserve and a desire to remain private."

"I am many things, sir. Not the least of which is this," —he finally remembered to remove his hat and in his fumbling haste almost dropped it— "I am a man in desperate and quite unaccountable love with your daughter."

Mr. Hathaway now tilted sharply forward, making recompense for his backward sway, but the adjustment was so severe that he had to save himself with one hand on the wall. "My...*my* daughter? Are you sure?"

"That's right." Harry held his hand horizontal to his chest. "About so high. Dark hair, freckles. Talks a lot."

"Good heavens."

Harry growled, "I'm sure it'll do nobody any good and Heaven has absolutely nothing to do with it."

* * * *

The invitation came almost two weeks after she left Woodbyne. Since she doubted her father would approve of her spending an evening away from the children for something so frivolous as a ball, Georgiana simply put the invitation away in her writing box and said nothing about it. Besides what did she want with balls, pretty dresses and dancing? She was a serious writer now, with a job to do.

Indeed, once her father announced that he would hire her properly to write for his paper, she had quickly discovered that a career was not nearly as adventurous and exciting as she'd always imagined. It was hard work and her father told her that he would have no fewer expectations of her than he had for any other writer who sold their stories to *The Gentleman's Weekly*. She must impress him. Finally she had a chance to earn his approval and she meant to seize her opportunity, as she would any other, with both hands. It may be considerably more taxing now that it was not merely an amusing hobby, but she loved every moment of it and each time she dipped her nib in the inkpot that thrill remained undiminished.

So why would she want to go to a silly ball and dance?

Her father, however, came to find her in the parlor where she was bent over her writing.

"Did you not receive an invitation to a ball at Woodbyne Abbey, daughter?"

She hesitated, poised in the action of mending her pen. "I did, father. I suppose the maid told you. She is remarkably nosy."

"You will go, of course."

"I had thought not to. I have so much to do here, with stepmother confined to her bed. You need me."

He reached over and took the pen from her fingers. "Did I not go to the expense of sending you to that school so that you might one day catch a husband of consequence? This ball sounds to be an ideal venue."

"But now I am a writer, papa. I have no need for a husband."

"You cannot be a writer and still dance? And here was I, certain you would shout at me for suggesting you might only be capable of one thing at once."

Georgiana thought of that time when she almost danced with Harry. A minuet. It was a chance stolen away by the arrival of his cousin. Max Bramley had spoiled several things for her and that was the first.

"You spent these last few weeks as a guest of Lady Bramley and her nephew. It would be rude now to decline the invitation," her father added. "I'm sure I can manage for one evening." He did not look too sure of that, but, for some reason he was determined that she should go to this ball. "You have a frock to wear? Something... suitable? Something that the fashionable folks wear?"

"Yes, indeed, I have an evening gown, papa." She chuckled, for he was never one to be interested in fashion, particularly not in anything *she* wore. As they grew up, her sister Maria was the one with all the good looks and so the money and effort was spent upon her.

"Then you must go to the ball, my dear. I insist. I will hear no argument." He laid an awkward hand on her shoulder, muttered a soft, "Well there we are," and left her alone.

Georgiana picked up the cat, which had been curled up on her desk beside her paper, and cuddled him gently. "What do you suppose that was all about, Foster?" The animal mewled into her shoulder, and she kissed the top of his head. "I daresay he is hoping I will change my mind about writing for his paper and become somebody's docile wife instead. That would save him a lot of bother."

Foster, knowing from whence his favorite treat of boiled fish heads came, agreed.

Chapter Twenty-Six

Since it was a three hour ride to Woodbyne and no young lady wanted to sit in a carriage for that long, getting her gown wrinkled, Mr. Hathaway arranged for his daughter to travel, on the morning of the great day, to an inn just a little more than half the distance between. Once there she could change, eat a light supper and then go on to the ball. Afterwards she could spend that night at the same inn and return to London the next day.

"But papa, would it proper for me to spend the night at an inn alone?"

"Alone? Who said anything about you traveling alone?"

She was utterly confused and he let her be for a while, because he did love his mischief at times, but eventually he added, "I understand your young friends, Miss Chance and Miss Goodheart, have also been invited, so the three of you can travel together."

"Papa!" She was so thrilled by the idea that she leapt out of her chair and startled the cat. "Are you sure they are invited?" After all neither girl had mentioned it to her in their last letters.

"Oh yes, I have it on very good authority."

Furthermore, the ladies were to be escorted on their trip by Captain Guy Hathaway, who she discovered next, was coming home on leave and had already been applied to for his services.

There was now so much happiness to be anticipated in this event, that Georgiana could barely sleep for the next few nights.

She had not seen her eldest brother in five years and their reunion was emotional on both sides— although only one would let it show.

"My darling brother! How wonderful it is that you are home."

He stood before her, very proud in his uniform blue coat. "Of course I must come home if my little sister needs an escort to a ball. I cannot have her going alone into the fray, can I?" Grinning, he stepped back to admire her full length. "You have grown so tall, sister. But I would still know that naughty face— even now it is clean and not covered in mud."

"You are taller now too, Captain Hathaway. And as handsome as ever."

"Nonsense. This is a face, sister, that halts ships and makes babe's cry."

She laughed. Her brother loved to make sport of himself, and of her, which had always given them a special bond. Maria was always too vain and thin-skinned, and Edward too easily offended for playful mockery.

"Now, are we sure you have all the weaponry you need, Georgie?"

"It's all packed." She motioned to the small trunk that was about to be lifted onto the back of the barouche their father had hired for the event.

But Guy, being a man of detail, insisted on opening her trunk and assuring himself that nothing had been left behind. "I know you, little sister, and we could turn up at Woodbyne Abbey with you in an ink-stained pinafore and a straw hat."

"Gracious such a lot of fuss about nothing!"

He sternly surveyed the inside of her trunk. "Evening gloves? Yes, good. Not too dirty yet at the fingertips. Petticoat? Yes. Dancing slippers? Ah, for once not grass stained." Then he straightened up and gave her person a similar assessment. "Teeth? Yes, all of a correct number. Curls? Suitably arranged. I declare myself shocked to find you so organized for once and traveling without your bow and arrows." He licked his thumb and ran it across her left eyebrow. "There, everything is now in place. Try to keep it thus and I think you might well make a conquest tonight, sister."

Again her mind went directly to Harry. The thought of dancing with him at last made her very anxious. Her palms were already damp. But there was no time to worry about herself for too long. Within half an hour the hired carriage was at the steps of the school and there they collected her friends.

"Emma! Melinda! The Ladies Most Unlikely are together again."

There was much crying and embracing, while her brother waited outside the carriage, clearly uncomfortable with such a display and impatient to be on the road. Really, it was very good of him to volunteer as their escort, she mused fondly, for she knew how little he enjoyed balls. And the chatter of excited young ladies always gave him a sore head.

Once she had introduced him to her friends, the carriage set off at last for Surrey, and the three friends set about catching up on all the news they had not yet had a chance to write about.

Georgiana soon learned that much had changed at The Pearl since the departure of Mrs. Lightbody.

"Lady Bramley has taken on much of the work overseeing the school," said Melinda. "She is a great manager."

Georgiana laughed. "Yes, I know this."

"And Emma has been appointed her assistant."

"Miss Emma Chance," she turned to accuse her other friend, "you never wrote to tell me!"

Emma blushed. "It has not long happened, and I have been very busy. Lady Bramley is a hard taskmaster." She was, as always, shy to beat her own drum. "I may still be sent away to be a governess, but for now I am reprieved." The idea of leaving the place she had known all her life and being all alone among strangers quite terrified the girl, a fact the old headmistress had well known, and used to hold it over her head.

Georgiana smiled and squeezed her hand. "You look very pretty with your hair in that new style."

"As do you. There is something different in your eyes, Georgie."

She supposed it must be maturity and all that she'd been through that summer. Although she longed to tell her friends about the proposal of marriage, she knew it was something she could never speak of. It rested in her heart. Another secret.

So many, lately, had fallen into her hands.

She stole another glance at Emma— the girl who was once left, as an illegitimate babe, to the "care" of Mrs. Lightbody, by a father who wanted nothing to do with the child, but paid her expenses. Probably paid too for Mrs. Lightbody's silence. That pact they had formed about the babe was perhaps only one of many other secrets Mrs. Lightbody had uncovered, and used, about the people she knew.

It sickened Georgiana that anybody would leave a baby in that woman's custody.

She thought of that small entry in the little book— *WF will not claim the child. He cruelly wanted Y to be rid of it, but she would not oblige. He has already found another lover.*

And a little later on the same page.

Y gave up the child when it was born. WF took it from her and said he knew of a woman who would raise it out of sight. He wants no mention made of it or he will silence her forever.

Eight or nine pages further on, a scribbled note along the very bottom, marked with the sketch of a tiny lily.

Y was buried today, taken by the pleurisy. Too delicate and good for this life.

In that house in Bethnal Green, where Mrs. Swanley once worked alongside "Salome Flambeau" there must have been many unfortunate young women, without family or fortune, struggling to survive in that hard world.

No doubt many illegitimate children were born of such places, sired by men who, for one reason or another, would not publicly acknowledge their responsibility.

Emma could be that child mentioned in the book. Her age was right and her father never showed any concern about her upbringing once he left her with Julia Lightbody.

She heard her father whispering in her head, *You have a great imagination, daughter, but this is all conjecture. One cannot make such an accusation without certain proof.*

They might never know the identity of Emma's father. But that did not change the fact that "WF" had a child out there, somewhere in the world, that nobody else knew about. A child he had callously wanted rid of.

* * * *

Harry took the box from his pocket and sat in his study, waiting. Sunlight drifted lazily through the window. At this time of the year it was burning itself out, mellowing to a rusty gold, lingering until it turned everything into the same color, just before it cooled and fogged to grey, then black. Harry may not know exactly which day it was, but he could tell the *time* of day to within five minutes, just by the color of the air. Yes, air had color; most people couldn't see it, but he could, having studied it for so long.

"You ought to be upstairs getting dressed for the ball," Parkes exclaimed, standing at his open door. "Your lady aunt has gone to all this fuss and bother. While all you do is sit here staring into space. I've said it before and I'll say it again, that lady has the patience of a saint."

"As you do too, to put up with me. All these years."

"Yes, well, somebody has to when she can't."

The light swung slowly around the room and she came with it, gliding. Her feet used to make a sound— that brisk clip he remembered from his childhood— but that memory was fading now, as were various parts of her form whenever she appeared.

"I have something I wanted to give you, Parkes," he said. "I wanted to give it to you many years ago, but I did not have the chance, of course."

She was at his desk now, looking annoyed. "Something for me? Why would you get anything for me? I'm sure I never—"

"It's to thank you for everything you ever did for me." He cleared his throat, opened the box and slid it toward her across his desk. "I bought it when I got my first command. I knew you'd be proud of me and...probably prouder than anybody."

Parkes looked down at the box and ran her hand over it, but she didn't pick it up. "You shouldn't have! You daft boy! The things you get into your head."

"I would have given it to you, but...well, I held on to it all these years." She was dead by the time he come on leave after that, and so the brooch of a silver galleon in full sail had remained in its box ever since. While cleaning out the clutter in his office recently, he found it again. "Parkes, I do not know what I would have done without you. I always wished I had..." he paused, swallowed, continued, "had the chance to tell you how dear you were to me. What you ...meant to me."

It was not the sort of thing men discussed. At least, not men like Harry, who preferred not to show particular affection for anybody. People had a habit of leaving him, once they knew he was fond. If he kept everybody at a distance he did not have to worry about that.

But this evening it had to be said.

She looked up then, her eyes shining in a ray of sunlight— a last burst before sunset— and she smiled. "That's what all this was about? Why you couldn't let me go? I knew. Of course I knew it, you daft boy. Don't you worry about that. Now you go upstairs and make yourself look presentable for once. Find a wife tonight, young sir, so that I can have a rest at last."

* * * *

The gravel approach to Woodbyne Abbey was lined on both sides with torches that evening. Horses and liveried servants milled about in the warm evening air, laughing and exchanging jests— probably about their masters'. A seemingly endless stream of ladies in exquisite gowns that trailed gently behind them, made their way up the stone steps into the house. It was all very grand, sumptuous, a perfectly glittering evening.

How different her arrival was tonight, to how it had been some months ago when a wild storm raged above and the house had seemed deserted!

As they entered the grand front hall, the ladies admired the festoons of flowers and greenery that seemed to be everywhere they looked— as if the outdoors had been brought inside.

"It's such a beautiful house," whispered Emma. "You never said how lovely it was."

Had she not? It was true that in the beginning she had not seen much beauty about the place. It was old, drafty and falling down. But Georgiana had come to appreciate the house, for all its creaks and groans. Rather like the master himself.

And there he was, greeting guests with his aunt.

Oh dear, the moment was almost upon her. Would she blurt out something silly, or lose her balance when she curtseyed? Was her hair tidy? Was her gown fashionable enough, or did it make her look like a Norfolk Dumpling?

She hiccupped.

Melinda nudged her in the side. "Stop that!"

"How does one stop hiccups?"

"Hold your breath."

So she did. As she curtseyed to their hosts, she could not speak for fear of making that dreadful noise. But it popped out anyway, and because she'd been holding it in, the sound was much louder than it might have been. Several faces turned to look at the source and Harry's eyes gleamed down at her in amusement.

"Miss Hathaway, you look so pretty tonight I almost didn't recognize you. Until that."

As she muttered an apology, he merely tugged the dance card out of her hand, wrote in it and gave it back to her.

"Aren't you going to introduce me to your companions?" he demanded.

But another series of hiccups overcame her. Fortunately Lady Bramley was able to do the honor for her friends, and once she had recovered, Georgiana obliged with the introduction of her brother.

"Ah, you are the Naval Captain of whom she is so proud," said Harry with a stiff smile and a bow. "I am delighted to meet you."

"And I you, sir," Guy replied, looking unusually awed.

Lady Bramley inquired into their stepmother's health and then they were moving along again with the crowd.

"If you hold a key on your tongue," said Melinda somberly, "that is suppose to help stop hiccups too."

"That's very nice, but I don't happen to carry a key around with me."

But it reminded her that she had never had discovered how Dead Harry got out of his room at night to go wandering after Brown locked him in. It was a mystery for which she might never have an answer, but in true life, she knew now, not everything could be explained.

She looked down at her dance card and saw that he had drawn a large X through most of it, with his initials marked on the first line.

Melinda, observing this over her shoulder, exclaimed, "He must be in love with you."

"Don't be ridiculous."

"He has been pining for you since you left, pacing his library and tearing out his hair. He looks the sort to fall in love quite dangerously. I suppose, in the end he'll carry you off and we'll never see you again."

"You have a great imagination, Miss Melinda Goodheart, but this is all terrible conjecture over a few pen marks on a dance card."

Emma softly agreed. "He could just want to save her the trouble of dancing as he knows she's not very skilled."

"Well, thank you very much! I do exceedingly well after a glass or two of wine," Georgiana exclaimed grandly. "Now I just have to find some."

But before any refreshment could be found— especially in the quantity required— the first dance was announced and Commander Thrasher made a direct course for where she stood, trampling on the trains of a few gowns as he came.

Her so-called friends swiftly abandoned her, and she was left utterly at his mercy.

* * * *

He could not know how, or when, the Wickedest Chit transformed into a beautiful, alluring woman. Some villainy, no doubt, was at foot.

"Miss Hathaway." He took her hand tightly in his, just as the first notes of the minuet began. "This dance has been long delayed."

"Yes." Her face fell sad for a moment, but then she managed a smile. "Your cousin is not here tonight?"

"No. Max is safely out of the way enjoying a house party in Devonshire." He glanced down at her. "I suppose you are disappointed."

Her smile gained strength. "Not at all. I am relieved."

"Oh? I thought you found him amusing. Like an overgrown puppy. Is that not what you called him?"

"Yes. But I do find he has a habit of spoiling my day,

whether he means to or not. I prefer to believe the latter and that he means well, but is merely clumsy in his delivery. Perhaps a hippopotamus would be a more accurate description of the way he blumberdumbers along."

"Blumberdumbers?"

She shrugged. "Sometimes I have to make a word up when the right one is not to be found."

Harry nodded, keeping his lips tight until he had tamed the urge to smile like a fool. "I understand your father has hired you to write some stories for his paper."

"He has."

"Then I must congratulate you, Georgiana. You are on your way to having everything you wanted. An independent life."

Her lashes lowered, then swept upward again, taking his heart beat with them. "Am I? Sometimes...I do not know."

"You do not know what?"

"Whether I knew what I wanted. *Everything* I wanted."

Hope sprung to life within him when she used the past tense. But he must proceed with care, not clumsily. "It is not always easy to know, when one is young, what one wants."

He wanted to hear her say she'd made an error, but perhaps because he wanted it so much that he read it in her eyes when it was not truly there.

She shook her curls and laughed lightly. "It doesn't matter now."

His thumb stroked across her gloved knuckles, wishing their hands were bare again, as they were the first time they touched. "My aunt has taken charge at your school. Perhaps you heard? She seems to have a new lease on life these days, keeps muttering about girls wasting their potential and how she could have done so much more with her own life. She's making up for it now."

307

"Oh dear, have I turned Lady Bramley into a revolutionary?" She dazzled him with her smile.

"I fear so." He couldn't smile back. For some reason his lips were too stiff, his throat was bone-dry and his tongue felt too large for his mouth. This was quite ridiculous, he thought angrily; he was a damned war hero who had died twice, and yet this girl left him tongue-tied. "She's not the only one making her mark anew. Have you heard about Mrs. Swanley?"

* * * *

He took her out into the hall and showed her the watercolor of Woodbyne Abbey as painted by the "artiste" Mrs. Evelyn Swanley. It was a mass of color in blobs and smears which, at first glance, appeared to be nothing more than accidental placement— the work, perhaps of four cat's paws that somehow got into the paint. But after standing for a moment, with one's eyes in a tight squint, the sight was able to transform those smudges of color into an image that was, in actual fact, almost recognizable.

"When the Parson's wife, Mrs. Darrowby, first saw it, she immediately persuaded her husband to a commission a portrait of the church in this 'new' style. After that, Mrs. Swanley's success grew in leaps and bounds. She is currently working on a still life for my aunt— some of her favorite gourds, I understand. Those you and your friends did not yet manage to destroy."

The longer one stood before the painting and studied it, the more the image transformed. "I am very happy for her," said Georgiana, still admiring the work. "It seems your aunt's owl was quite right when it gave her that fortune. *We know what we are, but not what we may be.*"

"Actually that fortune was meant for you," he replied quietly. "I meant for you to get the first slip of paper after mine, but she was too impatient and took the owl from me, if you recall."

She did not know what to say to that.

Harry was looking at the painting of his house, his profile turned to her. "But, as you say, it doesn't matter now."

In her peripheral vision she saw her brother watching them, and Lady Bramley too. The hall was crowded and loud, the very sort of thing he hated and tried to avoid. Yet he put up with it tonight. She must not let her imagination run away with her and think any of this suffering was was for her.

"Why did you draw all over my dance card?" she asked finally.

He looked down at her, his eyes as innocent as they ever could be. "Oh, did you want to dance with anybody else?"

"Not really."

"Not really?"

"No." It burst out of her with that patented lack of dignity. "I did not want to dance with anybody else." So much for aloof, she thought, remembering how Max Bramley had teased her.

"Good, because I would have to crush the fellow where he stood." Slowly he smiled and it felt as if a lightning bolt struck her senseless.

Lady Bramley swept across and took his arm. "Henry, you must not monopolize Miss Hathaway's attention. Now come here and let me find you some other ladies to dance with. They will all be insulted if you do not dance with them. We went to all this trouble to get you dressed up and shaved. It cannot all be for nothing, and I'm sure poor Miss Hathaway has had quite enough of you for one evening."

So she watched him being taken away from her. It was rare for him to go meekly at his aunt's orders, but that lady had indeed gone to a vast deal of trouble to get him this far. And he did look far too handsome to waste upon

309

Georgiana, in her old muslin.

She wandered around the dance and watched her friends enjoying themselves. Her brother gallantly danced with both girls and even managed to look cheerful, despite his general dislike of balls. And there was Harry, forced into dancing by his aunt, one fair lady after another. She even saw his lips move occasionally so he found something to say to them. Hopefully it was polite. Not too polite though.

"That's him," she heard somebody whisper behind her. "That's Dead Harry Thrasher. They say he's not all there in the head, you know. After what happened..."

"So I heard. Terribly unpredictable. The Navy did not know what to do with him and if they can't handle a man then nobody can."

Another woman giggled stupidly. "Well, I must say, I wouldn't object to trying."

"But he has a violent temper, they say. If you ask me, Amy Milhaven had a lucky escape."

Now came a low, lascivious chortle. "I doubt Amy Milhaven would agree. Admiral Shaftesbury is hardly a substitute for a man like that. I hear she's desperately unhappy in the marriage."

"And to know what she missed out on...what she might have had..."

A cloud of sighs swelled from the little group of gossiping women as they considered, in unison, the "terribly unpredictable", undeniably handsome, and wickedly fascinating figure of Not-So-Dead Harry.

This was the disadvantage of helping someone back to life, Georgiana thought, chagrinned. Suddenly he was more alive than she'd expected. These other women, with their elegant shoulders and ivory complexions, would never appreciate the many sides of that man. She was feeling quite annoyed about their suggestive whispers and cooing sighs, as they melted all over Harry.

Her Harry.

Eventually she realized she was twisting her dance card mercilessly in her fingers, smudging the pencil marks he'd made upon it. And that was another thing! While he had not wanted her to dance with anybody else, there he was cavorting with one pair of pushy bosoms after another. Did these women know nothing of being aloof? Where was their dignity?

Her pulse was very unsteady, as if she'd just fallen into the lake again.

Slowly she turned and began to walk. As the crowd around her thinned, Georgiana picked up her pace, until she had lifted up her skirt and broken into a most unladylike run.

Chapter Twenty-Seven

"Have you seen my sister?" Guy Hathaway came to him, concerned.

Harry had lost sight of her some time ago in the crowd and neither of her friends had seen her lately either. The four of them decided to look for her. How far could she have gone? Was there an answer to that question?

Although Harry said nothing to the others he feared she could be anywhere in his house. She might even be on the roof, knowing her propensity for trouble and that love of adventure. But when he ran into Brown, the old fellow was looking rather pleased with himself and readily pointed out the sinister glow of light shining from the island in the middle of his lake.

"We put no torches out there, did we?"

"No, sir, I reckon somebody must have rowed out there with one."

Harry eyed the fellow suspiciously. "Somebody? Brown, did you aid that woman in this mad enterprise? It's dark out there, and she could have fallen in!"

"I couldn't stop her, sir. No more than I could stop you getting out of your room at night."

"Have you been at the punch, Brown?"

"I might have had one or two. Thought I earned it after all these years." Then the old fellow chuckled. "There's the other boat standing ready, sir. Should you want to join the young lady. It's a night of moon and stars out there, sir. Quite as it should be."

"As it should be?"

"In a Grand Romance, the lady said."

Harry didn't wait to hear anything more.

* * * *

Brown was right; it was a night of moon and stars, not nearly as dark out on the lake as he'd thought. He removed his jacket, rolled up his sleeves and set off across the still water with as much speed as he could row. In the distance, the summerhouse glowed warmly, a beacon guiding his path. A gentle wind rustled the reeds and bulrushes, and, away across the lawns, slipping out through the doors to the terrace, dance music still played.

As he rowed, Harry tried to think of what he would say to her when he got there. Well, first he would admonish her soundly for taking such a foolish risk all by herself. Good thing it was a warm night. What could she be thinking? Nothing, probably, being a woman.

But by the time he reached the little island, he forgot all that. Because she was there, waiting for him.

* * * *

Georgiana had used her rush torch to light some candles inside the summerhouse, hoping he would see it from the Abbey. It was not long before she saw his white shoulders and shirtsleeves in the moonlight, heaving their way across the lake.

Tonight the island felt different than it had on that bright sunny day some weeks ago. Tonight it belonged just to the two of them.

"Miss Hathaway, you have a talent for drama," he muttered, breathless as he climbed out of the boat and leapt up the slight slope to where she stood. "What can be the meaning of this?"

She pointed up at the sky. "Look at the moon. It's huge."

"You lured me out here for the moon? We could have seen that from the house. Where it's dry and—"

"Harry, just shut up and kiss me before one of us dies for definite."

While he stood there looking alarmed, she reached up for his ears, tugged his face down to hers and lifted on tiptoe. She had not forgotten how wonderful it was to feel his arms around her, but it still made her heart leap when it happened tonight.

Despite his initial shock, he soon made up for the hesitation and kissed her as if his life depended upon it. The way he always did. As if she was the only woman on his island.

Suddenly the wind picked up, playfully tossing the bulrushes about around the edge of the island, making them sigh and whisper. Inside the summerhouse, although partly sheltered, the candle flames were tugged into a dance of their own and some were even extinguished.

"I love you, Harry," she exclaimed, the wind catching her the hem of her skirt and unsettling that neat arrangement of curls over which she'd taken such unlikely trouble. "I love you so much it terrifies me. I did not want to fall in love, but I have. Now it's too late. I don't know what else to do, but tell you. Being older and wiser, I thought you ought to know what to do about it."

His eyes flared, then narrowed, crinkling up at the corners. "I see." A little twitch at the corner of his mouth proceeded a wry smile. "You realize I don't believe, for a moment, that you think I'm wiser than you."

She struggled to keep her own lips steady and solemn. "Just older then. Experienced in these things."

A deep rumble of laughter escaped into the warm breeze. "Not that experienced. I've never been in love before either."

Did that mean he was now? Oh, her heart couldn't bear it another moment. "Can we go back to that day when we were last here and you asked me to marry you?"

"What on earth for? Do you want to wound me again? Make the pain linger even more by remembering all that?"

She scowled.

But then he laughed again and pulled her into his arms, squeezing the breath out of her. "I'm not letting you off this island tonight, until you say you'll marry me."

Perhaps because she was such a wicked girl, this immediately changed her plans a little and gave her an entirely new idea.

"Oh, really?" She gave an arch grin. "How are you going to persuade me then? I said I love you. It doesn't mean I think we should marry."

He gave her a look that quickly raised the temperature under her corset.

"What if someone sees us out here?" she muttered, backing away with a sudden qualm.

Harry was already unbuttoning his waistcoat as he strode slowly toward her, moving her into the summerhouse. "They won't," he murmured, blowing out the nearest candle and then the next.

"But...Brown—"

"Will keep anyone else away."

"Oh."

"Tonight it's just you and I on our island, Georgiana."

"What about my brother and my friends? They will wonder—"

"Brown will assure them that you're in safe hands."

And she was. In very safe, very large and very capable hands.

* * * *

She was surprisingly warm, even naked. He had removed her clothes slowly, piece by piece, the downward crumble of every fabric inch accompanied by the brush of his lips. About his own disrobing he was never as careful, she mused. It was as if he could not wait to get out of his clothing and be free. But when it came to her body, he unwrapped her like a long awaited, extremely expensive gift.

When he lay on the embroidered silk shawl that was still spread over the couch, he continued his kissing and exploring until she was dizzy with it and impatiently squirming. Then it was her turn to discover all his ticklish places, the dips and valleys, muscles and sinews she'd admired before but dared not touch. With her fingertips she traced the scars that marked his torso and then followed with her tongue, growing bolder as she went.

His skin was darker than hers— after years surviving a tropical island, it was no surprise— and it held many hints to the battles in his past. She discovered each scar, like another clue in the unveiling of a mystery.

"What happened?" she would ask. "How did you get this?"

After he told her, she kissed it and moved on to the next. His body was a book full of chapters. A book she wanted to pick up and read again and again.

Finally he rolled over to put her beneath him. He stroked a curl from her cheek. "I want to make love to you, Georgiana," he whispered.

"Gracious," she wriggled happily, "I hope so after all this."

"Then say 'yes'. Say you'll marry me and irritate me around my house for the rest of our lives."

"I still want to write for my father's paper."

"I know."

"You don't mind a wife with an occupation?"

He chuckled and his voice cracked when he replied, "If you do not object to a husband with the occasional aversion to clothing." He caressed her thigh and the sofa creaked as he adjusted his position over her. "A husband with a few eccentric habits and an overwhelming desire to mate with his wife at all hours of the day and night."

Georgiana slid her arms around his neck. "I think I can manage. But what changed your mind? I thought you didn't want a wife... that you only asked me out of duty."

He thought for a second, pondering her lips and then moving his gaze to her eyes, looking deeply into them. "I

316

didn't want the sort of wife I was supposed to have. But you..." he smiled in that slow way that made her melt, "you I want."

Then he entered her at last and she clung to him with a gasp that would have blown out any other candles, had they still been lit.

* * * *

She sat astride his hips and kissed him, her tongue trailing across his cheek where the stubble already sprouted again. "I want more."

"And I need to rest," he groaned, amused by her eagerness. "Are you not supposed to be the naive maiden?"

"I was." She pouted. "Until an hour ago."

Had it been that long? Not polite to be away from his guests this long. His aunt, if she had noticed, would be ready to shout at him. But here with Harry, on his island, was the most important guest. So should he not keep her happy? Who else mattered, but the Wickedest Chit?

Much to Harry's delight, she was very, very wicked.

"So how did you get out of your room every night after Brown locked you in?" she asked, nibbling his ear.

"That, my darling, is a secret you will have to try and pry out of me. Please subject me to every form of torture." He would enjoy her attempts, he mused. But he had no intention of ever telling her about the maze of secret passages and hidden doors built into the Abbey. Harry wanted to be sure he could continue surprising and thrilling his naughty wife, every day and night for the rest of their lives.

Epilogue

His may be an unfamiliar face at Boodles, but it was not unknown. An infamous reputation preceded the man wherever he went, and this gentleman's club was no exception.

The low murmur of surprised, "That's Dead Harry", comments swept the club just as quickly as he did. On a quest for one face in particular, he did not greet anybody or acknowledge the startled inquiries of the butler, who followed anxiously in his wake.

"Fairbanks," he growled, finally locating the man he sought. "I have something to say to you."

The Viscount looked over his shoulder and gave a languid yawn. "I am in the midst of a game, Thrasher, as you see."

But Harry was in no mood to wait. Much to the shock— and considerable delight— of the other patrons, he lifted Fairbanks, and the chair in which he sat. And shook it, as if to dislodge a stone from his boot. In a flurry of silk and ruffled lace, the other man tumbled to the floor and then scrambled hastily to his feet.

"How dare you?" His face was red as he turned to confront Harry, be-ringed fingers flashing while he checked the knot of his cravat. "I shall have you struck off the membership list. What can be the meaning of —"

With one hand Harry grabbed him by the throat and hauled him thus— his heels dragging across the floor— to the nearest wall. There he held the now white-faced fellow against the wallpaper, and said in a low, but clear voice, "I didn't give you permission to speak, did I? I believe I said that I have something to say to you."

The Viscount's eyes watered as that big, weather-worn hand tightened around his windpipe.

"I always think it's sad when a man cannot see himself," Harry continued in the same calm tone. "'Tis

318

even sadder when he can see himself, but does nothing to change for the better." He tilted his head, watching that heightened color drain from the silk-clad nincompoop's face. "*I* am the author behind *His Lordship's Trousers*, so if you wish to complain about that column in *The Gentleman's Weekly*, please do so to me, from now on. Otherwise I suggest that rather than whine loudly and make yourself even more embarrassingly conspicuous, you slink out of sight so that nobody even has cause to compare you with a fictional character."

Finally he opened his fingers and let the man drop. Hands to his neck, Fairbanks croaked, "You'll be sorry for assaulting me, Thrasher." But his shoulders sank against the wall and Harry suspected there was a damp patch staining the fellow's fashionable breeches by now.

"The only thing I'll ever regret is not finishing you off for good, long before this."

"I don't care for your tone." That was, apparently the most he could manage.

"I don't care for your face, your feet, or anything in between. But I tolerate your existence on this planet." He smirked, reached over and flicked a ruffle of the villain's shirt. "For now."

Fairbanks cringed away, sliding further down the wall. People had begun to gather and whisper. More than a few chuckles breezed through the informal audience. Of course, these folk were fickle and would cast their bet with whomever had the upper hand. Even the most devoted followers of Wardlaw Fairbanks took spiteful enjoyment in seeing him humiliated. Such was the changeable nature of this pathetic society of weasels and sycophants. But if one played in the pit with the snakes, one should be prepared to be bitten, and Fairbanks had played too long without a strike.

"From now on," Harry added with menacing softness, "I won't hear another sentence from you that doesn't end in either *sorry* or *thank you, sir*."

Fairbanks shut his pallid lips and bent his head.

It was concession enough for that moment and Harry felt that he'd spent long enough on the matter.

"Excuse me," he said, "I have a beautiful woman waiting for me to make love to her and she gets rather impatient."

Thus he left them all in various states of shock, amusement and wonder.

"There goes Dead Harry Thrasher," one elderly gent remarked with a chuckle and a shake of his head.

And his companion added wryly, "Not so dead after all, apparently."

Also from Jayne Fresina and TEP:

Souls Dryft

The Taming of the Tudor Male Series

Seducing the Beast

Once A Rogue

The Savage and the Stiff Upper Lip

The Deverells

True Story

Storm

Chasing Raven

A Private Collection

ABOUT THE AUTHOR

Jayne Fresina sprouted up in England, the youngest in a family of four daughters. Entertained by her father's colorful tales of growing up in the countryside, and surrounded by opinionated sisters - all with far more exciting lives than hers - she's always had inspiration for her beleaguered heroes and unstoppable heroines.

Website at:www.jaynefresina.com

Twisted E Publishing, Inc.
www.twistederoticapublishing.com